The Bear Went Over

the Mountain

The Bear Went Over the Mountain

TALL TALES
OF
AMERICAN ANIMALS

edited by Robert B. Downs

DETROIT
Singing Tree Press
1971

Reprinted by arrangement with the
author from the original 1964 edition first published in New York by
The Macmillan Company.

Library of Congress Catalog Card Number 73-148835

ACKNOWLEDGMENTS

Permission to quote copyrighted material is acknowledged to publishers
and authors as follows: American Folklore Society, Inc.—"The Angry Sailor"
by Norris Yates, copyright, 1949, American Folklore Society; *Atlantic Monthly*
—"Billingsley's Bird Dog" by Dillon Anderson, copyright, 1955, *Atlantic
Monthly*, "A Buffalo Named Woodrow" by Dillon Anderson, copyright, 1954,
Atlantic Monthly, "The Wonder Horse" by George Byram, copyright, 1957,
Atlantic Monthly, "The Perfect Bait" by Scott Corbett, *Atlantic Monthly* (re-
printed by permission of Willis Kingsley Wing, copyright, 1953, by Scott
Corbett); "The Surest Thing in Show Business" by Jesse Hill Ford, copyright,
1959, *Atlantic Monthly*; Caxton Printers, Ltd.—*Humor of the American Cow-
boy* by Stan Hoig, copyright, 1958, Caxton Printers, *Idaho Lore* edited by
Vardis Fisher, copyright, 1939, Caxton Printers; Columbia University Press—
The Devil's Pretty Daughter (1955), *Sticks in the Knapsack* (1958), *The
Talking Turtle* (1957), *We Always Lie to Strangers* (1951), and *Who Blowed
Up the Church House?* (1952) by Vance Randolph, copyright, 1951-1958,
Columbia University Press; Curtis Publishing Company—"The Duck That
Flew Backward" by Don Tracy, copyright, 1937, *Saturday Evening Post*
(copyright, 1949, by Don Tracy, reprinted with permission of Harold Matson
Company, Inc.); Duke University Press—*Bundle of Troubles and Other Tar-
heel Yarns*, edited by W. C. Hendricks, copyright, 1943, Duke University
Press; Harcourt, Brace & World, Inc.—*It Takes all Kinds* by Lloyd Lewis,
copyright, 1947, Lloyd Lewis, *Dear Baby* by William Saroyan, copyright 1944,
William Saroyan *Windwagon Smith and Other Yarns* by Wilbur Schramm,
copyright 1941, Wilbur Schramm (reprinted by permission of Harold Ober

iv

Associates, Inc.), *The Beast in Me and Other Animals* by James Thurber, copyright, 1948, James Thurber; Harper & Row, Inc.—*Love Conquers All* by Robert Benchley, copyright, 1922, Harper & Row, Inc. ("How Lillian Mosquito Projects Her Voice" reprinted by permission of the publishers), *My Life and Hard Times* by James Thurber, copyright, 1933, James Thurber, *Owl in the Attic* by James Thurber, copyright, 1931, James Thurber, *One Man's Meat* by E. B. White, copyright, 1942, E. B. White, *The Second Tree from the Corner* by E. B. White, copyright, 1951, E. B. White ("The Hour of Letdown" appeared originally in *The New Yorker*, "How to Cure Bird Watchers" by John Fischer, copyright, 1959, Harper & Row, Inc. (reprinted from *Harper's Magazine* by the authors permission), "Just a Simple Country Boy" by Priscilla D. Willis, copyright, 1958, Harper & Row, Inc. (reprinted by permission of the author), "A Little Wine of the Country" by Priscilla D. Willis, copyright, 1955, Harper & Row, Inc. (reprinted by permission of the author); Harvard University Press—*Jonathan Draws the Long Bow* by Richard M. Dorson, copyright, 1946, Harvard University Press; Alfred A. Knopf, Inc. —"Memoirs of the Stable" reprinted from *Heathen Days, 1890-1936* by H. L. Mencken, copyright, 1943, Alfred A. Knopf, Inc.; Random House—*Let the Crabgrass Grow* by H. Allen Smith, copyright, 1948, 1960, by H. Allen Smith (excerpted with the permission of Bernard Geis Associates); Charles Scribners Sons—*First and Last* by Ring Lardner, copyright, 1934, Ellis A. Lardner, renewal copyright, Ring Lardner ("Dogs" is reprinted with the permission of Charles Scribner's Sons); Story Magazine, Inc.—"Harold Peavey's Fast Cow" by George Cronyn, copyright, 1935, Story Magazine, Inc. (reprinted by permission of Story Magazine, Inc.), "Horse in the Apartment" by Frances Eisenberg, copyright, 1940, Story Magazine Inc. (reprinted by permission of Story Magazine, Inc.), "The Red Rats of Plum Fork" by Jesse Stuart, copyright, 1953, Whit and Hallie Burnett, "The Sea Serpent of Spoonville Beach" by Harold Helfer, copyright, 1953, Whit and Hallie Burnett; Texas Folklore Society—*Backwoods to Border*, edited by Mody C. Boatright and Donald Day, Dallas, University Press (1943), *Coyote Wisdom*, edited by J. Frank Dobie and others, Austin, Texas, Texas Folklore Society (1938), *Follow de Drinkin' Gou'd*, edited by J. Frank Dobie, Austin, Texas Folklore Society (1928), *From Hell to Breakfast*, edited by Mody C. Boatright and Donald Day, Dallas University Press (1944) *In the Shadow of History* edited by J. Frank Dobie and others, Austin, Texas Folklore Society (1939), *Tall Tales from Texas* by Mody C. Boatright, Dallas, Southwest Press (1934) *Texian Stomping Grounds* (edited by J. Frank Dobie and others, Austin, Texas Folklore Society (1941); University of North Carolina Press—*God Bless the Devil!* edited by James R. Aswell, copyright, 1940, University of North Carolina Press, *The Tree Named John* by John B. Sale, copyright, 1929, University of North Carolina Press.

The assistance of Elizabeth C. Downs in the preliminary process of searching and selection of materials for inclusion in the anthology is acknowledged with much appreciation.

CONTENTS

How it all began

Before launching upon one of the most delightful creations in American folk humor, "Jim Baker's Blue Jay Yarn," Mark Twain quotes Jim as remarking: "Animals talk to each other, of course. There can be no question about that; but I suppose there are very few people who can understand them."

Since time immemorial, man has tended to create animals in his own image, to imagine animals with the power of speech and human beings who have the ability to understand the language of birds and beasts. Perhaps originating in a primeval sense of kinship with lower members of the vast animal kingdom (of which man is merely the highest embodiment), the race has for thousands of years related beast fables for purposes of allegory, satire, and recreation. Peter Lum observes that "It was natural for primitive man to credit animals with powers far beyond his own. . . . Their speech, inarticulate though it might be, was near enough to man's own primitive language to leave him convinced that, could he only understand, the wail of the jackal and the chatter of the birds had a message for him."

Animal mythology is undoubtedly more ancient than writing. Evidence of man's preoccupation with the creatures around him is found, for example, in the prehistoric cave drawings of France and Spain. With the advent of recorded literature appear Aesop's *Fables,* telling of animals that talk and act like human beings; the Biblical episodes of Eve's talking serpent and Balaam's talking ass; the *Arabian Nights,* abounding in beast tales; Pliny's *Natural History,* describing, for example, dolphins carrying human riders; and the first of the fabulous monsters characteristic of every literary era.

But there was little of humor in either the animal literature or folklore of those early ages. Typically, real or imaginary beasts in such contexts possessed religious significance, reflected primordial superstitions or scientific ignorance, or served to illustrate moral lessons. Among writers of antiquity, perhaps the first and most renowned literary figure to indulge in natural history mendacity for amusement was the second-century Greek satirist Lucian, whose *True History*, the author says frankly, contains nothing but lies from beginning to end. Lucian's *Vera Historia* teems with gigantic "horse-vultures," sea serpents, dragons, and related monsters.

In more recent times, the champion prevaricator was a German adventurer, Rudolf Erich Raspe, whose *Baron Münchausen's Narrative of His Marvellous Travels and Campaigns in Russia,* published in London in 1785, is filled with colorful, highly preposterous yarns of hunting and similar exploits. Among the Baron's many perilous adventures is the pursuit of a fabulous bird, the Wauwau, through the deserts of North America.

The pioneer settlers who came to the New World in the seventeenth century in the first wave of immigration from Europe brought with them the folklore, the oral traditions and superstitions of the Old World. Strictly interpreted, little of American folklore is indigenous, except that of the Amerindians, which was present when the white man arrived. The English, Germans, French, Swiss, Swedes, Finns, Danes, Irish, Hungarians, Dutch, Spaniards, and all the rest contributed distinctive touches.

Under the influence of different ways of life, however, subtle changes began to occur almost immediately in the folk traditions imported from abroad. To the lore from their inherited backgrounds, the early colonists added new experiences and impressions. As they explored unknown wildernesses and moved steadily westward, virtually nothing seemed impossible to them. The wild frontier produced mighty boasters and heroes—Davy Crockett, Daniel Boone, Andy Jackson, Mike Fink, Kit Carson, Wild Bill Hickok, Sam Bass, Buffalo Bill, Jesse James, and a host of others—to whom the folk added such supermen as Johnny Appleseed (who talked to animals), Paul Bunyan, Tony Beaver, and Pecos Bill. Bold men created bold myths, and America became a land of marvelous stories both true and false.

The great spaces of "the wondrous west" also encouraged the rise of the tall tale. The Easterner was willing to believe that almost anything might happen in the West. As Van Wyck Brooks notes, "The West possessed the largest rivers; and were not the storms more terrible there; were not the bears more dangerous than anywhere else? No tales about the West could ever seem tall to anyone who saw the frontiersman with a rifle. He could perforate a milk-pail half a mile away, he could enlarge the tin eye of the cock on the steeple, he could split a bullet on a razor at a hundred paces and cut the string of a flag at three hundred yards."

A fertile field for lively flights of fancy was biological phenomena. The different flora and fauna of the New World vastly stimulated the growth of natural history folklore. Their dramatic effect on both oral traditions and written literature was evident from the outset. An extraordinary and fascinating lore relating to animal, bird, fish, insect, and plant life began to form. In time, folk and literary creations properly classifiable as apocryphal biology surpassed all others in vivid color, inventiveness, humor, and originality. "From Maine to Idaho, from the Adirondacks to Arkansas," as Ben Clough comments, "unlikely creatures crawl, prowl, whine, and roar through the jungles of America's imagination."

An influential factor in the development of such folklore, too, was a long tradition of oral storytelling, the importance of which was recognized by an English traveler, Andrew Lang, about seventy-five years ago. "All over the land in America," Lang wrote, "men are eternally 'swopping stories' at bars, and in the long endless journeys by railway and steamer. How little, comparatively, the English 'swop stories.' The stories thus collected in America are the subsoil of American literary humour, a rich soil in which the plant grows with vigour and puts forth fruit and flowers."

American folk humor has been characterized by one or another critic as boisterous, racy, irreverent, exuberant, zestful, Rabelaisian, full of gusto, and close to the soil. Springing from the grassroots, it is more intimately associated with the mass of the people than is any written literature. At the same time, the folklore heritage has been a potent force on more formal literary productions. A conspicuous example of a major author who drew extensively from this inexhaustible stream is Mark Twain. Much of Twain's genius and success as a writer lay in his ability to recall and utilize the Missouri and Mississippi River lore with which he had been surrounded as a boy and young man. Scarcely less indebted to folk traditions were Washington Irving, Herman Melville, Nathaniel Hawthorne, James Fenimore Cooper, Henry W. Longfellow, and innumerable lesser figures—limiting the field to the nineteenth century alone.

The beginning of the American tall tale may have been in the year 1000, when it is related that Thorwald, son of Eric the Red, was fatally wounded, in Nova Scotia, by a Uniped or One-Footer. Jacques Cartier in the sixteenth century also brought back from his

Canadian explorations reports of a land peopled by a race of one-legged folk. About the same time, Christopher Columbus made contributions to legend by reporting after his return home that he himself had seen three sirens leaping about in the sea, and "at a distance there were men with one eye only, and others with faces like dogs, who were man-eaters"—a whopper picked up from the Haitian Indians.

The state of scientific knowledge and the credulousness of America's colonial ancestors are indicated further by an incident reported as fact by Cotton Mather in 1712 to the Royal Society of London. As printed in the Society's *Philosophical Transactions*, Mather wrote: "A Person provoking a Rattle-Snake to bite the Edge of a broad Axe he had in his Hand; the colour, of the Steeled part bitten, was immediately changed, and at the first stroke he made with it in using his Ax, the so discoloured part broke out, leaving a gap in his Ax."

A leading chronicler of New England colonial folklore, Richard Dorson, recounts tales of sea serpents, mermen, two-headed snakes, and like exotic creatures; of a tulip tree so large that a man moved his household furniture inside; of a bear that killed a cow by biting into her hide and blowing air into the wound until she burst; of monstrous births and wonder-working demons. Again, however, these strange denizens and luxuriant, unfamiliar growths in the land, the wildly improbable stories were the fruits of naive superstition and pious gullibility, rather than attempts at humor.

Of a different character were several yarns invented by Benjamin Franklin to satirize the ignorance of Englishmen about the New World. Writing in 1765, Franklin relates: "The very tails of the American sheep are so laden with wool, that each has a little car or wagon on four little wheels, to support and keep it from trailing on the ground" (a fictional motif that goes back at least to Herodotus in the fifth century B.C.). Franklin continued: "Cod, like other fish when attacked by their enemies, fly into any waters where they can be safest; Whales when they have a mind to eat Cod, pursue them wherever they fly; and the grand leap of the Whale in that chase up Niagara Falls is esteemed by all who have seen it, as one of the finest spectacles in nature."

During the nineteenth century yarns of hunting, fishing, and outdoor pursuits were exceedingly popular. "America's favorite tall tale," says Richard Dorson, is "the Wonderful Hunt." Among numerous versions, one recorded by Harold W. Thompson from upper

New York State is representative. The hero and narrator is a famous
hunter, Mart Moody:

> One afternoon last season I was out in the woods when
> I saw five pa'tridges settin' in a row on the limb of a tree.
> I didn't have a gun with me; so pulled out my hunting-knife,
> took aim, and let her go. That danged knife split the limb
> so nice that all five birds were caught by the toes. That
> wasn't all. The knife went skimming across the brook along-
> side the tree and killed a bear that happened to be loitering
> on the other side. While I was wadin' across the brook to
> get the bear, I caught my pants so full of trout that a button
> busted off, flew forty rod, and killed a fox. I suppose you
> might call some of that Adirondack luck.

Neither have farmers been shy in adding their bit to the great
American brag. A rich Arkansas farm owned by a certain Captain
Billy Mansfield was the source of one such prevarication:

> "W'y, Gentlemen," Captain Billy declared, "I've growed
> cornstalks thirty foot high, with seven or eight big ears on
> ever' stalk. 'Stead of a tassel thar was a round dingus like
> a gourd, an' when I busted one of 'em open thar was 'bout
> a quart o' shelled corn in it, for seed! Hit run two hundred
> an' fifty bushel t' th' acre, an' maybe twenty bushel o' seed-
> corn in th' gourds. I've raised alfalfy ten foot high an' twelve
> cuttin's a year, an' cowpeas so all-fired big th' cows cain't
> git 'em in their mouth! Thar's jest one thing you cain't raise
> on my land, an' that's punkins. I planted a leetle patch o'
> punkins one year, an' th' vines growed up an' filled th' hull
> dang valley level full, plumb t' th' tops o' th' ridges. Th' hull
> country looked jest like a high prairie, an' so thick th' cattle
> couldn't find th' creek. But thar wasn't a single punkin,
> fur's we could find out. Th' vines growed so dang fast they
> jest wore th' punkins plumb out, a-draggin' 'em over th'
> rocks!"

Ferocious and gigantic mosquitoes have inspired a variety of
fantastic yarns. Paul Bunyan crossed mosquitoes with bumblebees;
the hybrid was far more dangerous and formidable than either of
its parents. Turning up in every region of the country, with minor
variations, is a tall tale of a narrow escape from pursuing mosquitoes.
An amusing version is attributed by Harold Thomson to John Darling, a legendary character of Sullivan County, New York. Darling
was working, as he tells it, in California in a sugar refinery, using
pans weighing one ton each for boiling down the sap:

Well, I was out in the woods working one day when I heard a sort of *roar, roar, roar* up in the sky that made me look for a place to hide. There wasn't any place except under the big sap-pan, laying bottom-side up on the ground; so I picked up one corner of it and jumped under. Less than a minute later there was a *crash;* a swarm of mosquitoes had hit that pan so hard that they drove their bills into it. There was some big stones on the ground under the pan where I was; so I picked up a stone and went around clinching all the bills of those mosquitoes onto the inside of the pan. The next thing I knew, they begun to clap their wings and make a sound like as if a big storm was coming. Then the sap-pan begun to lift up slow. It riz up graceful from the ground and over the tree-tops, and the last thing I saw of that sap-pan, it looked no bigger'n a baseball, on the way to China.

Several experts have essayed analyses of the tall tale—a dangerous enterprise, for any given specimen is likely to disintegrate and be spoiled by too minute study. "Humor can be dissected as a frog can," E. B. White warns, "but the thing dies in the process and the innards are discouraging to any but the pure scientific mind." Nonetheless, a brief glance at a few authoritative opinions may be enlightening. Walter Blair defines the tall tale as "an exuberant combination of fact with outrageous fiction." It is generally agreed that there is usually a tiny grain of truth somewhere in the most improbable story of this type. Ben Botkin, in fact, believes that "Improving on actual happenings rather than outright lying is the distinguishing feature of the tall tale," but he concedes that "the tall tale deals frankly with marvels, with the remarkable or prodigious." A long-time student of the subject, J. Frank Dobie, adds that the genuine narrator of tall tales considers himself an artist. "An authentic liar," Mr. Dobie says, "knows what he is lying about, knows that his listeners—unless they are tenderfeet, greenhorns—know also, and hence makes no pretence of fooling either himself or them."

Another branch of the American folktale, of ancient lineage, is the animal fable, exemplified by the Brer Rabbit stories of the Southern Negroes, and the paisano (roadrunner) tales of the Southwest. In the folklore, animals are given human characteristics. The best known are the Uncle Remus plantation stories from Georgia, as told in the eighteen-eighties by Joel Chandler Harris. Avid collectors for the past seventy-five years have added continuously to the store by scouring the byways of other Southern areas. The dominant theme of the Negro's animal fables, well summed up by Peter Haworth, is to project the "compensatory dreams of the subject races and serf-populations, expressed both in folk-tale and folk-ballad, which delight in the victory of the weak over the strong and in the triumph of brains over brute strength." Thus does a physical weakling like Brer Rabbit trick, outwit, and almost invariably triumph over such formidable antagonists as Brer Fox, Brer Wolf, Brer Bear, and their like. A sample of the technique is Elsie Clews Parson's "The Give-Away," recorded from the Sea Islands, South Carolina:

> Oncet Ber Wolf an' Ber Rabbit had a confusion-trouble over somet'in'. Ber Wolf an' Ber Tiyger was fixin' a plan to ketch Ber Rabbit. Ber Tiyger tol' Ber Wolf he mus' go in his house an' lay down, an' do like he was dead. Ber Tiyger he went out, an' tol' Ber Rabbit he mus' come to see Ber Wolf 'cause Ber Wolf wus dead. An' after Ber Rabbit went to Ber Wolf house, de firs' t'in he said was, "Dead people raise up some time." Ber Wolf raise up. Said, "I never seed a person what was dead could raise up." An' he ran all de way home.

If the present anthology demonstrates anything, it is that the animal story has universal appeal, at every cultural level from the lowliest illiterate to the most highly educated sophisticate. There is, for example, seldom an issue of the *New Yorker,* definitely a magazine for the cognoscenti and intelligentsia, without a cartoon of animals speaking to each other or to human listeners. Literary periodicals aimed at upper middle-brow or high-brow readers, such as the *Atlantic* and *Harper's,* not infrequently publish excellent animal tales in the tall category. And our top-bracket literary humorists—Mark Twain, James Thurber, Robert Benchley, Ring Lardner, Don Marquis, E. B. White, H. Allen Smith—have obviously enjoyed drawing upon the animal kingdom for some of their most amusing and imaginative fictional creations.

Meanwhile, Ben Clough remarks, "On a lower level, our weather stories, hunting stories, fish stories, impossible yarns, and sheer hoaxes go on. The great American liar is of no era, and of all; he is immortal."

Yankee Yarns

Major Brown's Coon Story

RICHARD M. DORSON

"I was down on the crick this morning," said Bill Gates, "and I seed any amount of coon tracks. I think they're agoin' to be powerful plenty this season."

"Oh, yes," replied Tom Coker, "I never hearn tell of the likes before. The whole woods is lined with 'em. If skins is only a good price this season, I'll be worth somethin' in the spring, sure's you live, for I've jest got one of the best coon dogs in all Illinois."

"You say you never hearn tell o' the like o' the coons?" put in Major Brown, an old veteran who had been chewing his tobacco in silence for the last half hour. "Why, you don't know ennything 'bout 'em! If you'd a come here forty years ago, like I did, you'd a thought coon! I jest tell you, boys, you couldn't go amiss for 'em. We hardly ever thought of pesterin' 'em much, for their skins weren't worth a darn with us—that is, we couldn't get enough for 'em to pay for the skinnin'.

"I recollect one day I went out a bee huntin'. Wal, arter I'd lumbered about a good while, I got kinder tired, and so I leaned up agin a big tree to rest. I hadn't much more'n leaned up afore somethin' give me one of the allfiredest nips about the seat o' my britches I ever got in my life. I jumped about a rod, and lit a runnin', and kept on a runnin' for over a hundred yards; when think, sez I, it's no use runnin', and I'm snake bit, but runnin' won't do enny good. So I jest stopt, and proceeded to examine the wound. I soon seed it was no snake bite, for thar's a blood-blister pinched on me about six inches long.

"Think, sez I, that rether gits me! What in the very deuce would it a bin? Arter thinkin' about it a while, I concluded to go back, and look for the critter, jest for the curiosity o' the thing. I went to the tree and poked the weeds and stuff all about; but darned the thing could I see. Purty soon I sees the tree has a little split a runnin'

3

along up it, and so I gits to lookin' at that. Dreckly I sees the split open about half a inch, and then shet up agin; then I sees it open and shet, and open and shet, and open and shet, right along as regular as a clock a tickin'.

"Think, sez I, what in all creation can this mean? I know'd I'd got pinched in the split tree, but what in thunder was makin' it do it? At first, I felt orfully scared, and thought it must be somethin' dreadful; and then agin I thought it moutn't. Next I thought about hants and ghosts, and about a runnin' home and sayin' nothin' about it; and then I thought it couldn't be enny on 'em, for I'd never hearn tell o' them a pesterin' a feller right in open daylight. At last the true blood of my ancestors riz up in my veins, and told me it 'ud be cowardly to go home and not find out what it was; so I lumbered for my axe, and swore I'd find out all about it, or blow up. When I got back, I let into the tree like blazes, and purty soon it cum down and smashed into flinders—and what do you think? Why, it was rammed and jammed smack full of coons from top to bottom. Yes, sir, they's rammed in so close that every time they breathed they made the split open."

A Very Friendly Horse

James M. Bailey

I don't really believe a yellow horse is any worse by nature than a bay horse, or a white horse, or a horse of any color or combination of colors; but our judgment of things in this world is often liable to be influenced by our prejudices. For this reason, perhaps, I cannot look upon a yellow horse with any feelings of delight.

A yellow horse was standing at the depot in Washington the time I came down the Shepaug road. Looking at the animal as he felt around casually with his hind foot for his owner's brains, my mind receded back to the home of my childhood.

It seemed so blessed to lean back in the seat, and with partly closed eyes give myself up to reveries retrospective.

I remember quite distinctly the day my parent brought home a yellow horse; in fact, I can without much difficulty pick out any day of the eight which that animal passed in our society. He was a comely beast, with long limbs, a straight body, and eyes that would rival those of an eagle in looking hungry.

When he came into the yard we all went out to look at him. It was an evening—clear, bright, and beautiful. My parent stood near the well holding the animal by a halter. We had a dog, a black and white, and if there ever was a dog who thought he had a head stowed full of knowledge it was that dog.

How plainly I can see him approach that yellow horse, to smell of his heels. He ought to have got more of a smell than he did, considering that he lost the greater part of one ear in the attempt. It was done so quick that it is possible we would not have known anything about it, had the dog not spoken of it himself.

He never smelt of that yellow horse again. The flavor wasn't what he had been used to, I think.

Three days later when he was turning around, to speak to a flea near his tail, as is customary with dogs, that yellow horse

5

unexpectedly reached down, and took a mouthful of spinal joints out of the dog's back, and the mortification from being thus caught preyed so heavily upon the dog's mind that he died in a minute or two.

That evening mother interested father with an account of Caper's death while he was waiting for her to replace the collar the yellow horse that afternoon had snatched from his best coat.

And thus time passed. But the horse lost none of it. There wasn't a neighbor within a half mile of our house but bore some mark of that animal's friendship. Like death he was no respecter of persons. He never stopped to inquire whether a man was worth a million dollars or ten cents when reaching for him. He may have had some curiosity about it afterwards, but he never showed it.

Finally people came to avoid him when they met him on the street. I don't think they did it purposely, but it seemed to come natural to them to rush through the first doorway or over the most convenient fence when they saw him approach. This inexplicable dread communicated itself to the very dogs on the street, but before they had come fairly to understand him, he had succeeded in reducing the price of a winter-breakfast luxury to almost a mere song.

After that they looked up to him with the respect exacted by a Hindoo god with two changes of underclothes, and no dog within three blocks of us would think of going to sleep at night without first coming over to see if that horse was locked up. It was instinct, probably.

My parent never enjoyed a single day of the eight he was the sole possessor of the animal. He nipped away some portion of him every once in a while. My parent was not a profane man, but he was sorely tempted to be every hour in the day. The man who lived next to us was a profound swearer. He owned a horse that was a model of goodness in every respect—as gentle as a lamb, and as lovable as a girl of sixteen. My father could never understand this. He always spoke of it as one of the inscrutable ways of providence.

There was only one person that had anything to do with the animal who came out of that fiery ordeal unscathed. He was the hired man, and he owed his salvation to a misfortune. He was cross-eyed. He was a great source of misery to that yellow horse. The misformation of his eyes was calculated to deceive even smarter beings. The beast kicked at him a few times when he was evidently looking the other way, but that was just the time he was bearing one eye strongly on him, and he missed; and when he really was not looking was just the time the beast thought he was, and so it went through the entire eight days, both stomach and heels yearning for a morsel of him, but never getting it.

I am sure there never was another such horse to kick and bite. He did it so unexpectedly, too. He would be looking a stranger square in the face, apparently about to communicate some information of value, and then suddenly lift his hind foot, and fetch the unsophisticated man a rap on the head that would make him see seventy-five dollars' worth of fireworks in a minute.

He would bite at anything whether he reached it or not; but in kicking, he rarely missed. He could use any leg with facility, but prided himself mainly on the extraordinary play of the left hind leg. With that limb he would break up a political meeting in five minutes and kick over the entire plan of the campaign before the last man got to the door.

The very air about our place was impregnated with camphor and the various new kinds of liniments. The neighbors came around after dark, and howled for the blood of that yellow horse like so many Indians clamoring for a pint of New England potash.

Matters commenced to assume a critical form. The people wanted the animal killed, and cut open so they could get back their things.

And so my parent determined to shoot the beast, but at the last moment his heart failed him. Pity triumphed, and he sold him to a man from a distance, and it was such a great distance that none of us were able to attend his funeral two weeks later, although earnestly invited to do so. He left a wife and three interesting children, and was struck just above the right temple, I believe.

The Sea Serpent
of Spoonville Beach

Harold Helfer

There was a statement from a preacher in the paper the other day complaining that people don't believe in anything anymore, so I thought I'd write this up to let everybody know there is at least one thing they can believe in. Sea serpents.

Of course, you're always reading that a sea serpent has been sighted off some beach or another but everybody knows that's just to drum up a little tourist trade. Somebody will say to somebody else, "Business has been kind of dull lately, hasn't it?" and then the somebody else will say, "Yeah, do you think we'd better send Mike out in the rowboat?" and the other guy will say, "Might as well." Then Mike will get in the rowboat and row out to sea and a few hours or so later he will come rowing back all excited and report he's seen a sea serpent. Then it gets in the papers and a lot of people come to the beach. Not that any of the people really believe there are such things at sea serpents but they're probably all set to go to some beach for a few days anyway and as long as they are going somewhere they figure they might as well get their money's worth and go to a beach where a sea serpent has been reported even if there really aren't any such things.

Of course, the guy's name who goes out in the rowboat doesn't have to be Mike. The main thing is he's got to be lean and hungry-looking and have a long, thin nose, the kind of a person, if there really were any sea serpents, he'd be the one to see them. On Spoonville Beach our rowboat man was a fellow by the name of Sam McGeever. He was pretty good too, and I remember once Moe Kopple saying that he was so good it was really almost a shame that there wasn't any real sea serpents, that he was wasting his talent. Little did we know then.

8

One day a number of years ago me and Moe Kopple and Freddie Smithson and Abe Damsky and some of the boys were having a little chinfest and somebody, Freddie Smithson, I believe, said, "Business hasn't been so good lately, has it?" Abe Damsky said, "For a fact, it hasn't—should we send Sam McGeever out?" We all looked at Moe Kopple, who owned the biggest restaurant of any of us on the beach and he nodded and said, "Might as well."

I happened to be at Moe's place when he sent Sam out. Sam was the handyman around the beach, picking up driftwood and collecting clams and one thing or another, and he always was glad to do something for somebody.

"Sam, you doing anything special this evening?" Moe asked him.

"Well, I was going out on the jetty and fish for a spell," Sam said. "But that can wait, Mr. Kopple. The fish haven't been biting too well lately anyway."

"How'd you like to get in the rowboat and row out to sea for a bit?" Moe said, lighting up a cigar.

"I'd be glad to," Sam said. Then very sympathetically he said, "Business falling off, Mr. Kopple?"

"A little," Moe grunted, switching his cigar to the other side of his mouth.

About 3 or so in the afternoon Sam McGeever got in the rowboat and started rowing away. I watched him get smaller and smaller until he was only a speck and pretty soon he wasn't even that anymore.

A few hours later, around 6:30 it was—the sun was coming down and there was a lot of purple and a lot of shadows over the water, which is the best time for this sort of thing—Sam came rowing back.

He was rowing as fast as he could and even from a distance his long nose seemed longer and there was a gleam in his eyes.

Moe and I were watching from a little way off and I remarked, "Old Sam seems to be in fine fettle today."

"He's got a way with him all right," said Moe.

"There's a sea serpent out there!" Sam cried, leaping from his boat to the beach and pointing with a trembling bony finger out to where he had come from. "A real sea serpent!"

In no time at all there was a crowd around him.

Nodding with satisfaction at one another, Moe and I proceeded to walk over to Moe's private office for a little ale and friendly palaver.

"You know something, Moe," I said to Moe after I leaned back in my chair. "I believe Sam gets better all the time."

"He puts his heart and soul into it all right," Moe agreed.

It was about a half hour later that Sam came knocking on the door of Moe's private office.

"Come in, come in," Moe said warmly to him. "Have a seat. You were fine today."

Moe had his feet on his desk and I had my feet on the desk. Moe and I always felt real good after one of these things.

"I bet we do a landslide oyster business," said Moe, lighting up a new cigar. "Sea serpent stories always bring out the oyster longing in people."

"I'm going to order a lot of shrimp too," I said.

"It was at least 300 feet long!" Sam said, "and it was blowing smoke out of its nose!"

"Another thing, Moe," I said. "I think I'll feature some crab meat specials."

Moe didn't answer me and I saw that he was staring at Sam. Then I stared at Sam. Sam was sitting down, his hands in his lap and his mouth a little open, and he wasn't staring at anybody, just space.

"Er, what was that, Sam?" Moe said.

"It was half as big as the jetty," Sam said slowly, spacing out each word as if it was coming to him out of a dream, "and it was blowing out of its nose."

"What was?" said Moe, watching Sam funny.

"The sea serpent," Sam said. "It had big ridges in its back, like a mountain range, and it was covered with green scales."

"You're all right, Sam," I said. "If I ever moved somewhere else and you reported a sea serpent, so help me I believe I'd drop everything and come to Spoonville Beach and strain my eyes looking out into the sea with the rest of the yokels, smart as I am."

"And it slithered around, sending out big waves everytime it swished its tail," Sam said, still not seeming to pay any attention to anybody or anything, but just staring out straight ahead at nothing.

Moe stuck his face and his cigar out closer to Sam and said, "Are you trying to say you actually saw a sea serpent?"

"Its eyes were big and bloodshot," Sam said. "They were the awfulest thing about it."

Moe relaxed back in his chair and said, "There's only one small point. How can you see something which isn't so?"

"Oh, Sam, you didn't really see a sea serpent," I scoffed. "Everybody knows there's no such thing. Sea serpents are like elfs and bogeymen and make-believe things you read about in books."

Sam suddenly quit focusing his eyes on nowheres and he looked from Moe to me.

"I know it doesn't sound like it could be so," he said. "But I saw it! I actually, positively saw it! I never was so scared in all my life. I thought I never would be able to move. It took all my will to start rowing back."

Smiling, Moe swooshed his cigar around in his mouth and said, "Well, anyway, Sam, you're getting really wonderful at this. How much do we usually give you for one of your sea serpent trips? Fifteen dollars? Tell you what—we'll make it twenty dollars this time. And if the oyster business is as good as I think it's going to be maybe we'll even add another fin."

"I appreciate that very much," said Sam. "But what do you think we ought to do about the sea serpent?"

"Now look, Sam," I said. "Sea serpents are even more unreal than mirages. At least mirages are something real which you think you see but don't. But sea serpents never were in the first place."

"I've been going out to sea to report sea serpents for years now," Sam said. "Have I ever before told you what I'm telling you now?"

Moe and I found ourselves suddenly looking at each other.

"I know it's hard to believe," said Sam. "I don't guess I'd want to believe it myself if I hadn't seen it with my own eyes. But nobody would have ever thought there was any such thing as the atom bomb either if it hadn't happened."

Moe and my eyes were meeting again.

"There's something in what you're saying, all right, Sam," I said, sounding a little doubtful, or at least that's the way I meant to sound.

"You say it had smoke coming out of its nose?" asked Moe, kind of cautiously.

"It was a gray smoke with flecks of fire in it," said Sam.

"This beats me," said Moe. "But I am bound to go back to my original premise. How can you see something which not only isn't so but never was?"

"I know you'll never believe me," said Sam. "Unless you see it with your own eyes. I'll take you out there tomorrow and show it to you."

"Well, I wouldn't mind going, except that I expect to be rather busy—" Moe said.

"I got to see about a shrimp order myself—" I said.

"Hold on, Sam," said Moe, smiling slyly. "If you really saw this sea serpent, then why would you want to go back out there? It is generally believed that, although there aren't any sea serpents, if there were, they'd be very dangerous."

"Because I want somebody else to see it besides myself so I'll be believed. I don't want to begin to doubt it myself and think I'm seeing things." Then Sam said grimly, "I got away from him before, I guess I can do it again."

"Oh, well, for that matter I really don't mind going," said Moe, still with that coy smile on his face. "It's been a long time since I've been rowboating."

Moe and Sam and me got in the rowboat the next afternoon about 3:30 and we started rowing out. Moe was plainly feeling very cocky and he kept saying witty things like, "We should of brought along a pot of coffee and hung it on the sea serpent's nose to warm."

I don't know how far we rowed out. There aren't any road signs on the sea.

I knew the thing was there even before I saw it. I was facing Moe and his face suddenly turned the color of his cigar ashes. He gulped and gasped and choked and then he pointed. His lips moved up and down for about a second but no words would come out of his mouth. Finally, though, he said, "There—there it is."

"That's it all right," said Sam and I bet a man's voice never shook so much before when he said something in triumph.

Then I turned around and saw it. I'm not good at describing things but it was just about like Sam said it was. It was very big and very green and it had awful-looking red eyes and it had big ridges and humps on its back. When it moved the water shook as if there was a squall.

I knew then what Sam meant when he said he got so scared he had a hard time budging. I suddenly felt like I was part of the petrified forest. I don't remember actually getting hold of the oars and rowing back but I know I did, we all did. And we must have done it in a hurry too because I really can't say for sure that I saw the smoke coming from the sea serpent's nose that Sam and Moe claim they saw. It seems to me I saw something all right, but it was more like vapor maybe, more like whatever it is that whales spout out. But Moe and Sam said they were sure it was smoke and Moe said it was a kind of steam smoke and he could see the heat shimmering through it.

This was something, however, we did not discuss there and then. None of us said anything for a long time, we were too busy rowing, I guess.

It wasn't until we got within sight of the beach that somebody spoke up. It was Moe.

"Let's not say anything about this to anybody," he said.

I was too preoccupied with my thoughts to say anything then but after we were in Moe's private office having some ale I said to him, "Say, Moe, why didn't you want us to say anything about what we saw? Seems to me the more publicity, the better."

"First of all," said Moe, "if we said anything it might look like we were horseplaying over what Sam reported yesterday. Sam was so good at it yesterday that anything we did might seem phoney, see what I mean? Also this is a big thing. We've got to think it out carefully. What you say we sleep over it tonight and talk about it further tomorrow."

Well, I tried to think what we ought to do about the sea serpent and about the best idea I could get was that we should try to get as much publicity as we could and then post signs with arrows in the water pointing to where the sea serpent was.

When I told Moe my idea the next day in his private office he listened respectfully but when I was through he shook his head.

"No," he said, "My idea is we shouldn't do anything."

"I don't get you, Moe," I said. "What do you mean not do anything? Why, a real sure enough sea serpent out there'd bring tremendous crowds to the beach!"

"For awhile," said Moe. "But once it gets established that there really are sea serpents people won't get so excited over them."

I began thinking this over.

"Remember when the automobile came out, how people would stare at one when it came down the street?" said Moe. "Nobody cares now!"

"But, Moe—" I said.

"Oh, sure a sea serpent would draw a crowd for awhile," Moe said. "But after awhile they'd get tired of it. Then what?"

Moe lit a cigar.

"I'll tell you what," he said. "Day in and day out why do people come to a beach? To go bathing in the water, right? But who's going to go into the water if there's a sea serpent around?"

"But what are we going to do about this sea serpent?" I asked.

"Forget him," Moe said.

"But you and I—and Sam—we know he's out there," I exclaimed.

"So what?" said Moe. "Is there a law that says if you see a sea serpent you got to do anything about it? Besides, Sam did tell everybody. It's in the papers. Can we help it if they print those things with their tongues in the cheek? Are we responsible for what position newspapers hold their tongues?"

"But maybe the sea serpent will come in to the beach and bite off somebody's leg or something," I said.

"Oh, I don't think so," said Moe. "For one thing, if he did come up to the beach, everybody'd be able to see him a long way off, with that steam cauldron he's got in his nose. And he seems to stay in the same spot all the time—maybe there's a mermaid out there he makes love to."

"Moe!" I said. "You don't believe in mermaids!"

"Why not?" said Moe. "There can be mermaids just as easy as there can be sea serpents."

Then Moe chuckled and said, "But don't let that give you any ideas. Even if you should find one, you couldn't keep it a minute from that wife of yours. But, seriously," Moe said, "I think the best plan for us is to just act like nothing's happened. I only got one further suggestion."

"What's that?" I asked.

"I don't think we should ever have Sam report a sea serpent again," he said.

"Why not?"

"Because there is one," said Moe. "Nobody believes there are sea serpents but at the same time everybody always is a little superstitious about everything and somebody is liable to be flying around low in a plane or happen to be out there in a yacht after one of Sam's sea serpent stories and then recognize it. But if they don't hear these reports from Sam they won't be thinking of sea serpents, so even if they see something out there they'll just think it's driftwood."

When Moe called Sam into his private office Sam was in a happy mood because he'd proved to us he really had seen the sea serpent, but his face got long when Moe told him to drop the sea serpent story as soon as he could and that he would rather he didn't ever give off with another one.

"Yes sir, if you say so." But Sam seemed real sad about it.

"Of course," said Moe, "we'll pay you the fifteen dollars or twenty dollars we've been paying you right along." With a little smile, Moe added, "If you like, you can consider yourself pensioned."

I noticed during the next few months that Sam walked around awful droopy-like, as if he might be moping over something. My restaurant faces right smack on the beach, and during lulls I'm always looking out [of] the window at the sea because I'd rather see that emptiness than the emptiness of my booths. Anyway, one evening while I was looking out of the window I saw a man getting into a rowboat.

He looked familiar, like Sam McGeever, in fact, and I went out there and, sure enough, it was.

I asked him where he was going and he said he was going to row out to sea.

"But, look here, Sam," I said. "Moe said he didn't want you to do it anymore."

"Oh, I'm not going to say anything about seeing a sea serpent," he said.

Lowering my voice a little, I said, "But hadn't you better not go out knowing what's there? You know you can stretch your luck too far."

"Well, after you've rowed out to sea and reported sea serpents for as long a time as I have," he said, "it gets in your blood. I just feel terribly restless and anyway, I thought I'd feel better if I rowed out a bit. Of course, I'll be careful."

I watched Sam row away, looking thinner and hungrier than ever.

He never came back. Neither he nor the rowboat.

So, like I say, if you don't believe in anything else these days, at least you can believe in sea serpents. If you have any doubt about any of this, you can check the Spoonville records of about ten years ago or so and see where a Sam McGeever went out to sea and neither he nor his rowboat ever were seen again.

Of course, you can believe, if you want to, that Sam just got lost in the waves or something. But the real proof is that Spoonville Beach has not reported seeing a sea serpent to this day and can you name any other beach that has not reported a sea serpent in ten years' time?

A Boston Terrier

E. B. WHITE

I would like to hand down a dissenting opinion in the case of the
Camel ad which shows a Boston terrier relaxing. I can string along
with cigarette manufacturers to a certain degree, but when it comes
to the temperament and habits of terriers, I shall stand my ground.

The ad says: "A dog's nervous system resembles our own." I
don't think a dog's nervous system resembles my own in the least. A
dog's nervous system is in a class by itself. If it resembles anything at
all, it resembles the New York Edison Company's power plant. This
is particularly true of Boston terriers, and if the Camel people don't
know that, they have never been around dogs.

The ad says: "But when a dog's nerves tire, he obeys his instincts
—he relaxes." This, I admit, is true. But I should like to call attention
to the fact that it sometimes takes days, even weeks, before a dog's
nerves tire. In the case of terriers it can run into months.

I knew a Boston terrier once (he is now dead and, so far as I
know, relaxed) whose nerves stayed keyed up from the twenty-fifth
of one June to the sixth of the following July, without one minute's
peace for anybody in the family. He was an old dog and he was
blind in one eye, but his infirmities caused no diminution in his
nervous power. During the period of which I speak, the famous
period of his greatest excitation, he not only raised a type of general
hell which startled even his closest friends and observers, but he gave
a mighty clever excuse. He said it was love.

"I'm in love," he would scream. (He could scream just like a
hurt child.) "I'm in love and I'm going *crazy*."

Day and night it was all the same. I tried everything to soothe
him. I tried darkness, cold water dashed in the face, the lash, long
quiet talks, warm milk administered internally, threats, promises,
and close confinement in remote locations. At last, after about a
week of it, I went down the road and had a chat with the lady who

16

owned the object of our terrier's affection. It was she who finally cleared up the situation.

"Oh," she said, wearily, "if it's that bad, let him out."

I hadn't thought of anything as simple as that myself, but I am a creature of infinite reserve. As a matter of record, it turned out to be not so simple—the terrier got run over by a motor car one night while returning from his amorous adventures, suffering a complete paralysis of the hip but no assuagement of the nervous system; and the little Scotty bitch returned to Washington, D.C., and a Caesarian.

I am not through with the Camel people yet. Love is not the only thing that can keep a dog's nerves in a state of perpetual jangle. A dog, more than any other creature, it seems to me, gets interested in one subject, theme, or object, in life, and pursues it with a fixity of purpose which would be inspiring to Man if it weren't so troublesome. One dog gets absorbed in one thing, another dog in another. When I was a boy there was a smooth-haired fox terrier (in those days nobody ever heard of a fox terrier that *wasn't* smooth-haired) who became interested, rather late in life, in a certain stone. The stone was about the size of an egg. As far as I could see, it was like a million other stones—but to him it was the Stone Supreme.

He kept it with him day and night, slept with it, ate with it, played with it, analyzed it, took it on little trips (you would often see him three blocks from home, trotting along on some shady errand, his stone safe in his jaws). He used to lie by the hour on the porch of his house, chewing the stone with an expression half tender, half petulant. When he slept he merely enjoyed a muscular suspension: his nerves were still up and around, adjusting the bed clothes, tossing and turning.

He permitted people to throw the stone for him and people would. But if the stone lodged somewhere he couldn't get to he raised such an uproar that it was absolutely necessary that the stone be returned, for the public peace. His absorption was so great it brought wrinkles to his face, and he grew old before his time. I think he used to worry that somebody was going to pitch the stone into a lake or a bog, where it would be irretrievable. He wore off every tooth in his jaw, wore them right down to the gums, and they became mere brown vestigial bumps. His breath was awful (he panted night and day) and his eyes were alight with an unearthly zeal. He died in a fight with another dog. I have always suspected it was because he tried to hold the stone in his mouth all through the battle. The Camel people will just have to take my word for it: that dog was a living denial of the whole theory of relaxation. He was a paragon of nervous tension, from the moment he first laid eyes on his slimy little stone till the hour of his death.

The advertisement speaks of the way humans "prod" themselves to endeavor—so that they keep on and on working long after they should quit. The inference is that a dog never does that. But I have a dog right now that can prod himself harder and drive himself longer than any human I ever saw. This animal is a dachshund, and I shall spare you the long dull inanities of his innumerable obsessions. His particular study (or mania) at the moment is a black-and-white kitten that my wife gave me for Christmas, thinking that what my life needed was something else that could move quickly from one place in the room to another. The dachshund began his research on Christmas eve when the kitten arrived "secretly" in the cellar, and now, five months later, is taking his Ph.D. still working late at night on it, every night. If he could write a book about that cat, it would make *Middletown* look like the work of a backward child.

I'll be glad to have the Camel people study this animal in one of his relaxed moods, but they will have to bring their own seismograph. Even curled up cozily in a chair, dreaming of his cat, he quivers like an aspen.

The Hour of Letdown

E. B. WHITE

When the man came in, carrying the machine, most of us looked up from our drinks, because we had never seen anything like it before. The man set the thing down on top of the bar near the beerpulls. It took up an ungodly amount of room and you could see the bartender didn't like it any too well, having this big, ugly-looking gadget parked right there.

"Two rye-and-water," the man said.

The bartender went on puddling an Old-Fashioned that he was working on, but he was obviously turning over the request in his mind.

"You want a double?" he asked, after a bit.

"No," said the man. "Two rye-and-water, please." He stared straight at the bartender, not exactly unfriendly but on the other hand not affirmatively friendly.

Many years of catering to the kind of people that come into saloons had provided the bartender with an adjustable mind. Nevertheless, he did not adjust readily to this fellow, and he did not like the machine—that was sure. He picked up a live cigarette that was idling on the edge of the cash register, took a drag out of it, and returned it thoughtfully. Then he poured two shots of rye whiskey, drew two glasses of water, and shoved the drinks in front of the man. People were watching. When something a little out of the ordinary takes place at a bar, the sense of it spreads quickly all along the line and pulls the customers together.

The man gave no sign of being the center of attention. He laid a five-dollar bill down on the bar. Then he drank one of the ryes and chased it with water. He picked up the other rye, opened a small vent in the machine (it was like an oil cup) and poured the whiskey in, and then poured the water in.

The bartender watched grimly. "Not funny," he said in an even

19

voice. "And furthermore, your companion takes up too much room. Why'n you put it over on that bench by the door, make more room here."

"There's plenty of room for everyone here," replied the man.

"I ain't amused," said the bartender. "Put the goddam thing over near the door like I say. Nobody will touch it."

The man smiled. "You should have seen it this afternoon," he said. "It was magnificent. Today was the third day of the tournament. Imagine it—three days of continuous brainwork! And against the top players in the country, too. Early in the game it gained an advantage; then for two hours it exploited the advantage brilliantly, ending with the opponent's king backed in a corner. The sudden capture of a knight, the neutralization of a bishop, and it was all over. You know how much money it won, all told, in three days of playing chess?"

"How much?" asked the bartender.

"Five thousand dollars," said the man. "Now it wants to let down, wants to get a little drunk."

The bartender ran his towel vaguely over some wet spots. "Take it somewhere else and get it drunk there!" he said firmly. "I got enough troubles."

The man shook his head and smiled. "No, we like it here." He pointed at the empty glasses. "Do this again, will you, please?"

The bartender slowly shook his head. He seemed dazed but dogged. "You stow the thing away," he ordered. "I'm not ladling out whiskey for jokestersmiths."

" 'Jokesmiths,' " said the machine. "The word is 'jokesmiths.' "

A few feet down the bar, a customer who was on his third highball seemed ready to participate in this conversation to which we had all been listening so attentively. He was a middle-aged man. His necktie was pulled down away from his collar, and he had eased the collar by unbuttoning it. He had pretty nearly finished his third drink, and the alcohol tended to make him throw his support in with the underprivileged and the thirsty.

"If the machine wants another drink, give it another drink," he said to the bartender. "Let's not have haggling."

The fellow with the machine turned to his new-found friend and gravely raised his hand to his temple, giving him a salute of gratitude and fellowship. He addressed his next remark to him, as though deliberately snubbing the bartender.

"You know how it is when you're all fagged out mentally, how you want a drink?"

"Certainly do," replied the friend. "Most natural thing in the world."

There was a stir all along the bar, some seeming to side with the bartender, others with the machine group. A tall, gloomy man standing next to me spoke up.

"Another whiskey sour, Bill," he said. "And go easy on the lemon juice."

"Picric acid," said the machine, sullenly. "They don't use lemon juice in these places."

"That does it!" said the bartender, smacking his hand on the bar. "Will you put that thing away or else beat it out of here. I ain't in the mood, I tell you. I got this saloon to run and I don't want lip from a mechanical brain or whatever the hell you've got there."

The man ignored this ultimatum. He addressed his friend, whose glass was now empty.

"It's not just that it's all tuckered out after three days of chess," he said amiably. "You know another reason it wants a drink?"

"No," said the friend. "Why?"

"It cheated," said the man.

At this remark, the machine chuckled. One of its arms dipped slightly, and a light glowed in a dial.

The friend frowned. He looked as though his dignity had been hurt, as though his trust had been misplaced. "Nobody can cheat at chess," he said. "Simpossible. In chess, everything is open and above the board. The nature of the game of chess is such that cheating is impossible."

"That's what I used to think, too," said the man. "But there *is* a way."

"Well, it doesn't surprise me any," put in the bartender. "The first time I laid my eyes on that crummy thing I spotted it for a crook."

"Two rye-and-water," said the man.

"You can't have the whiskey," said the bartender. He glared at the mechanical brain. "How do I know it ain't drunk already?"

"That's simple. Ask it something," said the man.

The customers shifted and stared into the mirror. We were all in this thing now, up to our necks. We waited. It was the bartender's move.

"Ask it what? Such as?" said the bartender.

"Makes no difference. Pick a couple big figures, ask it to multiply them together. You couldn't multiply big figures together if you were drunk, could you?"

The machine shook slightly, as though making internal preparations.

"Ten thousand eight hundred and sixty-two, multiply it by ninety-nine," said the bartender, viciously. We could tell that he was throwing in the two nines to make it hard.

The machine flickered. One of its tubes spat, and a hand changed position, jerkily.

"One million seventy-five thousand three hundred and thirty-eight," said the machine.

Not a glass was raised all along the bar. People just stared gloomily into the mirror; some of us studied our own faces, others took carom shots at the man and the machine.

Finally, a youngish, mathematically minded customer got out a piece of paper and a pencil and went into retirement. "It works out," he reported, after some minutes of calculating. "You can't say the machine is drunk!"

Everyone now glared at the bartender. Reluctantly he poured two shots of rye, drew two glasses of water. The man drank his drink. Then he fed the machine its drink. The machine's light grew fainter. One of its cranky little arms wilted.

For a while the saloon simmered along like a ship at sea in calm weather. Every one of us seemed to be trying to digest the situation, with the help of liquor. Quite a few glasses were refilled. Most of us sought help in the mirror—the court of last appeal.

The fellow with the unbuttoned collar settled his score. He walked stiffly over and stood between the man and the machine. He put one arm around the man, the other arm around the machine. "Let's get out of here and go to a good place," he said.

The machine glowed slightly. It seemed to be a little drunk now.

"All right," said the man. "That suits me fine. I've got my car outside."

He settled for the drinks and put down a tip. Quietly and a trifle uncertainly he tucked the machine under his arm, and he and his companion of the night walked to the door and out into the street.

The bartender stared fixedly, then resumed his light housekeeping. "So he's got his car outside," he said, with heavy sarcasm. "Now isn't that nice!"

A customer at the end of the bar near the door left his drink, stepped to the window, parted the curtains, and looked out. He watched for a moment, then returned to his place and addressed the bartender. "It's even nicer than you think," he said. "It's a Cadillac. And which one of the three of them d'ya think is doing the driving?"

The Perfect Bait

SCOTT CORBETT

This is the time of year when fishermen can't look at a page of print without seeing a column by some so-called expert telling us what kind of bait is best for what fish when; so while we're on that subject, I want to tell you about a little experience Judge Faggett and I had fishing on Cape Cod Bay.

We were out in the judge's skiff trolling for striped bass, and we weren't having any luck at all. The fishing had been terrible all week, and it hadn't improved any for us. We weren't getting a bite, we weren't getting a nibble. We weren't even getting a hard stare.

"Maybe we ought to try something else besides sea worms," I said. "We've tried 'em with spinners and spoons—maybe we should . . . Well, I don't know. Mac was telling me the fellows down that way have been using a blue nylon feather—"

"Poppycock!" snorted the judge. Judge Faggett is a large, imposing man, and his years on the bench somewhere—I never have found out exactly where—must have increased the powers of his voice. Nobody could have started out with a voice like that. His bald head was shaded by a discouraged old canvas hat, and he had on his usual fishing outfit—a set of garments which looked as if they had been stolen from some unusually slovenly sharecropper during the judge's recent swing through the South.

"All poppycock!" he went on. "Either they're biting or they're not. People never stop to think what may be going on down there," he added, pointing to the water. Judge Faggett has a low opinion of people. "Maybe just this morning a mess of stripers ran into a mess of sea worms and had a regular feast. They're lying on the bottom down there picking their teeth with crab claws and groaning. One of 'em says to another, 'Friend, I'm so stuffed I couldn't look another sea worm in the face!' Just then some simpleton like us lets down a sea worm he's paid 75 cents hard-earned cash money a dozen for.

24

What do the fish do? They take one look, burp quietly, and swim away fast as they can."

"I—"

"Stop talking so much and let's eat lunch," said Judge Faggett. "Get out the beer."

I stopped the boat, and we solaced ourselves with tomato-and-lettuce sandwiches and a few cans of beer.

"Another thing," Judge Faggett resumed. "People don't give fish credit for being as human as the next one. Fish are more like people than people think. They have fads just the same as people. One day some fish who's big and popular in the school decides he likes squid best, so for a while nothing will do but squid. It's all the fashion."

"Seems to me that that flies right in the face of your first thesis."

"My boy, you'd never make a judge," he said pityingly. "Hand me that sack of beer. And the opener."

I handed him the beer sack and the opener and dropped a piece of tomato out of my sandwich doing it. I picked it up off the floor boards and tossed it over the side.

There was a splash and a flip of a tail, and my eyes popped. "Judge! Did you see that?"

"See what?"

"That fish! It struck my tomato!"

Judge Faggett looked at the water and then he looked at me. "You're not getting any more beer," he said, rolling down the edge of the beer sack firmly.

"But I tell you it did! I threw out a hunk of tomato. The fish jumped. The tomato is gone."

"Took it down with him," snapped the judge.

With trembling fingers I picked another piece of tomato out of my sandwich. "We'll see," I said, and tossed it overboard.

Slosh!

"That was a worth-while fish," said Judge Faggett slowly, wiping the splash off his face. "How many more of those sandwiches have we?"

"Two."

"Get 'em out and let's bait up."

One hour later there wasn't footroom on the floor boards.

"What I like about it is, only the big boys seem to go for it," said the judge as we gaffed a 50-pounder over the side. Water was lapping at the top of the gunwales.

"Judge, we can't take any more fish," I said. "We don't dare.

Any more and we'll sink—boat, fish, and all—and have to swim for it."

Judge Faggett cast a sharp glance toward the shore. "Think we could swim it from here?"

"Well, I don't know about you," I said somewhat vainly, "but I could."

"Then start swimming," said the judge, turning back to his work. "I'm going to boat a couple more."

"Now, there's several possibilities we've got to consider," said Judge Faggett back at the house, while I was drying my clothes in front of the fire. He poured himself a few more fingers of my best liquor and cleared his throat with it. "First of all, is it the tomatoes they like, or is it the mayonnaise? Well, they must have seen tomatoes before, and they must have seen mayonnaise. Lots of fishermen take tomato sandwiches with mayonnaise on them and drop pieces of 'em in the boat and then heave 'em out the way you did. Therefore, it must be either the special kind of tomato or the particular brand of mayonnaise. Now, those tomatoes out of your own garden certainly are exceptionally well adapted to the purpose. They stay on the hook. Those tomatoes have the nastiest, thickest, toughest skins I've ever seen."

I decided to overlook this insult, since it happened to be true. "Yes, but—"

"Now, the mayonnaise. What brand of mayonnaise did you use?"

"Well, it's a new kind—"

"Ah!"

"It was on special. Cheaper than all the other brands at the supermarket, so my wife decided to try it."

"Now we're getting somewhere!" The judge rose and paced the floor for a moment, scratching his stomach thoughtfully, and then stabbed a finger at me. "Pick me up at 4 A.M. in the morning and we'll resume operations. Don't forget the mayonnaise. And the tomato. And the beer. Now let's drive down to the cove and go sell some fish."

We drove in the judge's jeep down to the out-of-the-way cove where we had beached his boat in order to keep the size of our catch a secret, and when we had loaded the stripers into the jeep we went out and sold part of them at each of four different fish markets, to keep anyone from getting wind of too much. During the fishing season, fishermen live in a police state of their own making. Every move a fisherman makes is watched. Meantime, he's watching all the others.

The second day we got the thing narrowed down in no time. Plain tomato got us nothing. Tomato with ordinary good mayonnaise got us nothing. But tomato with that bargain mayonnaise had our arms aching as we hauled them in.

"Prattley's Premier Mayonnaise," mused the judge, reading the label through his pince-nez, which were attached to his filthy fishing-jacket by a piece of 16-pound test Irish linen line. "I wonder if we could quietly pick up a block of stock in this concern? Well, that's for later. After we've completed our research. I can deduce part of this stuff's secret already, though. It's so goppy and gooky that even salt water doesn't wash it off the tomatoes. That's half the secret—it sticks."

Judge Faggett is a brilliant man. After all, he's a judge.

Well, the whole week went the same way. Every day we made a killing. Naturally, despite all our precautions, the other fishermen got suspicious and began to keep an eye on us, but we simply went off and fished in such unlikely places that they couldn't believe we'd get anything there. Wherever we went, though, the big ones followed. I suppose Judge Faggett and I are only flesh and blood, and prey to the same tendency to let success go to our heads as anyone else. It got so we were throwing back the 40-pounders.

The fifth day the wind came up a little too heavy to go out. "We won't let the day go to waste. We've got a job to do," said Judge Faggett, and we did it. We spent the day driving up and down the Cape buying up every jar of Prattley's Premier Mayonnaise we could find. We found 1263 jars. Judge Faggett was determined to corner the market if it took every cent I had.

The next day the weather leveled off and we went out again— and it happened. I knew something was wrong the minute I let out my line, because I ran out 75 feet without getting a strike. After I stopped my reel I still didn't get any action. Judge Faggett wasn't getting any either. We looked at each other, and the judge's nose seemed drained of color.

"I knew it! It was just a fad! A fish fad!" he groaned. "Now they've gone on to something else. The question is, what?"

"I'm not so sure," I said. "Something funny is going on here. I keep getting touches—extremely light touches. It's as if my tomato were out of balance. That's it! I'll bet there's something wrong with the mayonnaise today. I'll bet it's coming off!"

"Poppycock!" snapped Judge Faggett. "I tell you they've had enough of Prattley's. I *told* you this would happen," he added not quite accurately, as even judges sometimes will in the heat of a bad moment.

"Well, I'm going to reel in for a look at my bait," I declared, and began slowly reeling in. All the way, that strange action of my line continued. It was scarcely discernible, and yet it was there. Then, as the end of my line approached the boat—

"Great jumping Jeroboams!" the judge shouted under his breath, if you know how I mean. "Look at that monster!"

It was by half again the biggest striper we had ever seen. Long as the boat. Must have weighed a hundred. Sure world's record. And it was slowly and contentedly licking the tomato like a kid licking an ice-cream cone. "Judge! They don't want the tomato any more," I whimpered. "They've learned to lick off the mayonnaise!"

Judge Faggett collapsed from a half-standing position onto the center thwart, and his huge pot sagged in defeat. "We're whipped," he muttered. "Plain and simple whipped."

We've talked it over up one side and down the other ever since last summer, but we haven't been able to come up with anything yet. So if you can think of any way to put Prattley's Premier Mayonnaise on a hook and keep striped bass from licking it off we'll *give* you a jar. You can get in touch with us % General Delivery, Cape Cod.

Southern Sagas

Grinning the Bark Off a Tree

Davy Crockett

That Colonel Crockett could avail himself, in electioneering, of the advantages which well applied satire ensures, the following anecdote will sufficiently prove:

In the canvass of the Congressional election of 18—, Mr. ***** was the Colonel's opponent—a gentleman of the most pleasing and conciliating manners—who seldom addressed a person or a company without wearing upon his countenance a peculiarly good humoured smile. The colonel, to counteract the influence of this winning attribute, thus alluded to it in a stump speech:

"Yes, gentlemen, he may get some votes by *grinning*, for he can *outgrin me*—and you know I ain't slow—and to prove to you that I am not, I will tell you an anecdote. I was concerned myself—and I was fooled a little of the wickedest. You all know I love hunting. Well, I discovered a long time ago that a 'coon couldn't stand my grin. I could bring one tumbling down from the highest tree. I never wasted powder and lead, when I wanted one of the creatures. Well, as I was walking out one night, a few hundred yards from my house, looking carelessly about me, I saw a 'coon planted upon one of the highest limbs of an old tree. The night was very *moony* and clear, and old Ratler was with me; but Ratler won't bark at a 'coon—he's a queer dog in that way. So, I thought I'd bring the lark down in the usual way, *by a grin*. I set myself—and, after grinning at the 'coon a reasonable time, found that he didn't come down. I wondered what was the reason—and I took another steady grin at him. Still he was *there*. It made me a little mad; so I felt round and got an old limb about five feet long, and, planting one end upon the ground, I placed my chin upon the other, and took *a rest*. I then grinned my best for about five minutes; but the cursed 'coon hung on. So, finding I could not bring him down by grinning, I determined to have him—for I thought he must be a droll chap. I went over to the house, got my

31

axe, returned to the tree, saw the 'coon still there, and began to cut away. Down it come, and I ran forward; but d—n the 'coon was there to be seen. I found that what I had taken for one, was a large knot upon the branch of the tree and, upon looking at it closely, I saw that *I had grinned all the bark off, and left the knot perfectly smooth.*

"Now, fellow-citizens," continued the Colonel, "you must be convinced that, in the *grinning line,* I myself am not slow—yet, when I look upon my opponent's countenance, I must admit that he is my superior. You must all admit it. Therefore, be wide awake—look sharp—and do not let him grin you out of your votes."

Uncle Heber's Flytrap

W. C. HENDRICKS

There ain't no question 'bout my ole Uncle Heber being the goldurn-est laziest man in these parts, I reckon. Spent his full life trying to hatch up new ways of gitting outen work. Lots of folks 'cused him of shirking his dooties, and when he didn't make no comeback they said he didn't have no shame even, but I reckon the truth is he jes didn't have no energy to make argyment.

He never took no wife 'cause he was too lazy to go courting; and doing his own housekeeping like he done, he jes nacherly let his place go to rack and ruin. The shingles of his house all blowed off, and part of the roof caved in. Cracks come in the walls, and it rained in so hard that ever'thing in the house was wet. Uncle Heber stuck it out until the cracks got so big that the wind'd come in and blow the civers offen his bed. He caught cold and almost died 'cause he was too lazy to sneeze, even. At last the house sorta give up and caved in, and then Uncle Heber knowed he's got to move sommers else.

Feller told him 'bout a little island, eight mile up Brice's Crick, what nobody claimed, and Uncle Heber jes moved on up there. Was too lazy to explore it first, jes put his stuff together in a duffel bag, called his dog, and off he set.

The ground on that island was the richest, I reckon, anywhere could be found. No crops had ever been growed on it and it was made up of silt washed up from the crick. Uncle Heber was in the best piece of luck anybody ever heerd of, I reckon. All he had to do was push a stick in the ground, and goldurn if it didn't take root and grow. On the island was enormous trees of all kinds, some of 'em as thick in the trunk as a house. They was apple trees with apples as big as punkins, and persimmon trees with persimmons as big as your head and as sour as a old maid schoolteacher's mouth. The catfish in the crick was as big as alligators. Only trouble was that ever'thing

33

else was in perportion. The good things was the bestest, but the bad things was the worstest anybody ever heerd tell of.

Uncle Heber sure was in clover. He found a big holler tree what he makes into a house, and there's plenty of fruit and fish and ever'-thing he needs. He had brung along his old clay pipe and some fine-cut backer, and of course when he filled his pipe he spilt some backer and jes let it lay. Well, the backer took roots and growed up into the biggest and strongest backer leaves anybody ever heerd of.

He figgered out a good way to catch catfish and not tire hisself out. He'd balance his pole on a forked stick, and put a rock on the limb of a tree jes over the shore end of the pole. On the rock he tied a string. Then in the limb of the tree he rigged up a sharp knife atween two tater graters. He'd stretch hisself out on the crick bank, puffing on his pipe and cogerate hisself on how to cut down on his work. When he sees a nibble on the fishline, he pulls the string. The rock falls off on the end of the pole. This jerks the fish outen the water, 'crost the knife what guts it, and through the tater graters what takes off the scales. He didn't bother 'bout the heads and tails, jes cooked the fish thataway and left the rest for his dog.

Uncle Heber'd lost all his teeth when he was a young feller, jes 'cause he was too lazy to chew his food, I reckon, but he got 'round that all right. He traded a man outen a set of store teeth and then rigged up some clockwork to make the teeth champ up and down. Uncle Heber'd wind up the clockwork and put them in his mouth and let his jaw hang loose. Then he'd feed in his rations and the teeth'd chew it up for him. He used to keep the teeth in his hip pocket, but oncet they got started running in his pocket and bit a hunk outen Uncle Heber, and after that he kept 'em out on the table where he could see 'em.

Oncet he was laying on his back 'longside his fishpole on the crick bank, smoking his pipe and figgering how he was getting tired of catfish and wanted some fresh meat and how he could get some meat without trubble, when a big idee hit him. He 'membered 'bout a little plant he'd seen down near Wilmin'ton what folks call the Venus flytrap and this plant catches flies and little frogs. He figgered that in his fertile land mebbe one of them flytraps'd grow big enough to trap him some game.

After worrying 'bout it two or three months, he got up enough energy to push his raft acrost the crick, walk to the road, and pick up a ride to Wilmin'ton. He got a Venus plant and took it back to his island and planted it in a clear space.

In no time atall that plant begin to grow, and Uncle Heber see he had figgered proper and correct and the plant is going to be big as a live-oak tree. When the Venus plant was six foot high, it caught a rabbit one night. In the morning Uncle Heber see the jaws of the trap shet tight and a rabbit tail sticking out. He figgered and figgered how to git the rabbit out and fin'ly he hit on it. I be goldurn if he didn't light up his pipe with that strong backer and blow at the Venus trap. The plant got real white and began to shiver and opened up its trap and let the rabbit drop out.

Uncle Heber figgered this was the best luck of all. The Venus plant kept on catching him game, most every night, and in a few months it was big enough to catch a deer or a bear. Uncle Heber had so much game he didn't bother to fish no more, jes eat his fill on game. This went on for quite a spell, and Uncle Heber was sitting purty and the only thing he was worrying 'bout was how to find a easy way to dress his game.

Then late one night he was woke up by a awful yammering going on outside. He got up and crawled outen his holler tree, and it was bright moonlight, and he sees his dog chasing a big skunk 'round the Venus tree. The dog was right behind the skunk, but couldn't quite catch it. All a-sudden the tree reaches out one of its traps and grobs up the skunk and the dog in one gulp.

Now Uncle Heber thunk a lot of his dog. It was his onliest friend, and the only thing he could talk to, and he ruther have 'most anything happen to him 'cept lose his dog. So he runs back to his tree house to fetch his pipe so he can blow smoke on the trap and make it open up.

But I reckon that skunk was too goldurn potent for the Venus trap. When Uncle Heber come up, the Venus tree is shaking all over. It shake back and forth and dip up and down. Big gobs of sticky sap, like 'lasses, come oozing out and run down on the ground. First thing Uncle Heber knowed one of the traps dip down and grob him up entire.

The Venus tree keeps on shaking like it's sick to its stummick. Then it gives a powerful lunge and tore itself up by the roots and landed smack in the middle of the crick.

Iffen it hadn't been that Uncle Heber was smoking his pipe when the trap grobbed him he'd a-been a goner, I reckon. The Venus tree started down stream with him in one trap and the dog and the skunk in 'nother, and he jes puffed up a couple good puffs of that pipe and the Venus tree wilted right down in the water and opened up its traps, wide open. Uncle Heber landed in the water, and the skunk and the dog landed in the water, and the three struck off for shore. Uncle Heber smelt the skunk, and the skunk smelt Uncle Heber, and the skunk jes turned 'round and jumped back in the Venus trap.

Uncle Heber was a changed man after that. He moved to town and got a job in a livery stable, and he give up smoking. Said he couldn't stand that sissy stuff they sold in town and called it backer.

Bear Hunt in Reverse

W. C. Hendricks

Some men come down here in Onslow huntin' swamp bear, and sometime a man say to me, "Uncle Aaron, you wants to guide us on our bear hunt?" but I say, "No, suh, I don't guide nobody on no bear hunt. I has a good respeck fer them bear and all I ax is if the bear let me 'lone I lets the bear 'lone."

Them swamp bear are huge and pow'ful critters, sure 'nuf, and in the winter when they gits good and hungry they come outen the swamp and catches what they can and eats it. They come right in the pig sty and pick up a fat hawg and carry it off like nuffin' atall. They ain't no bear trap what'll hold one of 'em. I've seed bear traps all twisted to pieces where some big ole bear done pulled it offen his foot and beat it up on a tree or stump. Yes, suh, them swamp bear has got my respeck, and yo'all can hunt 'em all you please, but don't no cullud folks bother 'em none.

This time I's tellin' 'bout, when that bear hunt me, war eight year ago, in November. Mistah Bill Whitt had done kilt his hawgs and I help him, and Mistah Whitt say he pay me with fresh meat, sech as liver, and jowls, and haslets, and foots, and backbone, and some sa'sage, and chittlin's.

The day atter we butcher them hawgs, I hitch up my ole hoss to the car'yall, and drive the fo' mile to Mistah Whitt's place to git my meat. By time I had loaded up my meat, and help Mistah Whitt some 'bout the place cleanin' up, it war gittin' dark. Mistah Whitt he ask me did I have a gun, 'cause they might be some critters 'long the swamp road, but I say I don't have no gun, but iffen I move right 'long I reckon nuthin' goin' bother me none.

I gits 'long fine the first two mile, 'cause the moon shinin' bright and the road is out in the open, through cotton patches and cleared fields, but 'bout half-way home the road drops down through the woods and the swamp on both sides.

Soon's I gits in the woods, it plum black dark, like it poured outen a tar bar'l. I couldn't see the road at first, but atter while I begin to make out the ruts and mud holes. It so dark, I begins to think I made a mistook, and I should a-stayed at Mistah Whitt's till mornin'. The wind what had been cold out in the open, now die down account the trees, but I heered it messin' with the dry leafs and rattlin' the daid limbs, then I heered somethin' else.

'Twar somethin' a-tween a growl and a grunt, and I look 'round and I see the biggest bear I ever hope to see this side of jedgment. He war big as a cow, and right aside the road, and look like he a-squattin' on his haunches, fixin' to jump up in the wagon.

I knows he's a smellin' that fresh meat in the back of the car'yall, and I knows som'thin' else—that a bear know the smell of a cullud pusson and all bear like to eat cullud folks.

I hits the hoss a lick with the switch, and he jump and the bear jump at the same time. The bear done cotch hold of the tailgate, and he pullin' hisself up, and I do the fust thing what comes to my mind, I grabs up a hawg haid and I throws it outen on the road.

The bear he let go and hops back to the hawg head, and he starts to eat it up. I keeps whippin' up the hoss and we movin' 'long top speed, lickety bump, down the road. Afore I gits fifty yard that bear done et up the hawg head and he take out atter us agin. Seem like we standin' still the way that bear gain on us. I never knowed a bear could run so fast, but I sure knows it now.

When the bear gits his nose even with the tailgate agin, I throws out 'nuther piece of meat, but the bear jes grab that outen the air and swaller it with one gulp. Look to me like he goin' jump in the wagon, spite all I could do. I kept throwin' out the meat, but the more he got the more he wanted. I tied the reins 'round the footboard and let the hoss do his own runnin', 'cause the smell of that bear had done put him in top speed and he war doin' his bestest.

I crawl to the back of the car'yall, and jes set and throwed meat to the bear, but I could see these hunks was jes chickenfeed to him, and that all the hawg meat I had aboard wouldn't fill him up, and when all the hawg meat was gone they's nothin' left fer him but me and the hoss.

The hawg meat git lower and lower, and I git skeerder and skeerder. I thinks 'bout my burial 'surance, and how I's done paid fer a big funer'l, and morners, and ever'thin', but iffen that bear gits me they won't be nothin' left to bury.

When I throwed out the last piece of hawg meat, I begins to pray.

"Lawd," say I, "do somethin' and do it quick, else it'll be too late. This here bear ain't waitin' fer nuthin' and nobody, but please, Lawd, don't let this bear be in no bigger hurry than You is."

I lay flat on the wagon bed, jes as the bear leaped over the tailgate. He overshoot the wagon, and seat, and landed slap dab on the hoss. I sure hated to lose that hoss, but I figger it's the hoss or me, and I can spare the hoss better'n I can spare me. I hear the bear a-crackin' and a-munchin' on the hoss, and I wonders should I run fer it, but I jes can't make up my mind, 'cause I knows that bear'd cotch me in three shakes of a lamb's tail.

I lay there shiverin' and listenin', and all 'toncet the wagon begins to move 'long. I reckon we's on a hill and a-coastin' down grade, but I wonders what keeps the shafts from a-cotchin' in the road, less the bear done et up the shafts, too.

The wagon gits to movin' faster and faster, and then we comes outen the woods into the open, and the moon light all up, and I crawls up to the seat, and I'm blest iffen that'ar bear ain't in the harness, slicker'n a whissel, and a-pullin' the wagon 'long at a gallop.

He'd done et up the hoss, and he'd done et hisself all the way into the harness. The bridle was on his haid, and the bit was in his mouf. The bellyband was stretched tight 'round his middle, and the hamestraps was right on the whiffletree.

That war pie to me, and I drove him right on home as slick as you please, and lock him in the stable. He real quiet, and his belly is a-bulgin' full, and he lay right down in the straw and go to sleep.

I got the ole squirrel gun down, and I loaded it with all the powder and slugs I got, and I blowed that bear haid half off.

We never did miss that hawg meat, 'cause we got 'nuf bear meat to last all winter, and I didn't miss the hoss, nuther, 'cause I traded the bear skin fer 'nuther hoss. But that all the bear huntin' I want, and iffen they done leave me 'lone I's plum satisfied.

Young Melvin

James R. Aswell

After his pappy passed on Young Melvin decided he wanted to travel. He'd always lived back at the forks of the creek and he hadn't ever at no time been farther from there than the crossroads.

So Young Melvin put out the fire and hid the ax and skillet and called up his hound named Bulger and he was on his way. He went over the hill and a good piece further and he come to the crossroads. He went straight to Old Man Bill Blowdy's house there. He knocked on the door.

Old Man Bill Blowdy come to the door and stuck his nose out the crack. "Who's there?" says he, not daring to come out for fear it was somebody he'd beat in some deal.

"It's me," says Young Melvin. "Just me and my hound dog Bulger."

Old Man Bill Blowdy opened the door then and gave Young Melvin a sly look. "Come in and rest and eat a bite," he says, faint-like.

He was a great big fat red man that was always grinning and easy talking, like butter wouldn't melt in his mouth. And he was just about the slickest, double-dealingest old cooter in the country or anywhere else at all. Nobody could beat him in a deal—never had, anyway—or when it come to a law-suit. Always lawing somebody, Old Man Bill Blowdy was.

"Why don't you come in, Young Melvin?" he says.

"Because I'm on my way, Mister Old Man Bill Blowdy. I'm a-going to town for sure. It's forty miles and across two counties but I aim to see that town. That's why I come to see you."

Old Man Bill Blowdy started shutting the door. "Now, now, Young Melvin," he says. "I'm hard up for money right now. I couldn't loan my sweet mother, now in heaven praise be, so much as a penny."

40

"I don't want no money," says Young Melvin. "I ain't the borrowing kind."

So Old Man Bill Blowdy poked his head out again. "What can I do for you then?"

"Well, it's like this. You're my twenty-third cousin, my only kin in this world. I got a favor for you to do for me."

Old Man Bill Blowdy started sliding that door shut. "No, no favors. I make it a rule to do no favors and don't expect none from nobody."

"It's a favor I'm aiming to pay for," says Young Melvin.

"Oh," says Old Man Bill Blowdy, opening the door once more, "that's different now. Come right in, Young Melvin."

"No sir, no need to come in, for I'd just be coming out again. What I want you to do is keep my fox hound Bulger while I'm off on my travels. I'll pay his keep, I'll pay what's right when I come back to get him."

Old Man Bill Blowdy grinned all over his face. He thought he saw a way to make himself something extry or get him a fox hound one. Everybody knew Young Melvin was simple. Honest as the day's long but simple.

"Why yes," says Old Man Bill Blowdy. "Why yes, I'll keep Bulger for you, Young Melvin, and glad to."

So Young Melvin gave his hound dog over and bid Old Man Blowdy farewell. "I'll be back next week or month or sometime. I don't know how long it'll be, for it's forty miles and across two counties to town."

Well, one day the week or month or anyhow sometime after that, here come Young Melvin down the pikeroad to the crossroads, limping and dusty and easy in mind. He went straight to Old Man Bill Blowdy's house and knocked his knuckles on the door.

Old Man Bill Blowdy stuck his nose out the crack and says, "Who's there?"

"It's me, it's Young Melvin."

"How are you, Young Melvin?"

"Fair to piddling. I walked to town and saw all the sights and then walked back here again. Forty miles and across two counties. Don't never want to roam no more. I'm satisfied now."

Old Man Bill Blowdy started shutting the door. "Glad to hear it, Young Melvin. Next time you come down to the crossroads, drop in and say hello. Any time, just any time, Young Melvin."

"Hold there! Wait a minute!" says Young Melvin.

"I'm busy," says the old man.

But Young Melvin got his foot in the door. "How about Bulger, Old Man Bill Blowdy? How about him?"

Old Man Bill Blowdy kept trying to shut the door and Young Melvin kept shoving his foot in.

"See here!" says Young Melvin. "I mean my fox hound."

"Oh him? Why, I declare to my soul I'd almost forgot that hound dog, Young Melvin. I sure almost had."

"Where is he at?" says Young Melvin, still trying to keep the old man from closing the door.

"I'll tell you," says Old Man Bill Blowdy, still trying to shut it, "I feel mighty bad about it, Young Melvin, but your Bulger is no more."

"Howcome? What do you mean?"

"Why, he's perished and gone, Young Melvin. The first night after you left I sort of locked him up in that little busted-down house over in the Old Ground. Well sir, Young Melvin, those last renters of mine that lived there was powerful dirty folks. They left the place just lousy with chinch bugs. Them bugs was mortal hungry by this time. So they just eat that Bulger of yours alive. Eat all but the poor thing's bones by morning—and the bones was pretty well gnawed.

"It was my fault in one way. I ought to known better than put your dog in there, Young Melvin. But I done it. So I won't charge you a penny for his keep the night I had him. I aim to do the fair thing."

Well, Old Man Bill Blowdy stuck his sly eye to the crack of the door to see how Young Melvin was taking it. He knew the boy was simple. He figured he had him. Because Old Man Bill Blowdy had Bulger hid out and he aimed to swap him for something to a man he knew in the next county.

So Young Melvin stood there looking like the good Lord had shaken him off His Christian limb. Tears come in his eyes and he sleeved his nose. "That dog was folks to me," he says. "Them chinch bugs don't know what they done to me."

He pulled his foot out of the door and he backed down the steps. He started towards home.

Old Man Bill Blowdy eased out on the porch to watch him go.

About that time Young Melvin turned around. "Mister Old Man Bill Blowdy," he says, "my place is way over the hill and a good piece further. I'm beat out and tired. Wonder if you'd loan me your mule to ride on? I'll bring it back tomorrow."

The old man knew Young Melvin was honest as the live-long day. Besides, he was so tickled with how he'd got him a good hound to swap and it not costing anything that he just called across the way to the crossroads store and got a witness to the loan and let Young Melvin take the mule. It was a fine mule, too, with the three hind ribs showing, the best sort of sign in a mule—shows he's a hard worker.

Next morning Young Melvin never showed up and Old Man Bill Blowdy got worried. He got worrieder still in the middle of the day when no sign of Young Melvin did he see.

But along about afternoon he saw Young Melvin come walking over the hill and down towards the crossroads. He run out on his porch and yelled, "Hey, Young Melvin, where's my mule?"

Young Melvin kept walking. He just shook his head. "I feel mighty bad about that mule, Mister Old Man Bill Blowdy," he called. "I sure do."

"Hey! Wait there!"

But Young Melvin went on, heading for the store at the crossroads.

So Old Man Bill Blowdy was so mad he didn't wait to get his shoes. He just jumped off the porch and run across to Square Rogers, that good old man's house up the road a ways.

"Square," he says, "I want you to handle Young Melvin. He stole my mule."

The Square waked up his deputy and the deputy went down and brought in Young Melvin. Everybody at the crossroads come tagging along behind.

Square said, "Son, they tell me you stole a mule."

"No sir, Square Rogers, I never done it," says Young Melvin.

Old Man Bill Blowdy stomped his bare feet and shook his fists. "He's a bald-faced liar!"

"Curb yourself down, Old Man Bill Blowdy," says the Square, "and let the boy tell his side. Go ahead, Young Melvin."

So Young Melvin told his side, told how he borrowed the mule and started for home. "Well," he says, "you know I live over the hill and a good piece further. I rode that mule to the top of the hill. I was minding my own business and not giving nobody any trouble. Then all on a sudden I see a turkey buzzard dropping down out of the sky. Here it come, dropping fast and crowing like a game rooster.

"First thing I knew that old buzzard just grabbed Old Man Bill Blowdy's mule by the tail and started heaving and the mule's hind legs lifted off the ground and I went flying over his head and hit a rock head-on. I failed in my senses a minute. When I could see straight, I saw that buzzard sailing away with the mule, most a mile high and getting littler all the time.

"And that's how it happened. I sure am sorry, but there ain't much you can do with a thing like that, Square."

"Hold on there!" says Square Rogers, that good old man. "I've seen many a turkey buzzard in my time, Young Melvin, but never a one that could crow."

"Well," says Young Melvin, "it surprised me some too. But in a county where chinch bugs can eat up a full-grown fox hound in one night, why I just reckon a turkey buzzard has a right to crow and fly off with a mule if he wants to."

So it all come out and Square Rogers, that good old man, made Old Man Bill Blowdy fork up Bulger and then Young Melvin gave back the mule.

Old Man Bill Blowdy was mocked down to nothing. He just grieved and pined away and it wasn't no more than ten years before he taken sick and wasted away and died.

The Red Rats of Plum Fork

JESSE STUART

It's not been too long ago since it happened, but it was before we had heard of the guaranteed ways of getting rid of 'em. We didn't take any newspapers and we had to find our own way to destroy these rats which had come in such great numbers to our place. They multiplied so fast they'd about taken our place over. When I went to the henhouse to feed the chickens, rats came from the holes they'd gnawed through the floor. They'd look at me a full minute. I'd yell "shoo" at the rats and scare the chickens. The rats would walk across the floor while I kicked at 'em. They'd eat the corn I put in the feeder for the chickens. The chickens stood back and looked on with tiny glassy eyes from their little heads cocked sidewise.

We'd never seen anything like it. We lived the last house up on Plum Fork of the Tiber River. The Plum Fork jolt-wagon road came to our place and there it stopped. The semi-circled hills formed a barrier. And the giant cliffs walled us in until we didn't have to build a fence around our farm. All we had to do was build fences across the valley to make pastures for our cattle, horses and sheep. Then, we had plenty of limestone bottom land left to farm. And our land in this limestone valley produced more bushels of corn and tons of hay to the acre than any land in Greenwood County. We often had to leave corn in the fields. Pa said it was a good idea to leave some corn in the field to toll the rats away so our cattle, sheep and horses could have peace at feed times. But the rats came anyway.

The rats loved the warmth of the barn. That was before the first invaders' grandchildren started multiplying. And when this happened, they began to spread. They got under our floor. They got behind the rocks in the cellar under the house. They got in our smokehouse. They got into our granary. They gnawed holes through the weather-boarding on our house and climbed up the open space between the weather-boarding and the studding until they got into the garret.

Brother Finn and I slept upstairs. We'd lie awake and listen to a football game every night. We'd hear their fullback take off with a sweetpotato Pa had stored in the garret to keep until spring. And as the fullback carried the ball we'd hear the squeaky shouts of the spectators.

After much rolling and falling on the garret floor, the game would end. Then, the spectators would get into a brawl over the game. And this would be too much. Finn would get out of bed and pound on the ceiling with a broomhandle. He'd get back in bed and try to sleep and the brawl would start again. Then I'd get out of bed, my turn now, and I'd throw my shoes against the ceiling to break up the second brawl. It was this way every night.

One night a big brawl started. Finn pounded with the broom and I threw shoes. I don't know how many times Finn got out of bed and how many times I had to get up. Finally, Finn went downstairs and told Pa we couldn't sleep. Pa knew what it was. He and Mom and my sisters were disturbed downstairs by the rats climbing up and down inside the walls. Pa got his automatic pistol and came upstairs in his long flannel nightshirt.

"I can't help it if I do put a few holes through the roof," he said. "I'll break up that game they're a-playin' up there."

Pa emptied his pistol through the ceiling. He filled the chamber with cartridges and cut loose again after several of the rats must have felt the hot lead. And then he reloaded and shot again. Pa put so many holes through the roof that Finn and I could lay in bed and see the autumn stars in the big high blue sky above. It silenced the rats all right. But the next day, Pa, Finn and I worked all day fixing the roof.

We had nine cats. We had gray cats, yellow cats and brindle cats. Not a black one, because Pa was afraid of a black cat. He never wanted one to cross the path to the barn in front of him. If one ever did, he pulled off his hat, spit in it and mumbled some strange words. But the cats we had grew fat and lazy. And they couldn't multiply as fast as the rats.

But Pa did have a smart idea. He went to Blakesburg and brought home a rat terrier. Pa paid twenty-five dollars for Jerry. It was a little price to pay for getting rid of this world of rats. Jerry was everything Tobbie Bostock told Pa he was. Pa hadn't more than turned Jerry loose until he went to work. He ran a rat under the henhouse. But we had concrete block footers laid under the henhouse and that was as far as Jerry could dig unless we tore down the henhouse and went under the foundation. Jerry ran rats up in the big barnlofts. We couldn't fork over tons of hay and get the rats. Jerry ran them under our floor. They had holes dug under the foundations.

When Pa saw a hole rats had gnawed through the weatherboarding, he took off that strip and replaced it with another. Then he'd have to paint that strip of weather-boarding white to match the rest of the house. It was a lot of work, but Pa did it. Then the rats got wise and dug under the foundations and gnawed through the studding and came up the walls to the garret. Jerry would run them to these holes and here he stopped and started digging. We'd have to fill up the holes and smooth the yard. Often he dug down in one of Mom's flower beds and this caused more trouble. He ran rats under the granary and behind the rocks in our cellar. We did manage to catch seventeen rats with him. That's when he caught a rat out in the open taking a morning walk and he picked him up on the ground. Once he found a nest of rats in their summer home, which was back under the bank of the little creek that flowed down through our barnlot. Jerry dug them out and killed them all. He was as much against the rats as we and the cats were. Jerry worked all the time, but there wasn't much he could do.

On days when it rained Pa took his pistol, Finn and I took our rifles, and we went to the barn. We turned the horses and cattle from the barns and we sat on mangers and feedboxes waiting for rats. We killed thirteen rats the first rainy day. Pa thought we might thin them down this way. But we learned rats were smarter than we thought. The next day it rained and we took our firearms to the barn, turned the cattle and horses out, but we didn't see a rat stick his head from a hole.

Pa even talked about selling our farm and moving away. Selling the most fertile farm in Greenwood County, Kentucky, a farm which produced over a hundred bushels of corn to the acre! Anything would grow on our limestone bottom land. We had more corn in bins, more livestock, hogs and sheep than any farmer in Greenwood County. We had money in the bank. Pa had stocks and bonds. He had invested in many places. But, Pa also had rats. Pa wondered if the rats had been sent to plague him for something he had done. He read where the plagues had been sent on the Egyptians. Pa had always been a church-going man. But he had never tithed. He thought the rats were a plague sent on him because he hadn't tithed. So he started tithing.

"I'd give a third of my earnings to the Lord," he told Mom, "if it would only stop this scourge of rats."

But his tithing didn't stop the rats. They kept coming, and multiplying. Once Pa prayed for a plague to strike the rats. That didn't happen. We kept old Jerry and he did what he could. Our cats multiplied to thirty-three. Pa said we should have had more cats. He thought the rats had carried away the young kittens while the mother cats and the toms were out looking for the rats. The rats killed our young chickens, climbed the cherry and apple trees and robbed our birds' nests of young birds.

"When I even think of a rat," Pa said one morning when we were feeding the horses, "I see something red!"

For the rats came out and ate with the horses after we'd put corn in their feed boxes. They ate with the cows and with the hogs. They were under the big hog pen. And they ate with every living thing on our farm except the cats, Jerry, and with us.

The night that Pa saw the most red was when sister Essie screamed in bed. Pa jumped up, turned on the light and a big old rat ran across the room. It had gotten into Essie's bed and had bitten her little toe. Mom got some medicine. The toe was bleeding and Essie was crying. Mom tied the toe up and Essie got in bed with Pa and Mom. She was afraid to go back to her own bed in case the rat would come back and bite her again. Pa laid his loaded pistol on a chair beside his bed. And the next night Pa brought a dozen cats, inside the house to protect us. Finn put a loaded rifle beside our bed.

"I don't know why we'd get this pestilence," Pa said. "I can't think of any reason why it was sent upon me!"

"We're rich farmers, Mick," Mom told him. "Maybe we've had this good land long enough. Five generations of your people have owned this land and prospered and handed something down from one generation to the other!"

"I've paid my debts and taxes," Pa said. "I give a tenth to the Lord! If you think it just, I'll give more than a tenth to the Lord!"

"I think we'd better sell," Mom said. "Move away and let the rats have the place!"

"It breaks my heart to think of sellin'," Pa said. "I know every foot of ground on this farm. I know the trees and the great walls of white limestone cliffs. This farm is a part of me. I'd hoped to divide it and let my two boys carry on after I'm gone. My people never multiplied like these rats."

"People are laughing at us," Mom said. "It's funny to everybody. They know why you started tithing at Church, Mick. We're not fooling anybody. They know we have plenty. You know you loan corn to farmers like banks loan money."

"But why not?" Pa said, his face getting red as a turkey's snout as he sat at the breakfast table and sipped coffee. "My rate of interest is not too high on my corn. I loan ten barrels to a farmer in autumn, and the next autumn I take back twelve!"

"And if you loan two barrels," Finn said, "you take back three. That's more than six percent. If you loan four barrels, you get back six that next autumn. That's something like thirty-three percent isn't it?"

"But corn's not like money," Pa argued. "You can write a check for money and you have to barrel corn. It's a lot of trouble to transact a loan."

"And we've got the rats," I said.

"Other people don't have them," Mom said. "I know this plague has been sent on us for a purpose."

"Rats know a good place when they see it," Finn said. "We feed 'em well. That's why they come here. What other farmer in Greenwood County feeds his rats as well as we do? I think rats talk like people. I think they go visiting other rats and tell them what a fine place we have here."

"Son, that's about right," Pa said. "Help me to find a way to get rid of these boogers! All that stands between us and happiness are these awful pests."

"I'll help you all I can, Pa," I said.

"You'll never get rid of 'em until you give away everything we got," Mom said.

"I'm not givin' away any more," Pa said. "Givin' away a third now!"

"Old rats, I'm afraid of 'em," Essie said. "I'll never sleep in that room again!"

"It's a plague sent on us," Mom said as we left the breakfast table. "It might be something you did before I married you, Mick!"

"Women have funny thoughts sometimes," Pa said as we walked toward the barn.

That day we took two wagons down to the mouth of Plum Fork

to haul cordwood Pa had bought from Billy-Buck Everyman. Billy-Buck cut sycamores and waterbirches that shaded his Tiber creek corn bottoms. Each year he cut cordwood for Pa's fireplaces and traded the wood to him for corn and hay. One year he traded wood for a fat hog.

Billy-Buck climbed on the wagon with Pa and me when we reached his house. Finn followed us across the bottom toward the stacks of wood.

"You got any rats, Billy-Buck?" Pa asked.

"Not that I know of," he answered Pa. "Why? What made you ask me that?"

"They're about to take over my place," Pa told him.

"You feed 'em well, Mick," Billy-Buck said.

Then Billy-Buck Everyman, a big man, with red beard all over his face, laughed until his stomach shook. He slapped his overall patched thighs with his ham-sized hands. His big fingers were like small sticks of stove-wood. His thumbs were sticks of wood, weathered by the seasons, that had been chopped off too short.

"Rats," Billy-Buck bellowed between spasms of laughter. "Rats! I don't have a rat and I don't have a cat! You got my rats, Mick. They went up Plum Fork to live with you! And you can have 'em, Mick! Warm 'em under your hearths with this wood I'm tradin' you for corn so I won't have to pay you corn interest!"

Pa's red face turned white as a frost-bitten pawpaw leaf as we rolled over the wagon trail across the bottom land that wasn't fertile as our limestone land. Pa wasn't laughing. It wasn't funny to Pa. It wasn't funny to me either.

"Know anyway to get rid of the pests?" Pa asked.

"Get you some cats and a dog!" Billy-Buck laughed harder than ever.

"I've got thirty-three cats and a dog," Pa said. "I've still got rats! They're all over my premises and they eat with my livestock and my fowls, they even eat my birds and my kittens."

The way Billy-Buck laughed he must have thought Pa was joking. All the time we loaded the wood, Billy-Buck laughed. And when we'd driven across the bottom and he got off the wagon at his own house, he was still laughing. He stood and watched us drive up Plum Fork and we heard him laughing when we got out of sight.

"I'll stop up here and see what Frog-Eye Scott says," Pa said. "Maybe he's got some rats. His land's a little better and he's got more corn to feed 'em. Maybe he can give a man a sensible answer."

When we reached Frog-Eye's house, we stopped. Pa gave me the lines and he got off the wagon. He just got through the paling gate when Frog-Eye stepped off the porch. He was a big heavy man, with a white moustache, clean red face and a pair of brown eyes too big for their sockets.

"Howdy, Mick."

"Howdy, Frog-Eye!"

"Something I can do fer ye, Mick?"

"Yep," Pa said, with a smile. "I want to know if you got any rats."

"No, I ain't, Mick," he told Pa. "I've heard you got all the rats. And that is one bit of goodness ye've done for me. You feed yer rats, Mick. They tell me ye let them eat with yer chickens, livestock and hogs."

Pa turned and walked back through the gate and climbed onto the wagon.

"God almighty sent plagues more than two thousand years ago," Frog-Eye said, as he twirled his handle-bar moustache with his big soft hands. "Plagues are sent fer different things!"

"My hands are not soft as milkweed stems in July," Pa said as I gave him the reins. "My hands are hard as the bark on tough-butted white-oaks."

We drove on and left Frog-Eye Scott standing in his yard in his clean-washed overalls and blue work shirt.

"I never liked Soda Rife too well," Pa said, "but I'm goin' to stop and see if he'll give me a civil answer when I ask him about these pests!"

Soda Rife, a man as small as Pa and whose hands were as calloused as Pa's, was chopping stovewood when we stopped. Pa got off the wagon and walked over and asked him if he was bothered with rats.

"Ain't got a rat, Mick," he said. He stuck his ax in the block. He was willing to talk with Pa about our trouble. "I think all my rats went up to your house because you feed them better. They didn't starve when they were here but a onery rat goes where he can better himself. He'll go where he can get a better handout. He likes something for nothing more than any varmint in this world."

"I must have everybody's rats," Pa said. "They're about to ruin us."

"They're tellin' this thing everyplace that it's a plague sent on you, Mick," Soda said. He got up close and looked Pa in the eye.

"But I don't believe that. You're a good man and a good neighbor. You work hard and you save. You're free-hearted. Ye give to good causes. Give more to the Church than everybody else combined. You've got rats. That's all. Get rid of 'em!"

"But how?" Pa asked. "Tell me how and I won't charge ye any rent on the corn I've loaned you!"

"I know the answer, Mick," Soda said, almost getting close enough to whisper in Pa's ear. "I'll take ye up on that bargain. If it don't work, I'll pay you the corn interest this fall. Forty barrels principal. Eight barrels interest."

"It's a bargain," Pa said as Finn and I listened.

"Bonwock Bush's boy, Sach Bush, over on Little Frazier, has a ferret. Go over there and get that boy and his ferret. Put that ferret in the ratholes and stand back with clubs! Man, they'll run out of holes, pop up through the ground, scale the walls and the ferret will go right after 'em! Right up in yer garret!"

"That's wonderful," Pa said. "I believe Soda you've given me the answer to our future happiness! I must be on my way! Thanks. The deal is on!"

We trotted the team to the barn. Pa left Finn and me to unhitch the teams and unload the wood. He put a saddle on our sorrel mare, Kate, and a saddle on Bill. "Tell yer Ma, I've got the answer," he said. "I don't have time to tell 'er. I'll bring Sach Bush back in the empty saddle. Have clubs ready! Won't be gone two hours."

We did what Pa told us. We cut a half dozen nice clubs a little longer than baseball bats. And Pa and Sach came galloping up Plum Fork on the horses.

Pa climbed down from the saddle. "Boys, get yer clubs and get ready. This is going to be some fun!"

Sixteen-year-old Sach Bush was slower to get out of the saddle. In his hand he held a mealsack and something was squirming around inside.

"Boys, I ain't fed this ferret no meat," Sach said. "He craves blood."

"Fetch 'im here," Pa said. "Put 'im in this hole under the horses' manger. He'll get what he craves!"

Sach opened the sack, looked into it, reached down carefully and caught the long ferret by the nape of the neck. It was dirty-white, with pink eyes, little shoulders, short legs and a big stomach. Its big stomach was back near its short hind legs.

"Where he can put that little head, he can go," Sach bragged as he put his head into the hole and the ferret was off. "He can work that stommick backward and forward if he gets in a tight squeeze and needs to. Afraid to put my hand on 'im he's so hungry fer blood. Get ready with yer clubs!"

A rat broke up through the ground in the middle of the stall and Pa cut down on him with his bat. It was a home run. Another jumped up and Pa got him. Two home runs for Pa! He grinned like a possum. Then, Finn got a three bagger on one. But the second strike he polished him off. I got one with three licks. Two rats got past Sach and made for the hayloft. He was a strikeout both times. He wasn't as eager to win the game as we were. Pa lost his smile when the two rats got away. Then something happened. He waited for more rats. They didn't come. Mom, Essie and Grace came to the barn to watch us rid the place of rats. Now everything had bogged down. Sach got down at the hole and called his ferret pet names. But the ferret wouldn't come out.

"He never acts like that," Sach said. "Something's wrong. Got a mattock?"

"Yes, we have," Pa said. "Go fetch it, Finn!"

When Finn brought the mattock, Sach started digging. He followed the rat hole across the stall leaving a big trench in our barn. Then, he got warm and Pa dug a spell. Finn dug and I dug. And we got bach to Sach. Then Pa, Finn and I again. We dug across the barn stall and over into another stall.

"We're a-ruinin' my barn," Pa said.

"Can't help that," Sach said. "I've got to find my ferret."

Then Essie saw the ground move. She put her foot on the place, near where Sach was digging. He lifted some dirt with the mattock and there was the ferret. He had killed three rats. One was behind him blocking the rathole and two were in front of him. He couldn't go either way. Sach lifted him up and said pet-words. And then he saw one of the ferret's eyes was gone and he had been bitten near the other eye.

"Never heard tell of rats a-fightin' a ferret before," Sach said. "They've about blinded my ferret. This is enough!"

"Got the rats hemmed," Pa said. "That's why they bit the ferret!"

"They're old residenters," Finn said. "This is their home and they're fightin' to keep it. And it looks like this place will be their home!"

Sach Bush charged Pa twenty-five dollars. And when Pa climbed in the saddle to take Sach home, he was a sad-looking man.

"Guess I'll collect the corn interest from Soda," Pa said sadly. "I didn't want it. Not if I could get rid of these rats! It's our last chance. I don't know what else to do."

Then, we went back to Pa's old idea. We got a few more cats. We got another rat terrier that we called Rags. We got more ammunition for pistol and rifles. And Pa bought fifty steel traps. We tried to keep down the multiplication.

One night Finn, Pa and I set steel traps at the mouth of every hole we could find. The next morning we had twenty-one rats in our traps.

"Boys, we've been doin' everything," Pa said. "I believe we can lick 'em with traps."

Pa was pleased. And we set the traps again. Morning after morning we looked at the traps. Occasionally we caught a half grown rat but never an old one.

"A rat is a smart thing," Pa admitted. "They know where all our traps are set!"

Then, Pa put meat rinds on the traps for bait.

"I'll feed 'em something and see how it works," he said.

He caught six rats the first night with fifty traps. And these were all we caught with bait.

It was a bright sunny November day. Pa told Finn and me to paint the roof of the big barn where we kept the livestock. Said the weather was right and now was the time to paint for there were a few rust-leaks in the tin. Paint it before snows laid on the roof and leaked on the hay. Finn and I had just opened a big can of bright-red roof paint. We had our ladders and brushes and were about ready to begin work.

"I hate this color," Finn said. "Bright-red is the color of October shoemake, sweetgum and sourwood leaves. When I see them falling I think of drops of blood. I think of the paint as bright red blood. I just don't like red. What is there about red that reminds one of blood and falling leaves and bad weather?"

Just then I heard the jaws of a trap under old Bill's manger. I heard a rat squeak and I ran up the hallway and looked over. There was a big rat in the trap. The steel jaws had barely caught him by the hind foot. I took the chain loose, carried rat and trap over to the paint can.

"I hate a rat too," Finn said. "I see red when I see one. Hold up the chain so he'll swing in the air! I'll paint 'im!"

"Why paint 'im?" I said. "Why waste paint on a rat?"

"Why not have a red rat?" Finn said. "Why not one of a different color?"

I held the chain while Finn painted the rat. Finn put a bright red coat of roofpaint on the rat.

"Now what are we goin' to do with 'im?" I said. "Kill 'im?"

"Oh, no," Finn said. "Turn 'im loose and let's have a red rat running around this barn!"

When I set the trap down and pressed the steel jaws with my foot the rat freed himself and dove into a hole under the manger. Then something happened we'll never forget. This red rat's kinfolks didn't know him. When he ran into his home, he scared his kinfolks! They started poppin' up in all directions. They even forgot the steel traps we had setting for them. The jaws clicked all over the horsebarn. But we didn't have time to look about the traps. Finn climbed upon the manger and I jumped upon a five gallon can of barnroof paint to let the rats go by. I thought one might try to climb up and bite me! I never saw anything like it.

"A red rat," Pa screamed and dropped his ax on the woodblock.

I saw him take off toward the house screaming for Mom as the rats moved toward him, the red rat trying to keep up. It was a sight to see Pa running ahead of the rats.

"Oh, it'll work," Finn shouted. "Go to the traps and fetch me rats!"

I brought another big rat to Finn. The jaws of the trap held his hind leg. Finn put the red paint to him in a hurry.

"Turn 'im under the chicken house," Finn shouted.

I ran to the chicken house, set my foot on the steel jaws and freed him at the opening of a slick rat hole under the foundations. Talk about rats! They came from holes around the henhouse, up through the ground, leaped from the windows . . . from everywhere. They were on their way! They ran toward the cliffs but couldn't scale the steep limestone cliffs! Then they turned the way the others had gone down Plum Fork. And I ran back to get another rat for Finn to paint.

"Paint 'em red, paint 'em red," Finn shouted, shaking his tousled blond hair. "Paint 'em red until this paint-smell leaves a-swimmin' in my head!"

I carried more rats to Finn. Rats caught by one leg in the traps.

Those caught by both hind legs weren't any good. But the three-legged red rats could keep close to the four-legged rats. They followed them as they raced down Plum Fork between the cliff-walled valley. Finn kept on painting them. We put one behind the rocks in the cellar. We put one under the hay in each barn loft. One in each of the five corn bins! One in the granary. Then we had to wait to take two to the house. Jerry had run from the fleeing rats. First the terrier tried to kill them. But they kept coming and were running over him. The cats started work at first. Then, they knew something was wrong! When they saw the swarms of fleeing rats, each swarm pursued by a red rat, the cats took off with their long bushy tails riding on the wind! Many ran up the apple trees for safety!

When we got to the house, Pa, Mom, Essie and Grace were standing on the porch watching the rats go by. Pa might have been praying. I don't know. But I do know Finn hadn't spared the red paint on the two rats we had in traps. We put them in big slickworn holes under the house and sprung the traps. And then we waited. We didn't have long to wait. Rats came from under the house and from inside as they made their get-away. When they ran across the porch Mom screamed and jumped up into the porch swing. Pa jumped up beside her. They held to the porch chains as the swing rocked. Essie and Grace screamed as they climbed up into the chairs. Behind this swarm of rats, two red rats limped across the porch in hot pursuit.

"I told you, Mick, what was wrong," Mom said. "Now we can live in peace and happiness!"

"Wonder what Soda, Frog-Eye and Billy-Buck are thinkin' now? We've had their rats. Now, they've got 'em back."

"They can have 'em," Essie laughed.

"Come on, Shan," Finn said with a grin. "We'd better get back on the job. We've got a lot of paintin' ahead of us on that barn roof."

The Angry Sailor

NORRIS YATES

Not long ago I was pulling a liberty in Baltimore, Maryland. While I was wandering around town I was putting forth my share of stopping at all the local hooch joints. I had been in quite a few that day and had seen quite a few sights. By sights I mean the local characters and out-of-town ones as well. This one dump topped them all though. I was sitting there downing my third bourbon and ginger when in walks this little short swabbie [sailor]. He was so short that he had to stand on his tiptoes to see over the bar. The bartender walked over to him and quoted "What's yours sailor?" The sailor looked up at the bartender, who was a great big six-foot-six giant and said out of the corner of his mouth, "Give me a beer and a shot of whiskey." The bartender walked away and brought the drinks. Without a word the swabbie drank his beer and to the amazement of everyone poured the shot of whiskey in the breast pocket of his blue jumper. As soon as this was done the sailor turned to the bartender and said, "One more beer and one more whiskey." The bartender hated to see good whiskey go to waste but he hurriedly refilled the short sailor's order. Again without a word the sailor drank his beer and into the pocket went the shot of whiskey. By this time the sailor was the center of attraction and all the customers in the place had him as their center of attraction. The bartender went red as he saw the sailor repeat his mysterious actions. For the third time the sailor asked for the same order as before, not aware that all of the eyes in the place were focussed on him. This time the bartender asked him not to waste the whiskey. The sailor merely gave him a dirty look and drank his beer and poured the entire contents of the shot glass again into his pocket. This time the huge bartender just couldn't stand it. He rushed over to the swabbie and started reading him off. He asked the swabbie just what satisfaction he was getting by pouring good whiskey into his pocket. With this the little sailor reached

57

out to his full extent and grabbed the big bartender by the front of his shirt and pulled him to where he wasn't any more than six inches away from his nose. Then he says, "You're pretty damn nosey aren't you? If you bother me once more about how I drink I'll personally take you outside and beat the living hell right out of you." With that a little white mouse with a very red nose stuck his head out of the sailor's pocket and said, "Yeah and that goes for your goddam cat too."

Memoirs of the Stable

H. L. MENCKEN

Horses, taking one with another, are supposed to be the stupidest creatures (forgetting, of course, horse-lovers) within the confines of our Christian civilization, but there are naturally some exceptions, and they probably include the whole race of Shetland ponies. During the interminable epoch stretching from my eleventh year to my fourteenth I was on confidential terms with such a pony, and came to have a very high opinion of his sagacity. As the phrase ran in those days, he was as sharp as a trap, and also excessively immoral. The last word, I should say at once, I do not use in the Puritan or Freudian sense, for Frank was a gelding; what I seek to convey is simply the idea that he was also a cheat, a rogue and a scoundrel. Nearly all his waking hours were given over to deceiving and afflicting my brother Charlie and me. He bit us, he kicked us, he stepped on our toes, he crowded us against the walls of his stall, and he sneezed in our faces, and in the intervals he tried to alarm us by running away, or by playing sick or dead. Nevertheless, we loved him, and mixed with our affection there was a great deal of sincere admiration.

Where he was bred we never heard, and, boy-like, did not inquire. One day in the Autumn of 1891 a couple of carpenters appeared in Hollins street and began to throw up a miniature stable at the end of the long backyard, and by the time they got the roof on Frank was in it, along with a yellow go-cart, a tabloid buggy with fringe around its top, a couple of sets of harness, and a saddle. It soon turned out that there was not room enough in the stable for both the go-cart and the buggy, so the buggy was moved to Reveille's livery-stable two blocks away, where my father's horse John was in residence. Simultaneously, a colored intern was brought in from the same place to instruct Charlie and me in the principles of his art, for we were told that we were to have the honor of caring for Frank.

59

Inasmuch as we had been hanging about stables since infancy,
watching the blackamoors at their work, this hint that we needed
tutelage rather affronted us, but we were so delighted by the privilege of becoming hostlers—the dream of every American boy in
that horsy age—that we let it pass, and only too soon we learned
that there was a great deal more to servicing a Shetland pony than
could be picked up by watching blackamoors service full-grown
horses.

Charlie, I believe, got the first kick, but I got the first bite. It
was delivered with sly suddenness on the second morning after the
intern from Reveille's had graduated me *cum laude* and gone back
to his regular job. He had cautioned me that in currying any sort of
horse it was necessary to pay particular heed to the belly, for it
tended to pick up contamination from the stall litter, and he had
added the warning that the belly was a sensitive area, and must be
tackled gently. I was gentle enough, goodness knows, but Frank, as
I was soon to learn, objected to any sort of currying whatsoever, top
or bottom, and so, when I stooped down to reach under his hull—he
was only nine hands high at the withers—he fetched me a good nip
in the seat of my pants. My reaction was that of a coiled spring of
high tension, and it was thus hardly more than a split second before
I was out in the yard, rubbing my backside with both hands. When I
tell you that Frank laughed you will, of course, set me down a nature-
faker; all the same, I tell you that Frank laughed. I could see him
through the window above his feed-trough, and there were all the
indubitable signs—the head thrown back, the mouth open, the lips
retracted, the teeth shining, the tears running down both cheeks. I
could even hear a sound like a chuckle. Thereafter I never con-
sciously exposed my caboose to him, but time and again he caught
me unawares, and once he gave me a nip so severe that the scar
remains to this day. Whenever I get to hospital—which is only too
often in these later years—the sportive young doctors enter it upon
their chart as a war wound.

Frank quickly developed a really marvelous technic of escape.
He had a box-stall that, considering his size, was roomy, and Charlie
and I kept it so clean that the hostlers from all the other stables in
the alley would drop in to admire it. There was a frame of soft red
clay to ease his forefeet, and a large piece of rock-salt to entertain
him on lazy afternoons. He got hearty meals of substantial horse-
victuals three times a day, and in cold weather the water used to mix
his mill-feed was always warm. Through the window above his

trough he could look out into the yard, and a section of it about twenty feet square was fenced off to give him a paddock. In this paddock he was free to disport a couple of hours every day, save only when there was snow on the ground. But when he was in it he devoted most of his time to hanging his head over the paling-fence, lusting for the regions beyond. Just out of his reach was a peach tree, and beyond it a pear tree, both still young and tender. One fine Spring day, with both trees burgeoning, he somehow cracked the puzzle of the catch on the paddock gate, and by the time he was discovered he had eaten all the bark off the peach tree, from the ground to a height of four feet. Charlie and I found it hard to blame him, for we liked the peach gum ourselves and often chewed it, flies and all, but my mother wept when the tree died, and the paddock gate was outfitted with an iron bar and two chains.

Frank never got through it again—that is, by his own effort. But one day, when a feeble-minded hired girl left it open, he was in the yard instantly and made a killing that still lives in the family tradition. Rather curiously, he did not molest the pear tree, but by the time he was chased back to his own ground he had devoured a bed of petunias, all my mother's best dahlias, the better part of a grape vine, and the whole of my father's mint patch. I have been told by eminent horse-lovers that horses never touch mint, but I am here dealing, not with a horse, but with a Shetland pony. Frank gradually acquired many other strange appetites—for example, for ice cream. Every time it was on tap in the house he would smell it and begin to stamp and whinny, and in the end it became the custom to give him whatever happened to be left. Once, when the hired girl got salt into it and the whole batch was spoiled, he devoured all of it—probably a gallon and a half—and then drank two buckets of water. He also ate oranges (skin and all), bananas (spitting out the skin), grapes, asparagus and sauerkraut. One day Charlie tried him with a slab of rat-trap cheese, but he refused it. Another day Charlie gave him a piece of plug tobacco wrapped in a cabbage leaf, but again without success. This last trick, in fact, offended him and he sought revenge at once. When he bit through the cabbage into the tobacco he gave a sudden and violent cough, and the plug hit Charlie in the eye.

When we were in the country in Summer Frank had my father's horse John for a stable-mate, and they got on together well enough, though it was plain to see that Frank regarded John as an idiot. This was a reasonable judgment, for John, who was a trotter, was actually

very backward mentally, and could be easily scared. Whenever the
two were in pasture together Frank would alarm John by bearing
down upon him at a gallop, as if about to leap over him. This would
set John to running away, and Frank would pursue him all over the
pasture, whinnying and laughing. John himself could no more laugh
than he could read and write. He was a tall, slim sorrel with a long,
narrow head, and was so stupid that he even showed no pride in his
speed, which was considerable. Life to him was a gloomy business,
and he was often in the hands of horse-doctors. If there was a stone
on the road he always picked it up, and when we were in the country and Charlie and I had charge of him we never bedded him down
for the night without investigating his frogs. In the course of an
average Summer we recovered at least twenty nails from them, not
to mention burrs and splinters. Like most valetudinarians he lived
to a great age. After my father's death we sold him to an animal
show that had Winter quarters in Baltimore, and he spent his last
years as a sort of companion to a herd of trained zebras. The zebras,
I heard, had a lot of fun with him.

One night, an hour or so after midnight, there was a dreadful
kicking and grunting in our stable in the country, and my father and
Charlie and I turned out to inquire into it. We found John standing
in the middle of his box-stall in a pitiable state of mind, his coat
ruffled and his eyes staring. Frank, next door, was apparently sleeping soundly. We examined John from head to foot, but could find
nothing wrong, so we contented ourselves with giving him a couple
of random doses from his enormous armamentarium of medicine
bottles, and talking to him in soothing tones. He seemed quite all
right in the morning, and my father drove him to and from town,
but that night there was another hullabaloo in the stable, and we had
to turn out again. On the day following John was put to grass and
Charlie and I went for a colored horse-doctor in Cross Keys, a nearby
village. He advised us to throw away all of John's medicines, and
prescribed instead a mild course of condition powders, with a handful of flaxseed once a day. This was begun instantly, but that night
the same dreadful noises came from the stable, and again the night
following, and again the night after that, and so on for a week. Two
or three other horse-doctors were called in during that time, but
they were all baffled, and John took to looking seedy and even
mangy. Meanwhile, my father began to suffer seriously from the
interruptions to his sleep, and talked wildly of having the poor horse
shot and his carcass sent to a glue-factory. Also, he began to discover

unpleasant weaknesses in his old friend Herman Ellis, from whom John had been bought. Ellis, hitherto, had been held up to Charlie and me as a model, but now it appeared that he drank too much, kept two sets of books, was a Methodist, and ought to be expelled from the Freemasons.

Charlie and I, talking the business over at length, came to the conclusion eventually that there must be more to it than met the eye, and so decided to keep watch at the stable. There was already floating through our minds, I think, some suspicion of Frank, for we were at pains to prevent him learning what we were up to. At our bedtime we sneaked into the carriage-house on tiptoe, and there made ourselves bunks in the family dayton-wagon. We were soon sound asleep, but at the usual time we were aroused by a great clomping and banging in the stalls adjoining, and turned out to take a stealthy look. It was a moonlight night, and enough of the gentle glare was filtering into the stable to give us an excellent view. What we saw scarcely surprised us. All the uproar, we discovered, was being made by Frank, not by John. Frank was having a whale of a time flinging his heels against the sides of his stall. The noise plainly delighted him, and he was laughing gaily. Presently poor John, waking in alarm, leaped to his feet and began to tremble. At this Frank gave a couple of final clouts, and then lay down calmly and went to sleep—or, at all events, appeared to. But John, trying with his limp mind to make out what was afoot, kept on trembling, and was, in fact, still half scared to death when we announced our presence and tried to comfort him.

My father had arrived by this time, his slippers flapping, his suspenders hanging loose and blood in his eye, and we soon made him understand what had happened. His only comment was "Well, I'll be durned!" repeated twenty or thirty times. We soon had a bridle on Frank, with a strap rigged from it to his left hind leg, and if he tried any more kicking that night he knocked himself down, which was certainly no more than he deserved. But we heard no more noise, nor was there any the next night, or the next, or the next. After a week we removed the strap, and then sat up again to see what would happen. But nothing happened, for Frank had learned his lesson. At some time or other while the strap was on, I suppose, he had tried a kick—and gone head over heels in his stall. He was, as I have said, a smart fellow, and there was never any need to teach him the same thing twice. Thereafter, until the end of the Summer, he let poor John sleep in peace. My father fired all the horse-doctors, white and black, and threw out all their remedies. John recovered quickly, and a little while later did a mile on the Pimlico road in 2.17½—not a bad record, for he was pulling a steel-tired buggy with my father and me in it, and the road was far from level.

In that same stable, the next Summer, Frank indulged himself in a jape which came near costing him his life. To recount it I must describe briefly the lay-out of the place. He inhabited a box-stall with a low wall, and in that wall was a door fastened by a movable wooden cleat. He was in the habit of hanging his head over the door, and drooling lubriciously, while Charlie and I were preparing his feed. This feed came down from the hayloft through a chute that emptied into a large wooden trough, and he often saw us start the feed by pulling out a paddle in the chute. One night either Charlie or I neglected to fasten the door of his stall, and he was presently at large. To his bright mind, of course, the paddle was easy. Out it came, and down poured an avalanche of oats—a bushel, two bushels, and so on to eight or ten. It filled the trough and spilled over to the floor, but Frank was still young and full of ambition, and he buckled down to eat it all.

When Charlie and I found him in the morning he was swelled to the diameter of a wash-tub, his eyes were leaden, and his tongue was hanging out dismally, peppered with oats that he had failed to get down. "The staggers!" exclaimed Charlie, who had become, by that time, an eager but bad amateur horse-doctor. "He is about to bust! There is only one cure. We must run him until it works off." So we squeezed poor Frank between the shafts of the go-cart, leaped in, gave him the whip, and were off. Twice, getting down our hilly road to the pike, he sank to his fore-knees, but both times we got him up, and thereafter, for three hours, we flogged him on. It was a laborious and painful business, and for once in his life Frank failed to laugh at his own joke. Instead, he heaved and panted as if every next breath were to be his last. We could hear his liver and lights rumbling as we forced him on. We were so full of sympathy for him that we quite forgot his burglary, but Charlie insisted that we had to be relentless, and so we were. It was nearing noon when we got back to the stable, and decided to call it a day. Frank drank a bucket of water, stumbled into his stall, and fell headlong in the straw. We let him lie there all afternoon, and all of the night following, and for three days thereafter we kept him on a strict diet of condition powders and Glauber's salt.

The bloating that disfigured him, when it began to go down at last, did not stop at normalcy, but continued until he was as thin as a dying mule, and that thinness persisted for weeks. There came with it, perhaps not unnaturally, a marked distaste for oats. His old voluptuous delight in them was simply gone. He would eat them if nothing else offered, but he never really enjoyed them again. For a year, at least, we might have made him free of a feed-trough full of them without tempting him. What John thought of the episode we could never find out. My guess is that he was too dumb to make anything of it.

A Little Wine of the Country

Priscilla D. Willis

Nobody urged me to buy him. The touts didn't mutter behind knuckly, red fingers that I'd be making an awful mistake if I let him get away; the auctioneer didn't extol the virtues of his breeding; and the horsemen, those pantologists with the gin-clear eyes focused now upon the colt in the ring, didn't nod sagely, and tell me he looked as sound as a bell of brass to them. Nobody sold me the horse. I bought him. The auctioneer knocked him down to me before I had lowered my chin.

The sales catalogue stated that he had started once that year, at two. The racing chart showed that he had finished twenty-third in a field of twenty-four.

"I didn't think race tracks were wide enough to start twenty-four horses all at once," Charles said. "Still, if the others were all as narrow as he is, I guess it would be possible."

To the astonishment of the examining veterinarians, the colt, whose name was Wilson Pusey, recovered from the innumerable and unrelated ailments plaguing his wretched brown body. He even got over the cough which threatened to blow his head off the end of his long, ropy neck.

At three he wasn't exactly strapping, but he could stand up without staggering, and his hair coat commenced to show a faint polish. After a while he was galloped on the track in the mornings; once he breezed six furlongs in 1:21. Watching him, his trainer shook his head. "Never saw a horse move like that one; his legs all go in a different direction at the same time. It's a wonder he don't trip himself."

His second race was better than his first. He was sixth in a pack of seven, but still it was a better race.

He started half a dozen times after that, and then his trainer said we ought to put him up for the rest of the season. "We'll let him grow," he said. He intimated he was running out of jockeys. "The colt has a dead mouth. The boys can't rate him at all. They just have to sit there and let him run the way he wants to. They don't like that; it's an uncomfortable feeling."

Back in his stall in the shed-row I had many visits with Wilson Pusey. I never tried to touch him, for the boy who ponied him told me, "Missus, if you go to patting that one, you'll bring your arm back without a hand."

Soon I gave up inquiring about the boys missing from the stable gang. The answer was always the same: "George, 'e got 'is this morning. Knocked the feed tub right out of 'is 'and, 'e did, and sunk 'is bloody teeth clean up to the gooms in old George's arm." Or: "Sam, he liked to get hisself killed. That old colt, he let him have it with bof' hind feet whilest he were amuckin' out de stall." The blacksmith had had it; the dentist had had it; and the vets on their routine check-ups peered briefly over the stall guard and said, "He looks fit enough; let's see the next one." And they moved on up the row.

Even the dogs and the cats, the chickens and the goat that hung around the barn taking their ease in the stalls of the other horses circled away out from under the shed-row when they passed his. It seemed as if Wilson Pusey didn't want to be friends with anyone.

I used to stand at his door and watch him for a long time. Mostly, he stood with his back to me, his head hung in a dark corner. Thinking, I guess. But sometimes he would turn around and pinning his ears back, rush at me, his lips rolled up above his small white teeth. Occasionally he'd stand still and just stare back. It was then that I could see the torment in his face, the tense, pinched look as if something was hurting him. I thought about it for a long time.

A day came when I had a chance to accompany my husband to Louisville. I took it. I knew that Wilson Pusey's sire and his dam lived nearby. Surely one or the other might be able to give me a clue to the colt's behavior!

Business completed, Charles offered to drive me out to the country in spite of the fact that he had one of his sinus headaches coming on. He cursed himself for leaving his new pills at home; they helped him a lot.

We found the sire of the colt down on his knees in one corner of his paddock. He had thrust his head under the lowest board of the enclosure and was nibbling a fringe of green grass inaccessible to

him except for his extraordinary posture. He was an agreeable horse
and obviously smart. We patted him and fed him a package of
square gumdrops. "He likes them licorish ones best," his groom said,
so we saved the black one till last.

The mare lived on a twenty-five hundred acre farm so elaborately beautiful that it made us feel like whispering. We tiptoed
across the macadam courtyard surrounded by a clipped yew hedge,
to the vine-covered stable where twin white cupolas glistened like
spun sugar ornaments at either end of the long, slate roof. Every
knob, latch, and hinge sparkled like gold.

"How do you suppose any animal raised on this place can be so
god-awful ornery?" Charles asked.

The tack room to which we were directed was as imposing as
a financier's library. We sank into a soft leather sofa and waited to be
presented. Finally a groom nodded to us. We stepped out upon a
flagstone terrace where an old Negro, shank in hand, stood at the
head of a large, deep-bellied brood mare.

At once I noticed the same pained, tight look about her face
that her son had. If she'd been a woman she would have had a deep
frown running down her forehead. Her eyes were red-rimmed, and
she fastened them threateningly upon us, at the same time swelling
her fluted nostrils. The Negro tightened his hold on the shank, but
the mare reared and commenced to box the air just above our heads.
When the groom, dangling as he had been on the other end of the
lead-shank, had regained his footing I asked him how her disposition
was, side-stepping a sudden thrust from a hind leg. "Generally
speaking," I added, over the knot of terror in my throat.

He shook his old, graying head slowly. "She's kinda hateful,
miss," he replied softly.

At this moment a gentleman stepped out of the tack room onto
the terrace. He spoke cordially and explained that he was Rufus
Tate, the owner of the farm. "I drove down from the house when I
heard you were here," he said pleasantly. He was a tall, heavy-
shouldered man dressed in vintage tweeds plastered with leather
patches. His face, seamed with many lines under the patina of a
clear, tanned skin, was like old mahogany whose fine scratches lie
deep beneath the surface polish. His smile was wide and friendly.

"My wife," Charles told him, "owns a son of your mare, here; a
colt named Wilson Pusey."

"Is that so?" Mr. Tate responded politely, but I saw him flinch
just a trifle. "I've often wondered what happened to that one." His

tone of voice suggested that he had made his first and only comment on the subject, and that any further discussion would be distasteful to him. "Come on up to the house," he invited, taking me by the arm, "and have a drink before you go. Some people have just dropped in."

The narrow road, bordered by trees on both sides, meandered upwards for perhaps a mile through gently rising fields of grass divided by old stone fences into a checkerboard of pastures where cattle and horses were grazing. It ended on a high ridge in front of an ante-bellum mansion overlooking the valley.

We walked up the low, wide-flung steps and crossed the white-columned veranda. Inside, Mr. Tate took us through a superbly proportioned drawing-room and led us into a library where pictures of many horses hung. A few people were gathered around the fire; they all seemed to be talking at once. Introductions performed, Mr. Tate handed each of us a silver cup.

"A little wine of the country?" He raised his eyebrows amiably.

The whisky went down like maple syrup. I sipped mine pleasurably, somewhat surprised that Charles emptied his almost immediately. Alcohol, he has said many times, only inflames his sinuses.

I sat down beside a diminutive lady who wore her many years as carelessly as the toque, fashioned of velvet pansies, upon her marcelled waves of coral-colored hair. She was perched as a pipit might have perched, on the edge of a soft cushion. Her name was Mrs. Buffington.

"You horse people?" she asked brightly, including Charles with a quick jerk of her head which almost dislodged the pansies.

"Well, not really," I replied. "One swallow doesn't make a spring, you know, but as a matter of fact . . ."

"I've had dozens of them!" she interrupted before I could explain about Wilson Pusey. "Got cats now. More fun. Horses always have something the matter with them. Never can run when you want them to." She pointed a small, straight finger at a chubby-cheeked, balding man in a double-breasted checked suit standing by the fire extending his cup for another drink. "That," she announced, "is Mr. Sydney Gassoon-Smith, one of the best authorities on cats in the world. I brought him over from England to give me his opinion of my Abyssinians. Much cheaper than taking a hundred and seventy-eight cats abroad. Less trouble, too. They are very susceptible to colds." I nodded sympathetically, and emptied my cup.

Next to Mr. Sydney Gassoon-Smith, Mrs. Buffington's other

house guest, a ruddy gentleman from Canada whose large mustache was the color of wild strawberries, was speaking with great animation to a dismal-looking fellow who was trying terribly hard to buy a Bimelech filly he had seen on a nearby horse farm. Every little while he would go to the phone and offer the owner a few more thousand dollars, and he could be heard whining in the mouthpiece, "But *why* won't you sell her?" And when he returned he looked more dismal than ever.

"All my people are Canadians," the man with the mustache was saying briskly. "We've lived there forever, you might say. My grandmother was a Guelph."

"Really?" the Bimelech man said absently. "I thought they were extinct."

Charles was fingering the coin silver cups Mrs. Tate was showing him, explaining how she had found each one. His face was rather flushed.

"By Gad, that's good whisky!" exclaimed the Canadian, striding over to the bar where Mr. Tate was uncorking another bottle. "Where do you get it?"

Rufus Tate told him that each year he took a few of his own barrels to a friend in a small distillery and had them worked over. "Just for our own use, and for our friends," he said. "It tests around a hundred and seventeen proof. Of course," he added looking dubiously at his guests, "you don't stay with it all evening."

"None of that fire-water for me!" Mrs. Buffington called over from the sofa where we were sitting. "At least not when I'm driving. Last time I left here I sheared off my bumper and a front fender before I got to the main road. Rufus, you must do away with that grove of what-you-macallums at the third turn near the bottom of the hill. They're an unpleasant challenge."

Mr. Tate laughed. "For you, Lavinia, I may do just that, but I'm pretty fond of those trees. Great-grandaddy planted them himself." He looked fondly at the portrait above the mantel where the likeness of a benign old man hung between an engraving of Flora Temple, the trotting mare, and a primitive painting of Bulle Rock, the first thoroughbred imported to this country from England. It was obvious that Mr. Tate loved the three equally.

Mr. Gassoon-Smith was holding forth on a breed of cat unfamiliar to me. The name, as he said it, sounded like "Bwemerishes."

"A peculiar thing happened in this breed," he said, swaying uncertainly back and forth like a cattail on a broken stalk. "They turned white, absolutely white. Albinism crept in, nobody knows why. Very baffling to the geneticists. But the whole goddam breed turned white." He was very impressed. "However," he continued, "they can still be found in certain parts of Asia, the mountain regions, I believe."

I looked across the room at Charles. He was seated now in a wing chair by the fire. His head was resting against the crewel embroidery. His eyes were closed. I could see the torment in his face, the tense, pinched look he got when his headaches were upon him. All at once his face commenced to blur; his features seemed to be disappearing entirely, and his head moved slowly from one shoulder to the other like a pendulum, one, two, one, two. Putting my drink down on the table I sat up straight and opened my eyes wide. Charles was gradually taking shape again, but when his head stopped moving it didn't in the least resemble his own. The chin was elongated far below his collar and the knot of his tie; brown ears stood up on either side of his poll; his nostrils quivered in agony. Bare teeth gleamed savagely in his opened mouth.

"Wilson!" I exclaimed, jumping up, "Wilson Pusey!"

I got Charles to his feet with some difficulty. We disengaged ourselves from Mr. Gassoon-Smith who was speaking now on the coat of Abyssinian cats, holding an imaginary hair between his thumb and forefinger. "Each hair shaft," he was saying, "has three distinct colors, running 'orizontally." He clicked his nails. "Like a pousse-café, rather. . . ."

Before taking our leave of the Tates we promised to arrange better quarters for Mrs. Buffington's cats the next time a cat show was held in our city. "The last time," she said, "it was so cold and draughty they started coughing the night before they were to be judged."

"We'll put you all up at The Racquet Club," Charles said thickly, holding onto his throbbing head.

A few weeks later I was at the racetrack again where the colt was training. I visited him three times a day, taking the lumps of sugar I had filled with my husband's sinus pills.

The first time I stood at his stall with the proffered sugar cube my hand shook so badly I dropped it. The colt was interested. He watched me bend down, pick it up, and place it again in my hand, palm up. He raised and lowered his head with every move I made. When at last he took the lump he dropped it from his mouth and

I had to pick it up again, but soon we both caught on. It was not long before he nickered when he saw me coming down the shed-row.

His trainer said one morning, "That colt's finally beginning to come to himself. Guess it's a good thing we put him up last season. He worked six in one sixteen and no change this morning, and he's beginning to run like a race-horse. Not such a roughneck as he used to be, either." I smiled and doubled the dose.

Then came the afternoon when half a dozen cubes fell out of my purse and the pills, rolling out of the small holes I'd wedged them in, scattered on the ground. The trainer rushed at me. For a few seconds he stood sputtering, growing very red in the face. When the words finally came he wanted to know just what the hell I thought I was doing. "Giving him his medicine," I answered. "He has sinus headaches."

"Sinus trouble! A horse?" he bellowed. "I never heard of a horse with a headache!"

"That doesn't mean they can't have them."

"But I don't think horses *have* sinuses." His anger turned to uneasiness because he had been training for thirty years and didn't know whether horses had sinuses or not. "Of course," he admitted, "if it *was* possible, it might be the reason he quits so bad. Can't get enough oxygen to his lungs. But that's ridiculous. The whole thing's ridiculous!" Then he turned on me like a feist. "You had no business doing this. It isn't regular at all. I could get into a lot of trouble!" He turned still redder. "How do you know what's in that medicine?"

"I don't," I said, "but it helps my husband when he has headaches and when he has them he looks exactly like Wilson Pusey."

The trainer walked a few feet away. He stood there thinking. I picked up the pills and put them back in the sugar.

"Wait!" He lunged at me and grabbed both my wrists. "Don't give him any today! I'm going to run him Thursday and a horse can have no medication of any kind for forty-eight hours before he races. It's a rule at every racetrack."

"All right," I agreed. "But we'll steam his head out the morning of the race. That helps sometimes, too. There's no rule against that, is there?"

He didn't answer. Instead, he dropped into his canvas chair under the shed-row and didn't say another word to anybody the rest of the day. Just sat there brooding and staring into space.

The day of the race Wilson Pusey threw his jockey before he had even left the saddling enclosure. He acted as mean as ever. "Anything that happens today is your fault, not mine," the trainer hissed at me panting from the exertion of tightening the girths.

The odds board showed the colt at eighty to one.

"Last time," Charles said, stepping up to the corner of the grandstand porch from where the trainer and I were going to watch the race, "he was ninety to one. This is a good sign." He did not call my attention to the handicapper's comment after his name in the newspaper, which read, "Miserable sort."

The colt broke on top. He opened up a lead of about five lengths. I dug my elbow in the trainer's ribs. "Don't mean a thing," he said, out of the side of his mouth. "He'll be all through at the half, just like always."

But Wilson Pusey wasn't through at the half. He wasn't through until he coasted under the wire, the winner by two and a half lengths.

"I said that colt had come to himself, didn't I?" the trainer cried, stumbling down the stairs in his hurry to get to the winner's circle.

My sides ached from my husband's embrace. "How much did you have on him?" He shouted like a small boy on Christmas morning.

I shook my head. "Not a thing."

But Charles didn't hear me. Holding firmly to his mutuel ticket, he was pushing his way through the crowd toward the cashier's window.

The Surest Thing in Show Business

JESSE HILL FORD

Things didn't pan out in Texas, so my wife, Jerry, and me, we come East in our old car, hauling a trailer loaded with three hundred pounds of snakes, an old cheetah, and a bear cub. We found this place we could rent on the highway, jut outside the Great Smoky Mountains National Park, on the Tennessee side, so we decided to give her a try. It had a large clear space for parking and was on a long mountain grade going into the Smokies. A long grade that way will get you traffic that stops because the motor gets overheated, and then too, the kids will be yelling they want to see the snakes. So between the radiator and the kids, Daddy, he can't do nothing but stop.

Jerry, my wife, she helped me paint the signs, thirty-nine of them, all bright yellow and red enough to dazzle your eyes, and we tacked them up for two miles along the road on either side of the place, but mostly on the downgrade side. I was able to pick up three fair-size iguana lizards and a couple of pretty good Gila monsters from other reptile folks passing through on the way to Florida, and by the time traffic started really coming through in June, Jerry and me had a nice palisade wall, an admission booth, a free ice-water fountain, a free radiator water tank, and a Cherokee squaw named Lizzie who held down the candy, cigarettes, and souvenir stand.

Lizzie was okay, only she cussed and swore when she got excited, which had got her fired from her job at a souvenir joint inside the park. And, too, she was somewhat of a problem at first because she wanted to call me a swear word, and I don't like to have nobody but myself to swear around Jerry. What Lizzie called me sounded like *sumitch*, all one word: "Gimme some change for this goddam drawer, sumitch." She wouldn't call me by my own name,

74

Jake, so finally we hit on a sort of middle bargain. "How's about just calling me Mitch?" I says. And after some practice it worked out okay, and that's how come we changed the name to Mitch and Jerry's Reptile Show in place of Jake and Jerry's. For in show business you got to be ready to wheel and deal and bargain a little if you make it. And any show around the Smokies that don't have at least one real Indian is like a kite without no tail.

By July we was going full blast, and I had took on an old man and a boy to milk a couple of afternoons a week so I could tend to building more animal cages and ordering hot snakes in place of the old ones we brought with us. The old man couldn't do no more than hang a snake's mouth over a milk jar and grin—I mean he didn't actually milk out no venom and never learned—but he had a good line of gab and always drank a little dab of colored water he hid in the jar ahead of time, and the crowd liked him. Another thing, the old man put on he was more feeble than he really was and made his hands look real shaky so they figured he was going to get bit any second. And that's the whole secret. You go in there to make them believe you might get bit. But now the kid, he milked good and he handled them good and took all kinds of chances, but he made it look too easy and he never got the attention the old man did. The kid never got the point that you can't make it look too easy.

So on the Fourth of July the stranger showed up, one of those long pale guys in a shiny blue suit too small for him, wearing shoes that were never meant for walking—the pointed kind that might have been yellow when they were new—and of course he had walked about a hundred miles. He stayed around the Cherokee's counter for about two hours until she told him to get the hell away from there. Then he hung back a little distance like a stray dog and just stared and waited. Then about noon he got some free ice water and hiked on and I just wrote him off of my mind like a bad debt and patted myself on the back for having got a smart Indian out front like Lizzie, even if it did mean changing my handle a little bit. About four o'clock that afternoon he was back. He marched right up to the ticket window like he had money and asked Jerry, my wife, if the boss was around. He didn't need to explain that he was down on his luck. I guess the thing was that he had a Texas drawl and an unexpected soft voice. All of those fellows' voices will startle you, though. The voice never sounds like the guy looks. It's the road that does it. Jerry just pointed at the palisade gate with her thumb, and he slipped right on in on me. I could hear Lizzie swearing when he opened the gate. You would have thought some of the animals was loose. But Lizzie didn't have no use for white men in any form or fashion, especially his kind. They don't take too kindly to walking tourists up in the Smokies, for the walking ones never want to buy nothing and are always looking to put an honest Indian out of her job.

He come in and closed the gate behind him and give a sidelong glance at the cheetah, which was napping on his sawdust bed in one corner of his cage. I was just through with the three-thirty show and was trying to make a six-foot diamond-back get on in his box. He was a new snake and was still hot as hell. I just kept coaxing him with my snake hook and holding that tail, and the other guy waited real polite till I had the diamond-back in the box.

"Well?" I says. He was a pitiful sight. With everything else he had a blond mustache. It made him look like the next rain would dissolve him. But then he spoke up, brighter and more eager than I looked for.

"I need a stake," he says, waving one long hand like he was fending gnats away from his eyes. They were bright and yellow, like the Western sun, and Texas was right there in his voice so that he got to me fast, like remembering home and the old folks. But us show people are soft-hearted anyway.

"I found a little hick place over the ridge there," he went on, "talked them out of the high school auditorium for this evening to do a reptile show." The hand went hunting down into his pocket, the back pants pocket of the blue suit, and I couldn't hardly believe my eyes when it came out again. "I already collected fifty dollars in advance." He unfolded the bills one right after the other on top of the glass reptile case at his elbow. The snakes raised up and rattled a little and then laid right back down. They were the last of that original three hundred pounds, and they were getting wore out in a hurry. The most of them don't live over six weeks.

"Hey," I says, "I'd call that a pretty good stake already."

"Yeah," he says, "only I ain't got any snakes."

And there it was. He had located a school and store and a clump of houses up there on the edge of the park, and in three hours he had to be back up there ready to put on a full-feathered reptile show and he didn't have so much as a frog in his pocket. It wasn't any wonder to me at all, because if I've learned one thing after twenty-five years in show business, it's the fact that there ain't a single living

American that ain't had a great-grandaddy or a stepuncle or some connection like that who was swallered whole by a rattler. Understand, they never *knew* him, but Granny told them about it, which makes the rattlesnake the surest money-maker in American show business. They will pay to see what swallered Grandaddy every time. Of course you have to expect the comments. If you have an eight-foot snake—it's another story, but me and my brothers did have one once, a Florida diamondback, and we was so scared of him that we would have almost rather been shot at than to work him. It took three of us to handle him, and never a show went by that some smart bastard didn't pipe up and remark how he killed 'em bigger than that with his bare feet every morning, right by his kitchen door. "You call *that* a snake?" they yell. But then that's part of why they pay, and in show business you got to roll with the punches.

So he just stood there with the money laid out on the glass over them dying snakes, and I finally says, "And they even let you leave with the money."

"Yeah. I told them my truck was broke down and I had to get it fixed before I could bring up my reptiles."

"When is the show for?" I says.

"Seven o'clock," he says, "in the Hartsville High auditorium."

"You handled reptiles much?" I says.

"You bet your boots. Hell, it's practically all I ever done."

"You want hot snakes?" I says. There was two kinds, the fresh hot ones, straight up from the Mexican border and feisty as a coon dog pup, and the old ones, so weak you couldn't hardly put them into a coil unless you just took and wound them up like a piece of old rope.

"Whatever you can spare. Snakes, lizards, anything you can lend me. I'm willing to pay. The money's right there," he says, tossing his long sand-colored hair out away from those eyes where it had drooped while he was looking down.

The crowd was grouping up real nice about the arena next to us. I could see the glare off the white sand floor lighting their faces. I took a red balloon out of my pocket and blew it up and tied it. Then I stepped out into the middle of the arena and let it drift down onto the sand floor. Their eyes all went after it like a bunch of bees swarming with their mother queen. "Now folks, the show starts in just a few minutes," I says. Nothing can get quiet so quick as a crowd around a snake arena.

Then a kid yells: "Where are the snakes?"

"Now just be patient, Sonny. I'll be rounding up the stars of the show right away," I says, and this woman give a hysterical laugh, something like a coyote, and I ducked back into the reptile shed. The stranger had put one of the hot snakes into a coil, a four-foot Mexican green rattler.

"Now there's a hot one, ain't he?" I says, trying to cheer him up.

"Yeah," he says, "he's a jim-dandy." He turned his eyes on me and brushed his hair back from his forehead. "How much?" he says.

"I ain't going to charge you nothing," I says. "I know what it's like to be down."

"Well say, that's mighty swell. I ain't no beggar, understand."

"Naw," I says, "I'm glad to do it. Only thing, I don't see how I could get anything over there to you much before seven-thirty, daylight lasting like it does now. But if seven-thirty won't be too late, I'll box up some stuff and hustle it over to the schoolhouse for you in my car. How's that sound?"

"I can hold them thirty minutes easy."

"Well, I got to get started. This here is a continuous show all afternoon, so I'll see you at half past seven."

"Couldn't be better," he says. "Mind if I watch your act?"

"Help yourself," I says. I saw him sticking his money back into that rear pants pocket as I picked up my snake box. I left him there in the shed and stepped back into the arena and put my box down. They were still watching the balloon. I took out my snakes and put them each one in a coil by slapping my foot down at them, making a semicircle of coiled rattlers and starting my spiel. I looked up and saw he had elbowed his way to the rail. When I looked up the next time he was gone.

Before the milking act I took out one of my new iguana lizards. You got to be careful about how you hold an iguana because he's got a bite like a bulldog. The only difference is he don't give you no warning first, no growl, no frown, no hiss. He don't even quiver his eyes or show his tongue before he bites the very *bee*-devil right out of you. I held his head with all the iron I could get into my grip, and when I was done I took out a Gila monster. The old Gila was strong as a young steer. I held him the same way because a Gila is just like an iguana, only worse—once he gets his fangs into you he starts chewing like you was a plug of tobacco or something and you haven't got no alternative but to cut his head off to get him aloose. By then you're poisoned sure enough. So I was glad when I had worked the lizards and got them back in the box. I announced the milking act, and the old man came stumbling out with the kid right behind him and damned near scared the crowd to death. The kid brought the little milking table with the cocktail glass clamped to it, and I milked one and the old man did one, or made out like he did, and then I squirted a little stream of it right out in the air, just to prove to them it was real, squirted it right out of the snake's fang and got another coyote laugh out of the woman. I had just turned around when the old man started to howl and stuck his hand in his mouth. The crowd laughed some because they all thought it was a phony. They always think the real thing is phony, but I didn't even have to look at his hand to know it was real. The old man's face looked like a batch of cold grits at four A.M.

"Oscar," I says to the kid, quiet-like, "drive him to the hospital and don't worry about blowing out no tires." They went out and directly I heard the car take off outside and I had lost my best helper, probably for the rest of the season. I had it to myself for the rest of the afternoon, for when Oscar come back from the hospital he was too shaky to do nothing but stand around trembling like a tramp in January. He said the old man was in awful shape, that he was having a rigor and they had cut his arm open and all. "Don't tell me about it," I says. "I've been bit before." But he kept on, which is the trouble with them natives in the Smokies, that they can't shut up once they get shook. So finally I had to either tell him to go home or get my own self bit just to get away from him. So on the Fourth of July, like it will always happen in show business, I lost my extra help and had to clean out the cheetah's cage and tend to the armadillos all by myself and doctor the bear cub's paw where some tourist had give him a lighted cigar, until I was plumb whipped.

If Jerry, my wife, hadn't asked what that guy wanted I guess I would have forgotten him all the way. As it was I didn't start putting anything in the boxes until seven-thirty, and then it was harum-scarum. I just grabbed up the first things I could lay my hands on and marked the cardboard boxes on the lids. Since I hadn't had no assistants to go behind the crowd and start them clapping, there hadn't been no applause all afternoon and Jerry could see I was whipped out. It's that applause that keeps you going in show business anyway. I went on marking the boxes, and Jerry says, "I hope he realizes what a favor you're doing him, after what all happened. You look wore out, Jake."

"Look," I says, "will you just start putting these here boxes in the car? I promised him seven-thirty. He's up there on the ridge now trying to hold his audience." I was in a hurry, so I just put on MG for Mexican green and TDB for Texas diamondback and G for Gila monster and so on, right on the top where he could read it before he took the lid off. I took the hottest stuff we had and piled it in the back seat and grabbed a snake hook and we took off, me and my wife, Jerry, fast as the old car would run. The last word the Cherokee yelled when we left was one I don't like to hear said around Jerry. I could tell that Indian squaw was against us giving any helping hand to a walking tourist. "He had a nice way of talking," Jerry said while we rolled up the mountain. "Texas," I said back to her and reached out for her little hand and give it a big squeeze.

I guess it was eight o'clock anyway before we got to the schoolhouse, and he had crowded more natives into it than I would have thought was staked out in all them hills. Not only that but they were waiting just as faithful and polite as a bunch of treed house cats. A few had stood up and were jawing a little, but when Jerry and I came in they sneaked on back and sat down like they was trained that way.

The reason was right up there on the Hartsville High School auditorium stage, and when he opened his mouth it wasn't any wonder. If his spiel was a little wild, it was anyway one of the best I ever heard. Before Jerry and I could get the car unloaded and get the boxes on the stage, he had me believing I really was his "assistant," as he called me. Not only that, me and Jerry both hurried whenever we went out to the car for more boxes, so we wouldn't miss too much of what he said in his introduction. It wasn't any question but what he was good. And every time I took him a box onto the stage I tried to take him aside to explain about the markings on top, and every time he gave me the most elegant my-good-man treatment, waving me off and telling me where to set the box, until I just finally gave up.

I'll say this much for him. He did save us two seats down front which I appreciated, for I was in a notion to have a little nap during the show. In fact, if somebody had of told me anything could keep me awake, I would of laughed. But we hadn't sat down good and I hadn't closed my eyes quite shut, listening to him run on about Africa and Tibet and Peru and Norway and jungles and all, until Jerry's elbow, which is a sharp little thing, come into my side like a pool cue. I snapped open my eyes and started to say something rough to her, and then I looked at the stage and swallered my words whole. For he had put a Mexican green ratler into a coil and set a four-bit piece on its head. I heard him say it three times: "Now folks, I'm going to push that fifty cents off on the floor with my nose."

"Aw, why don't he *do* something," the woman on the other side of me says.

Jerry had hid her face against my shoulder. There just wasn't no way for the Mexican green to miss hitting him in the face. I figured we wouldn't get him outdoors until he'd be dead. And there his crowd was, already bitching and griping and him up on the stage like somebody bobbing apples without no tub, right over that snake's head, and it rattling so fast it was singing. He was doing a stunt that I had not seen or heard of, and which I knew I would not ever see again. In show business you always save your best stunt until last, and so I knew then what he was and where he had probably escaped from. It was the kind of stunt to end your life, instead of your act. I kept wondering if he had got the idea somewhere that their fangs had all been pulled out. The snake missed him three times and three times he put his four-bit piece back on its head. The last time he got his nose down and pushed the money off. By then it had sort of got through to the crowd what he was up to, and when that money hit the floor the last time, you could hear it roll. Then the snake struck and missed. It struck right through his hair, where it was hanging down, and I saw him brush it back with that quick flip of his head. He started up his spiel again, and I started wondering if maybe he used his hair that way on purpose. I didn't have to wait long. He was talking and opening boxes and the snakes were getting out mostly by themselves. Sometimes he stomped at them and put them in a coil, and other times he just let them come on out like they would or even dumped them. Then he reached in a box and hauled out the iguana by its tail. He held it up right in front of his face and laughed.

"Folks," he says, "I'm going to be honest with you. I don't know what this thing is." It was the truth, because he scratched it on the head. I kept waiting to hear him scream. But the iguana just hung there like he was in a tree at home and let that guy do anything he pleased.

Then he found the Gila monster. "Now," he says, "I do know what this here one is. This here is a Gila monster."

He handled it like it was stuffed and had its jaws wired. In fact he sort of waved it about while his spiel went on. I could feel my heart jumping, and Jerry's fingernails dug into my arm until it was starting to get numb. "You've heard lots of folks say Gila monsters is poison? Well, my friends, this little old lizard is not poison at all. People have told a lie on him all these years, and this evening I'm going to prove it to you. I'm going to show you he's ab-so-lute-ly harmless. Yes, friends and neighbors, I want you to watch me now. I'm going to stick my own tongue into this little feller's mouth."

"Anybody knows *they* ain't poison," the woman next to me says. "He sure is a gyp, ain't he?"

"Well, what did you expect?" says her old man.

It's the only time I ever left Jerry alone like that since we been married, but I just took her fingers aloose. "You ain't leaving?" she says.

"Yes," I says. "I'll be just outside if you need me."

"I'll holler for you when the monster latches on," she says.

"No need," I says. "I ain't going more than a mile. I'll hear him okay."

There was several guffaws as I walked out and I turned just once to look, and sure enough, he had that lizard up and was trying to poke his tongue in its mouth. I just hurried on outside and leaned up against the wall of the school building, feeling dizzy. I felt to make sure I had my pocketknife. Somebody would have to catch him and hold him while I cut the lizard's head off and then prized it off his tongue. I didn't know if I'd be up to it, and it was right there, the first time, that I wondered if I could stay on with show business. Inside they was busting gussets in all directions, laughing like a bunch of stooges. Then I heard his spiel again and risked a look inside the door. He had put the Gila monster up and was moving into something else. He had put a Texas diamondback around his neck like a scarf. I went on back in and sat down by Jerry.

"Everybody knows he's yanked the teeth out of every last one of them pore varmints," the woman by me says. "A fake, that's all in the world he is."

"What happened?" I says to Jerry.

"He couldn't make the lizard open its mouth," she says.

After a few more things, like milking venom straight into his mouth, he wound up his show and Jerry and I started the applause. It was kind of seedy. I didn't say anything. I just helped get everything off the stage and back into the boxes. Then we loaded the car and he crawled in the back seat instead of sitting up front like I asked him, and we started back down the mountain. I figured he wanted to get in the back so he could pet the iguana some more.

Anyway I was too sore at him to say anything for a while. Finally I asked him what his name was.

"Doug," he says.

"Where did you say you worked reptiles before, Doug?" I says.

"I ain't going to lie to you," he says. I guess he thought it over then, for he paused before he finally said the truth. "Tonight was my first time," he says.

And then he told us he had worked around oil fields mostly and was just coming East when he saw our place there on the road and saw Lizzie behind the souvenir counter. I felt like stopping the car right there and kicking him off the side of the ridge, but in my business you can't always yield to temptation and make a go of it. I had to bear in mind that the old man was in the hospital snake-bit and Oscar was so shell-shocked over it there was no telling when *he* could go back to milking again. So I waited awhile until I could get a hold on myself. We passed the first one of our signs. It drifted by in the headlights. "Doug," I says, soft as I could manage, "how would you like to learn the reptile business?"

"By gummy, Mitch," he says, "I was hoping you would ask me that."

Brer Rabbit and His Friends

Why Brer Rabbit Doesn't Have to Work Any More

John B. Sale

"Dishyere tale is 'bout howcome hit is Brer Rabbit don' ha' t' wuck no mo'. Dat come 'bout dissaway:

"In dem days, mos' lak whut dey does now, folkses all live in settlemints en sich. En dey wuz p'utty good neighbors to one 'nudder, dey wuz, too, en b'lieved in havin' a good time.

"Things 'uz gwine 'long mighty well, dey wuz, twel a big boss li-yon—'de boss uv de woods,' he call hisse'f—move into de settlemint whar Brer Rabbit en Brer Fox en Brer Coon en all de folkses live at. En he didn' do nothin', he didn', but jes lay roun' en 'stroy pigs en goats en things, twel atter w'ile hit look lak he 'uz gwi plum ruin de whole neighborhood en eve'ything in it.

"De folks all got t'gedder, dey did, en hilt a meetin'. En atter a heap uv argymints, fus' dis' way en den dat, dey 'cided dey'd jes ha' t' tell Brer Li-yon dat dey jes couldn' stan' hit no longer, 'ca'se ef he kep' up doin' lak he had been doin', dat fus' en las', dar wouldn' be nobody lef' but jes Brer Li-yon. Dey said dey'd 'gree t' feed 'im, dey would, 'ca'se hit wa'n't right t' starve nobody t' death, but ef dey did feed 'im, he sho ha' t' stay in his house en 'have hisse'f. En ef he didn' wan' t' do dat, dey 'uz gwi be fo'ced to have de law on 'im en maybe put 'im in de callyboose, too.

"Den Brer Fox, he jump up en say, 'Well, gentermens, us is got dis part uv it all settled now. De nex' thing is: Who's gwine cah'y de news to Brer Li-yon?'

"Dat started anudder argymint, 'ca'se dey knowed Brer Li-yon wuz a bad man to fool wid, en dey all wuz skeered.

"Brer B'ar said he wouldn' min' gwine down to Brer Li-yon's house tellin' 'im whut de folkses say, but he say he 'uz already

87

behime wid 'is corn plantin' in 'is new groun', en he jes didn' had de time.

"Brer Fox say he ha' t' go en dig a well 'fo' his stock all pehish fer water, en he couldn' go.

"Dey all gi'n fus' one kin' uv scuse en den anudder. Brer Goose say he jes ha' t' git in 'is fiel' en cut grass; en Brer Gobbler say Sis Turkey wuz down sick wid a mis'ry in 'er back en he had t' git home right away en ten' t' de chillun. Brer Pig said he ha' t' go en root up 'is gyarden 'fo' hit come a rain. Hit look lak all uv 'em had some 'portant business t' ten' to en couldn' none uv 'em cah'y de news to Brer Li-yon.

"Den Brer Rabbit jump up, he did, en pop 'is heels t'gedder, en he say, 'By Gollies, folkses, ef y'all is skeered uv 'im, Ah ain't.'

"Now, Baby," said the old woman, "Brer Rabbit wuz a mighty good man, he wuz, en a mighty smart un, too; but he sho would cuss w'en de 'casion come up. He sho would do dat."

"But, Ai' Betsey," said the puzzled boy, "I didn't know good folks cussed. Uncle John don't do it; an' you don't do it; an' Unc' Alfo'd don't do it."

"Well, you see, Baby, w'en Ah says Brer Rabbit 'uz a good man, Ah means he wuz a good neighbor en kin'-hearted. You never could rightly call Brer Rabbit a good Chris'chun man, you couldn', en 'sides dat, in dem days things wuz some diff'unt f'um whut dey is now. You see?"

John nodded his head in complete understanding.

"Well," Aunt Betsey went on, "Brer Rabbit he say, 'Folkses,' sezzee, jes shakin' 'is haid f'um side t' side lak he 'uz mad, 'a man's jes a man, en he ain' no mo'n nobody ilse. Um's a man, Um is, jes lak whut Brer Li-yon is. Ah don' kyere ef y'all is skeered uv 'im, Ah ain't. Ah'll take de news to 'im m'se'f.'

"Den de folkses all says, 'Aw shucks, Brer Rabbit, you know you's got more sense 'n t' do dat. Brer Li-yon is two three times bigger'n whutchu is, en he'll eat chu up en won' know he done had a mou'ful. Ain' chu skeered?'

" 'Skeered? Who? *Me?* Why, Gawd bless yo' souls, folkses, Ah thought y'all already knowed Ah ain' skeered uv nothin' ner nobody. En jes to prove hit to you, Um's gwine down dar en tell dat ole mangy-hided Brer Li-yon jes zac'ly whut us gwine do fer 'im, en jes zac'ly whut us ain't. En ef he don' lak it, he kin jes lump it. You wait hyere fer me, folkses,' sezzee, 'en Ah'll show you.'

"Wid dat, Brer Rabbit tucked 'is britches-laigs down in dem red-top boots uv his'n, pulled his white duck-cloth cap to one side uv 'is haid, en den wid a big see-gyar sho't stickin' out'n 'is mouf he sa'ntered off down de road twoge Brer Li-yon's house, jes lak he 'uz gwine to a picnic.

"Brer Rabbit walk mighty biggity, he did, ez long ez de folkses could see 'im, but w'en he got roun' a ben' in de road, he rub dat see-gyar sho't out 'g'inst a stump en put 'tin 'is pockit, en he straighten' de cap on 'is haid en f'um den on, he walk mighty diff'unt, 'ca'se he wuz skeered en 'is knees 'uz shakin'.

"W'en he got t' de li-yon's house he crope up to de do', he did, en he knock on it easy-lak, 'tap—tap—tap,' en he say 'Mist' Li-yon, Uh-r-r Mist' Li-yon.' En his voice 'uz so weak en trem'ly he couldn' hardly hyeah it hisse'f.

"But de li-yon hyeahd, he did, en he come th'owed de do' op'm en he hollered out *big*, 'WHO IS YOU EN WHUTCHU WANT?'

"Brer Rabbit 'uz jes shakin'. 'Dis is jes me,' he sez, 'hit's jes Brer Rabbit, Mist' Li-yon. De folkses done had a meetin',' he sez, 'dey done had a meetin' en dey sont me down hyere t' tell you dat—to splain to you dat dey done 'cided—'cided dat, seein' dat you is de big boss uv de whole worl', hit ain' right fer you to ha' t' go out en git yo' vittles. En—en dey done tole me to tell you dat—dat ef you'll stay in yo' house all de time en don' go out fohagin' none, dey'll sen' you sump'm t' eat—dey'll sen' yo' sump'm t' eat down hyere to you. En dat's jes zac'ly whut dey tole me t' tell you, Mist' Li-yon,' he say, squattin' en gittin' ready t' run.

" 'WELL, AH GOT TO HAVE FRESH MEAT THREE TIMES A DAY,' de li-yon hollered at 'im, 'EF DEY'LL DO DAT, AH'LL STAY IN DE HOUSE. BUT EF DEY DON'T, UM GWI 'STROY EVE'YBODY.'

"Brer Rabbit, he say, 'Yassuh, y-a-s-s-u-h, Mist' Li-yon, y-a-s-s-u-h! Dey do dat, sho! Dey gwi feed you good, too, 'ca'se Um's gwi see t' dat m'se'f,' he say.

"Wid dat, Brer Rabbit tuck off down de road, he did, lickety-split. Soon ez he wuz out uv sight uv Brer Li-yon he stop en knock de dus' off'n 'is boots, pull de cap down on de side uv 'is haid ag'in, en wid dat ole see-gyar sho't stickin' out one cornder 'is mouf, he strutted back to whar de folkses 'uz waitin' fer 'im at.

"W'en dey seed Brer Rabbit comin', dey all run to meet 'im. 'Is you see 'im?' dey ax 'im. 'Is you seed Mist' Li-yon? Whut he say?'

"Den Brer Rabbit say, right biggity-lak, 'Is Ah seed 'im? Well,

Ah went down dar to see 'im, didn't Ah? Howcome you thinks Ah ain' seed 'im, den? Co'se Ah's seed 'im.'

"Den de folkses say, 'L-a-w-d-e-e, Brer Rabbit! You d-i-d? Whutchu tell 'im? Wa'n'chu skeered?'

"W'en dey ax 'im dat, Brer Rabbit snatch 'is cap off'n de side uv 'is haid en th'owed hit down on de groun' en stomp it. 'Skeered,' sezzee, 'whut in de name uv Gawd kin' uv foolishmint is you talkin' now? Why, folkses,' sezzee, doublin' up 'is fis' en shakin' it in all dey faces, 'Um's a man, Um is. A m-a-n, a m—a—n, Ah tells you. En being's Um is a man, Ah ain' skeered uv nothin' ner nobody, en dat means Brer Li-yon en all de res'.'

"Den de folkses jes beg Brer Rabbit t' tell 'em all 'bout it.

" 'Well,' sez Brer Rabbit, 'W'en Ah went down to ole Brer Li-yon's house, Ah knock on de do', Ah did, en w'en he op'm it, Ah went in en sot down by de fiah. En Ah tole 'im dat us had done had a meetin' en 'cided dat he wuz raisin' too much 'sturbance in de neighborhood. En Ah tole 'im us done 'cided he'd ha' t' stay in his house en 'have hisse'f er ilse 'uz gwi beat 'is Gawd-lested liver out, en de Lawd hisse'f only knowed whut ilse. Den Ah tole 'im us 'ud feed 'im. Ah tole 'im us didn't wan' t' see nobody suffer en starve, so us 'ud feed 'im, us would, but he'd ha' t' take jes whut us wan' t' gi' 'im en be satterfied wid it, er ilse he could jes lump it.'

"Den de folkses all say, 'Lawd, Brer Rabbit, you s-h-o i-s b-r-a-v-e!'

" 'Um's jes a man, folkses,' sez Brer Rabbit, en he pick up his cap en knock de dirt off'n it en sot it back on de side uv 'is haid. 'Jes a man, folkses, dat's all. Ole Brer Li-yon, he pitch en he cuss en he ro'd, but dat didn' skeer me none; en w'en he seed Ah meant business he say he'd do jes whut de folkses tell 'im. En dat's jes how 'twus.'

"Den de folkses tried to 'cide who gwi be de fus' un t' go en feed Mist' Li-yon. Eve'body said to eve'body ilse, 'You go fus', you go fus', you go fus',' en dar dey stuck.

"Dey arg'ed en qua'el 'mongst d'se'fs twel Brer Rabbit tole 'em, 'Le's draw straws, en de one whut gits de sho't un feeds de li-yon.'

"Dey 'greed t' dat, dey did. Brer Rabbit hilt de straws, en Brer Goose, he drawed de sho't un.

"W'en Brer Goose seed he had de sho't straw, he 'gun to shiver en shake 'is whings en he say, 'N-a-a nah! N-a-a nah!'

" 'Y-e-h yeh!' sez Brer Rabbit, sezzee, 'Y-e-h yeh! Git on down dar en feed Brer Li-yon lak you done 'greed t' do.'

"So Brer Goose went on down dar en Brer Li-yon et 'im up.

"De nex' feedin' time, Brer Pig drawed de sho't straw. W'en he seed he 'uz de nex', he started crynin' en holl'in', 'W-a-i-t! W-a-i-t! W-a-i-t! W-a-i-t!'

" 'W-a-i-t! de devul!' sez Brer Rabbit, sezzee, 'You git on down yon'er en feed Brer Li-yon lak you done 'greed to, ilse us'll beat you half t' death en drag you dar.'

"So Brer Pig went on down dar en Brer Li-yon et *him* up.

"Now Brer Fox en Brer Allygater soon seed dat ez long ez Brer Rabbit hilt de straws he 'uz gwi sen' eve'ybody ilse, cep'm hisse'f, down de road t' feed dat li-yon. So at de nex' feedin' time dey fix it so dat Brer Fox hilt de straws. En sho 'nough, dis time Brer Rabbit, he drawed de sho't un!

"W'en he see he done got de sho't straw, he say t' hisse'f, he did, 'Dar Gawd! Ef Ah ain' sho done got my business in a twis' now.' Den he say out loud, 'Folkses,' sezzee, 'hit sho do look lak my time done come. Us is done had a heap uv fun en frolics t'gedder, us is,' sezzee, 'but dat's behime us now. En now Um's got t' go en feed dat ole li-yon's belly. Ah's been a good frien' t' y'all, folkses,' he sez, 'en a good neighbor, too. Ah vis'ted de sick en fed de hongry en he'p to bury de daid. But now hit looks lak my time's done come, en Ah wants you all to pray fer me en promus me dat w'en yo' time comes you'll all meet me in de Promus' Lan' whar d'ain' nobody goes but de pyo' in heart. Goodbye, folkses, goodbye, eve'body,' sez Brer Rabbit, en den he started walkin' off down de road, slow en mo'nful.

"Brer Rabbit soun' so pitiful dat all de folkses started crynin', en jes 'fo' he got out uv sight roun' a ben' in de road, Brer Houn' Dawg, whut wuz de gospel cah'ier, started singin',

> 'Am I bawn to die,
> To lay dis body down?'

en eve'body j'ined in.

"Brer Rabbit, he walk along mighty slow, he did, en den he 'cided dat, even ef ole Mist' Li-yon did ha' t' wait fer his dinner, he 'uz gwi look over his big plantation one mo' time anyhow.

"Soon ez he 'cided dat, he tuck off th'ough de woods to 'is house. W'en he got dar, he went all roun' en roun'. He went t' whar he wuz bawn at, en he went t' de barn en de hawg-lot en de gyarden, en he said goodbye to eve'ything. En den he went t' de well fer a las' drink a water. He look over in dat ole deep well uv his'n, he did, en w'en he seed his own face shinin' up at 'im f'um de bottom, hit gi'n 'im a idee.

So he slap his laig wid his han's en slam de kiver shet, he did, en put
out th'ough de woods fer de ole li-yon's house. W'en he got dar hit 'uz
way atter one by de clock.

"He knock on de do', he did, en he say, 'Mist' Li-yon,' he say, en
his voice 'uz weak en trem'ly, 'U-r-r-r Mist' Li-yon, hyere yo' dinner.'

"De ole li-yon th'owed op'm de do', he did, en he ro'd out,
'WELL, HIT'S A MIGHTY LI'L DINNER YOU DONE FOTCH
ME, EN HYERE HIT IS 'WAY ATTER ONE O'CLOCK.' En den
Brer Li-yon pull out his big gol' watch en look at it, en he showed
Brer Rabbit his tushes.

"Brer Rabbit look at dem big ole tushes stickin' out'n Ole Brer
Li-yon's mouf en 'is knees shuck wuss'n ever. Den he say, 'Yassuh,
Mist' Li-yon, yassuh. Ah jes couldn' gitchere no sooner, Ah couldn'.
Um is mighty sorry, Mist' Li-yon, ef Ah ain' enough fer yo' dinner;
but ef you is r-a-l-e hongry—hongry, Ah knows whar dar is a h-e-a-p
uv good fresh—fresh meat Ah done save fer you. En Ah'll show hit to
you, too, ef'n you'll come go—go wid me. En dat's de Gawd's trufe,
Mist' Li-yon, hit sho is,' sezzee.

"'WHAR IS DAT MEAT AT?' de ole li-yon ax 'im.

"'Hit ain' fur, Mist' Li-yon,' sez Brer Rabbit, sezzee, 'hit ain' but
jes a li'l piece—jes a li'l piece over t' my house whar Ah got—got hit
put up fer you.'

"'WELL, HIT BETTER BE ENOUGH!' sez de ole li-yon,
sezzee, en wid dat, him en Brer Rabbit put out th'ough de woods to
Brer Rabbit's house.

"Brer Rabbit op'm de well, he did, en look in it en fell back!
'L-a-w-d G-a-w-d!' sezzee, 'ef he ain' in dar eatin' yo' vittles right
now!'

"When Brer Rabbit say dat, de ole li-yon knock 'im 'way f'um de
well en look down it hisse'f. He thought he seed anudder li-yon
lookin' up at 'im en he hollered, 'WHO IS YOU?'

"De voice come back up out'n de well, 'WHO IS YOU?'

"Ole Brer Li-yon 'gun to git mad an he hollered down de well
ag'in, 'WHO IS YOU, AH SAY?'

"En de voice come back up out'n de well, 'WHO IS YOU, AH
SAY?'

"Den Brer Rabbit nudge de ole li-yon in de side en he say, 'You
hyeahd 'im, didn'chu, Brer Li-yon? Didn'chu hyeahd 'im mockin' you
lak dat? Gawd-lest 'is soul!' sez Brer Rabbit, sezzee, doublin' up 'is
fis' en dancin' roun' t' de udder side uv de well f'um de ole li-yon. 'Is
you gwi take dat? Is you? Is you gwi take dat slack talk f'um 'im,

Brer Li-yon? C-o-r-n-f-o-u-n' 'is fresh-meat-stealin' soul,' sezzee, 'ef he'll come up hyere Ah'll whup 'im m'se'f!' he say.

"De ole li-yon look over in de well ag'in en he hollered, 'WHO-O-O-O-O-O-O-O-O-O—!'

"De voice come back up out'n de well, 'WHO-O-O-O-O-O-O-O—!'

"Den de li-yon say, 'STAN' BACK, BRER RABBIT,' sezzee, 'HE'S MY MEAT!' En in he jump.

"Soon ez Brer Rabbit hyeahd 'im hit de water—Kerchug!—he slam de kiver shet en lock it. Den he pulled his cap t' one side uv 'is haid, tuck dat see-gyar sho't out'n 'is pockit en lit it, en den he sa'ntered on down de road to whar de folkses wuz 'batin' 'bout who wuz t' feed de li-yon nex'.

"When dey fus' seed Brer Rabbit comin', dey thought he wuz a ha'nt, en dey started to run. But he stop 'em, he did, en den dey all ax 'im en say, 'Lawd, Brer Rabbit, ain' Mist' Li-yon et you up?'

"En Brer Rabbit say, 'Et who up? Me? N-a-w Gawd! Ah wa'n't aimin' to be et up by dat durned ole li-yon ner nobody ilse.'

" 'But whut he s-a-y, Brer Rabbit? En whut de do? Ur-r-r my Lawdy, Mist' Li-yon gwi come up yere terreckly, jes lak he say, en 'stroy all us!'

"Den Brer Rabbit laugh mighty biggity, he did, en he say, 'D'ain' no nuse in you folkses bein' skeered uv nothin' ez long ez you got a man wid you,' sezzee, 'en dat's me. Um's a man, folkses, jes lak Ah said. En w'en Ah sez Um's a man Ah means Um is a man, en Ah kin prove it. Dat big ole fool li-yon ain' said nothin', he ain' done nothin' en he ain' gwi 'stroy nothin', 'ca'se w'en he tried t' git raw wid me, Ah beat de low-down scoun'l half t' death en th'owed 'im in my well en drown 'im.'

"De folkses wouldn' b'lieve 'im, dey wouldn', twel Brer Rabbit tuck 'em all over to 'is house en op'm de well en showed 'em de ole li-yon down in de bottom all drownded.

"Den dey all say, 'Brer Rabbit,' say dey, 'You is too smart a man to be anything cep'm a kang. En f'um dis time on, you ain' nevuh gwi ha' t' wuck no crop, 'ca'se us is gwi do it fer you.'

"En dat's jes zac'ly howcome hit is, dat f'um dat day twel dis, Brer Rabbit been livin' on udder folkses' goobers en taters en things."

The Animals' Spring

WILLIAM H. VANN

One summer a long time ago, when all the animals used to be real friendly with each other, it got so hot and dry that none of them could get any water to drink. The springs ran dry, the wells gave out, even the creeks and rivers stopped running. It got so bad that finally Mr. Lion called all the animals together to see what they could do about it.

They all came—Mr. Lion himself, of course; Mr. Tiger and Mr. Bear and Mr. Elephant; Mr. Deer and Mr. Rabbit; Mr. Dog and Mr. Pig; Mr. Snake and Mr. Frog and Mr. Terrapin, and all the others. When they all got together and talked about it, they decided the only thing to do was to dig a new spring, one deep enough to be sure to get a plenty of fresh water.

"Now everybody must help dig," said Mr. Lion. And they all said they would, except Mr. Deer. He somehow didn't like the idea, and wouldn't promise to do anything at all.

"Then you can't have any of our water," said Mr. Lion. "Anybody who won't dig can't drink."

"Well, you all just go ahead," said Mr. Deer. "Maybe I can get some water somewhere."

So all the other animals started in to digging. They brought their spades and shovels and hoes, and some would dig while others would rest. And after two or three days, sure enough they came to a deep, cool spring, with plenty of water for everybody. They were all so glad that they had to have a party to celebrate.

Of course, Mr. Deer was not invited to the party, and Mr. Deer did not get any water. But that night, after all the animals were gone and there was nobody to see him, he decided he would just have to have a drink. So he sneaked off through the woods until he came to the spring. Then he tip-toed up to the edge, stuck his nose in, and got all the water he wanted.

Next morning when Mr. Bear came to get a drink, he saw tracks in the sand around the spring. So he called Mr. Lion.

"Come here!" he cried. "Somebody has been drinking our water; look at these tracks!"

Mr. Lion was not very excited, though. "Those are just your own tracks," he said. "You go look at them again."

So Mr. Bear went back and looked at them; but they were not like his tracks at all, and he made Mr. Lion come look himself. When he did, sure enough he saw they couldn't be Mr. Bear's.

"They look like Mr. Pig's," said Mr. Lion. "I guess he came down early this morning." So they called Mr. Pig; but he was still asleep, and when they got him waked up, he showed them that the tracks were a whole lot too big for his feet.

About that time Mr. Frog hopped up. "I know whose they are," he said. "Those are Mr. Deer's hoof-prints."

The more they looked, the more sure they were that Mr. Deer had been stealing water from the spring.

"We'll have to put somebody to watch it," decided Mr. Lion. "Mr. Frog, you live near the spring; you watch tonight and catch Mr. Deer if he comes."

Mr. Frog said he would. He was almost asleep, though, when way late he heard somebody coming, real soft and easy. Sure enough, it was Mr. Deer. When he stuck his head down and was getting a big swallow, Mr. Frog jumped up at him. It scared Mr. Deer a little, but when he found it was just Mr. Frog he went right on drinking.

Next morning Mr. Lion came down early to see what had happened. "Did Mr. Deer come last night, Mr. Frog?" he asked.

"Yes, he did, and I tried to stop him, but he was just a little too big for me."

"Well, we can't let him get any more water," said Mr. Lion. "Mr. Terrapin, you watch tonight."

So Mr. Terrapin hid in one corner of the spring, and when Mr. Deer came to drink, he nipped him right on the nose. Mr. Deer snorted, and shook his head, but he couldn't get him off. He tried again, but Mr. Terrapin still hung on. Finally Mr. Deer got mad, put his nose down to ground, and stomped on Mr. Terrapin. That broke a hole in his shell, and of course Mr. Terrapin had to turn loose.

When Mr. Lion came around next morning, and called Mr. Terrapin, it was a long time before he crawled up.

"What's the matter?" asked Mr. Lion. "You don't look very lively this morning. Did you see Mr. Deer last night?"

Poor Mr. Terrapin could hardly talk. "Yes, I saw him," he finally said.

"Well, did you catch him?"

"I tried to, Mr. Lion, but he mighty near ruined me."

"That's too bad, Mr. Terrapin," said Mr. Lion. "But we've just got to catch Mr. Deer. Mr. Snake, suppose you try tonight?"

That night when Mr. Deer got down to the spring, he didn't notice anything, and nobody tried to keep him from drinking. But when he started to go, he felt something heavy on one leg. He tried to shake it off, but it wouldn't come off—because it was Mr. Snake. Then he tried to run away, but he couldn't get away, because one end of Mr. Snake was wrapped around his leg and the other end around a tree. Mr. Deer kicked and pulled, and pulled and kicked, but he couldn't get loose. And there he was next morning when Mr. Lion came around.

"Well, Mr. Deer," he said, "we got you at last, didn't we? You wouldn't help us dig, and you thought you'd get ahead of us; but we've got you now."

So Mr. Lion had Mr. Deer's legs tied, and they took him up to the big pasture. All the animals came, and they made a big ring, with Mr. Lion at one end and Mr. Frog at the other; and they put Mr. Deer in the middle.

"Let's make Mr. Deer perform for us before we kill him," said Mr. Dog.

"That's a good idea," said Mr. Bear. "What can you do, Mr. Deer?"

"Well, I could dance a little, if one of my legs was loose."

"Will it be all right to let one leg loose?" they asked Mr. Lion. He said it would. So Mr. Deer began to hobble around, doing the best he could, and he sang a little song:

> Folly-wolly bacon,
> Folly-wolly bacon,
> Way down in Peggy's old field,
> Where I'm bound for to sing, dear,
> Sing.

"Look at him," they all said. "Mr. Deer can dance, sure enough, even with three legs tied up."

"Shucks, that's not dancing at all," replied Mr. Deer. "You just ought to see what I could do with two legs loose."

"All right, let him have another leg loose," they said. "He can't get away with all of us around him."

So they untied another leg, and this time Mr. Deer cut a caper sure enough. He danced all around the ring; but he didn't try to get away, and he sang his same song. The animals all thought he was just wonderful.

"Now if you really want to see some fancy dancing," said Mr. Deer, "just let me have three legs loose. I don't need four—three will be enough to show you the best dancing you ever saw."

Of course when he had three legs loose, the other one would be loose, too. But they didn't think about that. Mr. Lion asked them all if they would be careful and not let him get away.

"Can you stop him if he tries to get away, Mr. Bear?" said Mr. Lion.

"Yes, sir, he can't get past me," said Mr. Bear.

"How about you, Mr. Frog?"

He said the same thing, and so did all the others. So when he had all his legs loose, Mr. Deer was just tickled to death. He danced real slow at first, then he danced a little faster. And the faster he danced, the faster he sang:

> Folly-wolly bacon,
> Folly-wolly bacon,
> Way down in Peggy's old field,
> Where I'm bound for to sing, dear,
> Sing.

All the time he was getting farther and farther from Mr. Lion and Mr. Bear, and presently he got around to where Mr. Frog was. Well sir, right then he gave one great big jump, and was out and gone before they knew it.

Mr. Frog started after him, hoppity-hoppity-hop; but he couldn't catch him. "You catch him, Mr. Dog," shouted Mr. Lion. Mr. Dog ran as hard as he could, yelping all the time, but Mr. Deer was a little too fast for him, too. Then Mr. Tiger came along and passed Mr. Dog. He was making great big jumps, and he was gaining on Mr. Deer all the time. He got closer and closer; and when Mr. Deer looked back, Mr. Tiger was almost up with him.

But Mr. Deer knew he was just about back home. So he ran a little bit harder, and presently he came in sight of the house. Just then his daddy and all his brothers saw him, and they ran out with

guns and knives and pitch-forks, and made Mr. Tiger turn around and
go back. The very next day, there came a big rain, and all the wells
and springs and creeks were full again, and Mr. Deer didn't have to
bother any more about the animals' spring.

How Mr. Rabbit Fooled Mr. Possum

WILLIAM H. VANN

Long time ago, when Mr. Rabbit used to be good friends with all the animals, except of course Mr. Fox, why, he was mighty fond of fish. Only he was powerful lazy, too.

One day Mr. Possum came along the road, and saw Mr. Rabbit sitting on his front porch.

"Howdy, Mr. Rabbit," he said. "Come along and let's go fishing."

Mr. Rabbit didn't answer for a while, then he said, "It's too hot to fish, Mr. Possum."

"Oh, shucks, it ain't either," said Mr. Possum. "Don't you like fried fish for supper? Better come on with me; they tell me the fish are biting mighty good these days."

"I like fish all right," said Mr. Rabbit, "but I got something else to do today." 'Course he didn't have anything to do; he was just plain lazy.

"Well, if you don't come you won't get any fish." And Mr. Possum went on down the road.

All day Mr. Rabbit kept thinking about those fish, how good they would taste, and wondering how he was going to get any. Sure enough, along about evening, here came Mr. Possum with a nice string—perch, and catfish, and chubs. He saw Mr. Rabbit and yelled at him, "I told you how you ought to come with me—look at my nice fish!"

Mr. Rabbit didn't say anything; but he'd been studying about it all day. And just as soon as Mr. Possum was out of sight, he lit out through the woods. He ran and got ahead of Mr. Possum, and lay down in the road right where Mr. Possum would be coming along, and acted like he was dead. Pretty soon Mr. Possum came along, and when he saw Mr. Rabbit, he stopped a minute, and said to himself, "Well, here's an old dead rabbit. Wonder what was the matter with him?" Then he went on down the road.

As soon as he was out of sight, Mr. Rabbit ran and cut through the woods again, and lay down just like he did before. Mr. Possum stopped and poked at him with his fishing pole, but didn't do anything. So Mr. Rabbit did the same thing one more time; and when Mr. Possum came along, he stopped and said, "Well, I just declare—here's another dead rabbit! Looks like the one I asked to go fishing with me, too—just too lazy to live. Guess I might as well eat these here rabbits; I'll go back and get the others, too."

So he laid down his pole and his string of fish, and went back up the road. Of course, as soon as he was out of sight, Mr. Rabbit picked up the fish and ran off with them, and had fried fish for supper after all.

Well, when Mr. Possum got back, and didn't find any rabbits or any fish either, he knew Mr. Rabbit had played a mean trick on him; and he was just about the maddest man you ever saw. The more he thought about it, the more he got riled, and the more he knew he just had to get even with him. Finally he decided to have a big party, and invite everybody except Mr. Rabbit.

So he sent out the invitations to all his friends, and told them it was going to be about the biggest party that ever was. When Mr. Rabbit heard about it, and thought he wasn't going to be there, he began to wish he hadn't ever got those fish; because if there was anything he liked better than a party, he didn't know what it was. The closer the day came for the party, the more he got worried.

Finally, however, he figured out how he could get to go. The afternoon of the party, he ran and jumped in the horse trough; then, while he was still wet, he wallowed in the ash pile, until he looked just like a possum. He put on some extra special clothes, screwed up his face, and started out.

When he got to Mr. Possum's house and knocked at the door, they wanted to know who he was. So he told them he was from across the river, and they could just call him Uncle Poss. He went on in, and began to dance, but they all kept on looking at him, and then they asked him what made him look like that.

"Uncle Poss, what makes your ears so long?"

"Well, when I was a little boy, my mammy used to pull them so hard when she washed them, that they haven't ever been short like other possums' ears."

"But how come your tail so short, Uncle Poss?"

"Why, that's because one day I was fishing, and my tail was hanging out of the boat, and a turtle snapped it off and it didn't ever grow back."

So Mr. Rabbit went right along, and danced with the ladies, and ate and drank, and had a big time in general, until finally it came time to go home. Mr. Possum hadn't suspected anything, so he asked Mr. Rabbit to spend the night with him.

"No, I guess I better get on home," said Mr. Rabbit. "I live a far piece, and I better be going."

"Oh, come on and spend the night," said Mr. Possum. "It's too far for you to go. You can leave early in the morning, right after breakfast."

Mr. Rabbit knew he ought to go on home, because in the morning the ashes would all be brushed off, and they'd know who he was. But he was still mighty lazy; so he decided he'd stay and get up real early, before anybody else was awake.

But the next morning when he waked up, the sun was shining right in the window so strong that he knew he had overslept himself. He heard the dishes rattling on the table downstairs, and presently Mr. Possum told his little boy, "Go upstairs and tell your Uncle Poss to come to breakfast."

Well, Mr. Rabbit knew then he was in trouble sure enough. When the little possum came in, Mr. Rabbit didn't know what to do, and he just lay up there in the bed with his eyes about to pop clear out of his head. The little possum looked at him real hard, and then ran back downstairs.

"Daddy," he said, "that ain't no possum—it's an old rabbit!"

"Shut your mouth, boy," said his daddy. "You go back up there and tell Uncle Poss that breakfast is ready, like I told you."

So the little possum came back again, and Mr. Rabbit just lay there, plumb scared to death. Then he went back downstairs again.

"Daddy, I know it *is* a rabbit—it ain't no possum at all! You come and see, and if it ain't, you can whip me!"

Mr. Possum wasn't so sure, but he said, "All right, I'll go—but if it's not a rabbit, I'm going to fix you sure enough."

When Mr. Rabbit heard Mr. Possum coming up the stairs, he knew he just had to do something then. So he pulled the covers over the bolster, then climbed out of bed and got behind the door. When

Mr. Possum came in and went over to the bed, Mr. Rabbit jumped out, ran down the stairs, and lit out for home.

Yes, he got there, all right, but since that time, rabbits and possums never have been friends any more.

How the Burro Tricked the Buzzard

Genoveva Barrera

One day Mr. Burro was lying under the shade of a big black oak tree. He had just had some nice green grass and some cool water, and he did not have any work to do; so he was very content and satisfied with himself and with life and with all the world in general. He had been there some time when Mr. Lion came along. Mr. Lion had just had a good meal too, and, like Mr. Burro, was satisfied with himself and with life. He came up to Mr. Burro and, noticing his look of contentment, said, "You look very happy, Mr. Burro."

Mr. Burro did not bother to get up; he just turned his head to face Mr. Lion, raised one ear and said, "And why shouldn't I be very happy? Am I not the cleverest and strongest animal in the world? And don't I have all the green grass and all the cool water I can eat and drink?"

"Why, you foolish one!" replied Mr. Lion. "Who has made you believe you are the cleverest and strongest animal in the world? And as for being owner of all the green grass you want, why, who cares? For my part, I want none of it."

" 'Tis a fact that I'm the cleverest and strongest animal in the world," said Mr. Burro lazily.

This made Mr. Lion very angry, for he claimed to be the king of the country-land.

"You are wrong!" shouted Mr. Lion. "I am the cleverest! Can't I catch any animal I want? I'm never hungry and I do not have to go far for my food. But should I have to, I would go quickly; whereas you are both stupid and lazy!"

By this time Mr. Burro was getting slightly bored. Besides, he was much too lazy to argue. He laid his head back and would have gone to sleep had not Mr. Lion been making so much noise. Mr.

Lion had been talking all the while but Mr. Burro was not listening. At last Mr. Lion saw some buzzards flying overhead.

"Look!" he said. "There are some buzzards. The one who can catch a buzzard and take it alive to the other is the cleverest and the strongest. We'll have three days to do it. In three days we will meet here. If you win, you'll be the cleverest and the strongest, but if I win, I'll eat you up, for I'll have no one saying or even thinking he is stronger than I am."

"That suits me," replied Mr. Burro. "Now, please go away and let me sleep."

Mr. Lion went away to his den to plan some way of catching a buzzard. He was laughing to himself, for he had no doubt that he could do it. But one day went by and he couldn't catch one, try as he would. Two days went by and still he hadn't caught one. By this time Mr. Lion did not even bother to eat, for he was afraid of losing time. He was very hungry and very thirsty, but he couldn't waste time eating and drinking. Anyway, he was going to have a fine meal of Mr. Burro. The third day came by and Mr. Lion was frantic. He ran here and there, doing this and that, but all his little tricks and all his clever plans failed. At last he started off toward the tree where they were to meet. It was quite a way, and he was so weak that it would take some time to get there. Anyway, he comforted himself, that stupid old burro surely hadn't caught a buzzard; the time for the contest would have to be extended.

And Mr. Burro?—Well, after Mr. Lion went away, Mr. Burro fell fast asleep and woke just in time to eat and drink before the sun went down. Then when the sun went down, there wasn't anything to do but to go back to sleep, which he did gladly. He forgot all about catching a buzzard and it wasn't until the third day that he remembered about it. He was lying under the same tree, which was his favorite place, trying to bring himself to begin to think of some plan, when he saw many buzzards flying over him. They had been seeing him there for so long that they thought he surely must be dead. Many of them got together and decided to make it a party. They flew down to Mr. Burro.

Now when he saw this movement he closed his eyes and opened his mouth. The buzzards started pecking at him, but my, he was tough! Maybe they should have waited a while longer. One saw his pretty tongue and, thinking it would be soft, stuck her head in the mouth. All Mr. Burro had to do was to close it, and he did! The other buzzards flew away, saying that they had never cared for donkey meat anyway. Now all Mr. Burro had to do was to keep his mouth closed. This he did and went back to sleep. The poor buzzard tried hard to get away but couldn't, and her head started getting redder and redder, and all the feathers were coming off.

At last Mr. Lion came creeping along. He was hungry and tired. Imagine his surprise when he saw Mr. Burro with the buzzard! Mr. Burro opened his mouth and laughed. "Is there any doubt now?" he asked.

Mr. Lion shook his head slowly and sadly, and walked away to get something to eat, for he was so hungry. Mr. Burro went back to sleep. He was very content and satisfied with himself and with life and with all the world in general.

And the buzzard? The poor old buzzard flew away as soon as she was released. Her head was red from shame and pain and all the feathers were off. Since that day it has remained that way, and no buzzard will stick its head in a dead burro's mouth.

Señor Coyote and Señor Fox

Dan Storm

In this certain country of which I am telling you there was a great rock very tall standing alone in the center of a plain. Looking at it from a distance, one would think that it was perhaps a church tower that had come straight up through the ground. But upon approaching closely to this strange thing, anyone could see that it was a great cliff higher than any church.

One day when Señor Zorro was traveling through this country he lay down to sleep in the shade close to the wall of this cliff and close to one corner. But Mister Fox never sleeps in the daytime with both eyes closed, and this is why he saw Señor Coyote before that very smart animal saw him. When he saw the Coyote's shadow appear around the edge of the cliff, the Fox sprang to his feet and started pushing against the wall of the cliff.

"*Pues, mira no mas!* just look!" exclaimed the Coyote. "After all the times you have escaped from me, here we are at last met again. Aha, do not try to climb the cliff, man. Stay for dinner. It is meal time for me."

"*Cuidado!*" yelled Mr. Fox, pushing against the face of the cliff and skidding his feet on the ground. "Look out! This cliff is falling. Help me hold it up. Hurry!"

Mr. Coyote looked up to the top of the high cliff, and as he was standing right almost against it, it did seem to be toppling slowly over.

"It is falling, sure enough," he gasped and with a leap was at Mr. Fox's side pushing against the cliff and grunting and pawing a hole in the ground to hold his feet.

"We can't continue this for a very long while," said the Coyote between puffing and blowing. "We will perhaps stay here until our bleached bones will be propped here holding up this rock."

"I tell you what we will do," said the Fox. "It is certain that we

106

must hold this cliff up. We cannot try to run to safe ground, because we cannot outrun this cliff when it once really starts falling. It is only trying to topple now. You keep on bracing the rock up and I will run and get some help and also some food."

"Oh, no," said the Coyote quickly, "it is necessary for both of us to be here to hold up this cliff."

"You saw me holding it alone when you came up," Señor Fox gravely replied. "Surely, you with your strong muscles can hold it about half an hour. And that is the very most time that I will be in returning with some of my friends bringing log props and food and pulque."

"All right," said the Coyote. "I suppose I could hold this thing for half an hour. I guess I do not know my own strength. But only hurry. And remember, half an hour, Brother Fox."

"Yes, yes," said Mr. Fox, easing away from the cliff, "only push harder, now that I am not helping you. Harder! Harder!" And Mr. Coyote strained and put his shoulder to the cliff, digging his feet deeper into the ground.

"Until half an hour, no more, Brother Coyote," called the Fox over his shoulder. And he was off galloping with light jumps across the level desert, away from Mr. Coyote sweating and panting against the cliff.

A half hour passed. And no Señor Fox. Señor Coyote was still at his post pushing with all his might. An hour passed, and still Brother Fox did not appear. Mr. Coyote became terribly tired and impatient. From time to time now he began to glance up to the top of the cliff and relax his hold for just an instant. But every time he relaxed, it seemed that the cliff would begin falling. So he would almost fall himself in his haste to push harder.

The sun went down behind the distant hills and up came the moon over the mountains to the east. And Mr. Coyote turning his head painfully over one shoulder and then the other could not see Mr. Fox or anyone else anywhere on the landscape.

All night long while the moon traveled overhead to the other horizon, Señor Coyote was pushing against the cliff and howling and calling for the Fox. But he got no answer.

The moon went down and up came the sun where the moon had come before, and what did the sun see but Señor Coyote up past his knees in the hole his feet had dug. There he stood whimpering and gasping for breath and cursing, and yelling for Mr. Fox.

"I have no strength left in my arms to hold this cliff," he half sobbed aloud. "Maybe with good luck I can run faster than this cliff can fall. It is my only chance."

So Señor Coyote took a deep breath, shut his eyes, and sprang out of his hole and dashed from the cliff, running so fast he seemed to be flying with only his ears and tail for wings. When he was about a quarter of a mile away, he looked back expecting to see the great stone cliff lying on its side in an immense cloud of dust. But there it was, upright, as always before. Mr. Coyote could not believe his eyes. "It cannot be," he said, when he was able to get enough air to spare some on words. "How can it be?" He sat down on the ground, and when his strength returned came also his reason; and the idea came to him all at once that the Fox had fooled him another time. Up into the air he jumped cursing and yelling and shouting what he would do to Mr. Fox the next time he saw him.

And Señor Fox, where was he? *Quien sabe?*

The Doodang

Joel Chandler Harris

"I wish," said the little boy, sitting in the doorway of Uncle Remus's cabin and watching a vulture poised on motionless wing, "I wish I could fly."

The old man regarded him curiously, and then a frown crept up and sat down on his forehead. "I'll tell you dis much, honey," he said, "ef eve'ybody wuz ter git all der wishes, de wide worl' 'ud be turned upside down, and be rollin over de wrong way. It sho would!" He continued to regard the little boy with such a solemn aspect that the child moved uneasily in his seat on the doorstep. "You sho does put me in min' er de ol' Doodang dat useter live in de mudflats down on de river. I ain't never see 'im myse'f, but I done seed dem what say dey hear tell er dem what is see 'im.

"None un um can't tell what kinder creetur de Doodang wuz. He had a long tail, like a yallergater, a great big body, four short legs, two short years, and a head mo' funny lookin dan de rhynossy-hoss. His mouf retched fum de cen'er his nose ter his shoulder blades, and his tushes wuz big 'nough, long 'nough, and sharp 'nough fer ter bite off de behime leg uv a elephant. He could live in de water, er he could live on dry lan', but he mos'ly wallered in de mud-flats, whar he could retch down in de water and ketch a fish, er retch up in de bushes and ketch a bird. But all dis ain't suit 'im a 'tall; he got restless; he tuck ter wantin things he ain't got; and he worried and worried, and groaned and growled. He kep' all de creeturs, fur and feather, wide awake fer miles aroun'.

"Bimeby, one day, Brer Rabbit come a-sa'nterin by, and he ax de Doodang what de name er goodness is de matter, and de Doodang say dat he wanter swim ez good ez de fishes does.

"Brer Rabbit say, 'Ouch! you make de col' chills run up and down my back when you talk 'bout swimmin in de water. Swim on dry lan' ol' frien'—swim on dry lan'!'

109

"But some er de fishes done hear what de Doodang say, and dey helt a big 'sembly. Dey vow dey can't stan' de racket dat he been makin. De upshot uv de 'sembly wuz dat all de fishes 'gree fer ter loan de Doodang one fin apiece. So said, so done, and when dey tol' de Doodang 'bout it, he fetched one loud howl, and rolled inter shaller water. Once dar, de fishes loan't 'im eve'y one a fin, some big and some little, and atter dey done dat, de Doodang 'skivver dat he kin swim des ez nimble ez de rest.

"He skeeted about in de water, wavin his tail fum side ter side, and swimmin fur and wide. Brer Rabbit wuz settin off in de bushes watchin. Atter while de Doodang git tired, and start ter go on dry lan', but de fishes kick up sech a big fuss, and make sech a cry, dat he say he better gi' um back der fins, and den he crawled out on de mud-flats fer ter take his nap.

"He ain't been dozin so mighty long 'fo' he hear a mighty big fuss, and he look up and see dat de blue sky wuz fa'rly black wid burds, big and little. De trees on de islan' wuz der roostin place, but dey wuz comin home soon so dey kin git some sleep 'fo' de Doodang set up his howlin and growlin, and moanin and groanin. Well, de birds ain't mo'n got settle' 'fo' de Doodang start up his howlin and bellerin. Den de King-bird flew'd down and ax de Doodang what de name er goodness is de matter. Den de Doodang turn over in de mud, and howl and beller. De King-bird flew'd aroun', and den he come back, and ax what der trouble is. Atter so long a time, de Doodang say dat de trouble wid him wuz dat he wanted ter fly. He say all he want wuz some feathers, and den he kin fly ez good ez anybody. Den de birds hol' a 'sembly, and dey all 'gree fer ter loan de Doodang a feather apiece. So said, so done, and in a minnit er mo' he had de feathers aplenty. He shuck his wings, and ax whar'bouts he mus' fly fer de fust try.

"Brer Buzzard say de best place wuz ter de islan' what ain't got nothin but dead trees on it, and wid dat, de Doodang tuck a runnin start, and headed fer de place. He wuz kinder clumsy, but he got dar all right. De birds went 'long fer ter see how de Doodang 'ud come out. He landed wid a turrible splash and splutter, and he ain't hardly hit de groun' 'fo' Brer Buzzard say he don't want his feather fer ter git wet, and he grabbed it. Den all de birds grabbed der'n, and dar he wuz. Days and days come and went, and bimeby Brer Rabbit wanter know what done gone wid de Doodang. Brer Buzzard say, 'You see my fambly settin in de dead trees? Well, dar's whar de Doodang is,

and ef you'll git me a bag, I'll fetch you his bones!' And den Brer
Rabbit sot back and laugh twel his sides ache!"

"Anyhow," said the little boy, "I should like to fly." "Fly, den,"
replied Uncle Remus; "Fly right in de house dis minnit, ter yo'
mammy!"

Ozark Ozone

The Indestructible Razorback

CHARLES F. ARROWOOD

The razorback has been as distinctive of the southern swamps and pine barrens as the long-horned steer has been of Texas. He was a principal support of life in the region of the Dismal Swamp when Byrd and his party ran the dividing line, and he has been an important economic and social factor in the region ever since. Nothing tougher ever ran on four legs. The razorback may lack the speed of the wolf, the fighting equipment of a wildcat, the strength of a bear, but no wolf, cat or bear can exceed him in ability to absorb punishment and come back for more.

A farmer was clearing a new ground—grubbing up the stumps laboriously, by hand. A county demonstration agent came by and showed him how easily and cheaply the stumps could be removed by the use of dynamite. The farmer was delighted. He went to the store, bought dynamite, fuse, and caps. Coming home, he dug a hole by a big white oak stump, set a charge of dynamite under it, lighted the fuse, and went to his house for supper. The fuse went out, but by that time the farmer was clear of the new ground; so he decided to wait until the next morning before lighting it again.

The next morning, early, the farmer's big razorback hog got up and went foraging. He found that stick of dynamite and ate it. Then he saw the farmer about the barn lot and hustled up to see if he could steal a little corn from the mule's breakfast. He broke into the mule's stall, and made for the feed trough. The mule, naturally, kicked at him, and, for the first and last time in his life, connected. The dynamite, at last, went off.

A neighbor heard the explosion and hurried over. He found the owner leaning over the fence of his barn lot, viewing the ruins.

The neighbor heaved a sympathetic sigh. "It looks pretty bad, friend," he said, "pretty bad."

"Yes," said the victim, "it is bad. Killed my mule, wrecked my barn, broke every window out of one side of my house, and, brother, I've got an awful sick hog."

A Randolph Carnival

VANCE RANDOLPH

The Toadfrog

One time there was a pretty girl walking down the street, and she heard somebody say, "Hi, Toots!" But when she looked around there was nobody in sight, just a little old toadfrog setting on the sidewalk.

So then the pretty girl started to walk on down the street, and she heard somebody say, "Hello, Beautiful!" But when she looked around there was nobody in sight, just this little old toadfrog.

So then the pretty girl started to walk on down the street, and she heard somebody say, "You got anything on tonight, Baby?" But when she looked around there was nobody in sight, just this little old toadfrog setting on the sidewalk.

The pretty girl looked down at the little old toadfrog. "I know it ain't you a-talking," she says.

"It's me, all right," says the toadfrog. "I'm a handsome young man, by rights. But I'm turned into a toadfrog now, because an old witch put a spell on me."

The pretty girl studied awhile, and then she says, "Ain't there anything you can do to break the spell?"

The toadfrog says there is only one way, and that is for a pretty girl to let him sleep on her pillow all night. The pretty girl thought it was the least she could do, to help this poor fellow out. So she took the little old toadfrog home and put him on her pillow when she went to bed.

Next morning the pretty girl's father come to wake her up, and he seen a handsome young man in the bed with her. She told her father about the little old toadfrog, and the witch that put a spell on him, and how it all happened. But the old man didn't believe the story, any more than you do!

117

Grandpap Hunted Birds

One time there was some business men from Kansas City come down here to shoot quail. They stopped to ask a farmer if they could hunt on his land, and he says sure. But when one fellow started to turn the bird-dogs out of the car, the farmer says you better leave them dogs where they are at, and hunt with Grandpap instead. So here come an old man with long whiskers, and he could smell out quail something wonderful. He pointed them coveys steady as a rock, and fetched dead birds the slickest you ever seen. The city fellows never heard of anything like that before. They all got the limit easy, so everybody was happy.

When they got back to Kansas City them fellows told some other people about it, but the people just laughed in their face. So next season a whole bunch of hunters come down to the same place. Soon as they got out of the car, the young farmer says, "Where is your dogs?" The city fellows told him they didn't bring no dogs, because everybody wanted to see Grandpap hunt quail, like they heard about last year in Kansas City.

The country boy just looked at them people, and shook his head. "I'm afraid you're out of luck," says he, "because Grandpap ain't here no more." So then they all begun to ask what has become of Grandpap, but the farmer didn't want to talk about it. Finally he says, "Well, gentlemen, if you must know, the old son-of-a-bitch got to running rabbits, and we had to shoot him."

The Talking Turtle

One time there was a fellow named Lissenbee, and the trouble was that he couldn't keep nothing to himself. Whenever anybody done something that wasn't right, Lissenbee would run and blab it all over town. He didn't tell no lies, he just told the truth, and that's what made it so bad. Because all the people believed whatever Lissenbee said, and there wasn't no way a fellow could laugh it off.

If he seen one of the county officers going to a woman's house when her husband was not home, Lissenbee would tell it right in front of the courthouse, and so there would be hell to pay in two families. Or maybe some citizens liked to play a little poker in the livery barn, but there wasn't no way to keep it quiet, on account of that goddam Lissenbee. And when the Baptist preacher brought some whiskey home, there was Lissenbee a-hollering before the preacher could get the keg out of his buggy. After while the boys was afraid to swipe a watermelon, for fear old blabbermouth Lissenbee would tell everybody who done it.

The last straw was the time Lissenbee found a turtle in the road. It was bigger than the common kind, so he stopped to look at it. The old turtle winked its red eyes, and it says, "Lissenbee, you talk too damn much." Lissenbee jumped four foot high, and then just stood there with his mouth a-hanging open. He looked all round, but there wasn't anybody in sight. "It must be my ears have went back on me!" says he. "Everybody knows terrapins is dumb." The old turtle winked its red eyes again. "Lissenbee, you talk too damn much," says the turtle. With that Lissenbee spun round like a top, and then he lit out for town.

When Lissenbee come to the tavern and told the people about the turtle that could talk, they just laughed in his face. "You come with me," says he, "and I'll show you!" So the whole crowd went along, but when they got there the old turtle didn't say a word. It looked just like any other turtle, only bigger than the common kind. The people was mad because they had walked away out there in the hot sun for nothing, so they kicked Lissenbee into the ditch and went back to town. Pretty soon Lissenbee set up, and the old turtle winked its red eyes. "Didn't I tell you?" says the turtle. "You talk too damn much."

Some people around here say the whole thing was a joke, because it ain't possible for a turtle to talk. They claim some fellow must have hid in the bushes and throwed his voice, so it just sounded like the turtle was a-talking. Everybody knows that these medicine-show doctors can make a wooden dummy talk good enough to fool most anybody. There was a boy here in town that tried to learn how out of a book, but he never done no good at it. The folks never found nobody in these parts that could throw his voice like that.

Well, no matter if it was a joke or not, the story sure fixed old blabbermouth Lissenbee. The folks just laughed at his tales after that, and they would say he better go talk to the turtles about it.

Tobey the Kingsnake

One time there was a fellow named J. Frank Tooler, and he heard folks talking how a kingsnake can kill a rattlesnake easy. The old-timers say that kingsnakes put in most of their time a-hunting rattlers and killing 'em just for the hell of it. The story don't sound reasonable, because a kingsnake ain't got no poison, so it looks like the rattler would just bite the kingsnake once and that would be the end of it. J. Frank didn't go so far as to call anybody a liar, but he says he is going to try a experiment and settle the question once and for all.

The first thing he done was to catch a kingsnake and put it in a wire cage. He named it Tobey after our sheriff, which was a kind of a joke because the sheriff was scared to death of snakes. The whole Tooler family had to catch mice for the critter to eat, and it was considerable of a chore. J. Frank told the boys next time you find a rattler don't kill him, but just holler for me.

Things run along for quite awhile, and then one of the hands run onto a big yellow rattlesnake in the pasture. Soon as he heard the hollering, J. Frank grabbed the cage and run down there. When they turned Tobey loose he didn't pay no mind to the rattler at first. No sir, that kingsnake just went a-slithering around, sticking out his tongue and looking at the bushes. All of a sudden Tobey stopped in front of a little bunch of snakeweed, and wiggled as if to say, "That's what I been a-looking for!" And then he give a big jump and grabbed the rattlesnake.

There was brush tore up and bushes bit for a couple of minutes, and then the old rattler socked his fangs into Tobey. But Tobey just run back and bit off a chunk of snakeweed. Soon as he swallowed a leaf or two, the kingsnake was just as good as ever, and he tackled the old rattler again. And that's the way things went from then on. The rattler bit him four times, but a swallow of that weed was all it took to cure the poison. And finally Tobey killed the old rattler plumb dead, and then crawled back into his cage to rest up.

Well sir, J. Frank took the kingsnake all round the neighborhood after that, showing off how it could kill rattlesnakes. Tobey never would tackle a rattler till he seen a bunch of snakeweed a-growing right handy. Folks come for miles around to see them fights, and sometimes they would bet on the rattler. But Tobey always killed 'em, even if it took six or seven swallows of snakeweed to do the job.

Finally a fool boy from Burdock township pulled up the weed and moved it about thirty feet, just to see what would happen. Nobody paid no attention, because they was all watching the fight. But just then Tobey got bit, so he come a-slithering back to get a dose of snakeweed. And when he seen the weed was gone, Tobey just give up. J. Frank run to fetch the weed back, but it was too late. Poor Tobey took a spasm, and pretty soon he was dead as a doornail.

Some fellows up the creek got to catching kingsnakes and matching 'em to fight rattlers, but J. Frank never took no more interest in it after Tobey died. J. Frank says the experiment worked out just like he figured. There ain't no doubt that a kingsnake can kill a rattler all right, if he's got plenty of snakeweed handy to cure the poison.

The Mare With the False Tail

One time there was a fellow up in Missouri owned a big fine-looking saddle mare, except she didn't have no tail, as it had got cut off some way. But there was a wigmaker in Kansas City that fixed a false tail so good you couldn't tell the difference, and it was fastened onto the stub with eelskin and rubber.

The trader that owned the mare got a fine saddle and bridle with silver on it, and he rode around to all the fairs. He would sell the mare for a good price, but he never sold the saddle and bridle. Soon as he got the money in his pocket, he always took off the saddle and bridle, and then he would pull the mare's tail off. She just had a little stub about six inches long, and it was shaved smooth and dyed yellow. It sure did look funny, so all the people would laugh, and the fellow that bought the mare begun to holler for his money back. But the horse trader says the tail does not belong to the mare, because it come off another animal. He says he bought the tail separate in Kansas City, and he has got a bill of sale to prove it. False tails is just like a woman's bustle, and if any gentleman wants a artificial tail, they can go to Kansas City and see the wigmaker, says he.

So then he would go set in the livery stable, and pretty soon the fellow that bought the mare would come around talking turkey. Then the horse trader would say, "I always try to do the right thing, and not work no hardship on the customers. So I will take the mare back, if you will give me twenty dollars for my trouble." That's the way it went all over the country, and sometimes he would sell the mare three or four times in one day. The horse trader was a-living the life of Riley, and putting money in the bank besides.

One day he rode into a little town in Arkansas, and right away an old man bought the mare for two hundred dollars. When the horse trader pulled the mare's tail off, the old man didn't bat an eye, and he just laughed like the rest of the boys. The horse trader hung around the livery stable all day, but the old man never showed up. The horse trader stayed at the hotel that night, and the next day he borrowed a pony and rode out to the old man's place. He says he don't feel right about the sale, so he will take the mare and give the old man his money back, and no hard feelings.

The old man just laughed, and says he hasn't got no complaint, as a bargain is a bargain. He says he likes the mare fine, and he is going to braid a new tail out of corn shucks, and paint it blue to match his wife's eyes. The horse trader figured the old man must be out of his head. But he had to get the snide mare back somehow, so he offered to pay the two hundred dollars and give the old man ten dollars besides. The old man just laughed louder than ever, and he says the mare is worth four hundred dollars easy, and she ain't for sale anyhow. So the horse trader come back to town. He set around the hotel mighty glum, and all the home boys was laughing about it.

Next morning he went out to see the old man again, and says he will give two hundred and twenty-five dollars for the snide mare. The old man says, "Don't talk foolish, because me and my wife has got attached to the mare now, and she is just like one of the family." And then he says he knowed that tail was a fake all the time, because he used to swap horses with the Indians when he was a young fellow.

The horse trader thought about it awhile, and then he says, "Listen, that snide's all I got to live on, and feed a big family. Do you want to take the bread out of my little children's mouth?" The old man he says, "No, I wouldn't do nothing like that. Give me three hundred dollars, and you can have your mare back." The horse trader started to write a check, but the old man wouldn't take no check, so they went to the bank, and the horse trader give him three hundred dollars in cash. All the loafers was a-laughing about it, and the banker laughed louder than anybody. So then the horse trader put the mare's tail where it belonged, and he rode out of that town. He never did come back, neither.

Lots of people up North think the folks that live down in Arkansas are all damn fools. But it ain't so, particular when it comes to swapping horses and things like that.

Wolves Are My Brothers

One time there was a girl named Jenny, and she married a fellow that was part Indian. They lived away back in the woods, as he says the wolves are my brothers, and we don't need no neighbors. Her friends thought Jenny had led her ducks to a poor puddle, because that Indian was wild as a mink. So finally Jenny made up her mind to run off, and go back to her folks. Soon as the fellow went a-hunting, she put on her best clothes and started for the settlement.

She walked through the woods a ways, and here come a big wolf. The wolf was going to eat Jenny up, but she throwed down her bonnet. So the wolf picked up the bonnet and away he run.

She just walked on through the woods, and here come another big wolf. The wolf was going to eat Jenny up, but she throwed down her coat. So the wolf picked up the coat and away he run.

Jenny just kept a-walking, and here come another big wolf. The wolf was going to eat Jenny up, but she pulled off her dress and throwed it down. So the wolf picked up the dress and away he run.

She was feeling mighty funny, but Jenny walked right on anyhow. When the next wolf come along she throwed down her petticoat. So the wolf picked up the petticoat and away he run.

Poor Jenny was considerable slowed down now, but here come another wolf, and she had to pull off her drawers. It wasn't no time at all till the next wolf showed up, and took her undershirt.

So there was Jenny a-standing out in the woods, without a stitch on but her moccasins. "I sure can't go into town like this," she says, "and it's too cold for me to be walking around naked as a jaybird, anyhow." So then she started back toward her old man's house. Jenny was worried about what might happen, when he seen her clothes was gone. "If I tell him about them wolves, he'll think it is a lie," she says to herself.

Pretty soon here come a big wolf with the undershirt, and he throwed it down. So Jenny put on the undershirt and walked toward home. And here come another wolf with the drawers, and he throwed them down. So Jenny put on the drawers and walked toward home. Then here come another big wolf with the petticoat, and soon as Jenny put the petticoat on she began to feel better. Pretty soon another wolf brought her dress, and another wolf brought her coat, and finally here come the last big wolf a-carrying the bonnet.

When she got back to the cabin Jenny was all dressed, and the old man didn't say a word. He just looked at her, and grinned kind of wolfish. And she says to herself, "Maybe them wolves are his brothers, sure enough." So after that Jenny didn't run off no more, but stayed home and took care of the house, like she ought to have done in the first place. The folks all say that him and her raised a fine family, and lived happy ever after.

What Cows Do on Christmas

One time there was a little boy lived away back in the hills. His paw and maw was good Christian folks, but kind of old-fashioned. They told him that Christmas comes on the sixth of January, and on Christmas Eve the cattle fall down on their knees at midnight. And they said the cows could talk that night, just like people.

Well, everybody knows Christmas used to come several days later than it does now; some of them old settlers still have their Christmas in January, and they call it Old Christmas. That's history, and you can't get around history. But it ain't likely that the cattle are going to kneel down at midnight, because a cow don't know nothing about religion, and how could they remember what day it is, anyhow? Still, you got to admit that cattle can kneel down whenever they feel like it, so it might be the notion would hit 'em all at once on Christmas Eve. But we all know in reason that cows can't talk, because it is against nature. Them old folks didn't have no education, and they believed all kind of things that people don't take any stock in nowadays. So they told their little boy about it, and he thought they was telling the truth.

Well sir, when it come the fifth of January, nineteen hundred and four, that little boy never went to sleep because he wanted to hear the cows talk. And when the clock says a quarter to twelve he got up easy, and put on his clothes. And when the clock says ten minutes to twelve he unbarred the door. The old folks was sound asleep, as he could hear them a-snoring like somebody sawing gourds. The little boy stayed out at the barn quite a while, and when he got back to the house the clock says twenty minutes to one. The little boy barred the door again, and took off his clothes, and crawled back in bed. The old folks was still a-snoring. The boy never let on, but he knowed his paw and maw was both liars. And he didn't believe nothing they told him after that.

The folks made the little boy go to church every Sunday, but he figured everything the preacher said was a lie, just like that whopper about the cows talking on Christmas Eve. They kept telling him every boy ought to learn how to read and write, but he thought that was a lie too, and run away from school every chance he got. His paw told him not to fool with them white trash gals that lived up the creek, but he done it anyhow. And by the time he was fourteen years old that boy run off to Oklahoma. Near as the folks could find out, he just hung around gambling halls and whorehouses. Finally he shot a deputy marshal and it looked like they was going to hang him, so he went to Texas and nobody knows what become of him after that.

The church people never could figure out how come that boy to go wrong, but the truth is the whole thing started when his paw and maw told him that fool tale about the cows a-talking. From that time on he thought all the folks was goddam liars, and he didn't believe nothing anybody said. It just goes to show that you got to be careful what you say to little boys, because they take everything mighty serious. It's different with little girls, of course. Girls are a lot smarter than boys, and they don't pay no attention to their paw and maw anyhow.

The Big Rabbits

One day Tip Martin come into town, and he says, "Gentlemen, I have killed the biggest goddam rabbit in the world!" The folks just laughed, but when Tip pulled the critter out of his wagon, they didn't know what to think. That rabbit stood six hands high at the shoulders, with ears eight inches long. It was just a terrible big jackrabbit, of course, but nobody around here had ever seen one before. The whole country was swarming with cottontails in them days, but we didn't have no regular jackrabbits till just a few years back, when they begun to drift in from Kansas and Oklahoma.

The boys hung that rabbit up in front of the butcher shop, and everybody that come along just looked at it, with their eyes sticking out like doorknobs. Next week a fellow says he seen another one over on Kickapoo Barrens, and pretty soon rabbit stories was flying round thick as crows at a hog killing. To hear them boys talk, you'd think them big rabbits was eating us out of house and home. Old man Preston says they have gnawed off fenceposts to get into the corn, and was felling his apple trees just like beavers. Up on Leatherwood Creek they got so big the dogs was afraid to tackle 'em. When a man went to call his hogs the rabbits would come a-running and chase the pigs right out of the lot. They turned over the feeding troughs, and would upset the farmer too, if he didn't get out of the way.

It seemed like them rabbits was getting bigger at every jump, especially the bucks. They could do everything a jackass does except bray, and mares all over the country was foaling colts with feet like rabbits. Lots of them was nothing but undersized mules, and no great harm done, but some of the horse colts was fertile. They would just breed around promiscuous with jennies and mares and rabbits and whatever come handy. Pretty soon the whole caboodle was all mixed up, till a fellow didn't know what kind of stock he was raising.

Nobody could tell how much truth there was in them big stories, but any fool could see that things was going from bad to worse. The Lord only knows what would happen next, but all of a sudden them animals took sick, and it was what they call rabbit fever nowadays. Most of the critters died right in the fields, and then come a big snowfall, so the folks went out and killed the rest of 'em off with shotguns. Everything kind of quietened down then, and the grass come green in March the same as always. So that was the end of the rabbit panic.

It all happened a long time ago, and most of the people that remembered the stories are dead now. But everybody knows that Missouri mules are not like other mules. And several of the old-timers still believe that maybe them big rabbits had something to do with it.

Fabulous Monsters

There are many legends of gigantic beasts and fabulous varmints in the Ozark country. It may be that credulous backwoodsmen believe some of them even today, but I wouldn't know about that. At any rate, the stories are still in circulation. Hillfolk tell them to their children, just as parents elsewhere used to entertain their offspring with yarns about dragons, centaurs, griffins, mermaids, and the like. Perhaps the children don't really believe all this, but it sometimes amuses them to pretend that they do, and thus the tales are preserved and transmitted from one generation to the next. Some of these items seem to be local, confined to certain clans or family groups. Others are much more widely known, and have even been published in the newspapers.

One of the latter is concerned with an extraordinary reptile called the gowrow which terrorized rural Arkansas in the 1880's. Several stories about the gowrow were attributed to Fred W. Allsopp, sometime editor of the *Arkansas Gazette*, but I have been unable to find them in his published works. I asked Mr. Allsopp about this once, but he just laughed and said that all he knew of the gowrow was what he read in the Missouri papers. According to the legends, the gowrow was a lizard-like animal about twenty feet long, with enormous tusks. There is a persistent report that gowrows hatched from eggs, soft-shelled eggs as big as beer kegs. Some say that the female carried its newly hatched young in a pouch like a possum, but the old-timers do not agree about this. The gowrow spent most of its time in caverns and under rock ledges. It was carnivorous, and devoured great numbers of deer, calves, sheep, and goats. Perhaps the creature ate human beings, too.

A traveling salesman named William Miller was credited with killing a gowrow somewhere near Marshall, Arkansas, in 1897, and many wild stories were told about this exploit. There is no record that Miller ever showed the carcass of the animal to any local people. Miller once declared that he shipped the gowrow's skin and skeleton to the Smithsonian Institution in Washington, D.C. But a newspaperman who interviewed the officials at the Smithsonian was unable to confirm Miller's claim.

Otto Ernest Rayburn reprints an unidentified newspaper account of Miller's encounter with "a gowrow of the goofus family" in Searcy County, Arkansas. Miller had been unable to overtake the gowrow, but lay in wait for it at the entrance of a cavern.

> This cave was evidently the home of the animal [the newspaper story continues] as here were found many skeletons, skulls and bones, as well as parts of human flesh of recent victims; but the monster had not returned to its lair. Miller

and his posse laid in wait, trembling in their shoes. Presently
the earth swayed as if another earthquake were taking place.
The waters of the lake began to splash and roar like the
movement of the ocean waves, and they realized that the
monster was approaching. As it came within range, all hands
fired, and after several volleys were discharged, succeeded
in killing it. But it died hard. A couple of huge trees on the
bank were lashed down, and one of the assailants was killed
by it before it breathed its last. The gowrow was twenty feet
in length, and had a ponderous head with two enormous
tusks. Its legs were short, terminating in webbed feet similar
to but much larger than those of a duck, and each toe had a
vicious claw. The body was covered with green scales, and
its back bristled with short horns. Its tail was thin and long,
and was provided with sharp, blade-like formations at the
end, which it used as a sickle. The animal was a pachyderm,
with long incisors and canine teeth, which apparently
showed its relationship to the ceratorhinus genus, supposed
long since to have disappeared from the earth.

In the same magazine story Rayburn repeats a tale which he had
from Clio Harper, of Little Rock. It seems that there is a very deep
fissure called the Devil's Hole, near the Self postoffice in Boone
County, Arkansas, on land owned by E. J. Rhodes. In trying to
explore this cave Rhodes descended by means of a rope, landing on
a ledge some 200 feet below the surface, but could go no farther.
Later several men went to the Devil's Hole with 1,000 feet of
clothesline. They fastened a heavy old-fashioned flatiron to the end
of the line, and let it down into the hole. When the weight reached
a depth of about 200 feet it struck something, probably the ledge
discovered earlier by Rhodes.

It was at this point [according to Harper's story, that] things
began to happen. The men heard a vicious hissing sound as
if it were some angry animal whose den had been rudely
intruded. The rope was pulled up and it was found that the
handle of the iron was bent. Jim, the guide, swore he could
see the marks of teeth upon it. A large stone was then attached as a weight and thrown in. Again the sibilant sound
when it struck the ledge, and when the rope was drawn up
the stone was gone. The rope had been bitten in two as clean
as though it had been cut with a knife. Fastening another
stone to the line, we cast again. Again it ran out to the 200-
foot ledge, again the hissing sound was heard and when the
rope was drawn up the stone was gone and the rope was
found to have been cut in two as clean as by a knife. The
marks of sharp teeth were clearly discernible. For the third

time the cast was made, and the third time the rope was
bitten in two.

Disregarding a local theory that the mysterious phenomena of the
cave were caused by the spirit of a dead Indian, at least one member
of the party, according to Rayburn's account, contended that a gowrow must be responsible. It might well be, he argued, that Miller's
posse had not killed the gowrow. Maybe the great beast had
"played possum" and fooled 'em. Perhaps, after Miller's departure,
the gowrow migrated to Boone County and settled down in the
Devil's Hole, where it may be living to this day.

I have met elderly men in Missouri and Arkansas who publicly
declared their belief that a few specimens of the gowrow may have
survived into the 1920's. But whether these fellows were in earnest,
I do not pretend to say.

My old friend Pete Woolsey, who used to run a restaurant in
Bentonville, Arkansas, was a little offended when I grinned at his
version of the gowrow story.

"I don't see nothin' so unreasonable about it," said he. "Them
scientists over at the State University are tellin' people that there
used to be elephants right here in Arkansas. *Elephants,* mind you,
with red wool on 'em two foot long!"

"That's different," I answered. "That was thousands of years
ago."

"Would you rather believe them professors, talkin' about red
elephants in Arkansas before America was *discovered* even, than my
Grandpaw's story of what happened in his own life-time?"

"Listen, Pete, did your grandfather ever see a gowrow?" I asked.

"No, he didn't. I never seen a painter, neither. But lots of old-
timers did see painters, an' killed 'em too, right here in this county.
I've listened at them hunters a-talkin', an' there ain't no doubt in my
mind that there was plenty of painters here in the early days. My
Grandpaw heerd about the gowrow, just like I've heerd about
painters."

Pete began to look kind of indignant, as if somebody had intimated that maybe his grandfather was a liar. Pete Woolsey was not
a man to be pushed too far. So I suggested that we take a drink,
which we did, and said no more about gowrows.

A gentleman at Mena, Arkansas, told me a long story of a
Missourian who claimed to have captured a gowrow alive. This
fellow had somehow induced the animal to eat a wagon-load of
dried apples, which had swelled its body to such a degree that the

beast could not get back into its burrow. He was exhibiting it in a tent, charging twenty-five cents admission. There was a horrible painting of the monster out front, showing it in the act of devouring an entire family of cotton farmers. When a good crowd was seated, there came a terrible roaring noise backstage, with several shots and a loud clanking of chains. Then the showman staggered out in full view of the audience, his clothes torn to shreds and blood running down his face. "Run for your lives!" he yelled, "the gowrow has broke loose!" Just then the back part of the tent collapsed, with more thunderous roars and chains rattling and women screaming. The spectators rushed away in a panic, without stopping to get their money back.

Eleanor Risley, author of *The Road to Wildcat,* was present when I heard this tale. She remembered that a similar yarn had been popular years before in Alabama. The name gowrow was not used in the Alabama version, though; it was some other sort of wild animal that the fellow pretended to have in the tent.

Down near Argenta, Arkansas, the old-timers used to speak jokingly of a mythical anachronism known as the jimplicute. This was a kind of ghostly dinosaur, an incredible dragon or lizard supposed to walk the roads at night, grab travelers by the throat and suck their blood. It is said that the jimplicute was invented by white people shortly after the War between the States, to frighten superstitious Negroes. Oddly enough, the name of this bloodthirsty beast seems to have struck the fancy of newspapermen. Walt Whitman, writing in the *North American Review* mentioned a Texas newspaper called *The Jimplicute,* and it is said that a *Weekly Jimplicute* was published at Illmo, Missouri, as recently as 1940.

Another apochryphal varmint was the famous high-behind, a lizard as big as a bull, whose hind legs were ten times longer than its forelegs. This creature, according to some children I met near Big Flat, Arkansas, lies in wait for human beings on the trails at night and "laps 'em up like a toad-frog ketchin' flies." Some people call it the "hide-behind," because it always hides behind some object so that nobody ever gets a really good look at it. Woodsmen say that the beast can "suck in its guts" so that it is slender enough to stand up behind a tree and be almost concealed. A man named Burke, in Joplin, Missouri, told me that the correct name of the creature is "*nigh*-behind," but the significance of this was not explained to me. Under whatever name, the high-behind is dangerous and an enemy to all humanity. In Taney County, Missouri, one of my friends learned that the sheriff had a warrant for his arrest, so he ran off to California and has never been heard from since. Some of this man's kinfolk said later that the poor fellow "unthoughtedly" walked up the Bear Creek road at midnight and failed to return. They found a few drops of blood and some mighty peculiar "sign" in the trail next day, so they "figgered the high-behind must have got pore Sam." Or at least that's what they told the authorities, and never cracked a smile in the telling.

The kingdoodle or whangdoodle is another big lizard, doubtless related to the gowrow, the jimplicute, and the high-behind. One night near Waco, Missouri, a drunken possum-hunter and I heard a strange booming sound in the woods along Spring River. "What's that noise?" I asked. The possum-hunter listened for awhile. "I don't know," said he, "but it sounds like a whangdoodle a-mournin' for its dead." One of my neighbors in McDonald County, Missouri, told his children that the kingdoodle looks very much like an ordinary mountain boomer, except for its great size. The mountain boomer, or collared lizard, seldom attains a length of more than ten inches, while the kingdoodle is "longer'n a well-rope, an' fourteen hands high." It is strong enough to tear down rail fences and pull up saplings, but is not bloodthirsty, and I never heard of its killing livestock or attacking human beings. Not far from Jane, Missouri, my wife and I stopped to look at a small building which had fallen off its stone foundation and rolled into a ditch. Probably a high wind was responsible, but a little boy who lived nearby didn't think so. "I reckon the old kingdoodle must have throwed it down, in the night," he said soberly.

The gollywog, as described to me by White River guides who claim to have seen it, is a giant mudpuppy or waterdog, which means salamander in the Ozarks. But a full grown gollywog is often eight or ten feet long, as big as an alligator. It spends most of its time in the water and moves about only at night, which explains why it is seldom seen except by illegal giggers and commercial fishermen. The gollywog upsets boats sometimes, but its main business seems to be the destruction of fishing-tackle, particularly trammel-nets and trotlines.

Looking through a collection of old letters and newspaper clippings in Greene County, Missouri, one finds occasional cryptic references to the willipus-wallipus. Asked where he was bound, a celebrated Missourian replied that he was going out to fight the willipus-wallipus, meaning that it was none of the questioner's damned business. I thought at first that the willipus-wallipus must be another legendary animal, but learned that it was a large road-building machine, a sort of roller propelled by a powerful steam engine. When a big stone statute was sent on a flatcar to Springfield, Missouri, to be set up in the graveyard, it was so heavy that several teams of horses failed to move it. But the old willipus-wallipus dragged the thing from the freight depot right through the town to the cemetery. An old resident of Springfield assured me that the machine was always known as the willipus-wallipus, and said that he had never heard it called by any other name. I queried May Kennedy McCord about this, and she commented upon the question in the KWTO *Dial.* "Whenever there's something you have no name for," she writes, "you just call it a willipus-wallipus. It is on record that a long time ago in Springfield they had a road-making machine listed in official documents as a willipus-wallipus." . . .

The bingbuffer has no part in our oral tradition nowadays, so far as I know, but one still finds references to it in old newspapers. The *Missouri Historical Review* reprints a piece from the Jefferson City *Daily Tribune,* where the following description is credited to Colonel W. J. Zevely.

> The hinge-tailed bingbuffer is nearly, if not quite, extinct at this time [said the Colonel]. I think the last one was killed in Osage County about 1881 or the spring of 1882. The animal is shaped something like a hippopotamus, only considerably larger and has a flat tapering tail which sometimes reaches the length of forty feet. Its legs are short and owing to the great weight of its body locomotion is necessarily slow. But nature supplies the hinge-tailed bingbuffer with the means of obtaining food. Underneath the jaws is a pouch that will hold at least a bushel. When in quest of food the animal fills its pouch with stones weighing from two to three pounds each. Where the tail joins the body there is a hinge, and when the animal desires to kill anything it takes a stone from the pouch with its tail, and hurls it with wonderful accuracy and force to a distance of several hundred yards. Talk about the accuracy and execution of a rifleball! You just ought to see a hinged-tail bingbuffer throw a stone. . . .
> As I said before, I believe the last one was killed some years ago.

Robert L. Kennedy, old-time newspaperman of Springfield, Missouri, used to tell the story of the orance, which he said was brought into prominence by Lee Holland and John G. Newbill. "These two wags of half a century ago," said Kennedy, "would be talking quietly about the orance, which would be mumbled so as to catch the attention of someone who was trying to overhear the conversation. Then when one or the other moved away he would be told in a louder voice 'They have taken it over to Joplin.' Most people thought it was an animal that was referred to, while others figured it must be some sort of projected factory that Springfield was trying to get, and had lost it to Joplin. Sometimes a man with a good ear would catch the word 'orance' clearly, and would want to know the details. He would be asked if he were not informed on the subject, and would reply that he was not. Then he would be told that the matter was of such grave importance that it should not be discussed in public. This would be kept up until the victim discovered that he was being played with. Some fellows would get furiously mad, and walk off mumbling words which did not sound like 'orance' at all." The whole thing was only a rib, probably limited to a few business men in Springfield, and never had any wide circulation. Oddly enough, the name orance is still known to some old settlers in southwest Missouri, but nowadays it means only a peculiar sort of legendary wildcat, more commonly called the wampus.

The most dangerous wild animal that ever really lived in the Ozarks was the panther or painter. The pioneers feared these beasts, and apparently with good reason. No less an authority than Wayman Hogue says that when he was a boy in Van Buren County, Arkansas, painters used to kill children occasionally, and would even climb down the chimney after a newborn babe. Because of their genuine fear of painters, the pioneers were frightened by any noise which suggested the screams of these animals. There are several stories of backwoodsmen who, when they heard the whistle of a steamboat or a locomotive for the first time, thought it must be some enormous wild beast. Doubtless some of these tales are based upon real incidents.

Jean Graham tells of the *Flora Jones*, the first steamboat that came up the Osage River to Harmony Mission, in Bates County, Missouri. It was in the spring of 1844. An old settler plowing in his clearing heard "a long wailing cry, followed by an angry roar," and figgered it must be some kind of super-painter. Stopping only to get his rifle, he rode madly into Papinsville. The people there had heard the terrible screams, and all able-bodied men gathered with dogs and guns.

> They pictured a varmint of gigantic size, to match the volume of its howling voice [writes Graham]. They figured

> it must be an unheard of species from the Rocky Mountains or some other remote region. The daughter of the house where they had congregated had just gone down to the river three or four hundred yards away for water. While the men made ready the unearthly sound came to them again from the direction of the river. The devoted father and others of the men mounted their horses and dashed after the girl, to rescue her from the beast. She met them half way, her eyes wild with terror and her hair streaming behind her as she ran. They saw her safely home, and her father bade her stay inside the cabin while they were away.

The dogs apparently failed to pick up any odor, but the varmint was certainly approaching. The hunters cocked their rifles and "made ready for the monster which they could hear puffing, blowing and roaring as he floundered along," evidently following the river. When the *Flora* finally steamed into view the backwoodsmen were so astonished that no word was spoken for a long time. Some of the settlers may have heard rumors of steamboats back East, but the *Flora Jones* was the first that any of them had ever seen. There were many such boats on Missouri rivers after that, for the Osage was navigable as far up as Oceola in those days.

Masterson quotes a story from the New York *Spirit of the Times* about an Arkansas planter who moved across the border into the wilderness of the Indian Territory. One evening he heard several very loud, shrill screams. The noise frightened the cattle, set the dogs to barking, and scared the womenfolk into fits. Everybody said it must be a painter, and a tremendous big painter at that. The planter took six Indians, four Negro men, and nine hound-dogs; they hunted through the whole country from Grand River to the Verdigris, but found no painter sign. Later it was learned that the mysterious sound was the fog whistle of a steamboat, the first steamboat that ever came up Grand River.

Panthers were common in the 1850's and 1860's, perhaps even later. But they were very rare in the Ozark country by 1900. The last Missouri panther was killed in 1927, according to the Missouri Conservation Commission. As for Arkansas, the official guidebook published in 1941 says that "only a few remain, and these in the most remote sections" (*Arkansas,* 1941, p.15). For all practical purposes panthers are extinct, but the hillfolk are still afraid of them. Hardly a month goes by without a panther being reported in some part of the Ozark country, and people always get pretty much excited. . . .

Most of the backwoods yarn-spinners have something to say about the side-hill hoofer. According to one common version of the tale, the hoofer is similar to a beaver in appearance, but very much larger, about the size of a yearling calf. It lives in a burrow on some steep hillside. This animal always runs around the hill in the same direction, since the legs on one side of its body are much longer than those on the other side. If by any accident the hoofer falls down into the flat country it is easily captured, since on level ground it cannot walk or run at all. The female lays eggs as big as water buckets, and one egg will furnish breakfast for twenty-five men. "But they taste kind of strong," an old man said soberly. Oscar Ward, a deer-hunter from Kansas, told me privately that the real Ozark hoofer has two big grabhook claws on its tail, so it can hang to the crest of a ridge and rest its legs.

Hawk Gentry, of Galena, Missouri, remarked that the side-hill hoofer is "kind of like a kangaroo, only built sideways." Gentry says that some of them run around the hill clockwise, the others anticlockwise, and there's an awful fight when the two varieties meet; they can't easily dodge one another, for the hoofer can only move *around* the hill, and goes up or down by means of long gradual curves. In other words, a hoofer can run rapidly on one level, but it's difficult for him to gain or lose altitude. These creatures sometimes attack men, just as a bull does, although they feed only upon vegetable matter. It is easy for a man to avoid the hoofer's attack, since he need only walk straight uphill or straight downhill for a few steps. They say that when a hoofer falls over on its side it is unable to get up, and just lies there and screams until it starves to death. Many are killed by falling off hillsides, and I have heard of one particular hollow in Marion County, Arkansas, which is half full of hoofer bones.

There are old tales also of the side-hill slicker and the side-hill walloper, but I have been unable to learn much about these animals. It may be that they are identical with the side-hill hoofer.

Another of these side-hill stories concerns the baldknob buzzard, an enormous vulture which they say was formerly common in White County, Arkansas. The man who told me this one is a resident of St. Louis, but he had the tale from his grandfather who lived near Bald Knob, Arkansas. The bird was much larger than the turkey-buzzard or the black vulture, and must have been something like the condor of the California mountains. But the outstanding feature of the baldknob buzzard is that it had only one functioning wing, the other being rudimentary. Because of this disability, the bird was always a little out of balance and could fly in one direction only. It always circled the hilltops from left to right. "Do you suppose your grandfather really believed all that about the baldknob buzzard?" I asked. My informant looked a bit shocked. "Believe that stuff? Of course not. It was just one of those old stories. But he always *acted* as if he believed it. That was part of the joke, you see."

A half-witted boy near Rolla, Missouri, rushed into the crossroads store to report a wild turkey "big as a cow," that ate up ten acres of corn in one evening. The village loafers were delighted, and began to elaborate upon the boy's story. A few days later, it was said that the big turkey was finally caught in a bear-trap baited with two bushels of popcorn. The great bird uprooted the post to which the trap was attached, but the woods were full of hunters by this time, and the turkey was riddled with bullets before it could get under way. Butchered like a steer, it weighed 150 pounds to the quarter, 600 pounds altogether. The women who picked it got feathers enough to fill seven bedticks, and old man Suggs used the quills to pipe water from the spring to his new barn. Two of the local strong men ruptured themselves trying to pull the wishbone, but they never even cracked it. An old settler kept that pulley-bone for many years, and it is said that he used it as a yoke for breachy steers, to keep them from busting through the fence. This is the story as I heard it in 1934. God only knows how the Phelps County whackers have dressed it up nowadays.

Over at West Plains, Missouri, there used to be a story about a very large bird, known as the giasticutus. Some of the old settlers said that it was the invention of a bunch of jokers in St. Louis; others thought that Mark Twain had something to do with it. One man told me that it all began in an anecdote related by Eugene Field when he was very drunk one night in the Planters' Hotel. Whatever its origin, there is no doubt that some country folk believed the tale. Only a few years ago there were men and women still alive who claimed to have seen the monster, which had a wingspread of about fifty feet. It was a bird of prey, like a prodigious chicken-hawk, with a great boat-like beak and a habit of carrying off full-grown cattle. But all this happened so long ago, I was told, that one cannot obtain any definite facts about the giasticutus today.

A man in Chicago wrote me at length about his experience with the giasticutus in Christian County, Missouri, many years ago. He says he used to be a college professor in Missouri, and repeats the

story of a man named Moorhouse who lived at a place called Windy
City, somewhere near Sparta, Missouri. Walking in his pasture one
Sunday, Moorhouse found a black feather fourteen feet long, with
a quill as thick as a man's leg. The professor declares that he has
"seen and hefted" this feather, which is now fastened with baling-
wire to the rafters of a certain hay-barn near Highlandville, Missouri.
I used to know some people in that neighborhood, and I queried
them very cautiously on this subject. But not one of them had ever
heard of the giasticutus, or the man named Moorhouse, or the four-
teen-foot feather.

A few giasticuti have been reported from Greene County, Missouri, but they were comparatively small. Floyd A. Yates, in a
pamphlet called *Chimney Corner Chats* tells of a hawk twenty-four
feet from tip to tip, which carried off a yearling calf. A pretty big
bird, all right, but less than half the size of the giasticutus of Howell
County. A yearling calf is quite a load, but a 1,600-pound Harlan
bull is something else again.

I have not heard the giasticutus story from the windy-spinners
in Carroll County, Arkansas, but have reason to believe that such
tales are still current here. In 1946 a newspaperman from New Jersey
came to see me in Eureka Springs, and asked if it were true that
some chicken-hawks in this region have a wingspread of sixteen feet.
He said he had heard some farmers discussing such a bird at a wagon
yard near his hotel. I suggested that the story was probably told for
his benefit, but the poor fellow did not think so. "Those chaps never
even glanced at me," he said earnestly. "They were talking among
themselves, all about crops and the like." Finally I said flatly that
there are no sixteen-foot hawks anywhere in the world, and let it
go at that. The man thanked me and went his way, but I'm afraid he
was still inclined to believe the whopper he had "overheard" in the
wagon yard. . . .

Frank Payne, an old-time guide at Galena, Missouri, had several
good stories about the galoopus, a big black eagle which nested in
the bluffs over the James River. This bird lays square eggs, since
ordinary eggs would roll to destruction before they could be incu-
bated. Frank told me that in the early days he and W. D. Mathes
used to gather galoopus eggs by the dozen, boil them very hard, and
paste playing-cards neatly on the sides. Mathes operated the float-
trip company in those days, and Frank sold the eggs to the tourists
for poker-dice. One of Frank's cronies said the galoopus was so big
that its shadow wore a trail in the stony soil of Barry County, Mis-

souri, almost paralleling the gravel road now called Highway 44. Payne himself would not vouch for this. "The trail's there, all right," said he, "but I ain't sure the galoopus is responsible. Maybe the Injuns done it, for all I know." . . .

The fishermen in Taney County, Missouri, still tell tourists about the clew-bird, that sticks its bill in a gravel bar and whistles loudly through its rectum. "It looks like a crane, only bigger," one old settler remarked. "Mostly it sets its bill solid in them gravels, an' then spins round like a top, so fast you cain't tell what color it is." My friend Allen Rose, of Springfield, Missouri, who used to direct float trips on the James and White rivers, says that his guides called this creature the milermore bird, because its whistle can be heard for a mile or more.

Along the western border of Arkansas the milermore bird is apparently unknown, but many old-timers remember the noon-bird, said to inhabit the Kiamichi Mountains of Oklahoma. It whistles like a fire engine exactly at noon, hence the name. Some enthusiasts claim that it blows a reveille at 5 A.M., and even a curfew at 9 P.M., but these additions to the tale are frowned upon by the best story-tellers.

I have heard some mention also of the waw-waw bird, the thunder-bird, the yow-ho bird, and the toodalong buzzard, but they are only names to me. I have been unable to find anybody who can describe their characteristics or way of life.

Some of the tales about aquatic monsters are more alarming than any of the bird stories. At a certain fish-camp near Branson, Missouri, the guides used to talk about an island that suddenly appeared in Lake Taneycomo, just after a great storm. At the same time a strange rhythmic rise and fall of the waters occurred. Every two or three minutes the water level would suddenly rise about four feet, then recede slowly. Some boatmen who investigated the matter discovered that the new island was really a gigantic turtle. Every time the monster breathed, the waters rose and fell. This story came to me at Columbia, Missouri, and I drove down to the lake to see about it, but the turtle was gone when I arrived. George Hall told me privately that Captain Bill Roberts, of Rockaway Beach, had killed the great reptile with a harpoon, and was serving the meat to his guests, who thought it was bootleg venison. But George Hall was a great joker, and I don't believe that Captain Bill had anything to do with the disappearance of the Taneycomo turtle.

Will Rice recalls a turtle killed in the Buffalo River near his home at St. Joe, Arkansas, which "made a meal for forty families, with two barrels of soup left over." An even larger turtle in the same vicinity swallowed a mule that was swimming the river; when this monster was shot four years later, the mule shoes were found in its stomach. Really warmed up by this time, Rice goes on to tell of a big turtle that got under a thirty-ton power crane used in building a bridge and carried the whole business upstream on its back. The man who was operating the crane saved his life by jumping onto a gravel bar.

Stories of big turtles are not new in the Ozark country. The Reverend D. A. Quinn, a Catholic missionary who worked in Arkansas in the 1870's, is quoted as saying that along the railroad between Memphis and Little Rock he saw "mud turtles, some *as long and wide as an ordinary door,* wallowing in the mire." According to *Ozark Life* a man named Messinger caught a turtle in the Black River, in Arkansas, that weighed 186 pounds; it was taken alive, and shipped to a zoo in Indianapolis. The biggest turtle I ever saw in this region was a snapper killed by Jess Lewellan and Wilfred Berry, in White River, near Hollister, Missouri, in 1936. It was nearly four feet long, and they said it weighed 70 pounds. Jim Owen, of Branson, Missouri, exhibted the shell of this turtle in his store for several years.

From the earliest times there have been tales of big bullfrogs in the Ozarks. Captain Jean François Dumont de Montigny records that in what is now Arkansas he captured a frog two feet long and 18 inches thick, weighing 36 pounds. It bellowed like a calf, he says, but could not jump at all because of its great weight. De Montigny reports another frog, even larger, but did not set down its exact weight and measurements.

More than a hundred years after Captain de Montigny's time, hardy Arkansawyers were telling of a pioneer whose oxen were killed by the Indians. Desperate because the plowing must be done without delay, this man yoked up a team of big bullfrogs. They worked pretty well, although they would jump and miss a thirty-foot span sometimes, while the plow and the cursing plowman were lifted clear off the ground. But by plowing the field both ways, most of the unbroken spots were caught the second time around. Plowing was no job for an old man, in them days.

A boatman on White River once sold me a mess of very large frog-legs. I remarked upon their phenomenal size, but the man replied that the really big frogs had been killed off years ago. "When

I was a young-un," said he, "the croakers in these here bottoms was big as full-grown steers. We used to butcher 'em just like hogs, an' salt 'em down for winter. They was so God-awful big we had to slice up their legs like a quarter of beef, an' cut through the bone with a bucksaw. When they got to bellerin' of a night, they'd rattle the winder-glass ten mile off. Them big 'uns could jump two hundred yards, easy. I've saw 'em jump one hundred yards, straight up in the air, to ketch a chicken-hawk."

I asked a storekeeper near Calico Rock, Arkansas, if he had ever seen frogs as big as oxen. "Well," he said slowly, "I reckon they was as *heavy* as steers, but not so tall. They was built kind of chunky an' low to the ground. I recollect Pappy killed one once. We just chopped off one hind leg an' drug it home, an' let the carcass lay there for the buzzards."

Will Rice tells of a man on Buffalo River who "grabbed a big frog by the leg. It jumped clear across the river with him hanging on, so that he had to walk a half-mile upstream to a shoal where he could wade back." Marion Hughes was inclined to minimize everything in the state, but even he admits that near Horatio, Arkansas, "there was bull frogs that you could hear crocking for three miles." *Crocking* is the way he spelled it, too. As recently as 1949 gamewarden Rayburn Brooks of Maries County, Missouri, investigated a report that a local fisherman had killed a bullfrog weighing 21 pounds. He learned that the frog had been caught in 1948 instead of 1949. Also, he writes, it turned out to be "twenty pounds of bull and one pound of frog."

Many fantastic stories have been told about the Lake-of-the-Ozarks country, but one of the wildest broke in June, 1935. Five men in two motorboats came tearing into port, white-faced and trembling. They had seen a gigantic animal, with one great eye like a punchbowl of green fire, a snakelike neck that rose twenty feet above the surface of the water, and a long red tongue that crackled like sassafras wood a-burnin'. One fellow was close enough to note the thick greenish scales on the creature's head and swore that its horny neck was studded with knobs the size and color of new basket balls. Charles Love, a deputy circuit clerk at the courthouse in Kansas City, took a party of armed men out in his launch. They searched the lake for miles, firing with rifles and revolvers at suspicious-looking objects in the water. But they didn't find the "Camden county sea-serpent." Love finally expressed the opinion that the monster was nothing more than a huge log, with one projecting branch which turned upward as the log rolled over in the current. But men who had seen the thing scoffed at this rational explanation. There are sober men in Missouri today who affirm that they encountered the varmint at close range, and others who saw it at a distance, "a-churnin' up the water like a God damn' steamboat," as one bug-eyed fisherman told me. I once thought I saw something like a young submarine myself, near Warsaw, Missouri, in the summer of 1936. But I could never be quite sure of it. The thing was quite a distance off, and we were all a little drunk that day, anyhow.

The Arkansas newspapers gave a great play to the "behemoth" which appeared in White River, early in June, 1937. A farmer named Bramlett Bateman rushed into the town of Newport, Arkansas, crying that there was a whale in the river "as big as a boxcar, like a slimy elephant without any legs." A lot of people hurried out to look, and several reputable citizens declared that they saw the creature. Newspaper reporters described the beast at great length, but the press photographers drew a blank. I drove down there myself and stared into the river for hours, but saw nothing but a lot of muddy water. The Newport Chamber of Commerce combined with Bateman to fence in the place, and then charged twenty-five cents admission. Signs were put up along the roads for miles around, THIS WAY TO THE WHITE RIVER MONSTER.

Groups of local sportsmen, armed with rifles, patrolled the banks day and night. These fellows wanted to kill the monster with dynamite, but the gamewardens wouldn't allow it, saying that the Arkansas law permits explosives to be used only to recover a human body. After a week of wrangling, Charles B. Brown, a professional diver, was employed to "beard the behemoth in its lair." This enterprise was sponsored by the Chamber of Commerce. They built a dance platform on the bank, with fiddlers and banjo-pickers from all over Jackson County. Local people sold soft drinks, sandwiches, and fruit. A public address system was set up, so that the crowd could hear a round-by-round account of the battle between the diver and the monster at the bottom of the river.

Finally Brown, wearing his diver's helmet and carrying an eight-foot harpoon, descended into the water. "There are some fish down there," said he, "also a lot of weeds, sunken logs, big rocks and pieces of old boats, but no sign of a monster." Later in the day he made another descent, which was equally fruitless. The crowd still watched the river and danced and drank far into the night. Brown dived again on the following day, but the crowd was pretty thin, and the refreshment concessions did very little business. About noon the Chamber of Commerce gave up the battle, and Bram Bateman went back to farming.

An Associated Press dispatch from Little Rock, dated Feb. 23, 1940, quotes Secretary D. N. Graves of the Arkansas Game and Fish Commission, who now believes that the "monster" was an overturned scow. It appears that a certain local shell-digger found a valuable bed of mussels at that point, very large shells used for making knife-handles and the like. Fearing that other diggers would muscle in on his discovery, this man sank the old scow and hitched it to a compli-cated set of wires. At one end the wires were fastened to the sub-merged roots of a tree; at the other end they led to a hiding-place behind some bushes on the south bank of the river.

> The story goes that the old man started the tale of a monster in the river himself [said Graves]. When one or two persons would come down there, he would hide in the bushes and pull the "monster" up for a few minutes. But if a crowd was on hand, the monster didn't appear, because the shell-digger was afraid of being discovered. All this time the old man was working at night, digging the shells. Due to the crowds, the situation got clear out of hand, so one night he slipped in and cut the wires, letting the monster ramble on down the river. By that time—about two weeks—he had the shells all dug, anyhow.

The few persons who actually saw the monster noted that it had "hide like a wet elephant," and Secretary Graves says that the moss-covered bottom of a scow would have this appearance. Graves told reporters that he got this explanation from a filling-station attendant in Newport, who had it from the old shell-digger himself. "The story has the ring of truth," said Graves, "and I am convinced that it is true."

The filling-station story which convinced Mr. Graves does not altogether satisfy me. Awaiting further light, I am content to string along with the agnostics for the present. Let the White River monster join the distinguished company of the jimplicute, the gow-row, the snawfus, the kingdoodle, the giasticutus, the whistling wampus, and other fabulous critters that live only in the tales that are told around campfires in the big timber.

Texas Tall Talk

Tall Tales for the Tenderfeet

A. W. PENN

When a year or so ago I was asked to address the Texas Folk-Lore Society on the subject of the ornithryncodiplodicus, the whifflepooffle, the milamo bird, and certain other remarkable fauna of the district known as the Conical Mountain Region of Central Texas, I was at first very certain that some mistake had been made. Folk-lore, according to Webster, is that body of rural superstitions, tales, and legends passed from generation to generation orally, mainly from the mouths of grandfathers sitting on the doorsteps at sundown while the grandchildren gather around and marvel at the good old days. Not of this nature are the coldly scientific facts regarding the ornithryncodiplodicus and other little known animals of the Conical Mountain Region of Central Texas. Parenthetically, it may be said that they are little known for two reasons: first, because of the innate laziness of the inhabitants of the region; secondly, because of the protective methods employed by these animals that they may not be seen or disturbed. The only similarity between the records which I am here setting down and the records that have already been printed in the *Publications* of the Texas Folk-Lore Society is that I can claim no more originality in recording them than the real Texas folk-lorists claim for recording certain of our most interesting and beautiful legends.

Know then that the region west of Austin was at one time a high rolling plateau in nature very similar to the prairie land north and east. In fact, the geologists claim that the two regions were in the distant past identical in form, one the continuation of the other. They say that as a result of a great break, known as the Balcones Fault, either the prairie lands to the east and north dropped down several hundred feet or the region west of the Colorado River was elevated an equal amount, producing such radical effect on the togopraphy as to affect the animal life of the region.

145

Of the animals that roamed this upland region before the change
in topography the strongest and the most peaceable was the orni-
thryncodidiplodicus; but as time went on and the erstwhile flat
region over which he roamed became more and more hilly, his disposition became correspondingly rougher and rougher. He became,
indeed, a savage creature. Nevertheless he retained his methodical
habits—the kind of habits always associated with peaceableness.
This methodical turn of mind had from the earliest times caused
each individual ornithryncodiplodicus to graze exclusively on his
own particular area without infringing on the rights of his neighbors;
then as erosion and elevation made of the ornithryncodiplodicus
habitat a series of cone-shaped hills and as each of the animals
found his particular plot becoming a hill, he continued in his
methodical way to graze on it. This meant that he grazed around
and around the hill. The inevitable result was that his uphill legs
became shorter than his downhill legs. Such a disproportion in
anatomy further distempered the ornithryncodiplodicusical disposition. From a peaceful, kindly, docile grazer of the open plateau, the
animal became a ferocious destroyer of all life that came within the
limits of his range. This range, however, was very limited, for while
the downhill legs and the uphill legs enabled him to go evenly
around and around the hill, they precluded his mobility on level
ground or in any other than his predestined direction. Some of the
species could circumambulate in clockwise fashion; some in counter-
clockwise fashion. A kind of jealousy arose between the individuals
whose right legs were longer than their left legs and other individuals
whose left legs were longer than their right legs.

Soon after the Conical Mountain Region grew out of the plateau, and after the disposition of the ornithryncodiplodicus had
suffered such a grievous change, many of the native men were
trapped on the hillsides and horribly mangled by the ferocious
beasts. Not many of the natives, however, really knew anything
about the strange beasts, for most of them early adopted, in one
respect at least, the policy of the squirrel, always staying on the
opposite side of the hill from any visitor. The name of the fierce
animal came to be vulgarized into "mountain stem-winder," but the
more dignified appellation of ornithryncodiplodicus is not likely ever
to be supplanted.

In time the natives learned how to cope with the beast, and
only tenderfeet who strayed too far into the mountains never
returned. The native method was this. When a man heard the fero-

cious growls of a charging ornithryncodiplodicus and located the beast plunging towards him through the underbrush, he would go towards him with an innocent smile on his face, as if unaware of danger. Then when the onrushing peril was exactly within two steps of him, the native frontiersman would step two paces down hill. Of course the ornithryncodiplodicus, with two long legs on one side of his body and two short legs on the other side—at infinitely greater disadvantage than the kangaroo—could not follow. Nevertheless, impelled by his fierceness and his voraciousness, he would check himself, turn as best he could, and plunge recklessly after the native. Inevitably he tottered on his unequal legs for only a minute or so, and then he rolled screaming into the abyss below.

Such a downfall was always the occasion for great joy among all the beasts and birds of the region as well as among the people. The elephants would flit from bough to bough in fairy-like ecstasy. The humming birds would crash through the underbrush and set up a loud cackle around the body of the ornithryncodiplodicus. The perch and other fishes would float high above the mountain tops and hover over the scene. Eagles floated lazily in the shadowy waters, and the voice of every milamo bird in the country could be heard for a mile or more echoing and reverberating through the mountain fastnesses.

As the conical hills of this region elevated themselves and became mountains, circular lakes, as deep as the mountains were high and as wide as the mountains were broad, naturally developed. In these circular lakes lived the whiffle-pooffle, most prized of all mountain fishes and most difficult to catch. Only by means of a good rowboat, a very long auger and a faculty for telling stories, could any fisherman catch a whiffle-pooffle.

The fisherman would take his auger and row out to about the middle of the lake. Then he would bore a hole far down to the briniest depths of the deeps below. When the hole was adjudged to be sufficiently deep, the fisherman would pull up his auger and suspend a squidge over the hole. No other bait would entice the whiffle-pooffle, but when he smelt the delicious aroma of the squidge, he at once located the hole and climbed to the surface. The fisherman allowed him to devour the squidge. Now squidge after it is eaten has the effect of swelling the eater, in this respect resembling hard-tack and water. As a consequence, the gorged whiffle-pooffle when he sought to re-enter the hole and retire to his watery home, would find himself too bulky to get into the hole.

At this juncture the artistry of the fisherman was called into play. As soon as the whiffle-pooffle gave up the attempt to enter the hole, the fisherman would start telling the funniest story he knew. The whiffle-pooffle, having a very strong sense of humor, would crowd up close to the boat so as not to miss a word; of course this proximity was determined by the degree of funniness that the fisherman could put into the story. All the while as he talked the fisherman would be edging his boat towards shore. Then as he approached the point of his funny story, he would row very rapidly, at the same time pouring a bucket of grease out on the surface of the lake to make it slippery. Timing his story to conclude just as the boat was about to touch shore, the fisherman would turn sharply to the right, and the whiffle-pooffle, wiliest of fishes, would slide, helpless, high and dry on the bank—often, it is said, so convulsed with laughter that it never realized the fate awaiting it.

That the greenness of the tenderfeet might ever be kept verdant, the old-timers had tales of many other strange "animules" that once inhabited the wastes of Texas. The clubtailed glyptodont, which placed large rocks on top of small ones and then batted them to the top of high slopes just to see the rocks roll back, was one of the most entertaining inhabitants of the Conical Mountain Region. Evidences of his handiwork may be seen yet in the white streaks down the sides of the mountains where the rocks rolled back. The tail of this animal was hard and elastic and he rotated on his hind legs at a terrific rate and then "golfed" the teed-up rock far up the hillside. The eight-legged galliwampus, the tufted pocalunas, and the milamo bird often vicariously entertained those who cared to listen when the talk in the evening became serious and waxed scientific. Thus from the land of the tamale trees on the south to the barbed wire between Amarillo and the north pole, the stories of these strange survivors of the past have been handed on until the accurate details have been blurred with certain imaginary trimmings more appropriate to folk-lore than to science.

Pecos Bill and the Mountain Lion

MODY C. BOATRIGHT

Bill was a good deal like his old man. When he had killed all the Indians and bad men, and the country got all peaceful and quiet, he jest couldn't stand it any longer and he saddled up his hoss and started west. Out on the New Mexico line he met an old trapper and they got to talkin and Bill told him why he was leavin and said if the old man knowed where there was a tough outfit, he'd be much obliged if he would tell him how to git to it. "Ride up the draw about 200 miles," says the old trapper, "and you'll find a bunch of guys so tough that they bite nails in two jest for the fun of it."

So Bill rides on in a hurry, gittin somewhat reckless on account of wantin to git to that outfit and git a look at the bad *hombres* that the old man has told him about. The first thing Bill knowed, his hoss stumps his toe on a mountain and breaks his fool neck rollin down the side, and so Bill finds his self afoot.

He takes off his saddle and goes walkin on, packin it, till all at once he comes to a big rattlesnake. He was 12 feet long and had fangs like the tushes of a *javelina* and he rears up and sings at Bill and sticks out his tongue like he was lookin for a scrap. There wasn't nothin that Bill wouldn't fight and he always fought fair; and jest to be shore that rattlesnake had a fair show and couldn't claim he took advantage of him, Bill let him have three bites before he begun. Then he jest naturally lit into that reptile and mortally flailed the stuffin out of him. Bill was always quick to forgive, though, and let bygones be bygones, and when the snake give up, Bill curled him around his neck and picked up his saddle and outfit and went on his way.

As he was goin along through a canyon, all at once a big mountain lion jumped off of a cliff and spraddled out all over Bill. Bill never got excited. He jest took his time and laid down his saddle and his snake, and then he turned loose on that cougar. Well, sir, the hair flew so it rose up like a cloud and the jack rabbits and road runners thought it was sundown. It wasn't long till that cougar had jest all he could stand, and he begun to lick Bill's hand and cry like a kitten.

Well, Bill jest ears him down and slips his bridle on his head, throws on the saddle and cinches her tight, and mounts the beast. Well, that cat jest tears out across the mountains and canyons with Bill on his back a-spurrin him in the shoulders and quirtin him down the flank with the rattlesnake.

And that's the way Bill rode into the camp of the outfit the old trapper had told him about. When he gits there, he reaches out and cheeks down the cougar and sets him on his haunches and gits down and looks at his saddle.

There was them tough *hombres* settin around the fire playin *monte*. There was a pot of coffee and a bucket of beans a-boilin on the fire, and as Bill hadn't had nothin to eat for several days, he was hungry; so he stuck his hand down in the bucket and grabbed a handful of beans and crammed 'em into his mouth. Then he grabbed the coffee pot and washed 'em down, and wiped his mouth on a prickly pear. Then he turned to the men and said, "Who in the hell is boss around here, anyway?"

"I was," says the big stout feller about seven feet tall, "but you are now, stranger."

Blue Quail Dog

CHARLES F. ARROWOOD

A West Texas rancher had gone to New York on business, and, while he was there, was hospitably entertained by a New York lawyer. Learning that the New Yorker was an enthusiastic wing shot, the rancher insisted that he visit him on his West Texas ranch, and hunt blue quail. He explained that he was away from the ranch a good deal; but if the New Yorker wanted to hunt when he was away the ranch foreman would be able to look after him. The New Yorker accepted. He would go to Texas and hunt blue quail at the first opportunity.

A little later the lawyer was able to get away for a hunt. He wired the rancher, who answered that he had to be away from the ranch, but that he had arranged with his foreman to put the lawyer up, and that the New Yorker was to hunt as much as he pleased.

The lawyer took a train for Texas, only to find when he reached the lonely little town which was the railroad point for the ranch, that there was no one at the station to meet him. He went to the one little hotel which the town boasted and asked where he could find a car and driver to take him out to his friend's ranch. He was told that there was a Negro taxi driver in the town who could furnish a car. The New Yorker sent for the driver, and asked to be taken out to the ranch. The Negro agreed to take him, and when he learned that the lawyer planned to hunt he volunteered his own services as guide and services of his dog.

"Boss," he said, "it sure is a good thing you told me you is going to hunt blue quail. Us will sure find them. I'se got the best blue quail dog in Texas—the best blue quail dog in the world."

The New Yorker declined. He explained that he had brought

151

his own dogs, that they were excellent, and that he planned to work them.

"But Boss," the taxi man protested, "them is bob white dogs. They don't know nothing about blue quail. Now my dog is a blue quail dog. He's the best blue quail dog in Texas—the best blue quail dog in the world."

It was no use; though the driver argued, the New Yorker was firm—he would hunt with his own dogs. He asked the driver to be at the hotel early the next morning.

The next morning, however, when the driver showed up with the car, he had his dog—a huge, sad-eyed, big-footed, lop-eared hound—in the front seat with him. All the way to the ranch they argued, and the Negro prevailed. The New Yorker finally agreed to give the blue quail dog a chance.

At the ranch the baggage was taken into the ranch house, the Eastern dogs were penned, and a gun unpacked. Then the Negro took the New Yorker about three-quarters of a mile from the house, and posted him on top of a little ridge overlooking a valley. "We'll just stand here a little, Boss," he said. "Old Ring is hunting now." Sure enough, the dog was coursing. He ran down the side of the ridge on which they were standing, circled across the valley, coursed along the opposite ridge, recrossed the valley, and down the near ridge again. Soon it was clear that he was running in a circle, which he drew smaller and smaller. After a little the circle was on the valley floor—it was only a hundred yards across—fifty yards across —and suddenly Old Ring dashed in and abruptly sat down on his haunches.

The guide motioned to the hunter. "Come on, Boss," he said, "He's ready now."

He posted the New Yorker about fifteen yards behind the hound, which was looking over its shoulder at his master.

"Ready, Boss," said the guide, and lifted his right hand. When his master lifted his hand, the hound raised his right foot, and out flew a quail. The hunter fired; the quail fell. The Negro lifted his left hand, the dog raised his left front foot; a second quail flew out; there was a second shot and a second quail fell. This went on—up hand, up foot, out flies a quail—until six quail had been shot.

The hunter lowered his gun. "Tell me, boy," he begged, "what is happening? I hear the report, I feel the gun kick, and see them fall; so I know I'm not dreaming, but I can't believe my eyes. What is going on?"

"Boss," said the guide, "you see, it's like this. These blue quails, they don't like to fly. They'll run and hide if they can. I've taught Old Ring to round them up, and run them down a prairie dog hole. After he's got them penned he lets them out when I tells him."

The Musical Snake

ROY SCUDDAY

Jim Bridger, the old frontier scout and trapper, used to spin some really tall tales about Indians, bears, and hair-raising adventures, but I believe he missed this one which an old uncle of mine used to tell me for a bed-time story.

Everyone thought old Uncle Jerry was crazy. He had a little place out on Killdugan Creek—a quarter section of grazing land—and all he had on it was a few milk cows, some chickens, and two old hide-racks that passed as horses. Uncle Jerry had a rickety little cabin on his land, and he lived there by himself—he and his cows, horses, and chickens.

When the big drought hit, many of the little farmers and ranchers went under. They were either forced out by the drought or sold out to the big ranchers, who bought the land for a song. And all the folks really thought Uncle Jerry had lost his mind when he refused to sell out to Jesse Bradford, who had one of the biggest spreads in the section. And Jess offered a fair price, too, considering the circumstances.

But Uncle Jerry just sat on his tumble-down front porch, playing his harmonica, shaking his head and saying, "Nope, I ain't goin' to sell. This drought cain't last forever."

Now, old Uncle Jerry was a harmonica-playing fool. Nobody questioned his ability on the mouth organ. Whenever any of the folks gave a barn dance, Uncle Jerry was always asked to help provide the music. Hot or sweet, fast or slow, he could play any way you wanted.

Well, one hot afternoon in June, just before sundown, Uncle Jerry was sitting out on his porch serenading the chickens with his evening harmonica concert. He had just swung into "The Stars and Stripes Forever" when he happened to glance down at his feet—and there coiled up, with his big wicked head swaying to the music, was

154

the biggest, blackest diamond-back rattlesnake Uncle Jerry ever laid eye on. He swore later that it was seven feet long if it was an inch.

Well, Uncle Jerry nearly swallowed his harmonica, but he had sense enough to keep on blowing. He played every piece he knew, from "Turkey in the Straw" to the "Wedding March," and when he ran out of pieces to play he started over again. But he noticed that the rattler kind of perked up, and swayed a little more when he played the "Stars and Stripes." Pretty soon Jerry ran completely out of breath, so he put down his harmonica, and said, "Go ahead and bite me, you durned varmint. Damned if I'll entertain you any more."

But the snake, just as if he was completely satisfied, shook his rattlers a little as if he were applauding, and crawled off.

After that, every afternoon when Uncle Jerry came out to play, that snake would appear just in time for the concert. The old boy became attached to the snake, and named him J. P. Sousa, after the composer of the snake's favorite tune. He enjoyed all the music, but he seemed to really get a kick out of the "Stars and Stripes." He even learned to "rattle his rattlers" in time to the music, and thereafter many an enthusiastic duet was indulged in.

One afternoon J. P. Sousa failed to show up. Uncle Jerry tried to play, but his heart wasn't in it. It was just like an orchestra trying to play to an empty auditorium. Uncle Jerry hopefully kept an eye open for J. P., but finally gave him up for gone. After that, there were no more evening concerts.

The drought was finally broken with some good midsummer rains, just like Uncle Jerry said it would be. And the people began to wonder if he was quite as crazy as they thought he was. Killdugan Creek was full, and Jerry had one of the richest quarter sections of pasture land in the country.

One day Jess Bradford came out to look over Jerry's land. He offered a price that even Jerry himself hadn't dreamed of. But Jess had some new white-face heifers that he wanted to put out to graze on the good grass of Jerry's land, and he didn't mind paying a big price for it. So Uncle Jerry hitched his two old crowbait horses to his rickety buckboard and drove Jess over the pasture, showing him the best grazing and watering spots.

They were bouncing along, and as they neared a little hill, the sound of martial music came to their ears. It sounded a little familiar to Jerry, so he jerked his team to a halt, and scrambled out of the wagon, and started up the rise, as fast as his arthritic joints would allow.

When he finally reached the top, a strange sight met his eyes. On top of the hill was a big, flat rock. And on this rock were twenty-eight big diamond-back rattlers, grouped in a circle. In the center, his head waving proudly, and his rattles beating out the time just a little louder than the rest, was old J. P. Sousa, leading his musicians in a loud, but positive rendition of "The Stars and Stripes Forever."

A Buffalo Named Woodrow

DILLON ANDERSON

Out northwest of Amarillo there's a place where you can get up on a big rock by the side of the road and look a hell of a long ways. You can look farther and see less right there, I do believe, than you can anywhere else in the whole world—at least anywhere else in the State of Texas.

It was along toward the end of August that I and Claudie passed the place, and nothing would do but we should stop the car so Claudie could climb up on the rock and take a look. When he finally came down, he said, "They's a little old white cloud way off out there to the west, Clint."

I and Claudie had been in the Texas Panhandle all summer, shy the whole time of enough money to get out of there; and since only three clouds had come up the whole time that I could remember, I climbed up onto the rock myself. The morning sun had about burnt the little old cloud off. So I watched a whirlwind start close by, with only a few dry thistles and stickers stirring at first in the yellow dust; I watched it twist and weave and grow until it was a mile or more high and the bottom bouncing along like a bull whip against the rocky ground. Then it blew itself out.

I was about ready to climb down when I saw a sight that you will not believe, and I'll admit that I didn't either, at first. It was a buffalo—a real live shaggy buffalo, standing in a rocky red gully not over a hundred yards away, and he was looking right back at me. He pawed his front feet a couple of times, then started loping toward us with his big fuzzy head lowered and swaying from side to side in front of a big plume of dust he kicked up as he ran.

"Get on back to the road, Claudie," I hollered. "Hurry. There's a buffalo after us."

I climbed down from the rock and passed Claudie before it soaked in on him what I'd said. Then, instead of running for our car

157

so he could drive us off, Claudie pushed his way into our trailer house right after me.

"Just how," I asked him, "are we going to get away from any buffalo with both of us in this trailer house?"

Claudie could see his mistake by this time, and he started out to get in the car, but it was too late. The buffalo was standing just outside the trailer-house door, staring in at us through the isinglass. He was a pretty mangy buffalo, with curved horns grown way long and sort of rusty-looking. When he moved his head his eyes stayed right on us, and I could see the milky white around the edges of his big mud-colored eyeballs. Also, there was a little yellow foam along both sides of his mouth.

"Claudie," I said, "that old bastard don't look so mean to me now. Maybe he's only thirsty. Reckon we'd better give him a drink of water?"

"How?" he asked. "Where's any water?" and I remembered we didn't have a drop in the trailer house.

"Claudie," I said, "tell you what you do. Get that little stewer —you know, the one that don't leak—and drain some water out of the auto radiator for this buffalo."

"I can't get out; I'm skeered of him," he said.

"But no," I explained. "You can get out under the trailer right through this hole in the floor. You can crawl under the car to the place where we drain the radiator, and the buffalo can't get at you. Also, I will keep him busy back here looking at me."

Claudie was covered with dust and grease when he came back, but he had the stewer full of brown water, and I passed it to the buffalo without stepping outside the trailer house myself. And, of course, I was right. He was awful thirsty, and after he'd drunk the water he bawled for more, so I spoke to Claudie and said, "We've got us a pretty valuable animal here, and I believe you'd better get him one more stewer full of that water."

Well, it turned out that we had found a fine friendly buffalo. We gave him some apples and part of a loaf of bread that we ate the rest of ourselves—along with some sardines. Claudie said he wondered how the buffalo would act if we got outside, so I said, "Why don't you try?" He did, and sure enough, the buffalo acted like a pet.

By noon we'd got used to him, and he was used to us. Claudie even got on his back and rode him all around the trailer house. "All we need now," I said, "besides some water for ourselves, is a way to get this buffalo to Amarillo. He's probably worth a lot of money to a zoo or a circus."

Claudie was rolling a cigarette at the time, and before he could answer me or put his sack of Bull Durham back in his pocket, that fool buffalo grabbed it and ate it. That little round yellow tag on the string was the last thing I saw as he stood there chewing up Claudie's smoking tobacco.

"Was it a full sack, Claudie?" I asked him.

"Nearly full," he said, and then the buffalo snorted, bellowed, pawed up a lot of dust from the ground, and started bucking. He made for us with his head lowered, and we barely got indoors in time. He ran and butted the trailer house so hard I knew something had to give, and it was tin that gave, not that buffalo's horns. Then he settled down and so did the dust, and pretty soon he was his same old gentle self again. I and Claudie both got out and rode him some more just to prove it.

I declare, I don't know how we'd have fared if the two sheriffs hadn't come along about the middle of the afternoon. "Sheriff's Department, Potter County," it said around a big white star on the side of their car.

"Here's your buffalo, Chuck," the fellow that got out of the car said. Chuck got out too, and they came over to the trailer house, both wearing pearl-handled pistols and silver sheriffs' badges.

"What are you doing with this buffalo?" they both seemed to be asking all at once.

"We found him here," I said, "and we've been taking good care of him, too."

"Well, he belong to Quagmyer's Dog and Pony Shows," one of the sheriffs said—the biggest one of the two. "He got away after the show last night. We're going to take him back and collect the reward."

"How?" I asked, and Chuck, the little sheriff, looked at the other one without saying anything.

"Maybe you fellows can watch him until we can send a truck for him," the big sheriff said.

"And maybe you can give us about five hundred dollars of the reward," I said. "If we don't keep him, he's liable to go out there," and I pointed west where there was enough country for a buffalo to go and hide in forever.

"The reward ain't but twenty-five dollars," the big sheriff stated.

We settled for ten dollars out of the reward if we still had the buffalo when they came back for him, and we had him all right. The sheriffs came along about sundown in a truck and brought along some water I'd told them we needed for our radiator.

The next morning, with the ten dollars in my pocket, I and Claudie went all over Amarillo looking for Quagmyer's Dog and Pony Show, since during the night I'd turned up with such a fine idea about the buffalo and Claudie that it fairly dazzled me. But I found the show was not of the size to do as big a town as Amarillo. It played in small towns only, and I learned at the newspaper office that it would go on that night at Canyon, Texas.

Claudie drove us the seventeen miles down to Canyon, and I kept him quiet all the way so I could think my whole idea out. We got there before noon, and the first thing I did was to study the poster about the show pasted up on the side of a feed store. I wanted to see what the buffalo did in the show. The poster had a lot about Celeste Booker, the daring lady bareback rider, and it showed her picture in black tights and red hair; it had some colored pictures of trained lions and tigers sitting up on stools while a guy in bright green clothes cracked a whip at them, and clowns; but I liked to have never found anything about the buffalo. Way down in one corner where they'd run low on glue and the edge of the picture was flapping in the wind, it mentioned several wild animals, and along with Gila monsters, anteaters, two elks, and a boa constrictor, it sort of admitted they had a buffalo, too. No picture of him at all.

"What a shame! What a waste of talent!" I told Claudie.

"Howzat?" Claudie asked, but I didn't go into it any further since I hadn't yet told him anything about my idea. I only set about to find the head man in the show.

"Mr. Quagmyer," I went up to the man and said where they had pointed him out to me in a little green diner across the street from the show tent. It was a diner made out of an old streetcar, with the wheels off, and this guy was eating fried chicken at a table about where the motorman would have used to sit.

"Colonel Quagmyer, please," he answered without looking up. "Colonel A. Frisbie Quagmyer."

"Hightower is the name," I said, and I found I could hardly keep my eyes on the Colonel because the lady that was eating there at the table with him looked so familiar and pretty at the same time. I noticed, too, that she was eating with nice dainty manners and daubing around her mouth with the blue calico napkin every time she took a bite.

"Where have I seen that pretty face before?" I was wondering when the Colonel said—stern like—"I'll see you outside later. Right now I'm eating lunch with my little niece here."

"Your niece? Pleased to meet you, ma'am," I said, taking off my hat, but she didn't look up also.

"Outside!" The Colonel seemed almost peevish.

"Yes, sir," I said, catching one more glance at the Colonel's niece that he was eating chicken with.

Well, this niece came out of the diner first, and in the bright sunlight her hair was the color of corn silk, but fine enough to make corn silk look like old rusty bailing wire.

"Please, ma'am," I said, tipping my hat, "is the Colonel about through eating? We wish to talk some business with him—I and my associate. Hightower is the name, and—"

"Tell it to him," she said, and walked across the street to the show tent. I noticed her plum-purple dress was very tight in the waist.

"A man might like it at the time," I told Claudie, "but I could never really care for a lady that would be too friendly right at first." Then I saw the big billboard, and it all came to me where I'd seen that pretty face before. She was Celeste Booker, the lady bareback rider, but the picture didn't begin to do her justice.

"All right, men, what is it?" the Colonel was saying. He'd come out of the diner when we weren't looking, and I saw that he was a lot taller than he'd seemed sitting at the table. He was picking his teeth with a gold toothpick and holding his broad-brimmed straw hat in his hand. When he put it on, a lot of his hair, the color of a Palomino's mane, still showed behind like senators' hair.

"It's about the buffalo," I began. "We're the ones that found him."

The Colonel said, "But, dammit, I've already paid the reward." Then he looked across the street toward the show tent. He had little eyes, and the skin under them was pink and puffy like persimmons after a hard freeze.

"What," I asked him, "does the buffalo do in the show?"

"Old Woodrow?" he asked. "What the hell can any buffalo do besides be?"

"Be what?"

"A buffalo. He's almost extinct. That's the reason old Woodrow is with us."

"But Woodrow may not be so near to extinct as you'd think," I said. "He can act."

By this time some more people from the diner were hanging around, and the Colonel sized them up before he said out loud, "Well, I've played to overflow crowds in Madison Square Garden; I've given command performances before the crowned heads of Europe; I've been impresario to talent in the sparkling sawdust of the greatest shows on the globe; yet I have to be told in Canyon, Texas, that I have overlooked latent virtuosity in a tame buffalo. I bid you good day, gentlemen." And while everybody around laughed, the Colonel bowed and walked across the street to the show tent.

Trouble was, the Colonel didn't know me; a haughty spirit like that has always been just my dish. I walked right across the street with him, and at the main entrance to the tent I spoke. "Colonel, in Woodrow you have a feature attraction and don't know it. You have a bucking buffalo."

The Colonel threw back his head and laughed. "Why, Woodrow is gentle as a pussycat," he said. "The children all ride him. You're taking a lot of my time."

"Would you let us show you?"

"Now?" he said.

"Now," I told him. He was tough, but he saw he'd met his match. He agreed to let us put on our act inside the tent since the show didn't come off until that night, and by the time word went around among the show folks we had a pretty good crowd. Celeste, the Colonel's niece, came too, at the last minute, and one of the show flunkies marched old Woodrow out into the ring. He seemed to recognize me and Claudie; he mooed a little and came over to us, shaking his shaggy head.

"Who's going to ride this ferocious bucking buffalo?" Colonel Quagmyer asked, laughing, and all the show people laughed. In fact, about everything the Colonel would say seemed funny to them.

"My associate, Claudie," I answered; "as long, that is, as he can stay on," and they all laughed again. "But, first," I went on, "we need a few minutes alone with Woodrow."

The buffalo followed us out, and we took him into a little sideshow tent. I looked everywhere to see that nobody was around, and then I whispered, "All right, Claudie, slip him another sack of Bull Durham."

"But I ain't gunna ride him after he's et it," Claudie argued.

"Oh, yes, you are; we're in the money, Claudie. This is no time to be unreasonable."

Claudie didn't get the point until the show people started yelling for us to come out, but after I'd given him the ten dollars from the reward he agreed. He gave Woodrow the sack of tobacco, and damned if he didn't seem to like it even more than he had the day before. Then, with Claudie on him, I led Woodrow into the big tent.

"Ladieeees and gennntlemen," Colonel Quagmyer announced, "Woodrow, the bucking buffalo." He was laughing fit to kill, and all the show people laughed and laughed. Then it happened.

Woodrow snorted a couple of times and made for Colonel Quagmyer. The Colonel got behind a tent pole just in the nick; then Woodrow started to buck, and for a lot longer than you'd think, Claudie stayed on him. But about the fourth or fifth buck was a lollapalouza, and it sent Claudie sailing off through the air like a big old water bird of some kind. He landed in the steam calliope and then tumbled off limp onto the ground. But he got up and dusted himself off, and while he still looked a mite dazed and ruffled, he was coming around fast. And there stood Woodrow, licking the seat of Claudie's pants as friendly as ever again.

"Now, Colonel, I hope you see what I mean," I told him, loud enough for Celeste to hear. By this time all the show folks were cheering, and I figured like this: If people in the show itself take on like this over our act—people that are used to the best in entertainment and have been all their lives—what would the public do?

The Colonel tried to run down the act some, but when I said, "Okay, then; let's just drop the idea," he followed me to the tent door.

"How did you make Woodrow buck?" was the way he put it.

"Colonel Quagmyer," I said as all the show people stood around, and Celeste too, with her eyes very bright, "Woodrow comes from a long line of fierce and proud ancestors. His ancestors were here, kicking up dust, bucking and enjoying themselves long before our ancestors got up the *Mayflower* trip. All the time you've kept Woodrow in the cellar, using him for no act except to be, he's been building up the ginger that was born right in him from his ancestors. I and Claudie have simply brought it out. That's all."

"But how . . ."

"You couldn't be expecting to learn that and then use some

other bronco buster, could you, Colonel?" I cut in. Oh, I had him right where the wool was short.

"Certainly not," he said, acting like a Colonel with his feelings hurt.

"Another thing, Colonel," I pointed out. "Just imagine the billing 'WOODROW AND CLAUDIE, THE ONLY SHOW IN THE WORLD FEATURING A WILD BUCKING BUFFALO.' The act will put you in big towns like Amarillo and Lubbock. You're through with skirting the edges. You are in the big time."

You can see how, standing on such firm ground as this, I and Claudie made our deal to get on the Quagmyer pay roll and for our board, too.

Sure enough, our feature got us into bigger towns right away. At Lubbock the following week Colonel Quagmyer threw away all the old billboard signs and had some new ones made. Woodrow took some of the space away from Celeste, and after she saw the new billing she would not even look at Woodrow, she was so furious. It seemed to turn her against me and Claudie, too. At first, that is.

With being featured and all, Claudie soon let it go to his head. He wanted to wear a green uniform in his act, one with brass buttons and gold braid like the lion tamer's, so only to humor him, I made Quagmyer buy him one. Also Claudie wore a big ten-gallon hat in the act with a little blue feather in it, and pretty soon he was putting on all sorts of airs. When Woodrow would throw him, he'd lie there on the ground where he'd hit; he'd wiggle and squirm like a worm in hot ashes, all so as to scare the crowd; then he'd get up and bow, grinning like a jackass eating briers to make the people cheer more. It was almost disgusting, but I did notice that he began to look better and happier than I'd ever seen him before. So did Woodrow. I told Claudie the day we played Brownwood, "We must be about the finest influence that ever came into Woodrow's life. They're feeding him better, his mange is improving, and he's getting some exercise these days. Just to be is no life even for a buffalo. It's right next to being plumb extinct."

"Let's us give Woodrow a better brand of tobacco," Claudie urged. "He must be tired of that Bull Durham."

"The best," I told him, "is none too good for Woodrow." So the next day we took him out behind the tent and offered him his choice of several other kinds of tobacco. But he wouldn't touch a one of them. He had only the Bull Durham habit.

Celeste came around the corner of the tent about this time, and I asked Claudie to kindly take Woodrow away so I could talk to her some. This was something I was doing more and more of since my part in Woodrow's act left me with plenty of leisure time every day. I was finding out by this time that she was about the finest company in the whole show, with a nice personality and all, as well as the prettiest, whitest set of teeth I'd ever seen growing out of gums; and Celeste had been showing in several ways that she could care for me too. That was the day she said why didn't I come by her dressing room some night and talk to her after her act, and that was the night I went. Her act was over, and it wasn't near time for Woodrow to go on, since he was always last so nobody would leave and stop buying popcorn and stuff until the very end. And that was the night Celeste really lifted the scales from my eyes about Quagmyer. "Clint," she said, as she rolled a cigarette, "I'm afraid Colonel Quagmyer doesn't like you very much."

"Why?" I asked.

"He's jealous of you."

"How can that be, Celeste? He's your uncle."

"Well, confidentially, he ain't any uncle of mine. We only claim kin so the show people won't talk."

This really flabbergasted me. Just why Celeste would be telling me this I couldn't tell. I said, "Celeste, I haven't figured Quagmyer was all he was cracking himself up to be for some time now."

"He ain't," she admitted; then she started speaking in a very confidential way and said, "Colonel Quagmyer is sort of new to the show. He's been the owner for less than a year."

"How'd he get aholt of the show, anyway?" I asked.

"Well, he went to see the show last spring when it was playing in Tuscaloosa, Alabama. He was running a pool hall there at the time. The show had an elephant then—a little old flea-bitten elephant, a she. Quagmyer managed some way to get stepped on by the elephant—she stepped on his foot, I believe—and he fell down with a sprained back. So he sued 'em for fifty thousand dollars and tied up the whole kit and caboodle with liens and things. Quagmyer stayed sort of paralyzed until the case was tried and the jury in Tuscaloosa gave him forty thousand dollars. The whole show wasn't worth that much, so Quagmyer took it over."

"Are you pretty sweet on Quagmyer, Celeste?" I had to know by then, with her showing this way how much she cared for me and all.

"I haven't exactly quit him—yet. . . ." I remember she was holding my hand at the time she said this; then she went on, "Now, Clint, there's something I want you to tell me."

"Oh no, Celeste; you're a fine girl, and I'm getting fonder of you every way, but I'm not about to tell you that." I stood up and let her hand go.

"What?"

"How we make Woodrow buck. That's what you wanted to know, wasn't it, Celeste?"

"Oh heavens, no," she laughed. "I know how you make Woodrow buck." She was teasing me; I could tell from the look out of her pretty blue eyes. I know women. Then Celeste got very serious and said. "I only wanted to know that you really trusted me."

"It isn't that I don't trust you, Celeste. I do, but I can't tell you that," and she looked so hurt I thought she'd cry. If you want to know the truth right here, some tears did come into her eyes.

"Don't worry, Clint," she said, and her lips were pouty. "I would never tell Quagmyer."

The only thing I wanted to do right then was to kiss Celeste to make her feel better, but she pushed me away and said, "No, Clint, you don't trust me."

By the time we got to Waco, Colonel Quagmyer was beginning to show that he liked me less and less, but he was getting nicer to Claudie all the time; so I had to speak to Claudie about it, and he admitted that the Colonel had offered him his pay and mine too if he'd only tell how we made Woodrow buck.

"I have been tempted, too, Claudie," I said, "but you know what the Bible says about temptation. A man is not supposed to yield to it; specially if it might mean his job."

"But I'm the one this here buffalo bucks off every night. My joints is getting loose."

"Don't you see it's a trick, Claudie? Once the Colonel learned our trade secret, he'd fire you, too, and use Hung How, that little old Chinese cook. Hung How has been eying your job for weeks. He wants to wear that green suit."

"He'll never get it." Claudie looked his stubborn best when he said that, and I knew this fire was put out for a while.

It wasn't long after this that the telegram came from Houston asking us to go to the rodeo there and take Woodrow's act. After all, it was bound to happen; anything in Texas that is as good as Woodrow—and there is nothing else like it in the whole dadburned world

—is bound to wind up in Houston. It's the way the state is set up.

The Colonel wired back that he'd go if they'd take Celeste's bareback act too, and they agreed. Matter of fact, they'd have taken a temperance lecture if they'd had to, they were so anxious to get Woodrow.

I explained to Colonel Quagmyer that I and Claudie wanted just exactly one half of all he got paid in Houston, and he finally had to take us up on this, since I stood pat. But when he agreed, he was reddish-purple in the face, like a west-of-Amarillo sunset during a dust storm.

We wound up the regular circuit in El Paso a week before we were due in Houston, and by this time we had Woodrow famous. Even a little spell of indigestion he had in Laredo made the front page in the San Antonio paper. All this made Claudie more temperamental by the day—he got to where he wore his green suit all the time. Myself, I had to worry more and more about our trade secret, and not even telling Celeste, but it was breaking my heart not to, and hers also because I didn't trust her enough to tell her.

From El Paso we all went to Houston by train, except that I rode ahead with Celeste and Quagmyer on the fast train that had sleepers and diners and everything, while Claudie rode on a much slower train that brought Woodrow also. "Be sure nothing happens to Woodrow on the trip," I told Claudie just before we left El Paso.

All the way to Houston, Celeste teased me—the way people don't do, I figured, if they don't really like you—and right before Colonel Quagmyer too. She teased me in the club car, in the diner, and other places, too, on the train. The Colonel would listen to all of this he could stand; I mean until his face would twitch all over and the blue veins in his temples would stand out and quiver; then he'd get up and walk in the train aisles to cool himself off. What Celeste was teasing me about was still claiming she knew how we made Woodrow buck. She kept saying she'd spied on me and Claudie.

When we got to Houston, we found we were all over town—on posters, that is. The big billing was our act, of course, with pictures of Woodrow all blown up, his eyes blazing and blue smoke coming out of both nostrils.

While we waited for Woodrow and Claudie to get there, I found I was seeing less and less of the Colonel and more and more of Celeste. I found, too, that this was slap-dab exactly the way I wanted it. And long before Woodrow and Claudie came, I knew I had fallen for Celeste about as hard as a man has any business falling for anybody, except for one thing: why did she keep pestering me to tell her how we made Woodrow buck?

"You can prove to me that you love me," she said one day out at Hermann Park Zoo. "Just tell me about Woodrow." Her arm was around my waist as we walked along looking at the animals.

I watched a slippery old hippopotamus climb up out of his wallowing place, and while the red and yellow parrots squawked outside in the sun, I sat there and thought and thought—like about Samson that was so taken, and then taken in, by the Gaza woman, Delilah; also about Joseph that, according to the Bible, walked right off, leaving Potiphar's wife talking to herself there by the couch—and I said, "Celeste, I do love you all right, but Houston is a hell of a long ways from that trailer house in El Paso for a man to be sharing a trade secret with anybody."

Well, with all the rest we did in Houston, this was about where we left things until Woodrow's and Claudie's train finally got there. And by the time it did, the Houston people had decided to change the place where we were to go on. The Coliseum wouldn't hold our crowd, so they had it out at the big First National Bank Stadium near Rice Institute. And what a crowd! They were still gathering when Celeste got into her black tights and went on first with her bareback riding act. Matter of fact, it was a sort of a preliminary they made out of Celeste, and I didn't like it a dern bit.

I went around to Celeste's dressing room after her act to cheer her up for being done wrong by in the program. We had nearly an hour to wait while some other small-time calf roping and steer bulldogging acts were run off. Naturally, Woodrow wasn't to go on until last. I sat there by Celeste watching her comb out her pretty red hair and talking to her until all of a sudden it was later than I thought. What really brought the time up was that Claudie stuck his ugly face inside Celeste's dressing room.

He was all dressed up in his green suit with braid and brass buttons, but he had the same baffled look on his face as the guy I saw in a fine picture once, the guy with a hoe in his hand—except of course Claudie didn't have any hoe in his hand. Claudie's mouth was working, but he wasn't saying anything, he was so wrought up.

"Take it easy, Claudie," I said. "What's the trouble?"

"I haven't got it," he managed to say. "Have you?"

"You mean—" I said, and I knew what he meant. He'd forgotten Woodrow's tobacco.

"Hell, no!" I told him. "You're the one that's supposed to have it."

"But I forgot."

"What's the trouble, fellows?" Celeste asked.

"Oh, nothing; nothing at all," I told her. Then I turned back to Claudie. "Where's the closest store?" I found I was yelling at him.

"I've already asked about that," Claudie said. "The stores are a mile or more away, and they're all closed up this time of night."

"How long before we go on?" I asked him, and Colonel Quagmyer answered me as he walked into Celeste's dressing room. "Five minutes," he said, "but don't hurry. It may be six or seven. Woodrow is waiting for you in the little tent out there."

Outside there was the hum and the buzz of all that big crowd ready for our act, and the whole thing seemed to be pressing down on my insides like a sack of wet oats. I noticed that Claudie's color was awful bad and getting worse by the minute. The green suit only brought it out more.

"What's the matter, Claudie?" Quagmyer asked. "Stage fright?" But Claudie didn't have any answer. He was all froze up, and so was I.

Things got so quiet then that when Celeste spoke up I felt myself flinch. What she said was "I feel like a smoke."

Quagmyer offered her a ready-roll, but she said, "No, I'll just make my own, thanks."

She opened her purse, but what she took out wasn't the tin can of Prince Albert, the kind Celeste always rolled hers with; it was a brand-new sack of Bull Durham. When Claudie saw what I saw, his mouth flew open and his front teeth showed more than ever. Claudie's teeth never were very close together, and this time he looked like a man fixing to eat a pumpkin through a picket fence.

Celeste rolled, then fired up, her new cigarette and laid the sack there on the dressing table so that the little tag at the end of the string was hanging down over the edge. When she got up, she left the Bull Durham sack right where it was. She flashed a sweet cozy wink at me; then took Quagmyer by the arm. "Come on, Uncle Frisbie," she said, "let's go get ourselves settled in our seats so we can see the best part of this show."

And as they walked out I thought no knights in tin suits or heroes in Hollywood ever loved their women any more than I loved Celeste.

Billingsley's Bird Dog

Dillon Anderson

I well remember the year Billingsley acquired Old Ruff, his pedigreed pointer with lemon spots—the worthy son, as Billingsley often described him, of a champion bitch. The proprietorship of any bird dog with less than superior attainments was simply foreign to Billingsley's nature. I refer, of course, to Richard K. Billingsley, Esquire, that peerless poker player. Hart, Fielding, and I, as long-time poker and hunting companions of Billingsley's, had been invited to accompany him and Old Ruff on the first hunt of the season, which was to be held on a ranch in Atascosa County.

I shall never forget the conversation around the log fire the night before the opening; how it was dominated by Billingsley; and how his sole topic was Old Ruff, then a four-year-old with the prime of his life still ahead of him. We heard every detail of how he had been "finished off" in the early autumn by an expensive trainer in Illinois. Billingsley—who, mind you, had bought the dog in the spring and thus had never hunted over him—kept us up until a late hour talking about Old Ruff and his extraordinary abilities in the presence of the birds. His concluding remark, uttered as the fire burned out and we made ready to retire, was: "I think I will enter Old Ruff in the National Field Trials next year in Georgia. You'll see why tomorrow!"

Old Ruff spent the night straining at his leash, which Billingsley had affixed to a cedar stake driven in the rear of the camp house. A full moon was out, and Old Ruff howled and whined and barked all night long. I remember the occasion in starkest detail, for I rolled and tossed through the dark hours, unable to catch more than an intermittent doze. I could tell that Hart and Fielding had a bad time of it too. Not so, Billingsley. After a remark or two about how *really ready* Old Ruff was for tomorrow's hunt, he begin to snore, and this continued throughout the night.

Along about dawn things quieted down ominously outside, and Billingsley arose to see whatever might have happened to silence his pointer. From what he said to himself as he strode around outside, we gathered the dog had simply pulled up the stake and dragged it off with him. So, while we dressed, Billingsley stood on the rear stoop in his nightshirt calling Old Ruff, who from time to time could be heard barking in the distance. We were dressed and halfway through with the coffee before Billingsley came back into the camp house. Though nobody had the heart to comment on what was going on outside, we could plainly observe Old Ruff through the screen door, still dragging the leash and stake and hard at work consuming the remaining portions of the Dominecker rooster he had brought back with him.

The first day

Billingsley appeared to be refreshed from his sound night's sleep, and I noticed that Old Ruff showed no signs of weariness; after his meal he panted earnestly and seemed to be filled with that early-morning exuberance known to all lovers of the pointer breed. And he was truly a hale and handsome pointer with a big frame, a massive head, eager eyes, a long red dripping tongue, and a vigorous wag in his tail which seemed to sway his entire hindquarters.

After breakfast we were met outside by Wilbur, Billingsley's local friend who had agreed to take us through the fields and indicate the areas where the big coveys had been seen earlier in the fall. Wilbur, a sallow, unshaved young citizen with protruding teeth, brought along a puny, liver-colored pointer of his own—an unwelcome development so far as Old Ruff was concerned; Ruff growled, showed his teeth, and revealed in the bristling hair on the back of his neck a readiness to fight the local dog on the spot. In fact, only Billingsley's fast move in seizing Old Ruff's leash saved us the unseemly spectacle of a most one-sided contest.

Old Ruff's debut

Immediately he was unleashed, Old Ruff bounded off, barking, in the direction of a baygall and very shortly disappeared into it. Meantime Wilbur's Joe worked slowly down a very promising fence row that led away from the camp house, and within ten minutes he was obviously trailing closely on game. The covey was not far ahead, as later events disclosed, for Old Ruff reappeared just in time to bark up fifteen or twenty birds not a hundred feet ahead of Joe.

"Takes him a little while to settle down," Billingsley said airily, speaking of Ruff; then to Ruff he said, "Look close, boy. Steady." But the animal was already well out of earshot.

Old hunters will understand, I am sure, why I must abandon here any attempt to recount the actual sequence of events that opening day; why it is painful enough to set out the results even in summary form. The unvarnished truth is that though we saw no fewer than a dozen fine coveys of quail during that day's hunt, we never got one shot at a covey rise, and the only single shots we got were birds we flushed ourselves. Billingsley ascribed our bleak experience to our poor shooting, Joe's errors, faulty shells, inadequate cover for the birds, and even to a gentle drizzle that fell on us throughout the day; but he saw no fault whatever in Old Ruff's performance.

Several times Wilbur's Joe came down on quail and held the point with steady posture, but invariably Old Ruff would beat the hunters to the spot, rush headlong into the covey, and flush the birds while they were still far out of our range. And each time Billingsley's explanation was different. Once when Ruff went barging in ahead of Wilbur's Joe, Billingsley explained that the birds must have been running and were thus about to avert the slower dog's point. Then, when the covey rose all around Old Ruff about a hundred yards away, Billingsley asserted fiercely that they were only field larks—no lark could fool Old Ruff; not a dog with a nose like that!

Billingsley never had any explanation whatever—and apparently did not consider one necessary—for another vicious habit Old Ruff disclosed during the day; that of barking and chasing after the flying quail until they sailed great distances away, quite too far to be watched down for single hunting.

About noon we had wandered far from the camp house, and when we had come upon a most likely-looking meadow filled with ample Johnson grass cover, Wilbur's Joe froze in his tracks not fifty yards ahead of me. I called to the others, but Billingsley at the same moment summoned us all in the opposite direction. Old Ruff, he announced, had not been seen in some five or ten minutes and must therefore be down somewhere on game. Wilbur—who actually rents the ranch from Billingsley, I must say—whistled his Joe to come along, but that splendid, lean, and faithful hound would not move from his point. Meanwhile Billingsley continued to yell and bellow that we back up Old Ruff, that we honor his point. "You can ruin a dog," he proclaimed, "by leaving him alone on birds." So, finally, Wilbur whistled his Joe in, and the latter gave up, reluctantly, to follow us.

When we finally found Old Ruff he was on the far side of an adjoining farm marked POSTED. NO HUNTING. He was not on quail; he was in hot and raucous pursuit of the neighbor's flock of guineas. Nor could he be called off until the guineas found sanctuary on top of a strawrick.

"Glad to see him get all of this kind of foolishness out of his system while he's a young dog," Billingsley remarked as we returned. But before we could get back to the place where Wilbur's Joe had pointed the covey, Old Ruff chased a jack rabbit through the area, flushed about twenty-five fine quail, and ran off down a ravine after them, barking and jumping with insouciant glee.

Afternoon

At noon we ate our sandwiches and apples under a big live oak tree, while Old Ruff skirmished at crawfish holes on the bank of a nearby stream. He drenched himself thoroughly in a little blue hole there before coming back and shaking cold water over us all. Then, as we finished eating, Old Ruff lapped up all the crumbs, scraps, and apple cores in sight, and was actually eying Wilbur's Joe hungrily, I thought, when Billingsley spoke to him with the only note of even implied criticism I ever heard him use in regard to his dog.

"Ruff," he said, "I hope you settle down this afternoon. A dog with as fine a nose as yours has got to be steady. Steady—steady, boy."

It must have been midafternoon, and our bag of birds was still pitifully light, when we heard Old Ruff barking in a nearby field. Shortly thereafter we saw him come running our way with a big covey of quail in full flight ahead of him. We were in tall cornstalks, and the birds flew very close by us, affording several excellent but very fast shots. We knocked down four birds, of which we got three, and Ruff ate the fourth one whole.

I noticed a smug look on Billingsley's face as he narrowly beat his dog to the bird he'd shot; and as we walked away he said, "Well, we can thank Old Ruff for another covey. I wonder where Wilbur's Joe was on *that* one." He was smiling broadly.

Old Ruff's endowments

These events in Atascosa County took place seven years ago

last fall, and Old Ruff is now nearly twelve years old and is in semi-retirement. (Billingsley still takes him along on some hunts "for his judgment, though his nose is not what it used to be.") Since a bird dog's career is built upon the acuity of his sensory gifts, let me describe Ruff's several endowments.

Old Ruff is blessed with good teeth, an amply salivated maw, and a steady appetite. In the course of one day's hunting I have seen him devour two rabbits, a setting hen and her eggs, three cans of dog food, a field rat, the edible portion of a young armadillo, and uncounted quail. That particular day was, to be perfectly fair, perhaps the high point of his career. Likewise, I must add, lest I do Old Ruff an injustice, that in the late afternoon he threw up most of the armadillo.

Old Ruff's hearing

Any early evening, Old Ruff can hear the Billingsley back screen door slam at whatever distance he may have strayed from home, for this usually means that the master has returned from the office and is opening several cans of dog food. On the other hand, I will affirm that I never once observed Ruff heed, obey, or even pay the slightest attention to Billingsley's words in the field, or to anyone else who tried to hunt over him. As a matter of fact, whenever anyone else tried to speak to the dog, Billingsley would start talking to himself. "Just how Old Ruff knows which one of us to obey is more than I can see," he was always fond of saying on such occasions.

"Hold, Ruff; steady, boy; easy now, *easy*," or "Look close, Ruff; look now; dead; dead *bird*," I've heard Billingsley bellow after winging a quail, with Ruff all the while romping through the fields in his own happy, carefree pursuit of his next morsel of food. Then, never a man without a command appropriate to the action, Billingsley would yell at the top of his voice, "Hie away, Ruff; hie away, boy." This was usually followed by a prideful comment upon what a rangy dog Ruff was. "You can have your slower dogs—dogs for single shots, dead birds, and so on," he would aver. "You can have your setters to pick out a single here and there. But Old Ruff is already out there in the next county looking for another covey."

Old Ruff can see

A remarkable demonstration of Old Ruff's farsightedness took place in the fourth year we tried to hunt over him, and at a stage which Billingsley was describing as the height of his career. We hunted that winter in the cutover timberlands of a South Louisiana parish where the abundant quail hadn't been shot at for some time.

Our host, Pierre LeBlanc of the black mustache and booming voice, furnished a fine coal-black setter named Thibodeaux, whose work throughout the day was steady, consistent, and effective. Both Billingsley and Old Ruff appeared in the early stages to resent Thibodeaux's quiet ease and poise in the presence of birds, and Old Ruff in particular barked a great deal as he circled around the spots where Thibodeaux was at work. But as the day wore on, Billingsley seemed to accept the setter as a fair dog—for his breed, that was— and spoke quite a bit about the advantages flowing to a dog who hunted in the type of country he knew and was *used to*. "Wait," he said, "until Old Ruff gets acclimated here—gets the feel of things, I mean, in a strange place."

It was late afternoon before we approached our day's limit. We were, nevertheless, within one good covey shot of the mark and hopeful, since the last we'd seen of Thibodeaux, the black setter, he was working far off to our right near a likely-looking oak mott.

Pierre and I moved, almost instinctively, in that direction, while Billingsley, a little weary by now, trudged along behind. Then, to my utter amazement, we saw Old Ruff in the pointer's posture and stance which have brought that magic spine-tingling thrill to bird hunters through the centuries. Billingsley saw him about the same time and cried, "Old Ruff's on game," in a new vibrant voice. Confidence, pride, and stern discipline were implicit in his tones. His admonitions then to his dog were wonderful to hear, not to mention his asides to Pierre and myself. "Steady, Ruff; hold it, boy," he said; then to us, "What a point! Gad, that's a superb dog. . . . Hold back, men; easy! Can't you see he's right on the birds?"

At this state Billingsley, whose eyesight is quite erratic, say beyond the end of his gun barrel, went into an absolute transport of rapture.

"Look!" he cried. "Right ahead there. It's Thibodeaux, down on birds. He's frozen, and Old Ruff is *backing him up;* he's honoring his point! There's a *dog* for you."

This was the first time Old Ruff had ever given Billingsley leave to claim he'd honored another dog's point, and I thought Billingsley's inordinate rash of pride was understandable; at least until I recognized the object which Billingsley had concluded was Thibodeaux at point. That which had deceived both Billingsley and his dog was not the fine setter at all, for indeed he was nowhere about. It was a pine stump, burned black—the same color as Thibodeaux and only about twice as big.

And feel

Whether Ruff's remote threshold in this department is due to plain numbness or to a long-cultivated stoic strain in the breed is a point of sharp difference between myself and his master. But Ruff's insensitivity was extraordinary, I must say. There was, for example, the time in Kenedy County when we came upon Old Ruff in an attitude which Billingsley described as an absolutely classic point. He even took time out, while I held his gun, to photograph the point (a picture which, incidentally, came out so well that Billingsley used it that year as his Christmas card).

Then, as we edged forward to flush the birds, Billingsley broke the silence of the prairie with rapturous praise. "By God," he exclaimed, "Old Ruff might as well be set in concrete."

As a matter of fact he was not far wrong. Ruff was caught and held fast in a coon trap.

"Bound to have been painful—not a howl—not a whine—never even whimpered," Billingsley said as we extricated the still uncomplaining Ruff.

And smell

As anyone will tell you, a bird dog must have a good nose. Ruff has grown old, as I have said, and one day he will be gone; nevertheless, I shall put it down as I see it, and Billingsley can make the most of it—or the least. *In my opinion Old Ruff has not yet pointed his quail number one.* I contend that pure coincidence, propinquity to birds and other dogs, all in good quail country, more than explain every episode linking Ruff with quail—except, of course, as to cripples and dead birds which he ate.

This is a harsh conclusion, but it has not been reached lightly. On the other hand, I shall suggest a possible qualification, if only out of an exalted sense of fair play and in deference to Billingsley's steadfast belief that Old Ruff was for years without a peer in the field; and, indeed, there are a paltry few equivocal episodes where I could possibly have been wrong and Billingsley might have been right.

For example, let us take the hunt three years ago on the Dickson Ranch in Lavaca County, where the grass burrs are perhaps the worst and the quail the thickest of anywhere in the South.

It was about midmorning on a bright day, and though we'd seen many quail, we'd bagged only a meager few. Old Ruff's eager ebullience and prodigious pursuit of rabbits, stinkbirds, and other irrelevant game seemed to have had a contagious and deleterious effect on the local dogs furnished by our host, so that they had all run around wildly for the first hour or two.

Then Billingsley and I suddenly came upon Old Ruff standing still in a pasture of good bluestem cover. I had to admit that Old Ruff had assumed an attitude of a bird dog on birds. As we moved up, I could tell that Old Ruff was no more pointing birds than he was playing a French horn. It is true his hindquarters were immobile, and his right forepaw was raised from the ground, but from my particular angle of view I was able to see that he was inert simply because he was in the act of extracting with his teeth a grass burr caught between his toes. So I naturally approached the animal in desultory fashion—whistling, as a matter of fact—all to the palpable disgust of Billingsley.

I watched Old Ruff gnaw away at the burr as we came closer upon him; then suddenly the largest covey I had seen all season arose immediately in front of the startled dog. Billingsley killed one quail and winged another, though I must confess it all took place so unexpectedly that I was unable to get my gun up for a shot before the birds were out of range. Billingsley beat Ruff to the cripple and bagged it nicely.

For the balance of the day—in fact, for the balance of the season—Billingsley was absolutely unbearable. The talk he put out about the beauty of the point and the size of the covey grew all out of proportion to the facts. Nor did he omit the detail of my failure even to get a shot on the covey rise.

Any fair account of Old Ruff's career must include an event the season before last when Old Ruff retrieved a bird late one afternoon. It was toward the end of a day of failure after failure, and we had scratched out only a handful which we had flushed ourselves. We were approaching a little baygall, where I thought I'd seen a wounded bird fall, when Old Ruff came out of it with a quail in his mouth. This naturally perplexed me, for I had never seen Ruff fail to eat any quail within his hungry reach.

"That's another thing about Old Ruff," Billingsley said proudly. "You can always count on him to bring in a lost bird."

This remark was made just before Ruff came close enough for me to get the scent of the dead quail, which soon turned out to be awful. The poor creature had obviously been dead for several days, and was actually coming apart at the seams—a fact which Billingsley and I both pretended, each for his own special sporting reason, not to notice.

No account of Old Ruff's nose would be complete without a summary of that day rather early in his career when we sought to hunt over him in some Fort Bend County rice fields. Quail were prolific in that area, and it was still early in the morning (Ruff had flushed no more than three or four fine coveys out of our range) when our hero met and made a new friend. She was a fine specimen of Llewellyn setter—a beautiful spotted bitch whose owner had been less careful about her on the particular day than he might have. Old Ruff's nostrils flared and vibrated in the presence of this charming setter in ways that were thrilling to behold, particularly to one who is a lover of bird dogs. It soon became obvious that the setter was in a most attractive condition so far as Old Ruff was concerned, and the two of them went romping off together in the direction of a nearby pasture despite the roar of Billingsley's stentorian commands.

We hunted all the rest of that day without the benefit of Old Ruff, though Billingsley blew his ultra-high-frequency dog whistle and called him off and on throughout the hunt. We flushed enough birds to get our respective limits and returned about dark to the car, where we found Old Ruff asleep under the bumper. It took both of us to wake him up.

The Wondrous West

Jim Baker's Bluejay Yarn

Mark Twain

Animals talk to each other, of course. There can be no question about that; but I suppose there are very few people who can understand them. I never knew but one man who could. I knew he could, however, because he told me so himself. He was a middle-aged, simple-hearted miner who had lived in a lonely corner of California, among the woods and mountains, a good many years, and had studied the ways of his only neighbors, the beasts and the birds, until he believed he could accurately translate any remark which they made. This was Jim Baker. According to Jim Baker, some animals have only a limited education, and use only very simple words, and scarcely ever a comparison or a flowery figure; whereas, certain other animals have a large vocabulary, a fine command of language and a ready and fluent delivery; consequently these latter talk a great deal; they like it; they are conscious of their talent, and they enjoy "showing off." Baker said, that after long and careful observation, he had come to the conclusion that the bluejays were the best talkers he had found among birds and beasts. Said he:

"There's more *to* a bluejay than any other creature. He has got more moods, and more different kinds of feelings than other creatures; and, mind you, whatever a bluejay feels, he can put into language. And no mere commonplace language, either, but rattling, out-and-out book-talk—and bristling with metaphor, too—just bristling! And as for command of language—why *you* never see a bluejay get stuck for a word. No man ever did. They just boil out of him! And another thing: I've noticed a good deal, and there's no bird, or cow, or anything that uses as good grammar as a bluejay. You may say a cat uses good grammar. Well, a cat does—but you let a cat get excited once; you let a cat get to pulling fur with another cat on a shed, nights, and you'll hear grammar that will give you the lockjaw. Ignorant people think it's the *noise* which fighting cats make that is so aggravating, but it ain't so; it's the sickening grammar they use. Now I've never heard a jay use bad grammar but very seldom; and when they do, they are as ashamed as a human; they shut right down and leave.

"You may call a jay a bird. Well, so he is, in a measure—because he's got feathers on him, and don't belong to no church, perhaps; but otherwise he is just as much a human as you be. And I'll tell you for why. A jay's gifts, and instincts, and feelings, and interests, cover the whole ground. A jay hasn't got any more principle than a Congressman. A jay will lie, a jay will steal, a jay will deceive, a jay will betray; and four times out of five, a jay will go back on his solemnest promise. The sacredness of an obligation is a thing which you can't cram into no bluejay's head. Now, on top of all this, there's another thing; a jay can outswear any gentleman in the mines. You think a cat can swear. Well, a cat can; but you give a bluejay a subject that calls for his reserve-powers, and where is your cat? Don't talk to *me*—I know too much about this thing. And there's yet another thing; in the one little particular of scolding—just good, clean, out-and-out scolding—a bluejay can lay over anything, human or divine. Yes, sir, a jay is everything that a man is. A jay can cry, a jay can laugh, a jay can feel shame, a jay can reason and plan and discuss, a jay likes gossip and scandal, a jay has got a sense of humor, a jay knows when he is an ass just as well as you do—maybe better. If a jay ain't human, he better take in his sign, that's all. Now I'm going to tell you a perfectly true fact about some bluejays.

"When I first begun to understand jay language correctly, there was a little incident happened here. Seven years ago, the last man in this region but me moved away. There stands his house,—been empty ever since; a log house, with a plank roof—just one big room, and no more; no ceiling—nothing between the rafters and the floor. Well, one Sunday morning I was sitting out here in front of my cabin, with my cat, taking the sun, and looking at the blue hills, and listening to the leaves rustling so lonely in the trees, and thinking of the home away yonder in the states, that I hadn't heard from in thirteen years, when a bluejay lit on that house, with an acorn in his mouth, and says, 'Hello, I reckon I've struck something.' When he spoke, the acorn dropped out of his mouth and rolled down the roof, of course, but he didn't care; his mind was all on the thing he had struck. It was a knot-hole in the roof. He cocked his head to one side, shut one eye and put the other one to the hole, like a 'possum looking down a jug; then he glanced up with his bright eyes, gave a wink or two with his wings—which signifies gratification, you understand,—and says, 'It looks like a hole, it's located like a hole,—blamed if I don't believe it *is* a hole!'

"Then he cocked his head down and took another look; he glances up perfectly joyful, this time; winks his wings and his tail both, and says, 'Oh, no, this ain't no fat thing, I reckon! If I ain't in luck!—why it's a perfectly elegant hole!' So he flew down and got that acorn, and fetched it up and dropped it in, and was just tilting his head back, with the heavenliest smile on his face, when all of a sudden he was paralyzed into a listening attitude and that smile faded gradually out of his countenance like breath off'n a razor, and the queerest look of surprise took its place. Then he says, 'Why, I didn't hear it fall!' He cocked his eye at the hole again, and took a long look; raised up and shook his head; stepped around to the other side of the hole and took another look from that side; shook his head again. He studied a while, then he just went into the *de*tails—walked round and round the hole and spied into it from every point of the compass. No use. Now he took a thinking attitude on the comb of the roof and scratched the back of his head with his right foot a minute, and finally says, 'Well, it's too many for *me*, that's certain; must be a mighty long hole; however, I ain't got no time to fool around here, I got to 'tend to business; I reckon it's all right—chance it, anyway.'

"So he flew off and fetched another acorn and dropped it in, and tried to flirt his eye to the hole quick enough to see what become of it, but he was too late. He held his eye there as much as a minute; then he raised up and sighed, and says, 'Confound it, I don't seem to understand this thing, no way; however, I'll tackle her again.' He fetched another acorn, and done his best to see what become of it, but he couldn't. He says, 'Well, *I* never struck no such a hole as this before; I'm of the opinion it's a totally new kind of a hole.' Then he begun to get mad. He held in for a spell, walking up and down the comb of the roof and shaking his head and muttering to himself; but his feelings got the upper hand of him, presently, and he broke loose and cussed himself black in the face. I never see a bird take on so about a little thing. When he got through he walks to the hole and looks in again for half a minute; then he says, 'Well, you're a long hole, and a deep hole, and a mighty singular hole altogether—but I've started in to fill you, and I'm d—d if I *don't* fill you, if it takes a hundred years!'

"And with that, away he went. You never see a bird work so since you was born. He laid into his work like a nigger, and the way he hove acorns into that hole for about two hours and a half was one of the most exciting and astonishing spectacles I ever struck. He never stopped to take a look any more—he just hove 'em in and went for more. Well, at last he could hardly flop his wings, he was so tuckered out. He comes a-drooping down, once more, sweating like an ice-pitcher, drops his acorn in and says, 'Now I guess I've got the bulge on you by this time!' So he bent down for a look. If you'll believe me, when his head come up again he was just pale with rage. He says, 'I've shoveled acorns enough in there to keep the family thirty years, and if I can see a sign of one of 'em I wish I may land in a museum with a belly full of sawdust in two minutes!'

"He just had strength enough to crawl up on to the comb and lean his back agin the chimbly, and then he collected his impressions and begun to free his mind. I see in a second that what I had mistook for profanity in the mines was only just the rudiments, as you may say.

"Another jay was going by, and heard him doing his devotions, and stops to inquire what was up. The sufferer told him the whole circumstance, and says, 'Now yonder's the hole, and if you don't believe me, go and look for yourself.' So this fellow went and looked, and comes back and says, 'How many did you say you put in there?' 'Not any less than two tons,' says the sufferer. The other jay went and looked again. He couldn't seem to make it out, so he raised a yell, and three more jays come. They all examined the hole, they all made the sufferer tell it over again, then they all discussed it, and got off as many leather-headed opinions about it as an average crowd of humans could have done.

"They called in more jays; then more and more till pretty soon this whole region 'peared to have a blue flush about it. There must have been five thousand of them; and such another jawing and disputing and ripping and cussing, you never heard. Every jay in the whole lot put his eye to the hole and delivered a more chuckle-headed opinion about the mystery than the jay that went there before him. They examined the house all over, too. The door was standing half open, and at last one old jay happened to go and light on it and look in. Of course, that knocked the mystery galley-west in a second. There lay the acorns, scattered all over the floor. He flopped his wings and raised a whoop. 'Come here!' he says, 'Come here, everybody; hang'd if this fool hasn't been trying to fill up a

house with acorns!' They all came a-swooping down like a blue
cloud, and as each fellow lit on the door and took a glance, the whole
absurdity of the contract that that first jay had tackled hit him home
and he fell over backwards suffocating with laughter, and the next
jay took his place and done the same.

"Well, sir, they roosted around here on the housetop and the
trees for an hour, and guffawed over that thing like human beings. It
ain't any use to tell me a bluejay hasn't got a sense of humor, because
I know better. And memory, too. They brought jays here from all
over the United States to look down that hole, every summer for
three years. Other birds, too. And they could all see the point, except
an owl that come from Nova Scotia to visit the Yo Semite, and he
took this thing in on his way back. He said he couldn't see anything
funny in it. But then he was a good deal disappointed about Yo
Semite, too."

Ants

Mark Twain

Now and then, while we rested, we watched the laborious ant at his
work. I found nothing new in him—certainly nothing to change my
opinion of him. It seems to me that in the matter of intellect the ant
must be a strangely overrated bird. During many summers, now, I
have watched him, when I ought to have been in better business,
and I have not yet come across a living ant that seemed to have any
more sense than a dead one. I refer to the ordinary ant, of course; I
have had no experience of those wonderful Swiss and African ones
which vote, keep drilled armies, hold slaves, and dispute about religion. Those particular ants may be all that the naturalist paints
them, but I am persuaded that the average ant is a sham. I admit
his industry, of course; he is the hardest-working creature in the
world—when anybody is looking—but his leather-headedness is the
point I make against him. He goes out foraging, he makes a capture,
and then what does he do? Go home? No—he goes anywhere but
home. He doesn't know where home is. His home may be only three
feet away—no matter, he can't find it. He makes his capture, as I
have said; it is generally something which can be of no sort of use to
himself or anybody else; it is usually seven times bigger than it ought
to be; he hunts out the awkwardest place to take hold of it; he lifts
it bodily up in the air by main force, and starts; not toward home
but in the opposite direction; not calmly and wisely but with a
frantic haste which is wasteful of his strength; he fetches up against
a pebble, and instead of going around it, he climbs over it backward, dragging his booty after him, tumbles down on the other side,
jumps up in a passion, kicks the dust off his clothes, moistens his
hands, grabs his property viciously, yanks it this way, then that,
shoves it ahead of him for a moment, turns tail and lugs it after
him another moment, gets madder and madder, then presently hoists
it into the air and goes tearing away in an entirely new direction;

186

comes to a weed; it never occurs to him to go around it; no, he must
climb it; and he does climb it, dragging his worthless property to the
top—which is as bright a thing to do as it would be for me to carry
a sack of flour from Heidelberg to Paris by way of Strasbourg steeple;
when he gets up there he finds that that is not the place; takes a
cursory glance at the scenery and either climbs down again or
tumbles down, and starts off once more—as usual, in a new direction. At the end of half an hour he fetches up within six inches of the
place he started from and lays his burden down; meantime he has
been over all the ground for two yards around, and climbed all the
weeds and pebbles he came across. Now he wipes the sweat from his
brow, strokes his limbs, and then marches aimlessly off, in as violent
a hurry as ever. He traverses a good deal of zigzag country, and by
and by stumbles on his same booty again. He does not remember to
have ever seen it before; he looks around to see which is not the way
home, grabs his bundle, and starts; he goes through the same adventures he had before; finally stops to rest, and a friend comes along.
Evidently the friend remarks that a last year's grasshopper leg is a
very noble acquisition, and inquires where he got it. Evidently the
proprietor does not remember exactly where he did get it, but thinks
he got it "around here somewhere." Evidently the friend contracts to
help him freight it home. Then, with a judgment peculiarly antic
(pun not intentional), they take hold of opposite ends of that grasshopper leg and begin to tug with all their might in opposite directions. Presently they take a rest and confer together. They decide
that something is wrong, they can't make out what. Then they go at
it again, just as before. Same result. Mutual recriminations follow.
Evidently each accuses the other of being an obstructionist. They
warm up, and the dispute ends in a fight. They lock themselves together and chew each other's jaws for a while; then they roll and
tumble on the ground till one loses a horn or a leg and has to haul off
for repairs. They make up and go to work again in the same old
insane way, but the crippled ant is at a disadvantage; tug as he may,
the other one drags off the booty and him at the end of it. Instead of
giving up, he hangs on, and gets his shins bruised against every
obstruction that comes in the way. By and by, when that grasshopper
leg has been dragged all over the same old ground once more, it is
finally dumped at about the spot where it originally lay, the two
perspiring ants inspect it thoughtfully and decide that dried grasshopper legs are a poor sort of property after all, and then each starts

off in a different direction to see if he can't find an old nail or something else that is heavy enough to afford entertainment and at the same time valueless enough to make an ant want to own it.

There in the Black Forest, on the mountainside, I saw an ant go through with such a performance as this with a dead spider of fully ten times his own weight. The spider was not quite dead, but too far gone to resist. He had a round body the size of a pea. The little ant— observing that I was noticing—turned him on his back, sunk his fangs into his throat, lifted him into the air, and started vigorously off with him, stumbling over little pebbles, stepping on the spider's legs and tripping himself up, dragging him backward, shoving him bodily ahead, dragging him up stones six inches high instead of going around them, climbing weeds twenty times his own height and jumping from their summits—and finally leaving him in the middle of the road to be confiscated by any other fool of an ant that wanted him. I measured the ground which this ass traversed, and arrived at the conclusion that what he had accomplished inside of twenty minutes would constitute some such job as this—relatively speaking —for a man; to wit: to strap two eight-hundred-pound horses together, carry them eighteen hundred feet, mainly over (not around) boulders averaging six feet high, and in the course of the journey climb up and jump from the top of one precipice like Niagara, and three steeples, each a hundred and twenty feet high; and then put the horses down, in an exposed place, without anybody to watch them, and go off to indulge in some other idiotic miracle for vanity's sake.

Science has recently discovered that the ant does not lay up anything for winter use. This will knock him out of literature, to some extent. He does not work, except when people are looking, and only then when the observer has a green, naturalistic look, and seems to be taking notes. This amounts to deception, and will injure him for the Sunday schools. He has not judgment enough to know what is good to eat from what isn't. This amounts to ignorance, and will impair the world's respect for him. He cannot stroll around a stump and find his way home again. This amounts to idiocy, and once the damaging fact is established, thoughtful people will cease to look up to him, the sentimental will cease to fondle him. His vaunted industry is but a vanity and of no effect, since he never gets home with anything he starts with. This disposes of the last remnant of his reputation and wholly destroys his main usefulness as a moral agent, since it will make the sluggard hesitate to go to him any more. It is strange, beyond comprehension, that so manifest a humbug as the ant has been able to fool so many nations and keep it up so many ages without being found out.

The Dog That Was Pensioned by a Legislature

Anonymous

In the Territory of New Mexico the Legislature, by joint action, recently pensioned a dog for noble services. In that country there are many sheep farms, and shepherd dogs are so well trained in caring for the flocks of their masters, that it is their daily practice to take out the flocks in the morning to pasture, guard them all day, and, at night, return them to the fold or corral. This work of the Mexican dogs is so common and so faithfully performed that it is looked upon as a matter of course, and nothing more than should be expected from a well-trained dog. This being the case, it would appear that the dog worthy of a pension in that Territory, must have performed some very marvelous feat indeed, and something out of the common line of canine achievement. And he did. He did not save his mistress' life from the murderous fury of the savage, nor her child from being brained against a doorpost or being choked by a huge black snake, for his master was not married, and had no wife or babe, but led a solitary life in his solitary ranch in a very solitary part of New Mexico.

It chanced that the dog in question, on returning of an evening with his sheep to the fold, discovered that his master was not stirring about, but remained inside the shanty and kept very quiet. The next evening it was the same. The dog, when he penned up the sheep, repaired to the shanty, smelled through a crack in the door his master's presence, but the master was still quiet and did not breathe. The dog scratched, barked, and even howled, but no response came from within. The door remained closed; no smoke arose from the chimney to greet the early morn. But the dog, true to his appointed duty, went out with the sheep on the third day, and cared for them while they cropped the herbage on the hillsides. But he was getting hungry, and that night when he drove the flock into their pen, the last one to attempt to go in became the victim of his appetite. This method of providing for his own wants became a portion of the faithful dog's daily duty. Occasionally the last sheep to try to enter the fold was seized by him and served for supper and for breakfast and dinner the following day. As stated before, the ranch to which the dog belonged was in a solitary part of the Territory, and out of the track of travel and social intercourse or visitation.

For two years from the time of the master's death—as ascertained by data left by the latter—the faithful dog tended the flock committed to his charge, and had fresh mutton for supper every night. The flock was not decimated by this steady drain upon its resources. On the contrary, it increased its numbers, and when, at the end of two years from the time of the death of the proprietor the ranch was visited and the remains of the poor fellow found, the dog was still at his post of duty, jealously guarding his flock, and driving them to the best pastures every day, and to the fold at night, before which he slept, to keep the wild sheep-eaters of the plains at a civil distance. Such fidelity excited admiration wherever the story was told, and the Arcadian legislators of the Territory, in a fit of generosity and enthusiasm, at their session two years ago (they have biennial sessions in that happy country) granted a pension for life to that dog, to be paid from the State Treasury as a reward for his fidelity, and no doubt as an encouragement to all other shepherd dogs in that Territory to be good dogs and faithful.

A Family Pet

Vardis Fisher

Acme Sulphide came in from his prospect on Caribou Creek, bringing a big cougar to Larry Frazee's taxidermist shop. "Want him skun out and made into a rug?" asked Larry.

"No sir. Stuff him as is. I wouldn't think of walkun on Petronius."

"Why not? Just a cougar, ain't he?"

"Not by your tin horn. He's an institution, that's what he is. When he was just a kitten I ketched him by the mine shaft. Him and Pluto, they was great friends until Petronius growed up. Then one evening when I comes back, why Pluto was gone and Petronius wouldn't eat his supper. I was plumb mad, but I figgered Pluto was gettun old and wasn't so much account nohow. Then, by gum, I missed Mary, the goat. When I missed the last of the chickens and Petronius showed up with feathers in his whiskers, I made up my mind to shoot him. But I got to thinkun how that goat could butt, and the hens wasn't layun anyhow. So I let it go. But I shoulda bumped him then.

"Lydie, she's my old woman—or she was. Partner of my joys and sorrows for forty years. One evening when I gets back she was gone. No sign of her anywhere exceptun one shoe. And Petronius didn't want no supper agin. That got me mad, danged if it didn't, and I went for my gun to blast the varmint. Then I got to thinkun. Lydie wasn't much for looks and besides, she was about to leave me. She was all for hittun the trail, so I puts my gun up."

"Then what happened?"

"Well, last night he jumped me on the trail and took a big hunk right out of me. That was too danged much. So mount him up pretty. He represents my whole family."

192

Old Mitts

Lloyd Lewis

"Old Mitts" is the story of Tom Blevins, who lived alone, except for his pets, on a remote Colorado ranch.

What he liked to eat were prunes and pancakes. He would eat the bacon and the hams we would bring in to him twice a year, along with six months' supply of flour, buckwheat, syrup, salt, sugar, lard, and staples of that kind, but he didn't feel quite right about eating meat, for he did want to be a Pythagorean. Living there in the heart of one of the best of the big game countries, he refused to take life. The deer would trample the scrawling little garden he pretended to cultivate, but Old Tom would never shoot them. His big mongrel hound, Keno, would chase jack rabbits right up to the door, but Old Tom would never take down the rifle which had hung, unused, twenty years or more. His other dog, Friskie, was a white poodle who practically never went out of the cabin. Tom had quite a story about how he came by Friskie. It boiled down to, "Friskie was give me by that big, fat chippie who used to stay in the town of Red Onion. Can't recall her name; we all just knew her as 'The Covered Wagon.'"

Usually Old Tom had another pet—a cat named Old Mitts. If the cat died, he got another as soon as he could and called it Old Mitts, too. He said he always had one because he liked the way that first Old Mitts had behaved the time his wife left him.

Tom had got his wife through "The Heart and Hand" column in the *Denver Post* and, as he told it, had given her, on their wedding night, instructions as to what he expected.

"I wound that alarm clock, there," he told us, pointing to a long-dead timepiece on the log shelf, "set it fer six, and, as we climbed into bed, I told her, 'Now when that rings, I want to hear your feet flap on the floor.'"

After three months Tom's wife left him: "Said she was going

into Jensen to get some things, and I saddled up Old Cody and she rode off down through that draw. It was spring and the fireweed was over the hills. She waved as she went out of sight behind that rock, and I waved and turned around to go back into the house and there in the door stood Old Mitts, wavin' her tail goodbye, too."

Mrs. Blevins never came back, though she left his horse, properly enough, at the feedbarn with the note which explained her reasons for departing. Tom never revealed to us what the note contained. He kept her wedding clothes in a grain sack and every so often would take them out to burn, but would wind up cursing softly and stuffing them back in the bag again.

It must have been the sixth or seventh cat in that succession of Old Mitts which produced a temporary revolution in Blevins' soul. Monaghan learned about it one November when he rode in with Tom's winter supply of grub. The old man started goddamming before he could ask Monaghan to come in or how he was or how long he could stay.

"God damn 'em," he snorted. "God damn them coyotes; they've et Old Mitts. She's been gone a week now, and I've sent to town fer twenty steel traps and three dollars' worth of poison and 200 cartridges. I've oiled up the rifle, and I'm going to spend the winter killin' coyotes. They'll pay fer this."

He could talk of nothing else all that evening and next day and it was amid his profane volleys of promised revenges that Monaghan rode away to be gone till spring would let him come up through the mountain passes again.

When Monaghan did come back the next March, he halted the pack train as he neared the cabin. What had happened? The cabin looked like a carnival tent, with banners or something fluttering along its walls. He rode nearer and saw that the cabin was covered with coyote hides, their fur moving in the spring wind.

Monaghan shouted, and out came Old Tom looking as if he had been killing sheep.

"I guess I made a kind of a fool of myself, Jimmy," he said. (He always called Monaghan, "Jimmy.") "You remember when you left last fall I told you I was goin' to get even with them coyotes? Well, there they are, forty-five of 'em. I shot and trapped all winter— froze one foot, lost old Keno, lamed my horse, but I got 'em."

Monaghan said Tom looked at the trophies bashfully, scratched his bottom shyly, then added, "Well, day before yisterday that chinook struck and the snow melted and I said, 'I guess spring's here so I think I'll make my bed.' I carried it out here into the yard and give it a shake and out fell Old Mitts, pressed as pretty as a flower."

Just a Simple Country Boy

PRISCILLA D. WILLIS

"I don't aim to sell him," the cowboy said, gazing steadfastly into Charles' eager eyes. "Not exactly, that is. A good home for him means more to me than money. This horse is about my best friend; he always done everything I ever ast him." He shifted his narrow hips above his wishbone legs encased, like sausages, in blue denim levis. "Course," he added somewhat apologetically, "I reckon I'd have to have a little something for him."

"Of course," Charles agreed. "How much?"

"Well," the cowboy replied, drawing a tiny circle on the frozen ground with the pointed toe of his boot, "first thing is to see if you folks like him. Then we can git down to trading." He had his own method of doing business, and was not to be hurried out of it.

"But you say he's a good horse with cattle." Charles was a little impatient. "That's all I want." My husband has his methods, too. He buys and sells bonds and stocks by simply picking up a telephone, and the deal is consummated before you can say Dow Jones. Twenty-five years in a brokerage firm have left him with the impression that a quick trade is the expedient way to transact business, and prolonged conversation about anything makes him nervous. When he is nervous he rolls his fingers up into the palms of his hands and then unrolls them again, like window shades going up and down.

"Don't you want to see him rode, even?" the cowboy asked suspiciously. He took a cigarette from the pocket of his plaid woolen jacket and put it carefully in his mouth.

"Well, yes," my husband replied. "As a matter of fact, I was thinking of riding him myself."

Without taking his gentian-colored eyes off Charles' face the cowboy chipped the tip off a wooden match with his thumbnail, cupped his rough hands under the wide brim of his hat and held

196

the flame to his cigarette. Solemnly, he observed Charles' legs in his Newmarket boots like toothpicks sticking out of a baked potato beneath the alpaca-lined storm coat, bunched and belted at his waist which the good things of life have expanded to a bacchanalian forty-four. He regarded the cashmere scarf, knotted at his throat, the English cap above Charles' face empurpled by a cruel wind hustling through the empty shedrow.

"You ride pretty good?" he said at last.

"I've ridden all my life," Charles declared with briskness, and quickly sketched his qualifications as an equestrian from the time he was nine with his first pony, through the dude ranch days in Arizona, the bridle trails in the forest preserve, and more recently his necessity for riding on his farm in Alabama. "I've got to have a decent cow horse down there," he concluded.

The cowboy didn't seem especially satisfied. He swallowed his Adam's apple, and when it returned he said as if to reassure himself, "This is a made cow horse, all right; ain't nothing he don't know about cutting and roping; he's real gentle, too. Little kids has rode him—lots of times—and there ain't a pimple on him, neither. You can see for yourselves."

We turned to the horse whose brown face thrust over the stall door had been investigating us while we were talking. He had supernaturally bright eyes, set very wide apart, and the flat cheek and well-defined jaw of the quarter horse; his delicately pointed ears twitched back and forth as if trying to identify unfamiliar and not particularly agreeable sounds. He looked a great deal livelier in his stall than he had looked loping around the racetrack where we watched him during the summer with the cowboy on his back carrying the films from the patrol towers after each race. He stopped at the towers on the backstretch while the cowboy picked up the films, and then moving in close to the rail, galloped back to the grandstand where the films were delivered to the stewards.

"That," Charles had remarked on many occasions, "is a horse I would like to have. Look at him. He goes on a loose rein, and has a fine, easy canter. Looks like a first-rate cutting horse, too."

He arranged to meet the cowboy through a horse-trainer seated in the box next to ours, who told him he'd heard the cowboy wanted to retire the horse, and was looking for a good home for him. The cowboy, he said, was very fond of that horse; he didn't want to beat him up on the winter racing circuit as a lead pony or on the film patrol. If Charles could wait until the end of the meeting which would wind up racing in the North for this season he was sure he could get the horse for practically nothing.

Charles waited. The last of the race-horses had shipped out, and the barns were empty except for the film patrol horse. A cloak of cold silence hung over the stabling area; the racetrack was barren of its customary early morning life. There were no sets out galloping, no railbirds clocking works, no young horses being schooled from the starting gate. The grandstand across the oval from the barns was forlorn in its emptiness, as purposeless as an ant hill without any ants.

"I'll put the tack on him," the cowboy said. He took a slip-ear bridle from a peg and, picking up his stock saddle, balanced its weight against his thigh as he shuffled off into the stall.

In a very few moments the cowboy led out the horse who appeared to be walking on only three legs.

"He's lame!" Charles shouted into the wind. "He's dead lame!"

The cowboy curled his thin lips into an agreeable smile, revealing two rows of teeth as perfectly matched as the keys on a piano. "He ain't lame," he said. "Not really. He's always gimpy like this of a morning. He walks right out of it."

"Well," said Charles, as if he didn't believe it.

"Don't you ever get up of a morning feeling kind of kinky-like and stove up?" the cowboy asked as he tightened the latigo.

Charles admitted that he did.

"Same thing with this horse."

Charles looked as if he were back in the game again. He focused his wind-watered eyes upon the horse with obvious appreciation when the cowboy led him out from under the shedrow and posed him on the icy ground.

"He's a good type," my husband whispered; "looks like a model quarter horse."

"He is," said the cowboy who had picked up the whisper at twenty paces in the high wind. "He stood second in the halter class at Fort Worth."

Charles looked awfully pleased. "What," he asked, "is his name?"

The cowboy lowered his head in momentary embarrassment as if he had committed a minor indecency like belching in mixed company. "His registered name," he mumbled, "the name that's on his papers, is Excalibur, or some such foolishness, but I and my brother has always called him Sport."

"Sport," Charles repeated, tasting the word as if it were a very green wine. "Sport."

With a single, agile movement the cowboy was in the saddle, sitting easily, perfectly balanced. He walked the horse up and down on the frozen ground, jogged him, cantered him, stopped him abruptly, and worked through a figure eight on a loose rein.

"He pivots real good, don't he? You don't see him going gimpy, now, do you?"

We shook our heads and smiled.

"What did I tell you?" the cowboy laughed cheerfully, and cut an imaginary steer from a non-existent herd, changing the horse's leads with every stride.

Charles commenced to unbutton his storm coat. "Can I ride him?" he called.

"Sure thing." The cowboy dismounted with the grace of a feather floating to the ground.

Charles dumped his alpaca coat into my arms, and strode out from under the shedrow. He was wearing over two sweaters, a senescent tweed riding-coat tailored at the time waistlines were nipped in directly below the armpits, and skirts were cut in generous peplums rippling at the sides and stopping abruptly at the hips. With the passage of time the peg in his khaki breeches had slipped, for the only fullness in them now were two little pouches drooping around his knees.

"You just hang onto him," Charles instructed, gathering the reins in one hand, and turning the box stirrup toward his left foot with the other. It was a long reach from the ground, and in order to achieve sufficient momentum to hoist himself into the saddle he began hopping up and down on his right foot, gaining altitude all the time, but not quite enough.

"Can't do it," he panted, "trouble is, I've got too many clothes on. I feel stuffed. Isn't there a mounting block around here?"

"A what?" The cowboy was beginning to look frightened.

"Something I can stand on so I can get on him."

"I'll give you a leg up," the cowboy offered, and keeping hold of the bridle he bent down and seized Charles by his booted ankle. "Now!" he cried, and gave a mighty heave as he straightened his back.

There was a flash of coattails, a disproportionate expanse of khaki seat, a fleeting impression of arched legs thrusting in the rhythm of a swimming frog's, and Charles was in the saddle.

The horse steadied himself to accommodate the unaccustomed weight; then he humped his back slightly.

"Walk him out!" the cowboy cried. "Don't leave him git his head down!"

Charles closed his legs on the horse's sides and shook the reins.

The cowboy raised his weathered face to the slate-colored sky, and his eyebrows, like two furry caterpillars, crawled up under the band of his hat. "Sweet Jesus," he murmured.

The horse didn't move; he just stood there with the hump in his back growing bigger.

Exasperated, Charles gave the reins a sharp tug; the horse took ten steps straight back without stopping, leaving Charles, expecting to go forward, biting into the mane.

The cowboy was making a real effort to pull himself together. "Ain't he cuttin' the fool?" he laughed nervously, and clapped his large rough hands as if to make a joke of the whole thing. "Sport, he's pretending he's working against the rope you've throwed your calf with," he called. "He's showing you how a good cow horse can hold a critter. Look at him back up for you!"

"Open the gap onto the racetrack!" Charles' voice came from quite a distance, because Sport had backed to the very end of the shedrow and was still going, but when he saw the opened gap, he gathered his legs under him and, exploding past us, shot onto the plowed track, where he took the inside rail and shifted into high. He ran the first mile as handily as a racehorse with Bill Hartack up.

"I reckon I been graining him too heavy," the cowboy said morbidly, squeezing the outside rail with both hands until his knuckles turned white. "It don't look like he's ever going to stop."

The horse flashed by us again, his ears pinned to his head, his tail as plump as a plume on a drum major's hat standing out behind him. The thing hanging around his neck like a fur stole must have been Charles, but it was impossible to be sure; it was such a blur.

After several impressive laps Sport shortened stride approaching the gap, ducking through it so suddenly that Charles shifted like a cargo of bananas, slipping halfway down the side of the saddle where he clung to the leather thongs until the horse stopped abruptly.

"Great!" my husband gasped, letting go of the thongs. "A great ride! I let him stretch his legs a little, but I could have taken him back any time I wanted to."

He was breathing a good deal harder than the horse, and his face beneath the tangle of hair on his wet forehead was the color of California redwood. His cap had blown off at the sixteenth pole. "How much do you want for him?"

Without any hesitation the cowboy reckoned he'd take five hundred, because Sport would be getting a good home with nice folks.

"All right," Charles said, and the cowboy, profoundly astonished, studied him carefully. The expected counter-offer at a lower figure had not been forthcoming; this made him uneasy, almost suspicious, but he collected himself quickly, and showing his piano teeth in a wide grin when Charles asked how he could get the horse down to his farm, replied that that wouldn't be no trouble at all, because he was trailing a lead pony to Floridy and he'd take Sport along, dropping him off on the way. His time and the gas wouldn't amount to more than another couple of hundred, he added, striking while the iron placed in his hand by an agreeable if perplexing providence was still red hot.

Inside the cowboy's rusty sedan parked in front of the shed-row, Charles wrote a check and instructions how to reach his farm. The automobile looked as if it had been assembled in a hurry from odd parts lying around a junk yard; it had a nasty list, and jewel-studded mudguards that swept the ground.

"Only one thing you'd ought to remember," the cowboy said, folding the check and putting it in the pocket of his jacket, "don't never put no bit in this horse's mouth; he don't act good with bits."

"Really?" said Charles, and we noticed for the first time that the horse's bridle was rigged with a long shanked hackamore, a braided leather roll across the nose the only means of restraint.

When we reached our apartment in town, Charles telephoned his farmer, Fremont Pone, to tell him when the horse arrived, to put him in the shed with the milk cow where he could run out in her pasture. Then he sat down with his Saturday noon martini and spoke at length about how splendid it was going to be to have a good horse to ride instead of those swaybacked nags the colored boys used to count calves and mend the fences.

Fremont Pone, brought up in the tradition of the county that if work must be done at all it should be squeezed in between shooting birds in the day and hunting coons at night, reluctantly put away his shotgun during Charles' infrequent visits to his farm. This time, however, he was waiting for us in the barn lot. He turned his narrow face with its hash-browned complexion and slitty eyes toward the car and, moving with the same loose-jointed ease as the Blue Tick hound at his side, shambled over to greet us.

"Yawl know that horse?" he began. "Well, ah done lak you tole me, all right. Ah put him in wiv the milk cow, but he been carryin' on fierce wiv her, tormentin' her all the tahm. He goes to kissin' and luvvin' her up, hoppin' on her and peelin' her back wiv his shoes. She's took a fright, and doan let down no milk at all. Not a drop. Ah doan believe that horse eveh seen a cow before in his whole life."

"Nonsense!" Charles snapped, "he's a cutting and roping horse; he stood second in the halter class at Fort Worth."

"Mah, mah," said Fremont Pone, but he was not really impressed.

In the half light of the cow shed the milk cow trembled on her Queen Anne legs; her brown eyes, normally kind and patient, were glazed with terror. Behind her Sport was dozing, his nose resting possessively upon her striated hips. Hearing the door open, the horse picked up his head, twitched his ears, and swelled his nostrils to catch the scent of his intruders. He walked up to my husband and bumped him in the stomach with his nose.

"Hello, boy," Charles grunted, putting up a protective hand.

The horse bumped him again, harder.

"Now, now," said Charles, speaking as he used to speak to the children when they were little, "now, now."

Sport wheeled and, throwing his tail up impudently, trotted out the far end of the shed into the small pasture where he bucked and ran and, standing on his hind legs, boxed at shadows with his flinty hooves.

When the bridle with the hackamore Fremont Pone fashioned from some pieces of an old mule harness was completed, he adjusted it on the horse, and throwing a saddle on him led him over to the nail keg used for a mounting block. He stood with his mouth hanging open like a pocketbook idly patting the head of his hound dog as he watched Charles mount and jog off down the red road toward the upper fields where the beef cows were grazing with their calves. He followed them with his slitty eyes until they disappeared behind a stand of timber.

"Ah always reckoned one good mule were worth twenty horses inny day," he commented.

In half an hour Charles returned to the house holding his right shoulder with his left hand.

"I can't understand it," he said, dropping heavily into a chair, "this horse will only move in a circle."

"A circle?"

"Yes. He goes perfectly straight on a loose rein for a short distance, and then all at once, no matter where he is, he is seized by a compulsion to bend to the right and continue in a circular direction. The last time he turned into that planting of young pine with me." He rubbed his shoulder gently.

"The racetrack," I said.

"What do you mean, the racetrack?"

"He's accustomed to picking up the films from the towers on the straightaway of the backstretch, turning, and galloping back to the stands along the rail around the oval. Don't you remember?"

"That can't be it." Charles was stunned.

"It seems logical."

"Of course," he suggested unhappily, "it might be something I'm doing, or not doing. I believe I'll let some of the boys try him and see what he does with them."

It was soon evident that Sport's insistence upon galloping in circles had nothing whatsoever to do with Charles' riding. Fremont Pone was rubbed against a live oak and brushed neatly from the saddle within a matter of minutes. He limped back on a painful leg, brutally skinned. Benny Sawyer, whose arms and legs hung from his long, dark body like flags on a windless day, returned holding a throbbing shoulder.

"Da ho, ee crazy, da whuh," he observed.

Leroy Pollock and Geech Wiggins met the same misfortune, and finally, Major Emery Pugh, a neighbor, who with Mrs. Pugh dropped in one afternoon for a cup of tea.

"Clearly, this is a matter of proper training," said the major whose retirement from Fort Riley coincided with the mechanization of the U.S. Cavalry. "I can straighten him out in no time."

"But Imm'ry," his wife protested, "you haven't been on a howess fah yeahs." Her face beneath the large, lacy hats she always wore permanently expressed a look of pained surprise. "You maht get hurt rahdin' this howess."

"It is not a matter of riding, my dear," the major replied. "It is, as I have said, a matter of training. I shall begin on the ground, working him on a long line; when I feel he is ready, I will ride him, not before. If Charles will agree, I'll take the horse over to my place."

Charles agreed. "Don't ever put a bit in his mouth," he cautioned, "the cowboy said he didn't act good with bits."

"Rubbish!" the major snorted. "That's probably what's the matter with him. The proper bit will accomplish wonders."

A week to the very day Sport was back and the major was in the Phoebe Scott Memorial Hospital, in traction.

Sport commenced getting out of his pasture and roaming around the farm at nights. Every morning the top plank of the fence was on the ground.

"Ah believe he picks them spikes outen that board wiv his teeth," Fremont Pone observed. "Them nails is pulled cleah out eveh moanin'."

The horse learned to jump the cattle guards, eight-foot spans of railroad irons dividing the pastures, and reaching the upper fields he herded the mother cows and their calves, chasing them in a circle until the cows staggered with dizziness and the calves tumbled to the ground. He picked the locks on the barn doors, broke open the feed sacks, scattering the grain and tramping it into a mash; he hopped over wire fences as if they were croquet wickets, and when he was confined in a box stall he kicked his way out and, with tail held aloft, trotted over to the hog lot where he ran back and forth in the newly poured cement floor so that it looked like Grauman's Chinese. He continued to torment the milk cow until her nervous system was completely shot. The men spent so much time repairing buildings, mending fences, and salvaging feed that there was little time left to lime the fields and get the row crops in.

"At this point," my husband remarked one evening, "I stand to lose just double what I lost down here last year. I can't help feeling that that damned horse is responsible for it. It is an exasperating situation." His fingers commenced to roll and unroll rapidly in his palms. He was growing increasingly nervous as week after week went by.

Then came a day in the early spring which was to resolve the problem. It was one of those tranquil mornings when the new brilliance of the sun refreshes the winter-weary earth, extracting from it the very fragrance of growth. The pastures seemed suddenly to swell with their burden of clover, crimson oceans between forests of pine whose needles glittered as if they had been dipped in glycerin. It was the kind of day when you first realize that the sting of winter has left and will return no more; it was also the day which marked the opening of the racing season in the North.

A small car, riding very low to the ground, came slowly up the lane. Behind it was a horse trailer, obviously empty, for it was jumping skittishly from side to side.

"It's the cowboy!" Charles exploded. "It's that goddamned cowboy!"

"Howdy, folks," the cowboy said, climbing out from behind the sprung door of his rusty sedan, "I was just heading North, and I figured I'd stop in and see how you and Sport was getting along."

Charles shook the outstretched hand with something less than enthusiasm. "The horse," he declared, "is getting along fine; I cannot say the same for the rest of us."

The cowboy's face puckered in concern. "Is that so?" he said, but he didn't sound very surprised. He took a cigarette from the pocket of his plaid jacket, put it carefully in his mouth, and lighted it, waving the match until it was cool before throwing it to the ground. He stared thoughtfully at his boots stitched in an elaborate design of yellow tulips as he took a deep drag, and slowly hissed the smoke out between his teeth.

"What," he said finally, "seems to be the matter?"

Charles spared no details recounting the disasters perpetrated by Sport. "There are enough difficulties on a farm," he said with his voice climbing into its highest register, "without some goddamned horse wrecking everything! You can't even catch him any more." He pointed to the Pollocks' vegetable garden behind their small house where Sport was pacing the flimsy fence protecting the turnip greens whose tender leaves were pushing up through the red soil. "Look at him now; he'll be in that next!"

"Ain't that something?" the cowboy smiled fondly. "He's real smart, all right."

"He certainly is. He's so smart I'm going to get rid of him. I can't even look at him without losing my temper."

The cowboy shook his head sadly, but the corners of his mouth rose in a tiny smile.

"Do you aim to sell him?" he asked.

"How can I sell him?" Charles sputtered. "Everybody in the county knows what a rogue he is!"

"Why," said the cowboy, "I'd buy that horse back myself, I think so much of him, but to tell you the truth I'm a little short on cash. Tell you what I'll do, though; I'll take him back to the track with me up North. Maybe I can find a buyer for him up there. I'll sure let you know if I do."

"Take him!" Charles cried. "Take him right now—if you can catch him!"

The cowboy placed the tips of his little fingers in his mouth and exhaled one whistle.

Sport raised his head quickly. He hesitated for only an instant before he trotted over and buried his head in the sleeve of the cowboy's jacket.

"He sure looks good," the cowboy said. "Yes sir, he's wintered *real* good. Must have put on a hundred pounds at least." He encircled the brown head with a caressing arm. "Come on, boy," he said softly to the horse, "we're going home." He lowered the ramp of the trailer and Sport walked in. There was a rope net already filled with hay for the return journey.

The cowboy climbed quickly into his rusty sedan. "It's been real nice seeing you folks again," he said. "Maybe I'll git to see you at the races sometime this summer." He gunned the ancient motor and the car and trailer moved off down the road.

"You know," Charles said, fastening his eyes on the back of the trailer where Sport's well-rounded hindquarters were still visible above the tail gate, "that's a sight I shall never allow myself to forget. I'd give fifty dollars to shake the hand of the sucker who wintered that horse last year, and another fifty to know who that cowboy is going to get to do it next year. What is that quotation, something about East being East and West being West?"

"And never the twain shall meet."

"That's it," my husband replied, walking over to one of the sway-backed nags dozing in the sunshine at the hitching rail. "But it's all wrong. If that cowboy did his trading on Wall Street he'd be a millionaire in no time at all."

The Wonder Horse

George Byram

Webster says a mutation is a sudden variation, the offspring differing from the parents in some well-marked character or characters—and that certainly fits Red Eagle. He was foaled of registered parents, both his sire and dam descending from two of the best bloodlines in the breed. But the only thing normal about this colt was his color, a beautiful chestnut.

I attended Red Eagle's arrival into the world. He was kicking at the sac that enclosed him as I freed his nostrils from the membrane. He was on his feet in one minute. He was straight and steady on his pasterns by the time his dam had him licked dry. He had his first feeding before he was five minutes old, and he was beginning to buck and rear and prance by the time I got my wits about me and called Ben.

Ben came in the other end of the ramshackle barn from the feed lot. He was small as men go, but big for a jockey. Not really old at forty-two, his hair was gray and he was old in experience of horses.

Ben came into the box stall and as he saw the colt he stopped and whistled. He pushed back his hat and studied the red colt for a full five minutes. Even only minutes old a horseman could see he was markedly different. The bones from stifle to hock and elbow to knee were abnormally long. There was unusual length and slope of shoulder. He stood high in the croup and looked like he was running downhill. He had a very long underline and short back. All this spelled uniquely efficient bone levers, and these levers were connected and powered by the deepest hard-twisted muscles a colt ever brought into this world. Unbelievable depth at the girth and immense spring to the ribs meant an engine of heart and lungs capable of driving those muscled levers to their maximum. Red Eagle's nostrils were a third larger than any we had ever seen and he had a large, loose windpipe between his broad jaws. He would be able to

fuel the engine with all the oxygen it could use. Most important of
all, the clean, sharp modeling of his head and the bigness and luster
of his eyes indicated courage, will to win. But because of his strange
proportions he looked weird.

"Holy Mary," said Ben softly, and I nodded agreement.

Ben and I had followed horses all our lives. I as a veterinarian
and trainer for big breeders, Ben as a jockey. Each of us had out-
served his usefulness. Ben had got too heavy to ride; I had got too
cantankerous for the owners to put up with. I had studied bloodlines
and knew the breeders were no longer improving the breed, but I
could never make anyone believe in my theories. One owner after
another had decided he could do without my services. Ben and I
had pooled our savings and bought a small ranch in Colorado. We
had taken the mare that had just foaled in lieu of salary from our
last employer. Barton Croupwell had laughed when we had asked
for the mare rather than our money.

"Costello," he said to me, "you and Ben have twenty-five hundred coming. That mare is nineteen years old. She could drop dead
tomorrow."

"She could have one more foal too," I said.

"She could, but it's five to two she won't."

"That's good enough odds for the kind of blood she's carrying."

Croupwell was a gambler who raised horses for only one
reason: to make money. He shook his head. "I've seen old codgers
set in their thinking, but you're the worst. I suppose you've got a
stallion picked out—in case this mare'll breed."

"He doesn't belong to you," I said.

That needled him. "I've got stallions that bring five thousand
for a stud fee. Don't tell me they aren't good enough."

"Their bloodlines are wrong," I answered. "Mr. Carvelliers has
a stallion called Wing Away."

"Carvelliers' stallions cost money. Are you and Ben that flush?"
He already knew what I had in mind.

"You and Carvelliers trade services," I said. "It wouldn't cost
you anything to have the mare bred."

He threw back his head and laughed. He was a tall, thin man,
always beautifully tailored, with black hair and a line of mustache.
"I'm not a philanthropist," he said. "Do you really want this mare?"

"I said I did."

"You really think she'll get with foal?"

"I'll turn your odds around. I say it's five to two she will."

"I'll gamble with you," he said. "I'll send the mare over to Carvelliers'. If she settles I'll take care of the stud fee. If she doesn't, I keep the mare."

"And my and Ben's twenty-five hundred?"

"Of course."

"You're no gambler," I said, looking him in the eye, "but I'll take the bet."

Now, Ben and I were looking at a running machine that was something new on the face of the earth.

Our ranch was perfect for training the colt. It was out of the way and we took particular care that no one ever saw Red Eagle. By the time he was a yearling, our wildest estimate of what he would be had fallen short. Ben began to ride him when he was a coming two-year-old. By that time he had reached seventeen hands, weighed twelve hundred pounds, and could carry Ben's hundred and twenty-six as if Ben were nothing. Every time Ben stepped off him he was gibbering like an idiot. I was little better. This horse didn't run; he flowed. Morning after morning as Ben began to open him up I would watch him coming down the track we had dozed out of the prairie and he looked like a great wheel with flashing spokes rolling irresistibly forward. Carrying as much weight as mature horses are asked to carry, our stop watch told us Red Eagle had broken every world record for all distances and this on an imperfect track. Ben and I were scared.

One night when the racing season was close upon us, Ben said nervously, "I've made a few calls to some jockeys I know. Croupwell's and Carvelliers' and some others. The best two-year-olds they got are just normal, good colts. Red Eagle will beat them twenty lengths."

"You've got to keep him under restraint, Ben. You can't let anybody know what he can do."

"I can do anything with him out here by himself. But who knows what he'll do with other horses?"

"You've got to hold him."

"Listen, Cos, I've ridden some of the best and some of the toughest. I know what I can hold and what I can't. If Eagle ever takes it in his head to run, there'll not be a hell of a lot I can do about it."

"We've trained him careful."

"Yes, but if I've got him figured, he'll go crazy if a horse starts to crowd him. Another thing, any horseman will see at a glance what we've got. They'll know we're not letting him extend himself."

We were standing out by the pine pole paddock and I turned and looked at Red Eagle. Have you ever seen a cheetah? It's a cat. It runs faster than any other living creature. It's long-legged and long-bodied and it moves soft and graceful until it starts to run; then it becomes a streak with a blur of legs beneath. Red Eagle looked more like a twelve-hundred-pound cheetah than a horse and he ran the same way.

"Well, he's a race horse," I said. "If we don't race him, what'll we do with him?"

"We'll race him," said Ben, "but things ain't ever goin' to be the same again."

That turned out to be pure prophecy.

We decided to start him on a western track. We had to mortgage the ranch to get the money for his entry fee, but we had him entered in plenty of time. Two days before the race we hauled him, blanketed, in a closed trailer and put him into his stall without anyone getting a good look at him. We worked him out at dawn each morning before any other riders were exercising their horses.

This track was one where a lot of breeders tried their two-year-olds. The day of the race the first person I saw was Croupwell. His mild interest told me he already knew we had an entry. He looked at my worn Levis and string-bean frame. "What's happened these three years, Costello? You don't appear to have eaten regular."

"After today it'll be different," I told him.

"That colt you have entered, eh? He's not the bet you won from me, is he?"

"The same."

"I see by the papers Ben's riding. Ben must have lost weight too."

"Not so's you'd notice."

"You're not asking a two-year-old to carry a hundred and twenty-eight pounds on its first start!"

"He's used to Ben," I said casually.

"Costello, I happen to know you mortgaged your place to get the entry fee." He was looking at me speculatively. His gambler's instinct told him something was amiss. "Let's have a look at the colt."

"You'll see him when we bring him out to be saddled," I said and walked away.

You can't lead a horse like that among a group of horsemen without things happening. Men who spend their lives with horses know what gives a horse reach and speed and staying power. It didn't take an expert to see what Red Eagle had. When we took the blanket off him in the saddle paddock every jockey and owner began to move close. In no time there was a milling group of horsemen in front of where Ben and I were saddling Eagle.

Carvelliers, a handsome, white-haired Southern gentleman, called me to him. "Costello, is that Wing Away's colt?"

"Your signature's on his papers," I said.

"I'll give you fifty thousand dollars for his dam."

"She's dead," I said. "She died two weeks after we'd weaned this colt."

"Put a price on the colt," he said without hesitation.

"He's not for sale," I answered.

"We'll talk later," he said and turned and headed for the betting windows. Every man in the crowd followed him. I saw several stable hands pleading with acquaintances to borrow money to bet on Eagle despite the extra weight he would be spotting the other horses. By the time the pari-mutuel windows closed, our horse was the odds-on favorite and nobody had yet seen him run.

"I'm glad we didn't have any money to bet," said Ben, as I legged him up. "A dollar'll only make you a dime after what they've done to the odds."

The falling odds on Red Eagle had alerted the crowd to watch for him. As the horses paraded before the stands there was a rippling murmur of applause. He looked entirely unlike the other eight horses on the track. He padded along, his head bobbing easily, his long hind legs making him look like he was going downhill. He took one step to the other mincing thoroughbreds' three.

I had gone down to the rail and as Ben brought him by, heading for the backstretch where the six-furlong race would start, I could see the Eagle watching the other horses, his ears flicking curiously. I looked at Ben. He was pale. "How is he?" I called.

Ben glanced at me out of the corners of his eyes. "He's different."

"Different!" I called back edgily. "How?"

"Your guess is good as mine," Ben called over his shoulder.

Eagle went into the gate at his assigned place on the outside as docilely as we'd trained him to. But when the gate flew open, the rush of horses startled him. Breaking on top, he opened up five lengths on the field in the first sixteenth of a mile. The crowd went woosh with a concerted sigh of amazement.

"Father in heaven, hold him," I heard myself saying.

Through my binoculars, I could see the riders on the other horses studying the red horse ahead of them. Many two-year-olds break wild, but no horse opens five lengths in less than two hundred yards. I saw Ben steadying him gently, and as they went around the first turn, Ben had slowed him until the pack moved up to within a length.

That was as close as any horse ever got. Around the turn a couple of riders went after Eagle and the pack spread briefly into groups of three and two and two singles. I could see the two horses behind Eagle make their move. Eagle opened another three lengths before they hit the turn into the stretch and I could see Ben fighting him. The two that had tried to take the lead were used up and the pack came by them as all the riders turned their horses on for the stretch drive. Eagle seemed to sense the concerted effort behind him and his rate of flow changed. It was as if a racing car had its accelerator floorboarded. He came into the stretch gaining a half length every time his feet hit the turf.

When he hit the wire he was a hundred yards ahead of the nearest horse and still going away. Ben had to take him completely around the track before Eagle realized there were no horses behind him. By the time Ben walked him into the winner's circle, Eagle's sides were rising and falling evenly. He was only damp, not having got himself hot enough to sweat.

The first thing I remember seeing was Ben's guilty expression. "I tried to hold him," he said. "When he realized something was trying to outrun him he got so damn mad he didn't even know I was there."

The loudspeaker had gone into a stuttering frenzy. Yes, the world's record for six furlongs had been broken. Not only broken, ladies and gentlemen; five seconds had been cut from it. No, the win was not official. Track veterinarians had to examine the horse. Please keep your seats, ladies and gentlemen.

Keep their seats, hell! Every man, woman, and child was going to see at close range the horse that could run like that. There had been tears in my eyes as Eagle rolled down the stretch. You couldn't stay calm when you saw what these people had seen.

The rest of that day sorts itself into blurred episodes. First, the vets checked Eagle's teeth, his registration papers, his date of foaling, and finally rechecked the number tattooed in his lip to make sure he was a two-year-old. Then they found that he had not been stimulated. They also found measurements so unbelievable they seriously questioned whether this animal was a horse. They went into a huddle with the track officials.

There was loose talk of trying to rule the Eagle off the tracks. Carvelliers pointed out that Eagle's papers were in perfect order, his own stallion had sired him, he was a thoroughbred of accepted bloodlines, and there was no way he could legally be ruled ineligible.

"If that horse is allowed to run," said one track official, "who will race against him?"

Croupwell was seated at the conference table, as were most of the other owners. "Gentlemen," he said suavely, "aren't you forgetting the handicapper?"

The job of a handicapper is to figure how much weight each horse is to carry. It is a known fact that a good handicapper can make any field of horses come in almost nose and nose by imposing greater weights on the faster horses. But Croupwell was forgetting something. Usually, only older horses run in handicaps.

I jumped to my feet. "You know two-year-olds are not generally handicapped," I said. "They race under allowance conditions."

"True," said Croupwell. "Two-year-olds usually do run under arbitrary weights. But it is a flexible rule, devised to fit the existing situation. Now that the situation has changed, arbitrarily the weights must be changed."

Carvelliers frowned angrily. "Red Eagle was carrying a hundred and twenty-eight against a hundred and four for the other colts. You would have to impose such weights to bring him down to an ordinary horse that you'd break him down."

Croupwell shrugged. "If that should be true, it is unfortunate. But we have to think of the good of racing. You know that its lifeblood is betting. There will be no betting against this horse in any race it's entered."

Carvelliers rose. "Gentlemen," and the way he said it was an insult, "I have been breeding and racing horses all my life. It has always been my belief that racing was to improve the breed, not kill the best horses." He turned to Ben and me. "At your convenience I would like to speak with you."

Ben and I paid off the loan we'd used for the entry fee, bought ourselves some presentable clothes, and went up to Carvelliers' hotel.

"Hello, Ben; good to see you," he said. "Costello, I owe you an apology. I've disagreed with you on bloodlines for years. You've proven me wrong."

"You've been wrong," I agreed, "but Red Eagle is not the proof. He would have been a good colt if he was normal—maybe the best, but what he actually is has nothing to do with bloodlines."

"Do you think he's a mutation—something new?"

"Completely."

"How much weight do you think he can carry and still win?"

I turned to Ben and Ben said, "He'll win carrying any weight. He'll kill himself to win."

"It's too bad you couldn't have held him," said Carvelliers. "My God, five seconds cut from the record. Don't fool yourself, they'll weight him until even tendons and joints such as his can't stand it. Will you run him regardless?"

"What else will there be to do?"

"Hmmmm. Yes. Well, maybe you're right. But if they break him down, I have a proposition to make you."

We thanked him and left.

Ben and I planned our campaign carefully. "We've got to train him with other horses," Ben told me. "If I can get him used to letting a horse stay a few lengths behind, I can hold him down."

We bought two fairly good platers with the rest of our first winnings and hired neighboring ranch kids to ride them. We began to see men with binoculars on the hills around our track. We let the Eagle loaf and the boys with the binoculars never saw any great times.

The racing world had gone crazy over what Red Eagle had done to the records. But as time passed and the binocular boys reported he wasn't burning up his home track, the writers began to hint that it had been a freak performance—certainly remarkable, but could he do it again? This was the attitude we wanted. Then we put Red Eagle in his second race, this one a mile and a sixteenth.

It was a big stakes race for two-year-olds. We didn't enter him until the last minute. Even so, the news got around and the track had never had such a large attendance and such little betting. The people didn't dare bet against the Eagle, but he had only run at six furlongs and they weren't ready to believe in him and bet on him to run a distance. Because of the low pari-mutuel take, we were very unpopular with the officials of that track.

"If there's any way you can do it," I told Ben, "hold him at the gate."

"I'll hold him if I can."

By this time Red Eagle had become used to other horses and would come out of the gate running easily. When they sprung the gate on those crack two-year-olds that day, Ben had a tight rein and the pack opened a length on the Eagle before he understood he'd been double-crossed. When he saw horses *ahead* of him he went crazy.

He swung far outside and caught the pack before they were in front of the stands. He'd opened five lengths at the first turn. He continued to accelerate in the back stretch, and the crowd had gone crazy too. When he turned into the stretch the nearest thing to him was the starting gate the attendants hadn't quite had time to pull out of the way. Eagle swerved wide to miss the gate and then, as if the gate had made him madder, really turned it on. When he crossed the finish line the first horse behind him hadn't entered the stretch. I sat down weakly and cried. He had cut *ten* seconds off the world's record for a mile and a sixteenth.

The pandemonium did not subside when the race was over. Front-page headlines all over the world said "New Wonder Horse Turns Racing World Topsy-turvy." That was an understatement.

"The next time we run him," I told Ben, "they'll put two sacks of feed and a bale of hay on him."

Ben was gazing off into the distance. "You can't imagine what it's like to sit on all that power and watch a field of horses go by you backwards, blip, like that. You know something, Cos? He still wasn't flat out."

"Fine," I said sarcastically. "We'll run him against Mercedes and Jaguars."

Well, they weighted him. The handicapper called for one hundred thirty-seven pounds. It was an unheard-of weight for a two-year-old to carry, but it wasn't as bad as I had expected.

At home we put the one thirty-seven on him and eased him along for a few weeks. He didn't seem to notice the weight. The first time Ben let him out he broke his own record. I kept tabs on his legs and he never heated in the joints or swelled.

We entered him in the next race to come up. It rained for two days before the race and the track was a sea of mud. Some thought the "flying machine," as Red Eagle was beginning to be called, could not set his blazing pace in mud.

"What do you think?" I asked Ben. "He's never run in mud."

"Hell, Cos, that horse don't notice what he's running on. He just feels the pressure of something behind him trying to outrun him and it pushes him like a jet."

Ben was right. When the pack came out of the gate that day, Red Eagle squirted ahead like a watermelon seed squeezed from between your fingers. He sprayed the pack briefly with mud, then blithely left them, and when he came down the stretch he was completely alone.

During the next several races, three things became apparent. First, the handicapper had no measuring stick to figure what weight Eagle should carry. They called for one hundred forty, forty-two, then forty-five, and Eagle came down the stretch alone. The second thing became apparent after Eagle had won carrying one forty-five. His next race he started alone. No one would enter against him. Third, Eagle was drawing the greatest crowds in the history of racing.

There were two big races left that season. They were one day and a thousand miles apart. The officials at both tracks were in a dilemma. Whichever race Eagle entered would have a huge crowd, but it would be a walkaway and that crowd would bet its last dollar on Eagle, because the track was required by law to pay ten cents on the dollar. The officials resolved their dilemma by using the old adage: *You can stop a freight train if you put enough weight on it.* Red Eagle was required to carry the unheard-of weight of one hundred and seventy pounds. Thus they hoped to encourage other owners to race against us and at the same time they'd have Eagle's drawing power.

Ben grew obstinate. "I don't want to hurt him and that weight'll break him down."

"Great," I replied. "Two worn-out old duffers with the world's greatest horse end up with two platers, a sand-hills ranch, and the winnings from a few races."

"I know how you feel," said Ben. "The only thing you could have got out of this was money, but I get to ride him."

"Well," I said, trying to be philosophical about it, "I get to watch him and that's almost as good as riding him." I stopped and grabbed Ben's arm. "What did I say?"

Ben jerked his arm away. "You gone nuts?"

"Get to watch him! Ben, what's happened every time the Eagle's run?"

"He's broke a record," said Ben matter-of-factly.

"He's sent several thousand people into hysterics," I amended.

Ben looked at me. "Are you thinking people would pay to see just one horse run?"

"Has there ever been more than one when the Eagle's run? Come on. We're going to enter him."

We entered Eagle in the next to the last race of the season. What I'd expected happened. All the other owners pulled out. They weren't having any of the Eagle even carrying a hundred and seventy pounds. They all entered in the last race. No horse, not even the Eagle—they thought—had the kind of stamina to make two efforts on successive days with a plane trip sandwiched between, so they felt safe.

The officials at the second track were jubilant. They had the largest field they had ever run. The officials at the first track had apoplexy. They wanted to talk to us. They offered plane fare and I flew down.

"Would you consider an arrangement," they asked, "whereby you would withdraw your horse?"

"I would not," I replied.

"The public won't attend a walkaway," they groaned, "even with the drawing power of your horse." What they were thinking of was that ten cents on the dollar.

"That's where you're wrong," I told them. "Advertise that the wonder horse is running unweighted against his own record and you'll have a sellout."

Legally, they could not call off the race, so they had to agree.

On the way home I stopped off at Carvelliers'. We had a long talk and drew up an agreement. "It'll work," I said. "I know it will."

"Yes," agreed Carvelliers, "it will work, but you must persuade Ben to run him just once carrying the hundred and seventy. We've got to scare the whole racing world to death."

"I'll persuade him," I promised.

When I got home I took Ben aside. "Ben," I said, "every cow horse has to carry more than a hundred and seventy pounds."

"Yeah, but a cow horse don't run a mile in just over a minute."

"Nevertheless," I said, "he'll run as fast as he can carrying that weight and it doesn't hurt him."

"But a cow horse has pasterns and joints like a work horse. They just ain't built like a thoroughbred."

"Neither is Red Eagle," I answered.

"What's this all about? You already arranged for him not to carry any weight."

"That's for the first race."

"*First race!* You ain't thinkin' of runnin' in both of them?"

"Yes, and that second one will be his last race. I'll never ask you to ride him carrying that kind of weight again."

"You ought to be ashamed to ask me to ride him carrying it at all." Then what I had said sunk in. "*Last* race! How do you know it'll be his last race?"

"I forgot to tell you I had a talk with Carvelliers."

"So you had a talk with Carvelliers. So what?"

"Ben," I pleaded, "trust me. See what the Eagle can do with a hundred and seventy."

"All right," said Ben grudgingly, "but I ain't goin' to turn him on."

"Turn him on!" I snorted. "You ain't ever been able to turn him off."

Ben was surprised but I wasn't when Red Eagle galloped easily under the weight. Ben rode him for a week before he got up the nerve to let him run. Eagle was still way ahead of every record except his own. He stayed sound.

When we entered him in the second race all but five owners withdrew their horses. These five knew their animals were the best of that season, barring our colt. And they believed that the Eagle after a plane ride, a run the day before, and carrying a hundred and seventy pounds was fair competition.

At the first track Eagle ran unweighted before a packed stand. The people jumped and shouted with excitement as the red streak flowed around the track, racing the second hand of the huge clock that had been erected in front of the odds board. Ben was worried about the coming race and only let him cut a second off his previous record. But that was enough. The crowd went mad. And I had the last ammunition I needed.

The next day dawned clear and sunny. The track was fast. Every seat in the stand was sold and the infield was packed. The press boxes overflowed with writers, anxiously waiting to report to the world what the wonder horse would do. The crowd that day didn't have to be told. They bet their last dollar on him to win.

Well, it's all history now. Red Eagle, carrying one hundred and seventy pounds, beat the next fastest horse five lengths. All the fences in front of the stands were torn down by the crowd trying to get a close look at the Eagle. The track lost a fortune and three officials had heart attacks.

A meeting was called and they pleaded with us to remove our horse from competition.

"Gentlemen," I said, "we'll make you a proposition. You noticed yesterday that the gate for Eagle's exhibition was the largest that track ever had. Do you understand? People will pay to watch Eagle run against time. If you'll guarantee us two exhibitions a season at each major track and give us sixty per cent of the gate, we'll agree never to run the Eagle in competition."

It was such a logical move that they wondered they hadn't thought of it themselves. It worked out beautifully. Owners of ordinary horses could run them with the conviction that they would at least be somewhere in the stretch when the race finished. The officials were happy, because not only was racing secure again, but they made money out of their forty per cent of the gates of Eagle's exhibitions. And we were happy, because we made even more money. Everything has been serene for three seasons. But I'm a little concerned about next year.

I forgot to tell you the arrangement Carvelliers and I had made. First, we had discussed a little-known aspect of mutations: namely, that they pass on to their offspring their new characteristics. Carvelliers has fifty brood mares on his breeding farm, and Red Eagle proved so sure at stud that next season fifty carbon copies of him will be hitting the tracks. You'd never believe it, but they run just like their sire, and Ben and I own fifty per cent of each of them. Ben feels somewhat badly about it, but, as I pointed out, we only promised not to run the Eagle.

Cow Country Critters

Stan Hoig

Whenever cowboys weren't stretching their imaginations about the weather, they were generally dreaming up some wild yarns about the animals of the range country. Because cowboys lived close to nature, they understood and respected animal life. A range-wise man could foretell a bad winter by the coyote's extra-heavy fur or from noticing the beaver stocking up on saplings. Animals often offered the only companionship for long periods in the cowboy's life and, through intimate contact, he came to see their "human side" and to understand himself better as a "human animal."

Once a cow hand who had attended a fancy dinner party described himself as feeling like "an old ranch rooster flappin' his wings and tryin' to fly south in the winter."

Such application of human traits to animal life offered much possibility to the cowboys of the range and resulted in some of their most hilarious "windies." The intelligence of animals, for which the cowboy had a high regard, was generally the ignition subject for a barrage of high-soaring cowboy oratory which might include anything from hydrophobic skunks to rooter-dogs, a cross between a bulldog and a wild Mexican hog which was used to root out tarantulas and harvest goober peas. One story would lead to another until, at last, someone had produced the topper of them all.

A group of cowboys was sitting around arguing one lazy afternoon when one puncher began to brag about his dog, claiming that it was undoubtedly the smartest dog he had ever seen. He said that the dog had once been caught in a wolf trap by the tail.

"What yuh reckon that dog did?" he asked.

"Pulled up the stake and dragged it an' the trap back to the ranch," a waddie suggested.

The owner of the dog shook his head.

"Jes' turned around and bit his tail off," another tried.

"Naw, he didn't do none of them fool things."

"What did he do, then?"

"Why, he done jes' what any other sensible dog would've done. He jes' set up a howl and kept it up until I heard him and took the trap offen his tail!"

A cowboy who had been listening to the conversation shook his head.

"Wal, now," he said. "I reckon I've never owned such a smart dog, but I did own an ol' hoss one time that was about the *dumbest* critter I ever did see. I'll tell yuh what that fool horse did one night when I drunk too much likker and passed out in town. He picked me up and slung me on his back and carried me twenty miles to the ranch. When he got me there, he pulled off my boots with his teeth and nosed me inta my bunk. Then he went to the kitchen, fixed up a pot of coffee, and brung me a cup all fixed up with cream and sugar. Then the next day I had a hangover, and he went out all by hisself and dug post holes all day so's the boss would let me sleep. When I woke up and found out what that fool hoss had done, I cussed him fer two days without stoppin' and wished 'im off on a greener which was passin' by. It was good riddance, too!"

"I'd say that was a pretty smart horse," observed a listener. "What in the world did you get rid of him for?"

"Smart, heck! Who ever heard of a real cowboy usin' cream and sugar in his coffee? No wonder I had such a turrible hangover!"

"Thet reminds me," piped up another waddie, "of a hoss a friend of mine down in Texas once owned. This here friend was plum' foolish over quail huntin', but he didn't have any bird dog. But he got to thinkin' that, since a cayuse is supposed to be the smartest animal alive, it ought to be able to do anything that a bird dog could do, so he taught it to point birds. It worked out pretty well, and he used that ol' hoss all one winter to hunt quail. But, come spring, this friend needed some breakin' out clothes, and he sold the hoss to a neighbor. But when the man took the hoss, my friend plum' fergot to tell him about its unusual ability. The next day the man came back with the animal and demanded his money back.

" 'Whut's wrong?' my friend asks.

" 'Wrong?' sez the new owner who is plainly disgusted. 'Heck, I can't even get the fool animal in the barn. Ever' time I try, he stops dead still with one foot lifted an' sticks his tail straight up in the air.'

"My friend thinks this over for a minute, then asks, 'You don't by any chance have some chickens around yore place, do you?'

" 'Why, yes,' sez the other, 'as a matter of fact, I got a chicken pen right next to the barn. Why?'

" 'Wal,' sez my friend, 'You don't have a thing to worry about, then. The next time that ol' hoss balks at the door, all you gotta do is shoot off yore gun and holler, "Missed again!" and he'll go right on in.' "

After this had been digested by all concerned, another waddie cleared his throat.

"That brings to mind," he said, "ol' Peg-Leg Dooley, who onc't had a rattlesnake for a pet. Now, you gents may figger I'm tryin' to string up a bunch o' nonsense, but I'll explain 'zactly how it happened. An', by the way, how ol' Pete got that peg leg.

"It seems ol' Pete was up in Oklahoma Territory one fall an' had to make camp in that shinnery country. Wal, he had heard how that country was full o' rattlesnakes, so he figgered he'd tie a hammock up between two shinnery trees when he bedded down. It was pretty dark by that time, an' it was only after considerable gropin' 'round that Pete got his hammock tied up. Durin' the night he felt that hammock swingin' quite a bit, but he blamed it on the Oklahoma wind. But the next morning when he woke up, derned if he didn't find that he had tied that hammock up with a pair of live rattlers!

"Wal, ol' Pete was pretty skitterish after that an' packed up as quick as he could an' started to kite outa there. But about that time his hoss stepped in a gopher hole an' pinned him to the ground. Pete was in a turrible fix an' thought he was doomed to die right there, but he got an idea that saved his life. He walked to the nearest ranch an' borrowed an axe. Then he came back and chopped off his leg and set hisself free.

"Then, after Pete had cut him a peg leg outa a shin-oak tree, he skedaddled for home. When he got there, he found a baby rattlesnake which had struck him on the peg leg an' hadn't been able to get loose. It was a cute lil' critter, an' Pete decided to keep him for sort of a combination pet an' souveynir of his visit to Oklahomy.

"After that, Pete became real attached to that rattlesnake, which he named Elmer, an' Elmer to him. In fact, Elmer got so he was a regular watchdog an' guarded Pete's shack. One night, while Pete was gone, a thief busted into the shack, an' Elmer was on the job. He captured that ol' robber by wrappin' hisself around one o' the feller's legs an' a leg o' the table. Then he stuck his tail through the keyhole o' the door an' rattled until the law came.

"By and by Elmer grew up into one o' the biggest rattlesnakes anybody had ever seen. He wasn't so long, but he was about a foot thick. It got so he was the talk o' the whole country, an' ol' P. T. Barnum came down an' offered to buy him off Pete. But Pete was plum' sentimental about that snake, like I said, an' wouldn't let him go. But he got to thinkin' that he couldn't stand in the way o' fame an' fortune fer Elmer, an' agreed to loan him out to the circus.

"They stuck Elmer in a box an' hied him off in the baggage car of a train. Well, after a while Elmer got lonesome an' chewed his way outa the box. About that time the train started up a steep grade an' the couplin' busted. So what do you think ol' Elmer did? Why, he wrapped his head 'round one brake wheel and his tail 'round the other an' held the train together until they reached the next station! But all that strain on Elmer stretched him out until he was about thirty feet long. The circus had to advertise him as a boa constrictor instead of a rattlesnake!"

It was time for one of the older hands to clear his throat and lope off on a yarn.

"Onc't, about twenty-thirty years ago when I wuz jes' a button, I wuz ridin' fer ol' Jim Creagor down on the border. Ol' Jim wuz as good a boss as a man ever hired on with, but sometimes he got the craziest ideas you ever heard of 'n wuz as stubborn as a longhorn bull about 'em. But all of us hard-ridin', fast-shootin' riders of the range managed to overlook most of ol' Jim's crazy notions 'n got along fine. That is, we did until the day he went down to Mexico City 'n came home with this fightin' game rooster.

"Right away it's clear that this ol' rooster 'n us cowboys ain't goin' to get along. He seems to figger right off that he's the king of the camp 'n struts 'round like he owned the place. Not that we cow pokes wuz foolish 'nough to get jealous of a lil' ol' chicken, but it kinda got under our skin the way he stuck his nose up at us. Worse'n that, ever' time we'd get in his way, that rooster'd tie off into a real temper'mental fit 'n come at us with spurs flashin'.

"Course our legs wuz pertected by our boots, but it wuz kinda like havin' a town dog yappin' at your heels. It got so we wuz walkin' 'round with one eye peeled in fear this chicken'd stage one of his attacks. Wal, we finally had all of that we could take, so we held a meetin' of the crew 'n kangarooed that bird. The decision was to execute him fer gen'ral misbehavior.

"But the minute we took out after him, he saw we wuz up to no good fer him. After that, he wuz no easy bird to catch, 'n he sure gave us eighteen waddies a go fer our money. A big, red-headed waddie by the name of Charlie Graham almost had him trapped on the barn roof. Charlie made a wild grab 'n ended up on the corral floor with a busted leg. But finally we got that rooster trapped between the corral fence 'n the barn, 'n though he put up plenty of fight he was overpowered by the force of numbers. Let me tell you, we wuz a scratched 'n bleedin' 'n mad bunch of cowboys by the time we got that rooster under control.

"We tied a blindfold over his eyes an' stood him up against a haystack 'n lined up twelve of our best shots fer a firin' squad. But jes' then ol' Jim came ridin' up 'n stopped the whole show. He said we ought to be ashamed of ourselves fer pickin' on sech a poor, defenseless chicken, made us untie 'im, 'n swore he'd fire the firs' so-'n-so that molest'd that bird without just cause.

"Wal, as you can imagine, after that things got even worse. That got to be the most overbearin' fowl I ever seen in my life. He'd slip up between our horses' legs 'n crow 'n make them range-wild cayuses so skeerish that it wuzn't even safe fer a bunch of bronc-bustin' experts like us. An' sometimes he'd come to the bunkhouse winder at two or three o'clock in the morning, jes' when we wuz sleepin' the soundest, 'n start crowin'. But he wuz too smart to ever bother us when the boss was around. An' we knew it would mean our job if we molest'd that chicken without a good reason.

"Meanwhile ol' Charlie Graham had been laid up with that broken leg, 'n all he did wuz sit around all day 'n nurse his hatred for that loud-lunged fowl. Then, one day, he got an inspiration 'n promised the boys that when they came in from work that night there'd be no more Mr. Rooster at that ranch.

"The boys had a hard time keepin' their minds on their chores that day in their eagerness to get back 'n see what Charlie had up his sleeve. Some bet Charlie wouldn't have the nerve to buck ol' Jim's orders, but when we rode in that night the firs' thing we saw wuz the carcass of that rooster lyin' in the yard about thirty feet from its head. Charlie had a long, serious look on his face which warned us to keep our mouths shut about the hull thing. It wuzn't until later, in the bunkhouse, that Charlie started to laffin' so hard he doubled up on the floor 'n rolled around. Finally, when he got over his hysterics, he told us what had happened.

"After we had rode out, Charlie had gone to the barn 'n soaked a batch of blackberries in some rotgut whisky which he had cached away fer emergencies. Then he tossed a couple of handfuls out in the corral where that rooster jes' gobbled 'em up like they wuz a real delight. But after he had eat about fifteen blackberries, that ol' chicken began to wobble around on his legs 'n when he'd peck at a berry he'd miss it about four inches.

"About that time the boss came outa the house 'n started away on his horse. But he never got to where he was goin', fer jes' then that rooster saw him, threw back his head 'n let out a mighty crow you could hear the length of the Brazos. An' before ol' Jim knew what wuz goin' on, that rooster charged up 'n sank a spur into the shank of Jim's hoss.

"Wal, to hear ol' Charlie tell it, the boss musta had time to recite the Lord's Prayer twenty times 'twixt the time he left that hoss's back 'n when he landed on his chin in the yard. An' when Jim set up 'n saw his prize game cock chasin' his hoss around the yard, he wuz madder'n twenty-nine hornets fightin' over a dead grasshopper. He got up and went into the house, 'n when he came out he had his .30-30 in his hands. It only took one shot to fix up Mr. Rooster.

"It wuz then that Charlie wandered up 'n inquired, innocent-like, as to why the boss had gone and shot that poor, defenseless chicken. Ol' Jim didn't have any answer at firs', 'n then he got that stubborn look on his face 'n said, 'He wuz guilty of disturbing the peace!' An' that wuz the last word he ever said about his prize game cock."

It was then that the stranger stepped up and licked his lips solemn-like.

"Speakin' of chickens," he said, "calls to mind the time I decided to give up cowboyin' and go into the chicken business. And all because one day I got to thinkin' about how I could make a million dollars by mixin' up the breedin' a mite so's to get a chicken with a lot of thigh and breast and not much neck. I took one kind of chicken that was a squat little critter with a short neck and a big breast and crossed it with another kind that was built somethin' like a road runner, with big feet and long legs which made it stand about three feet tall. But somehow the product of my efforts wasn't at all like I expected.

"When the firs' bunch hatched, it turned out they was the strangest lookin' critters you ever saw. Their legs was so long and their necks so short that they couldn't reach the ground to feed themselves. I had to fix up a special table for 'em so's they wouldn't starve to death. And then next I found out that their feet was so big that ever' time the wind blew one over, it couldn't get back up by itself. It got so's I spent all my time runnin' around settin' em back right-side up.

"I was about to give the whole thing up but, luckily for me, that was the year of the great grasshopper plague. My chickens could catch about any kind of a bug that made the mistake of gettin' in the air, 'cause with them long legs they was the fastest things in the country. I used to set on my back porch and watch them chicks by the hour as they galloped to and fro around the hills catching grasshoppers, and I began to feel real proud and sentimental towards 'em.

"But the day came when I knew I had to start reapin' a return on my experiment, so I decided to take a bunch of the critters to market. I found, howsomever, that they was too tall to fit into a chicken crate like they was supposed to, and I had to turn the crate up sideways to get 'em in it. When I got to town I ran smack into a tourist party who was plum' astounded when I told that what I got in my crate is chickens. One lady decided to buy one of 'em as a souveynir of her trip out to the woolly West.

"It was about a month later that I got a letter from this Eastern lady tellin' me how that bird had died out of homesickness for the wide open spaces where it could run and romp in freedom. After that, I decided against sellin' any more of the birds unless the buyer promised to kill it and eat it quick, without makin' it suffer. But this lady also sent back the carcass of the bird which she had tried to eat, and requested that I get her teeth loose from it and send 'em back.

"Meanwhile, my other birds was gettin' friskier by the day, and I was havin' trouble keepin' 'em in their pens since they was gettin' so's they could run and jump clean over a ten-foot fence. They got so rambunctious, in fact, that I was wearin' myself out when I went to call 'em in for chuck. Finally, one day I got the idea of fixin' up a horn and trainin' those chickens to come runnin' at the honk-honk of that horn.

"You'd be surprised how quick my chickens was to learn about that honk-honk. I was real proud of 'em, and I named 'em the Honk-honk breed. We was gettin' along jes' fine until one day one of them automobeels came jarrin' down the road and, jes' as it passed my chicken ranch, it let out a honk-honk. Wal, you talk about a stampede! In a flash ever' last head of my Honk-honks sailed over my fence and took out after that car and outran it and scared the livin' daylights out of the driver.

"It got so's ever' time a car would come whizzin' by, my Honk-

honks would be waitin' for it and then outrun it jes' to show off. I saw my chance to make that fortune I was after, and I started puttin' my birds up against any man, horse, or machine in those parts and bettin' on 'em. It was then that my faith in my Honk-honk birds began to pay off in cash."

Someone coughed and finally asked the question.

"If you wuz makin' so much money, how come you ain't in the chicken bizness today?"

"Wal, it's like this," the stranger explained. "Them Honk-honk hens jes' wasn't used to all that success and glory. It was race suicide, that's what it was. They got so gawd-awful big-headed and haughty that they was too proud to stoop so low as to lay an egg."

In Dodge City, one of the woolliest of trail towns, a tinhorn made the mistake of arguing over cards with Dodge's marshal, Mysterious Dave Mather. Dave was no slow man with a six gun, having put six on the deceased list, all in one night and in one sitting. The gambler drew, and Dave drew faster. He not only hit his man, but the bullet continued on through his victim killing a hound dog that happened to be around the saloon.

Now, the incident would have been closed and forgotten if it had been merely a matter of burying one dead tinhorn gambler. But, as it was, the hound dog happened to belong to a man named Jim Kelly. Kelly owned only something less than a hundred dogs which he kept to chase jack rabbits, antelope, and coyotes. To some he was known as "Dog Kelly," but not to his face. Kelly was an Irishman with a Irish-sized temper and, when he heard that Dave had killed one of his dogs, he promptly went looking for him with a sawed-off shotgun.

Dave, however, had been hit on the top of his head by som plaster which had been knocked loose by the gambler's shot, and he had gone to get his head wound fixed. When Kelly stormed into the saloon, the boys tried to cool him off about the dog and convince him that it was just an accident. But Kelly claimed that Dave, marshal or not, had no business shooting his gun off in the saloon without first looking to see if any of Kelly's dogs were around. They finally pacified Kelly by promising to bury the dog with military honors and to hold an inquest for the dead critter.

Someone sent for O. B. "Joyful" Brown, the coroner, to hold the inquest. A jury was impaneled, and several witnesses testified that they had never seen the dog take a drink and therefore it was doubtful if it had any business in the saloon anyhow. Other witnesses testified that Dave's gun had hung fire, and that if the dog had been on guard it could have jumped out of the window. Anyhow, the dog should have been out chasing jack rabbits, or at least kept one eye on Dave's gun which had a habit of going off unexpectedly.

The jury brought in the verdict that the dog they were then sitting on came to its death by a bullet fired from a gun in the hands of Dave Mather, better known as "Mysterious Dave," and that the shooting was done in self-defense and was perfectly justified as any dog should know better than to go to sleep in a Dodge City saloon.

This cooled Dog Kelly off somewhat but, to further pacify the Irishman, a hearse was hired and the famous Dodge City Cowboy Band led a regular funeral procession to Boot Hill where the dog was buried. A sermon was said over it, and then the boys all joined together in singing "The Cowboy's Lament." When it was over, Kelly went home with tears flowing down his cheeks, and Mysterious Dave, the gun-slinging marshal of Dodge City, breathed a sigh of relief and ordered the undertaker to clean up the carcass of the gambler from the saloon floor. The tinhorn was buried quietly and without ceremony.

Harold Peavey's Fast Cow

George Cronyn

When Harold Peavey graduated from the State Agricultural College and won a prize in oratory on "The Plow Is Mightier Than the Pen," we all thought he was a pretty smart boy, but when he leased the Eppingwell place on shares we changed our mind. The last family that took it worked five years and then they owed Old Lady Eppingwell five hundred and the bank another odd thousand. Parks, the man's name was, told me all he got out of it was a lame back and three more kids to raise.

So, when I saw smoke coming out of the chimney after two years when there wasn't any, I went over to call on my nearest neighbor. He was just carrying in a load of apple wood as I came in the front gate and, seeing me, he put it down.

"Hello, Bud," I says, "how's tricks?"

"Oke," he says, grinning. He was a nice-looking kid, standing over six feet, with a good set of teeth and hair that needed pruning. "Are you Pete Crumm?"

"Same," I says. "I used to know your folks at Medford. Your dad did me on a lumber deal, but I guess he's got you well educated."

"I don't know," he says thoughtfully. "I know all the spray formulas and the life history of the Woolly Aphis but I guess I've got plenty to learn."

"You have," I says, looking out over the twenty-seven acres of Eppingwell's Folly that was called an apple ranch. "Plenty. Your trees will stand a little pruning."

"Yes," he says. "They're pretty brushy. I've been working a couple of days and I've got twelve trees pruned."

"Not bad," I says. "You've only got two months' work ahead of you pruning at that rate, and it's the middle of March now. And there's another three weeks repairing the irrigation flumes that are all shot to hell. And maybe a week or two clearing the meadow patch—"

"You mean, I've got work ahead of me?"

"Not more'n fifteen hours a day. Have you got a good plow team?"

"None better. I've made a deal with Morrison to work his team and plow one day a week in return for helping him three days."

"I see. That leaves you four days for your own work, counting Sundays."

"Sundays I got a job driving the Sunday school bus."

"Well then," I says, "everything's jake. You can just sit down and take it easy the rest of the time. When are you getting a wife to do the house chores and cooking?"

"Not till I've saved about three hundred dollars," he says.

"I see," I says. "You'd as leave stay a bachelor."

"No, I wouldn't. I'd like to start a family." He looked out over the place in a sort of dreamy way. "And I'd like to have·a cow." He picked up his chunks of apple wood and said, "It's a good view from the house here, with old Mount Sherman and Pine Butte and—"

"I see you've painted your hen house," I says.

"Yes," he says. "It matches up with the scenery. Morrison says he's got a good cow, a heifer. Black Jersey. I never heard of a black Jersey before. There can't be many of 'em."

"I've heard of *that* black Jersey," I says. "Her name is Mabel, but I don't know if I'd call her a cow."

"Why not?" he asks in surprise.

"Well," I says, "I don't know. It just never struck me that way. When are you getting her?"

"Tomorrow."

"I'll drive you over in my gas wagon." I says. "It's a mile and a half to Morrison's—quite a piece to lead Mabel."

So the next day about seven in the morning, after about a dozen flapjacks, I tuned up the old bus and drove over to pick up Harold. There was a lot of smoke coming out of the kitchen door and when I stepped inside at first I couldn't see nothing but I could hear Harold coughing and choking around the wood stove.

"Morning," I says. "How's tricks?"

"It's the prunes," he sort of gasped. "I left 'em to cook while I started running a ditch through the meadow. I guess there wasn't enough water."

"Maybe there was too much prunes," I suggested. "Can you salvage any?"

"Sure!" he says. "The top layer is only burnt on one side. Would you care for any?"

"No," I says. "Prunes is a fruit that just spoils in me. I swell all up."

"Well," he says, scraping off half a dozen from the top, "they're full of vitamins."

"I know," I says. "That's why we always buy 'em in the package. The vitamins don't get into the packages."

After he ate as much as he could stand of the prunes and drunk what he said was coffee we climbed in the bus and drove over to Morrison's. On the way over I asked him how much Morrison was asking for the heifer.

"Only $35.50," he said, "and she's just coming fresh."

"What's the fifty cents for?"

"That's for the rope, and a dollar for the halter, so she really only comes to $34."

"Cheap enough," I says, "if she milks."

"She'll milk all right," he says hopefully. "Morrison guarantees that."

"Morrison guaranteed me a Poland China sow once," I says. "She wasn't no good raising pigs but she made fair to middling bacon. Old man Morrison's girl Sadie has got considerable of a shape."

"I met her at the Grange dance," the kid sort of stammered, "and I noticed she had blue eyes."

"Blue as a new pair of jumpers," I says. "And them lips of hers are just made for pecking at. She acts sort of stand-offish but if a fellow would just grab her—"

"Look at the sun," he says, "on Mount Sherman. The way it hits that glacier is something pretty!"

Old man Morrison was standing in the front yard with his two boys and the extra hand. The older boy, Perley, was coiling a rope and the young one, Sid, was mending an old halter with a piece of bailing wire. Old man Morrison looked as mean as ever but when he saw us drive in he brightened up like a winter sunset.

"Hello, Mr. Peavey," he says. "Hello, Pete. You're up bright and early."

"The early buzzard catches the snake," I says. "How's all the lawsuits?"

"Them lawyers," he says, "keep ahounding me. In the end they take all. But what's a poor man to do?"

"Keep out of court," I says. "Where's the heifer?"

"Down in the pasture," he says. "We're all fixed to bring her in."

"I mean Sadie," I says.

"Oh she!" he grunts. "She stays abed 'till 'most noontime. Says the morning air is bad for her complexion. If I thought tanning her hide would do any good—"

"Here's ten dollars down," says Harold stiffly, "and I'll pay the rest at the beginning of next month."

"You wouldn't need a receipt, I take it, Mr. Peavey?"

He was starting to say no when I says, "You bet. Business is business. You just write out the receipt while we go down and fetch the heifer."

"The boys'll do that for you," he says, scowling at me. "They know her better."

We went on in the kitchen where Mrs. Morrison was cooking up a mess of apples. The kitchen was full of the week's wash, the tables was heaped with dirty dishes, and a couple of kids was crawling on the floor playing with the butcher knife and a meat chopper.

"You men must be hungry," she says. "Set down and have some apple sauce."

"I'm not hungry," I says, looking around the kitchen, "but maybe Harold here is. He's batching."

"Poor man! He must be starved," she says, and began to ladle apple sauce into a soup bowl that you could see just had oatmeal in it. Mrs. Morrison is good hearted even if she has got a figure like a female walrus.

Harold made a noise in his throat, meaning "No, thank you," but hunger got the best of him and he began wolfing down the sauce.

"Sadie has been speaking of you, Mr. Peavey," says Mrs. Morrison, throwing a bunch of diapers into the washtub. "She heard all about your taking the prize for that speech on 'The Club Is Mightier than the Pen,' and she thinks you dance real graceful. She'll be sorry to miss you. Maybe if I give her a call, she might come down."

"Oh," says Harold, gurgling into the apple sauce. "Don't—please don't disturb her!"

"It's all right," she says. "Sadie was going to town today anyhow." And rolling over to the upstairs door, she calls out, "Sa-die!"

After a few minutes, while I was trying to keep one of the kids from untying my shoelace, a voice like a sick cat calls down, "What do you want, ma? Can't you ever let me be when I'm trying to get a little rest?"

"There's a young man here to see you," says the Missus. "And he ain't got long to stay."

"Who is it? What does he want to see me for so early in the morning? Can't he come back in the afternoon? Who is it, anyway?"

"It's Mr. Peavey and he's taking his cow home."

"Oh!" said the voice, sweet as honey. "Tell him to stop a while and I'll be right down!"

I looked at Harold. He had his spoon full of apple sauce half way to his mouth and he'd forgotten about the next bit. His expression was like a calf when it hears the milk pail rattle—sort of eager and vacant.

"Gorry!" I thinks to myself. "The boy is caught! Hope Sadie don't fill out like her ma!"

Just then old man Morrison stuck his head in the outside door.

"The heifer's come up. You better take her right along. She's kind of restive."

Harold looked like he'd as lief stay there till moonrise but I took him by the elbow and he got up, pushing back the wobbly kitchen chair. I stooped down to tie the shoelace one of the brats had been playing with and when I looked up again Sadie was standing at the foot of the stairs. I will say, she looked pretty, if a man could stand her ways. Her hair was touseled but she'd thrown it up in a coil like a bundle of corn silk, and she had a pink kimono with yellow dots that set off her figure. There aren't many girls that look good just out of bed, but Sadie could get away with it, rubbing her eyes and half smiling at Harold.

"I'm so glad you came over to see me, Harold," she says, holding out her hand. "It was nice of you!"

"Well," says Harold, turning red, "I don't usually come around when people are in bed but I had to get my cow—"

"Oh," she says coolly, "the cow, of course! I hope you like her! Some day when your mind isn't taken up with your cow you might call around, if I'm home. Anyway, ma'll be here."

That's the way with the female, always trying to knock the pins out from under a man.

Harold gulped and I says, "He'll be back, missie, don't you worry. He don't give all his time to cows, he's—"

Right then we heard a commotion in the yard and old man

Morrison hollering, "Hold her, dod blast it! Keep her out'n them lilies!"

"Well, goodbye, Mr. Penney," says Mrs. Morrison, wiping her sudsy hands on a dish cloth. "I suppose we can call you Harry?"

"Sure, you could!" says Harold. "I'll be around—"

Old man Morrison stuck his head in the door. He looked sort of red-purple and his eyes was bugged out. "Better take the heifer right along home," he says. "She's feelin' skittish this mornin'.."

Harold looked calfish again at Sadie, we shook hands all around, and stepped out into the yard. The heifer was there waiting for us, and at first I couldn't make out exactly what they was doing with her. They had slung a hitch in the rope around her horns. One of the Morrison boys had a hold of one end and the other boy had a hold of the other end, and the extra hand was holding onto her halter rope. But what struck me as curious was the cow herself. The Morrisons had one of these rope swings hung from a big oak tree, that the three middle-size Morrison youngsters played in, and the cow was in the swing. I don't mean setting. She had got her front legs and forepart through it so that the rope was under her belly, and she would take a run, dragging the two Morrisons and the extra hand, until the rope brought her up sharp, then she'd back up, kicking like a steer.

Harold looked at her like he was sort of puzzled and says, "She's pretty active for a cow, ain't she?"

"If it was the deer season," I says, "she'd pass for a young buck."

The fact is, Mabel did look more like a deer than anything. She was small, shiny black, and built lean and slender. Pretty, yes. But I couldn't see her as a milker.

"She's all right," old man Morrison mutters. "She'll give milk that's more'n half cream."

"I'd say she'd give butter, the way she's churning," I says.

Mabel put her head down and stood quiet. Perley Morrison yells, "Pa! Slip the swing out from under! She's all tuckered out!"

Before the old man could get to her, though, she made a lunge and brought the swing down out of the tree. Off she went, headed for the road, with the three boys hanging on for dear life. Luckily, the rope swing hooked onto the gate post as she went through and that held her.

"Well," I says to old man Morrison, "she seems to be stopped at the thirty-yard line. Guess we might as well amble along with her. Would you think maybe she'd go better in front or behind the bus?"

"Back up your car and we'll tie her on behind," he says, sort of gruff. "I'll put a half hitch around her muzzle."

I backed up the Ford, Harold climbed in, and they tied her up to the rear springs, with only about three feet of lead rope. Then they got the swing rope out from under her and untied the other one from her horns. All the while she stood quiet as a lamb, like she was meditating.

"Take it easy," says the extra hand. "You don't want to strain her."

"No," I says, putting the bus into low, "I don't want to—"

Right then she made a dive for the car and tried to climb into the rumble seat where I had two sacks of lime, a peck of oats, and a job lot of tools I had lately bought in town. She had got her front hoofs onto the rumble seat and it looked bad for the car, which is an old sport model and none too strong.

"Keep her out," I says to Harold. "We don't want her riding with us."

There was a cant hook in the rumble seat and Harold managed to yank it out. He shoved the end of it against her chest and she got off the car and tried to climb over the right fender. When she found she couldn't make it she headed off the other way, and the car nearly went into the ditch. I put the machine into second and for the next two minutes she did 'most everything an animal can do without twisting itself into knots. She reared, she bucked, side-stepped, swung from side to side, and played the devil with both fenders. Finally she fell down on her knees and I dragged her a dozen feet before I could stop.

"What this heifer seems to want is exercise," I says to Harold, who was beginning to look grim.

"I'll give it to her!" he says between his teeth, starting to get out.

"What the hell are you doing, Harold?"

"Going to lead her!"

"Don't be a fool! We'll borrow a horse off Jake Lentz down the road a piece and you can herd her back home. It'll be less wear and tear."

"I was fullback on the Ag. eleven and captain of the track team," he says with a stubborn look, "and I'm going to lead my cow home."

"Oke!" I says. "It's your cow."

While he was walking around the car I untied her halter rope, and thinking he would need some extra line to pay out in case of trouble, I tied onto it a length of stout hemp rope, about thirty feet, that was tucked away in the rumble seat. Mabel never made a move. She was still on her knees, like she was praying.

"I'll stay behind you, Harold," I says as I passed over the rope to him, "and if she starts any monkey business, I'll be right there to help out."

Harold went over and gave her a kick and she scrambled to her feet sort of dazed. He began to pull her and she followed along like all the spirit had left her.

"See?" he calls out. "All she needs is the right handling."

He hadn't no more than got the words out of his mouth when that cow got into motion, and she had only one speed, which was high. She spun Harold around and the line started running through his hand like a hauser on a big boat but he had sense enough to wrap the end of it twice around his fist. Or maybe it wasn't such good sense either, for when the line was all paid out he started traveling. I guess he must have been a pretty good runner at college for he sure made tracks, sometimes not hitting the ground for a yard or so. When I caught up with them, my speedometer showed they was going exactly fifteen miles an hour. The road here ran straight for a half a mile before turning off to our places and for the first quarter Mabel didn't slacken a mite. Then she eased up a bit, to about twelve.

"Whoopee!" I yells. "Stick to her, kid! She's a good pace-maker!"

Harold must have begun to lose some of his wind because I noticed he was maneuvering. The orchards came down close to the road at this point, so that some of the trees hung over it. Harold was trying to pick up enough speed on the heifer so's he could swing off and take a turn around a tree with the line and bring her hard to. But every time he'd make for a tree and get part way around, the cow would be so much ahead that he'd be jerked back around and have to try for another tree further down. I saw he wasn't going to make it that way and for fear he'd go on past the turn I stepped on the gas and shot around them, and at the turn I swung the bus sideways, blocking the road. For a minute I thought Mabel was going to jump right over the car, but I yelled bloody Moses and she swerved off down the home stretch. At Harold's gate I pulled the same trick, and so headed her into his barnyard. In another five minutes the two of us had hauled her into the barn and had her tied tight to a post. Then Harold sat down on the manure pile, looking all in.

"Well, boy," I says, "she's beginning to know her master."

After breathing hard for a few minutes he managed to gasp out, "And believe me, she's going to!"

When he had rested a while we came back on up to my place to get some liniment for Mabel's knees that had been badly skinned and Minnie, my old woman, thinking he looked hungry, passed him out a platter of doughnuts and bowl of applesauce. He ate them with relish and drank three cups of strong coffee while he explained a new spray formula for Woolly Aphis. About half-past ten we came back down, as I had volunteered to hold Mabel while he bandaged the knees. I wasn't sure but that we would have to hobble her if she was anything like she had been. He was talking about planting nasturtiums in the front yard when we got to the barn.

"Nasturtiums in a center bed and patches of Golden Glow and maybe phlox—"

"It looks to me as if your barn door got kicked off its hinges, Harold," I says.

The barn was pretty old, a good ten years older than the house, and the barn door was lying flat and one plank had been knocked out of it. We looked inside but there was no Mabel. No cow and no post, either. The post she had been tied to was not a part of the frame; it was just a brace and probably not even toe-nailed. Anyway, it was gone. We looked down the wagon road that led to the meadow and we could see a furrow where she had dragged the post.

"She's a mighty strong and vigorous heifer you got, Harold," I says, "but she won't get far with that post. It's as good as a man could do to lift it, let alone a cow. Maybe it's just as well she took the post, she'll learn what it is to go pulling a man's barn apart. About the time she hits a stump or a ditch with that post, she's going to want to come back and be a nice cow."

Harold snorted. "I'll teach her to be a nice cow!" he growled.

"Is that your 'phone ringing?" I asked. Harold listened.

"Three rings—that's mine! Maybe somebody has caught her. Jake Lentz's place comes down to mine on the other side of the meadow. Maybe Jake has caught her and wants me to come and get her."

"I expect anybody that got her *would* want you to come and fetch her," I suggested.

"I'll go find out," he says.

He was gone quite a spell so I had time to smoke a pipeful, setting on the manure pile. I was thinking about the nature of cows in general, and how if they got off on the wrong hoof they are likely to run wild, like this one, same as some women folks, when he come running down, looking sort of wild-eyed and troubled.

"What's up?" I asks.

"Well! I don't know—damned funny! I can't make head nor tail of it. I guess I'm going nuts or else I didn't hear right."

"Has Jake got the cow?"

"No, but he saw her passing through his orchard. She took down a whole row of young Winter Bananas."

"That's no loss, Harold. The Winter Banana is mighty poor apple. It won't keep and it's losing out in the open market. Now, I had a patch of Winter Bananas that I yanked out—"

"He saw her and ran out of his house and started after her, yelling. She stopped and he thought he had her. He says she couldn't budge that post, walking. But then she made a run and got going with it again at a dead gallop, smashing a row of Delicious—"

"That's too bad! The Delicious is a first-rate fruit. Now, I took down a load—"

"And then she disappeared into the Larson place next to his."

"Well, now that's good! She'll never get across the Larson place. Too much barb-wire fences. They'll stop her! Did you call Larson?"

"Yes, I called Larson, and he said he'd go right out and take a look to see what she'd damaged, and—" Again that queer look came over him and he sort of choked out, "after a few minutes Larson rang me back and said—and said . . . that she was up in one of his trees!"

"Aw, now, Harold! Larson was just kidding you. Larson is a great kidder."

"He didn't sound like he was kidding. He sounded mad. He said, 'You come quick and take your goddamn cow out of my tree before she spoil him!' "

"So he was mad, eh? He shouldn't get mad about a thing like that! It couldn't be a very big tree if she was up in it."

" 'But that's it!' Larson said. 'That cow she's up in my biggest, best walnut tree. Up clear in the top!' "

I got up off the manure pile. "Look here, Harold," I says, "I don't know which of you is lying or is nuts, but we might as well go and find out. I can swallow anything but about a cow in a walnut tree. Why, I know those walnut trees of Larson and nary one is less than thirty feet tall, and it ain't easy to climb a walnut tree, even for a man, without a ladder. And I *know* that cow didn't go up no ladder—not with that post tied to her! Come on, let's go!"

The trail of Mabel was easy enough to follow. It went down into the meadow and then across the meadow to where she'd taken a panel out of the snake fence on the other side. Then we came into Lentz's orchard and we could see where she'd laid down a row of young Winter Bananas, just as if she'd planned to do it—which, no doubt, she had.

"They're not hurt bad," I says, "just scraped on one side, and they'll all have to be staked again."

We also saw where she'd barked the row of Delicious. She had run straight down the row, figuring, I guess that she couldn't turn a corner with that post. Right at the end of the row Lentz's orchard stopped, and all at once I had a hunch about the walnut tree. The orchards in our valley are all laid out on "benches," and some of them mark the boundary lines. Now Jake's place was on a bench lying about thirty feet on the average above Larson's place. It dropped off so sudden that there was just a narrow fringe of alder thicket between the upper orchard and the lower one. Larson was an economical Swede and he had planted right up to the line. Apples wouldn't do any good so close to a high bank so he had put in a row of walnuts and they generally brought in a paying crop.

When we pushed through the thicket we saw Mabel. She was astraddle of a crotch in the walnut tree and for once her head was hanging low, for the halter rope was still attached to the post; it was let out as far as it would go, and the end of the post just barely touched the ground. If the rope had been six inches shorter, Mabel would have broke her neck.

Larson was standing under the tree and when he saw us he began to yell, "Take her out! Do you think I want a cow in my best walnut tree? Do you want to make a fool of me, letting a cow in my tree?"

"Shut up!" I yells back. "You'll make her nervous!"

Jake Lentz had come up and no sooner saw what a fix Mabel was in than he said, "Why, that's nothing! I got a hog out of my sixty-foot well once! Don't cut her halter rope till I get back or she'll start to flounder."

He ambled off and after a while came back with his tractor and a lot of heavy ropes and straps. I climbed into the tree and rigged her out in a sort of harness, slung a strand over a higher limb to hold her from hitting against the bank, then Harold cut the halter rope and Lentz drew her out with his tractor. It took a couple of hours and didn't bother nobody much except Larson, who kept dancing around and cursing underneath the tree.

When Harold unhitched her finally and began to lead her home, she followed along as meek and subdued as any cow.

"How about them trees, and the hire of my tractor, and my own time?" Jake asked.

"Don't worry," says Harold, "I'll come over and work it all out."

"Looks to me, Harold," I says, "as if you was doing more work for that cow than she is for you."

"Never mind," he says, stubborn again, "I'll work it out of her!"

He began working it out of her the next morning and kept it up every day for the next three weeks. I was so busy with bud spraying I didn't have a chance to get over for about a week but I would see him go past with her around 6 A.M. and come back nearly an hour later. The first three mornings she led him, but after he got into training form he led her. And I'm saying, they *traveled!* There was a stretch of road the opposite way from Morrison's, about two mile and a quarter. He told me afterward he'd let her hit her stride the whole way down, then give her five minutes to catch her wind, turn her around and head her back. He didn't get much milk—about a quart a day—but he got plenty of exercise. You'd think Mabel would tire of it. If she did, she didn't give any sign, and he would have to hobble her hind legs when he turned her out in the meadow.

At that, she learned to manage her hind quarters so she could get around, with a motion something like a hobby horse. The funny thing was, so far as milking went, she was docile enough. Just so soon as Harold would set down on the old wobbly milking stool, she'd turn and look at him, contented and satisfied, and if she had been a cat she would have purred.

It came Sunday so I ambled over to see how Harold was making out. He was stirring up something in a big bowl that he said was going to be corn fritters but I told him my stomach was delicate and we fell to talking.

"How's the heifer, Harold?" I says.

"I don't give her any rest in the morning. First thing, I go down and give her a kick—"

"I mean Sadie. How are you and Sadie hitting it off?"

"Oh, Sadie's too high-toned for me. I called her up three times and she said she had a date each time. It's that lawyer, Murfree, from Portland. He's handling a couple of her dad's lawsuits and he's got a

Cadillac. I was coming back from Lentz's Wednesday when they passed me, going lickety-split. Sadie didn't even wave. Well, if she gets him I guess she'll be coming into a little piece of jack. It's jake with me. I guess when I've put in three or four years on this place, I'll pick me a girl who doesn't set too much store by mere wealth."

"If Sadie's set her cap for Murfree, she's not going to win no prize studhorse. He's slicker 'n a whistle and slipperier than a greased pig. Wait till he puts in his bill to the old man. Maybe she won't fancy him so well."

"It makes no difference to me who she fancies," he says. I could see he didn't want to talk about Sadie so I changed the subject to water coring and dry rot. After he had stowed away his mess of corn fritters, or whatever they was, he said, "I want you to come down and see a little contrivance I've rigged up for Mabel. I found something in the barn that's going to improve her disposition a lot."

"A goad?"

"No, I don't believe in using harsh methods in handling a cow. They're like human beings, you have to analyze 'em psychologically, then treat their complexes."

"I've always used Glover's Horse Tonic," I says. "It works for cows the same as horses."

"I don't mean that sort of remedy, Pete. It's for what is wrong in their heads. Now take Mabel. She's got a complex on running. Maybe she was repressed when she was a calf and couldn't run. Now she just *has* to run. Well to treat that, you have to let her run as much as she wants, but you have to direct her running, 'channel' it, as they say."

"I don't know," I says, "about channeling a cow to run. I'd rather channel her to milk."

"That will come later," he says.

We got to the barn and he showed me what he had fixed up for Mabel. It was a racing sulky, all painted bright and new, in green, with red trimming on the wheels.

"By gorry!" I says. "You ain't going to hitch the heifer onto that rig, are you?"

"Sure as shooting!" he says. "And I've greased the wheels and oiled up the harness. I had to adjust the harness. The belly band had to be lengthened, and of course there's no bit. You can't drive a cow like you can a horse—no use trying! And she doesn't need a check rein. She runs with her head up." It was plain that he was mighty proud of his work.

"I'm not throwing a wet blanket on your project, Harold," I says, "but how do you aim to stop her or turn her?"

"I won't have to. If I'm right about this, she'll stop herself and turn around. She does it every morning now. I've conditioned her to do it and she'll keep on."

"I hope you're right, Harold," I says, "but you had better be ready to jump—in case she don't stay in condition."

"I'll tell you, Pete, I intend to try her out tomorrow. I'm pretty sure she'll work into it all right, but I'd like to have you down at the end of the stretch, and if she starts to go through the fence where the road turns, you could stop her with a pitchfork."

"I don't know about stopping her, but I'll be mighty glad to be there and tell you when to jump."

So the next morning I told Minnie I had to have an early breakfast on account of going up to the head-gate to see about the irrigation, and at quarter to six I was driving down to the turn. I hadn't been there five minutes and was just taking the first puff on the corncob when I saw them coming over the rise about a mile away. I will say this for Mabel, she had lots of style and no end of speed as a racer. She had as pretty a pace as any gelding that ever come down a track and she never broke her gait in the whole two miles. When they got nearer it was a fine sight, with the rising sun making the new-painted wheels all a glitter of whizzing spokes and Harold holding onto the reins, which was more for decoration than use as they was fastened onto the halter.

I had jumped from the car and had my pitchfork ready. For a minute I thought I'd have to go into action and was just getting ready to holler to Harold to jump when she pulled up so sudden that Harold went right out of his little seat and landed plumb on her back. He fell off as Mabel came to a dead halt. Then, without his saying a word, she turned around. Off she went again, quick as lightning, and Harold, being taken by surprise, stood there with his mouth open.

"Oh well," he says, "it's no use my trying to catch her. She'll run right to the barn."

"Harold," I says, "you sure have got confidence in that cow!"

"It isn't confidence in her," he says. "I just know my psychology."

"Harold," I says, "I hope Larson isn't getting home from one of his all-night jags. If that cow passes him the way she's going, he's going right into d.t.'s!"

You might think that Harold Peavey's fast cow would get noised about the neighborhood but there were several things in the way of it. For instance, the hour of day, which was either milking or breakfast time. Then, it was the season when everybody was in a rush to get the spring work done and the first spray on the trees. Mainly it was because Harold and I were the only ones on our road except a shack that hadn't been occupied in ten years, and then only partly, the owner having been a half-wit. I didn't see much of Harold myself except Sundays while Minnie was taking herself to the United Congregation Church and that would give me a little time to rest. I found out in May that he'd gone so far in his cow-training that he was able to cut down the morning workouts to three times a week without Mabel getting restless, and he was getting two quarts of rich milk a day. As for his orchard, I've seen worse. Considering the time he had to work out for his neighbors, training Mabel, and thinking about Sadie, he didn't do so bad for the first year. At any rate, he rubbed off a lot he'd learned down at the Ag.

Sadie I saw a couple of times when her old man and me was negotiating over a boar-pig. Once I says to her, "Sadie, that young Peavey sure is a hustler! He's getting his place into jim-dandy shape. Wouldn't surprise me none if he went wife-hunting one of these days."

"Well!" she said, tossing her mop of corn-silk hair. "Now that's news! I thought he was a born bachelor. I hope he gets one that likes to cook and scrub dirty clothes and tend chickens and garden, for I don't!"

"Oh I don't know," I says. "Some girls like it better working when there's a husky young buck on the place than riding with an old codger that's half mummy!"

"Are you telling *me?*" she says saucily. "Thanks for your kind advice, Mr. Crumm! I prefer roses!"

"Humph!" I says. "To me they looks prettier on the vine than wired up in a florist shop!"

Old man Morrison, while he was arguing over the boar-pig, said that Murfree had gone back to Portland but was coming down again in June when one of his cases came to trial.

By the time June come along Harold told me he had cut the driving to once a week. He said Mabel didn't like it but he had irrigation on his hands and was in the middle of cultivating the orchard and an acre of carrots. Besides he was deep in cookery, studying cookbooks, and trying his hand at Birds'-Nest Pudding,

Aunty Phelps' Pie Crust, and such. I told Minnie he was looking peaked and she invited him to Sunday dinners.

One Sunday, the last week in June, Harold was at our place for dinner. While Minnie was putting the finishing touches to chicken with dumplings, he was pouring over the Sunday edition of the Tillamook *Gazette.*

"Say!" he said suddenly, sort of excited. "I see there's going to be big doings at Tillamook on Fourth of July."

"Always is. Parade and fireworks and speeches."

"And racing!"

"Yep! They open up the county fair grounds for some racing. But it ain't much. Just local talent. Still, there's some pretty fast horses in the county and sometimes you see quite a few fast heats. I remember last year—"

"Look here, Pete," he says, shoving the paper at me. "Read that and tell me what it says."

I took the paper and read, " 'Final Event. Free-for-all One Mile Race for Drivers. All classes of racers may be entered and any style gig. This classic event, for one heat only, takes a purse of $100. Entries accepted up to the last minute.' That," I says, "is the windup of the whole shebang. And what a sight it is! Plenty of fun, too. Usually a couple of wrecks and a few wheels lost. Now I remember the year the President stopped over—"

"Does it say anywhere in that announcement that the racers have got to be *horses?*"

I looked at Harold with my eyes bugged out. "Young feller," I says, "just what have you got on your mind?"

We kept the whole thing a dead secret. The rest was simple. I hooked the sulky on behind the Ford and drove over on July 3. We made a deal with Jake Lentz to take Mabel over in his truck the same day, telling him she had to be treated at the veterinary for milk fever. He was going over for a load of fertilizer anyway so he said he'd do it for $5, but we would have to get her back some other way.

It was a broiling hot day and Tillamook was jammed. There was a parade of Boy Scouts, firemen, and Knights of Pythias in uniforms that made them look sort of proud and desperate. There were plenty of speeches, ending up with a long one by Lawyer Murfree. He kept wiping his bald head with a silk handkerchief and talking about the Constitution till my throat went plumb dry and I had to find the nearest bar. We stayed there an hour or two drinking beers, then we ambled over to the fair grounds where I'd parked the sulky in a shed off in a patch of fir near the track. Harold had brought Mabel over there and while they were running off the first heats he curry-combed her until she shone all over like a black silk purse.

"The only thing that worries me, Pete," he says, "is whether she'll stick to a circular road. She's used to a straightaway, but if I can get her next to the fence I know she'll follow it because there's a fence runs along our stretch back home, and she's conditioned to a fence. How long is the track?"

"It's an even mile. How'll you stop her when she passes the judges' stand?"

"Oh, that won't matter. If she runs beyond, it makes no differ-ence. They can't disqualify her for going over the finish line a piece. Anyway, if she runs too far, I can make a jump from the seat and bull-dog her. I guess I could steer her by the horns if I had to."

"Well, Harold," I says, "I'll be rooting for you and her." I looked at my watch. It was a quarter to four and the free-for-all was scheduled at four sharp. "Guess we'd better hitch up," I says.

We hitched up, Harold took hold of the lead rope, and we pulled over toward the starting line. The grandstands were packed from top to bottom and about a thousand cars were parked around the track. The crowd was milling around so and raising such a hullabaloo over each entry, what with the various kinds of vehicles in the race, that they didn't hardly notice our entry till we pulled up before the judges' box. Then they busted loose plenty. Harold walked over, holding out a five-dollar bill, and says, "I'm entering my racer, Mabel."

One of the judges turned red as a beet, like he was mad, and the other two began laughing fit to kill.

"You can't enter a cow!" says the red-faced one.

"Oh yes I can!" says Harold, cool as a cucumber. He had the announcement with him and handed it over to the judge. "Read that," he says, "and see if it says anything about disqualifying racing cows."

"I say, you can't enter that animal!" bellows Red-face. "This is no cattle show!"

Just then Judge Olney, whom I knew personal, pushed his way through and says, "What's the trouble?"

"This man," the other judge bawls, "is trying to enter a cow in the last race!"

"Well," says Olney politely, "why not?" He winked at the other two judges. "It's a free-for-all, isn't it?"

"That's right, judge," says one of the others. "I guess a good-looking cow like that one has as good a right to run as some of them nags out on the track, that look like they was ready for the bone-yard!"

The upshot was, that the judges voted, two to one, to allow Mabel to run. Harold filled out a card and led her over to the starting line. If you had looked at her then, you would have said she was just getting ready to be milked, she was that docile. The rest of the entries was snorting and neighing and prancing, and the drivers was all yelling "Whoa!" or "Git up, there!" but Harold climbed into his seat and said nothing, and Mabel stood with her front hoofs just touching the line, as if she had her mind on green fodder.

One of the judges took a megaphone and hollered, "Now, men, there won't be no false starts. When the gun goes, you just lick in to it, and the first one home wins!"

Then the starter fired his gun and they started off. Mabel was three places away from the inside fence and for a minute I didn't think she'd start at all. She took a few short steps, then she sort of ambled for about ten yards, and finally she settled down to her pace. By that time the rest of the field was a good twenty-five yards ahead of her and there was nobody between her and the fence. She turned right in and stuck to it from then on. At the first turn the other drivers was still a good bit ahead of Harold, but the crowd was yelling like mad, throwing up their hats and ice cream cones, and leaning on each other laughing. On the far side of the track she began to pick up on them. At the other turn she had passed all but three of the horses, one of them being a big gray mare, a trotter, and in the professional class. I heard that she belonged to Murfree. Her name was Peaches-and-Cream, and they said Murfree was trying her out here before sending her south to the big tracks. Harold told me afterward that at the turn Peaches-and-Cream either caught a whiff of Mabel or heard the sound she made, which was a sort of fierce "moo!" At any rate, Peaches-and-Cream suddenly broke. She reared and jumped sideways, and Mabel passed her in a cloud of dust while the crowd went mad.

They came down the home stretch, Mabel running neck and neck with a sorrel gelding. That made me feel pretty good for in the first two minutes of the race I had placed two five-dollar bets on Mabel at ten to one.

She pulled away from the gelding and came over the line with three yards to spare. I guess you never heard such a rumpus!

When the yelling died down a little, the man with the megaphone yelled, "Mabel wins first place! Grand Mogul, second! Peaches-and-Cream, third!"

But Mabel was still going. If anything, she picked up a little speed on the second lap. I'm telling you, that was a cow! Nobody on the track or in the grandstand thought she'd keep up more than half way around, but she did. The finish line was like it is after a race. There was still gigs and sulkies standing around and little crowds milling around them, all talking and arguing when somebody hollered, "Look out! Here comes that cow!"

She drove through them like a whirlwind, stopped dead just beyond the judges' stand, turned around, and started back. By that time there was wild horses all over the place. Drivers was tangled up every way, and the loafers on the track broke and ran for cover like a flock of quail. When she come around the reverse way, some misguided fool, thinking the cow had gone loco, ran out with a horse blanket and tried to stop her by waving the blanket.

She hit the blanket square and it settled down over her and Harold but she kept right on going. I guess with the blanket over her head she must have lost her direction for she made a beeline straight off the track, taking out a section of guard rail, and headed for the cars that were parked all over the grounds. I heard a crash and started running.

When I got up where it happened there was a crowd standing around looking at Harold. He was sitting on top of a limousine, wrapped in a blanket; one of the shafts of the sulky had gone through the top and the other had busted off. Mabel wasn't nowhere.

He stuck his head up out of the blanket, looking sort of dazed, and asked, "Did we win?"

"Hands down!" I yelled, reaching up to help him down.

On the way back home, Harold was feeling pretty blue about losing Mabel. We had traced her as far as the edge of town but we couldn't get any word of her after that.

"Well, Harold," I says, to cheer him up, "she ain't a total loss! After all, you paid $34 for her and she brought in a hundred-buck prize, that leaves a good profit even deducting the damage to Jake Lentz's orchard."

"Yeah?" he says gloomily. "Didn't you hear that circus fellow offer me five hundred on the spot for her?"

About five o'clock in the afternoon of the fourth day after the race, Harold come running over to my place. I could see right off he was all steamed up about something.

"She's come home!" he panted. "Walked right into the barn and stood in her stall, waiting to be milked. She looks pretty worn down and she didn't give more than half a pint of milk, but hell! she's no milker, anyway; she's a racer! I'll fix up the old sulky, break her in again, and sell her for five hundred!"

Well, Harold went to work on her and I'll say he worked hard. He let her rest up two days, then he hitched her up, and took her out for a spin. But she wouldn't spin, no sir, not even a slow trot! She wouldn't do any more than an ordinary cow! He fooled around with her a while and I came out to help but it wasn't any good; she'd turn around and look at us, all meek and gentle, like she was asking what in the world we were up to, and then she'd start, the way cows do, at a walk so slow you could pick daisies and keep up with her! Just seemed like the old racing spirit was gone. After a week of trying, Harold gave up.

"I'm beaten," he said, "and plumb disgusted! She don't milk and she don't run; I guess I'll have to beef her!"

Luckily, while he was making up his mind and too busy to take her down to the butcher, she began to show signs of being in the family way. In another few weeks it was plain enough she was going to calve. Well, we talked it over and decided that on the way back from Tillamook she must have dawdled.

"I guess," said Harold, "her racing days are over!"

The piebald bull calf, when it came, was as pretty as a picture and built like a fawn. At first Harold thought of training it to be a racer like its mother and maybe breeding a strain of fast cows but I argued that after that race they'd never let another bovine enter a track with horses, so he gave the calf to Sadie, which was a good thing because Harold for all his studying hadn't really learned to cook.

He's got other cows now but they keep Mabel for sentiment.

From East to West

The Mule

Josh Billings

The mule is haf hoss and haf Jackass, and then kums tu a full stop, natur diskovering her mistake.

Tha weigh more, akordin tu their heft, than enny other kreetur, except a crow-bar.

Tha kant hear enny quicker, nor further than the hoss, yet their ears are big enuff for snow shoes.

You kan trust them with enny one whose life aint worth enny more than the mules. The only wa tu keep the mules into a paster, is tu turn them into a medder jineing, and let them jump out.

Tha are reddy for use, just as soon as they will du tu abuse.

Tha haint got enny friends, and will live on huckle berry brush, with an ockasional chanse at Kanada thistels.

Tha are a modern invenshun, i dont think the Bible deludes tu them at tall.

Tha sel for more money than enny other domestik animile. You kant tell their age by looking into their mouth, enny more than you could a Mexican cannons. Tha never have no dissease that a good club wont heal.

If tha ever die tha must kum rite tu life agin, for i never herd noboddy sa "ded mule."

Tha are like sum men, verry korrupt at harte; ive known them tu be good mules for 6 months, just tu git a good chanse to kick sumbody.

I never owned one, nor never mean to, unless thare is a United Staits law passed, requiring it.

The only reason why tha are pashunt, is bekause tha are ashamed ov themselfs.

I have seen eddikated mules in a sirkus.

Tha kould kick, and bite, tremenjis. I would not sa what I am forced tu sa again the mule, if his birth want an outrage, and man want tu blame for it.

Enny man who is willing tu drive a mule, ought to be exempt by law from running for the legislatur.

Tha are the strongest creeturs on earth, and heaviest ackording tu their sise; I herd tell ov one who fell oph from the tow path, on the Eri kanawl, and sunk as soon as he touched bottom, but he kept rite on towing the boat tu the nex stashun, breathing thru his ears, which stuck out ov the water about 2 feet 6 inches; i did'nt see this did, but an auctioneer told me ov it, and i never knew an auctioneer tu lie unless it was absolutely convenient.

The Poodle

Josh Billings

The poodle iz a small dog, with sore eyes, and hid amungst a good deal ov promiskuss hair.

They are sumtimes white for color, and their hair iz tangled all over them, like the hed ov a yung darkey.

They are kept az pets, and, like all other pets, are az stubborn az a setting hen.

A poodle iz a woman's pet, and that makes them kind ov sakred, for whatever a woman luvs she worships.

I hav seen poodles that i almost wanted tew swop places with, but the owners ov them didn't akt to me az tho they wanted tew trade for enny thing.

Thare iz but phew things on the face ov this earth more utterly worthless than a poodle, and yet i am glad thare iz poodles, for if thare wasn't thare iz some people who wouldn't hav enny objekt in living, and hav nothing tew luv.

Thare iz nothing in this world made in vain, and poodles are good for fleas.

Fleas are also good for poodles, for they keep their minds employed scratching, and almost every boddy else's too about the house.

I never knew a man tew keep a poodle. Man's natur iz too koarse for poodles. A poodle would soon fade and die if a man waz tew nuss him.

I don't expekt enny poodle, but if enny boddy duz giv me one he must make up his mind tew be tied onto a long stick every Saturday, and be used for washing the windows on the outside.

This kind of nussing would probably make the poodle mad, and probably he would quit, but i kant help it.

The Intelligent Steer

Edward H. Mott

It was a chilly morning. A farmer from the hoop-pole fields of Chucktown stopped his yoke of steers in front of the tavern, and went in the barroom to get a ten-cent piece changed. The dog Cæsar occupied the only bit of sunshine that had as yet found a place on the front stoop. The Squire came out with his chair. He kicked Cæsar into the street.

"Blast a lazy dog," said he, "that's always a-loppin' around in the sun."

Then he sat his chair on the patch of sunshine, sat himself on the chair, and gazed pensively at the yoke of steers. The Sheriff came up from a late breakfast of buckwheat cakes and sausage, and remarked to the Squire that there was frost in the air this morning.

"You'd hardly think," said the Squire, still taking in the points of the Chucktown cattle—"you'd hardly think, to look at one, that a five-year-old steer, especially a brindle one, know'd any more than enough to chaw its cud, and kick with its off hind leg at any fool of a dog that got within ten foot of it."

Cæsar, a steer's hind foot, and a howl suggested the concluding sentence of the old gentleman's remark.

"But don't you make no mistake," he continued. "Take a steer that's got enough to eat, and whose agricult'ral trainin' has been somethin' more than haulin' hoop poles to market, and he'll be as cute as a coon, if he's a mind to, and have a heap o' fun in him bigger'n a haystack. But you'd hardly believe it, to look at them steers yonder."

"Oh, I don't know," said the Sheriff. "I remember—"

"You remember!" interrupted the Squire. "Yes, of course you remember. You remember too durned much. If one quarter o' the wonderful things you remember had ever happened, you'd be older than Methuseler, and the history o' Pike County couldn't be got into twenty-eight volumes bigger'n dictionaries."

The Squire likes his meals on time. He had been up since four o'clock, and his breakfast wasn't ready yet.

"Now, you take Bloomin' Grove steers," he continued, "and you won't find many lunk-heads among 'em. I'll never forgit one that Mose used to have. It's a funny thing, but that steer was too smart to die, and at the same time he was too smart to live. I'll explain that to you by one or two little things that I remember about him.

"Mose bought this steer to fat and kill. He was as slick as a beaver, and in good condition to start with, but Mose wanted him a leetle fatter. Mose was always wantin' things a leetle better than they was. If he went to a hoss trot and see a hoss go in two-ten he'd say it was pooty good, but he thought it ought a gone in two-nine, and it would if it'd been druv right. So we went to stuffin' this steer to make him fatter, but we wa'n't long in noticin' that the more victuals we turned into him the thinner he got. Of course, we had talked right before the steer what we intended to do with him. About the same time there was some sportin' men from New York puttin' up at Mose's, and they was talkin' most o' the time about the exercise some fellers was takin' to keep down their flesh to be in condition for fightin', or rowin', or walkin', and so on, and about the diet of Graham bread and other chip victuals they indulged in. The steer didn't eat half we give him, and kept gittin' thinner and thinner. I noticed that every day he'd walk down the road, and in about two hours came back foamin' with sweat, and tired most to death. So one day I made up my mind to see what in the great nation he was up to, and follered him, keepin' back so as he couldn't see me. He stopped about two mile down the road. I hid in the woods, in a place where I could see him. After lookin' up and down the road for a spell, as if he wanted to see whether any one was watchin', he started on a tight run up the road. He tore along for half a mile, and then turned and tore back agin. He kep' that up for an hour, and then started back hum as wet as a bog medder, and as tired as a livery horse in 'lectioneerin' time. This strange perceedin' was too many fur me. I thought the steer was crazy, but I kept it to myself, waitin' to see how it would turn out.

"Well, one day the steer started up the road to'rds the tan'ry store. Thinks says I, this is a new move, and I'll see what it means. I follered him, and he never stopped till he got to the store. He squared himself around in the road, facin' the store, and begun to

beller as if his heart would break. We couldn't drive him away, and
couldn't make out what ailed him. All of a suddent I noticed a sign
on the side of the store. In big letters it said:

GRAHAM BRAN SOLD HERE

"Then the hull blame thing was as plain as day. That steer had took
in all we'd said about fattin' him to kill, and all that the sports had
said about keepin' flesh down and Graham feed. He had been takin'
violent exercise every day by runnin' up and down the road, and, to
cap it all, had concluded to try the Graham business. That was what
he wanted at the store, and seein' the sign, was bound to have the
diet. I jist ordered a bushel o' that bran quicker'n a buck rabbit could
spile a cabbage. When I shouldered the bran and started for hum
that steer come very near eucherin' himself by dyin' with joy. When
I told Mose about the cuteness o' the steer, it knocked him all in a
heap.

"'That steer,' said he, 'is too smart to die, and I'll tell him so.'

"From that time the steer begun to git fat, and he was in condition to kill in two weeks.

"Well, it went along, and the steer got to be a big favorite.
About that time Dutch Franz got it in his head that there never was
a better scheme than to stock Mose's trout pond with pickerel. Franz
was workin' there then, and he meant well, but he didn't know. So
one day he caught a lot of pickerel over in Bloomin' Grove Pond, and
unbeknown to any one turned 'em into the trout pond. The first we
know'd the only fish we could git out o' the dam was whoppin' big
picker'l. The only thing that can live where there's picker'l is
snappin' turtles, and if they wa'n't so humly the picker'l'd soon
gobble them. The fellers use to come and have lots o' fun trollin' for
picker'l in the dam. One day I see our steer watchin' a couple o'
fishermen trollin'. The next day I was walkin' over that way, and
what should I see but the steer standin' in the water up to his flank.
He had his face to'rds shore, and was switchin' his tail slowly to and
fro over the surface. There was a pleased expression on his face. I
stopped to see what the deuce he was up to. Suddently I see him
give his tail a quick jerk, and kerplunk dropped a big picker'l down
by my feet. 'Fore I got over my s'prise out come another picker'l.
There was the fact right 'fore my eyes or I never could have believed
it. That steer was standin' there trollin' for picker'l with his tail, and
in less than twenty minutes he had yanked out thirty-two of the
biggest ones there was in the dam. Then he come out, and jist rolled

and rolled on the bank, and bellered till the tears rolled down his cheeks, the fun tickled him so.

"Well, he kept that up for several days. One Sunday we missed him. We didn't think much o' that, but when he didn't come home at night we got uneasy. We hunted the woods for nearly a week, but never found him, and made up our minds he was stole. A month or so arterward I was fishin' for picker'l in the pond. I caught an old socker, and when I went to take him off my hook I see he had a spur —a regular spur, about two inches long, and curved like a rooster's, comin' plumb out o' his back, about eight inches from the tail.

" 'Here's a curiosity, certain,' says I.

"I took him hum and put him in a hogshead of water. It got noised around the country, and so many people flocked to the house to see it that Mose got mad one day and took the picker'l out and chopped its head off. I was mad, of course, but couldn't help myself. I took the fish and .went to cleanin' it. When I cut it open what should I find but a horn that belonged to our lost steer. Then the mystery was solved. The picker'l in the pond had tackled the steer on one of his fishin' excursions, surrounded him, run him out into the pond and drownded him, and then eat him up. The picker'l I had caught had swallowed one o' the horns. The little end o' the horn had pushed its way out o' the fish's back, and that was what I thought was a spur.

"So you see," concluded the Squire, "that steer was too smart to die and too smart to live."

The breakfast bell rang, and the Squire went in.

Prehistoric Animals of the Middle West

JAMES THURBER

Many residents of that broad, proud region of the United States known as the Middle West are, I regret to say, woefully ignorant of, not to say profoundly incurious about, the nature and variety of the wild life which existed, however precariously in some instances, in that part of North America before the coming of the Red Man (*Homo Rufus*) or of anybody else.

The only important research which has been done in this fascinating field was carried on for the better part of thirty-two years by the late Dr. Wesley L. Millmoss.* For the last twenty years of the great man's life, I served as his artist, companion, counsellor and assistant. In this last capacity, I did a great deal of heavy lifting, no doubt more than was good for me. During the years I spent with Dr. Millmoss, he devoted most of his time to digging in all parts of the Middle West for the fossilized remains of extinct animals. From bits of a thigh bone, or one vertebra, he would reconstruct the whole animal. My drawings of his most famous reconstructions accompany this treatise.

For the past twelve years I have striven without success to have his findings, together with their accompanying illustrative plates, published in one or another of the leading scientific journals of this and other countries. I lay my failure directly at the door of Dr. Wilfred Ponsonby who, at the meeting of the American Scientific Society in Baltimore in 1929, made the remark, "The old boy (Dr.

---

* While on a field trip in Africa in 1931, Dr. Millmoss was eaten by a large piano-shaped animal, to the distress of his many friends and colleagues.

258

Millmoss) has never dug up half as many specimens as he has dreamed up."

Although Dr. Millmoss, quite naturally, was unable to perceive the wit in this damaging observation, which hung like a cloud over his last days, he was not without a sense of humor, and I believe, if he were alive today, he would take no little satisfaction in the fact that for the last five years Dr. Ponsonby has labored under the delusion that he is married to a large South African butterfly.

However, this is scarcely the place for an exploration of the little feuds and fantasies of the scientific world. Let us proceed to an examination of the remarkable fauna of the prehistoric Middle West. If in doing so, I present no formal defense of the Millmoss discoveries, put it down to a profound reverence for the memory of Wesley Millmoss, who used so often to say, "A Millmoss assumption is more important than a Ponsonby proof."

All the plates reproduced here were drawn by me from photographs of original life-size models constructed by Dr. Millmoss out of wire, *papier mâché* and other materials. These models were all destroyed by fire in 1930. "All that I have to show for them," the good doctor once told a friend, "is two divorces."

According to all scientists except Dr. Millmoss, the famous mounds of Ohio were built by an early race of men known as Mound Builders. The doctor, on the other hand, contended that the mounds were built by the Mound Dweller (Plate I). This primitive

Plate I.

creature was about the size of the modern living room. The Mound Dweller's body occupied only one third of the space inside his shell, the rest of which was used to carry the earth as he dug it up. The creature's eye was an integral part of its shell, a mistake made by Mother Nature and not, as has been claimed,* "a bit of Millmoss butchery-botchery." The Mound Dweller is of interest today, even to me, principally because it was my friend's first reconstruction, and led to his divorce from Alma Albrecht Millmoss.

In Plate II, I have drawn the Thake, a beast which Dr. Millmoss was wont to refer to lovingly as "Old Laughing Ears." It represents

* Dr. W. Ponsonby, in the *Yale Review*, 1933.

perhaps the most controversial of all the ancient creatures recon-
structed by the distinguished scientist. Dr. Millmoss estimated that
the Thake had inhabited the prairies of Illinois approximately three
million years before the advent of the Christian era. Shortly after
Dr. Millmoss gave his model of the Thake to the world, Dr. Ponsonby, in a lecture at Williams College that was notable for its

lack of ethical courtesy, asserted that
the Thake bones which Dr. Millmoss
had found were in reality those of a
pet airedale and a pet pony buried together in one grave by their owner, *circa*
1907. My own confidence in the authenticity of the Thake has never been
shaken, although occasionally it becomes
a figure in my nightmares, barking and
neighing.

In Plate III, we have the Queech,
also known as the Spotted, or Ringed,
Queech—the only prehistoric feline ever
discovered by Dr. Millmoss in his mid-

Plate II.

western researches. I find no record in the doctor's notes as to the

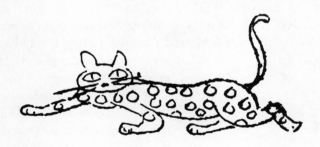

Plate III.

probable epoch in which it flourished. Like so many of Dr. Millmoss'
restorations, the Queech was made the object of a particularly unfriendly and uncalled-for remark by Dr. Ponsonby. At a dinner of
the New York Society of Zoologists, held at the old Waldorf-Astoria
some fifteen years ago, Ponsonby observed, "There is no doubt
in my mind but that this pussy cat belongs to the Great Plasticine
Age."

As to the authenticity of the Cobble-tufted Wahwah (Plate IV), even the sardonic Dr. Ponsonby could offer no slighting insinuations.* Like all other scientists, he was forced tacitly to admit the brilliant precision with which the old master had restored this antediluvian fowl. The Wahwah bird, in spite of its mammoth size, measured nothing at all from wing tip to wing tip, since it had only one wing. Because of its single wing, its obviously impractical feet and its tendency to walk over high rocks and fall, it is probable, Dr. Millmoss believed, that the species did not exist for more than a hundred and seventy-five years. Dr. Millmoss once told me that, if the bird made any sound at all, it probably "went 'wahwah.'" Since this embarrassed me for some reason, the celebrated scientist did not press the point.

Plate IV.

In Plate V, we come upon my favorite of all the Millmoss discoveries, the Hippoterranovamus. One of Nature's most colossal errors, the Hippoterranovamus ate only stork meat and lived in a land devoid of storks. Too large to become jumpy because of its predicament, the 'novamus took out its frustration in timidity. It almost never came out completely from behind anything. When I asked Dr. Millmoss how long he figured the 'novamus had existed as a species, he gave me his infrequent but charming smile and said in his slow drawl, "Well, it never lived to vote for William Jennings Bryan." This was the only occasion on which I heard the great man mention politics.

Plate V.

Plates VI and VII represent, respectively, the Ernest Vose, or

Author's Note: My research staff has since established that Dr. Ponsonby was enjoying a two-year sabbatical in Europe at the time the Wahwah model was completed.

Long-necked Leafeater, and the Spode, or Wood-wedger. Neither
of these animals has ever interested me intensely, and it is only fair to
say that I am a bit dubious as to the utter reality of their prove-
nance. At the time he constructed
these models, Dr. Millmoss was being divorced by his second wife,
Annette Beggs Millmoss, and he
spent a great deal of his time reading children's books and natural
histories. The tree at the back of
the Spode is my own conception
of a 3,000,000-year-old tree. The
small animal at the feet of the
Ernest Vose is a Grod. Dr. Millmoss'
notes are almost entirely illegible,
and I am not even sure that Ernest
Vose is right. It looks more like
Ernest Vose than anything else,
however.

Plate VI.

The final plate (Plate VIII) was one of the last things Wesley
Millmoss ever did, more for relaxation, I think, than in the interests
of science. It shows his idea, admittedly a trifle fanciful, of the
Middle-Western Man and Woman,
three and a half million years before the dawn of history. When I
asked him if it was his conviction
that Man had got up off all fours
before Woman did, he gave me a
pale, grave look and said simply,
"He had to. He needed the head
start."

Even in death, Dr. Wesley
Millmoss did not escape the sharp
and envious tongue of Dr. Wilfred
Ponsonby. In commenting upon
the untimely passing of my great
employer and friend, the *New York*

Plate VII.

Times observed that explorers in Africa might one day come upon
the remains of the large, piano-shaped animal that ate Dr. Millmoss,
together with the bones of its distinguished and unfortunate prey.

Upon reading this, Ponsonby turned to a group of his friends at the Explorers' Club and said, "Too bad the old boy didn't live to reconstruct *that*."

Plate VIII.

The Pet Department

JAMES THURBER

The idea for the department was suggested by the daily pet column in the *New York Evening Post,* and by several others.

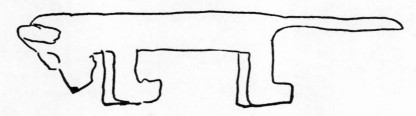

Q. I enclose a sketch of the way my dog, William, has been lying for two days now. I think there must be something wrong with him. Can you tell me how to get him out of this?

MRS. L. L. G.

A. I should judge from the drawing that William is in a trance. Trance states, however, are rare with dogs. It may just be ecstasy. If at the end of another twenty-four hours he doesn't seem to be getting anywhere, I should give him up. The position of the ears leads me to believe that he may be enjoying himself in a quiet way, but the tail is somewhat alarming.

Q. Our cat, who is thirty-five, spends all of her time in bed. She follows every move I make, and this is beginning to get to me. She never seems sleepy nor particularly happy. Is there anything I could give her?

Miss L. Mc.

A. There are no medicines which can safely be given to induce felicity in a cat, but you might try lettuce, which is a soporific, for the wakefulness. I would have to see the cat watching you to tell whether anything could be done to divert her attention.

Q. My husband, who is an amateur hypnotizer, keeps trying to get our bloodhound under his control. I contend that this is not doing the dog any good. So far he has not yielded to my husband's influence, but I am affraid that if he once got under, we couldn't get him out of it.

A. A. T.

A. Dogs are usually left cold by all phases of psychology, mental telepathy, and the like. Attempts to hypnotize this particular breed, however, are likely to be fraught with a definite menace. A bloodhound, if stared at fixedly, is liable to gain the impression that it is under suspicion, being followed, and so on. This upsets a bloodhound's life, by completely reversing its whole scheme of behavior.

Q. My wife found this owl in the attic among a lot of ormolu clocks and old crystal chandeliers. We can't tell whether it's stuffed or only dead. It is sitting on a strange and almost indescribable sort of iron dingbat.

Mr. Molleff

A. What your wife found is a museum piece—a stuffed cocka-

too. It looks to me like a rather botchy example of taxidermy. This is the first stuffed bird I have ever seen with its eyes shut, but whoever had it stuffed probably wanted it stuffed that way. I couldn't say what the thing it is sitting on is supposed to represent. It looks broken.

Q. Our gull cannot get his head down any farther than this, and bumps into things.

H. L. F.

A. You have no ordinary gull to begin with. He looks to me a great deal like a rabbit backing up. If he *is* a gull, it is impossible to keep him in the house. Naturally he will bump into things. Give him his freedom.

Q. My police dog has taken to acting very strange, on account of my father coming home from work every night for the past two years and saying to him, "If you're a police dog, where's your badge?", after which he laughs (my father).

ELLA R.

A. The constant reiteration of any piece of badinage sometimes has the same effect on present-day neurotic dogs that it has on people. It is dangerous and thoughtless to twit a police dog on his powers, authority, and the like. From the way your dog seems to hide behind tables, large vases, and whatever that thing is that looks like a suitcase, I should imagine that your father has carried this thing far enough—perhaps even too far.

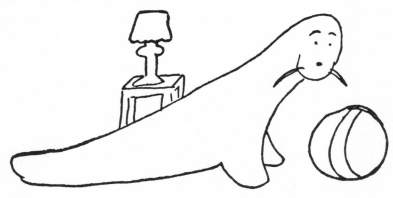

Q. My husband's seal will not juggle, although we have tried everything.

GRACE H.

A. Most seals will not juggle; I think I have never known one that juggled. Seals balance things, and sometimes toss objects (such as the large ball in your sketch) from one to another. This last will be difficult if your husband has but one seal. I'd try him in plain balancing, beginning with a billiard cue or something. It may be, of course, that he is a non-balancing seal.

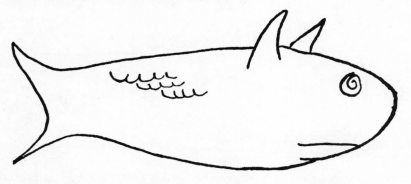

Q. We have a fish with ears and wonder if it is valuable.

JOE WRIGHT

A. I find no trace in the standard fish books of any fish with ears. Very likely the ears do not belong to the fish, but to some mammal. They look to me like a mammal's ears. It would be pretty hard to say what species of mammal, and almost impossible to determine what particular member of that species. They may merely be hysterical ears, in which case they will go away if you can get the fish's mind on something else.

Q. How would you feel if every time you looked up from your work or anything, here was a horse peering at you from behind something? He prowls about the house at all hours of the day and night. Doesn't seem worried about anything, merely wakeful. What should I do to discourage him?

MRS. GRACE VOYNTON

A. The horse is probably sad. Changing the flowered decorations of your home to something less like open meadows might discourage him, but then I doubt whether it is a good idea to discourage a sad horse. In any case speak to him quietly when he turns up from behind things. Leaping at a horse in a house and crying "Roogie,

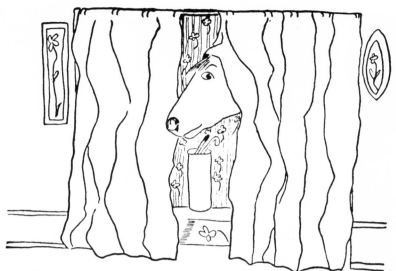

roogie!" or "Whoosh!" would only result in breakage and bedlam. Of course you might finally get used to having him around, if the house is big enough for both of you.

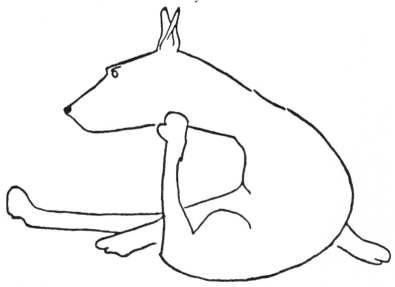

Q. The fact that my dog sits this way so often leads me to believe that something is preying on his mind. He seems always to be studying. Would there be any way of finding out what this is?

ARTHUR

A. Owing to the artificially complex life led by city dogs of the present day, they tend to lose the simpler systems of intuition which once guided all breeds, and frequently lapse into what comes very close to mental perplexity. I myself have known some very profoundly thoughtful dogs. Usually, however, their problems are not serious and I should judge that your dog has merely mislaid something and wonders where he put it.

Q. We have cats the way most people have mice.

MRS. C. L. FOOTLOOSE

A. I see you have. I can't tell from your communication, however, whether you wish advice or are just boasting.

Q. No one has been able to tell us what kind of dog we have. I am enclosing a sketch of one of his two postures. He only has two. The other one is the same as this except he faces in the opposite direction.

MRS. EUGENIA BLACK

A. I think that what you have is a cast-iron lawn dog. The expressionless eye and the rigid pose are characteristic of metal lawn animals. And that certainly is a cast-iron ear. You could, however,

remove all doubt by means of a simple test with a hammer and a cold chisel, or an acetylene torch. If the animal chips, or melts, my diagnosis is correct.

Q. My oldest boy, Ford Maddox Ford Griswold, worked this wooden horse loose from a merry-go-round one night when he and some other young people were cutting up. Could you suggest any use for it in a family of five?

MRS. R. L. S. GRISWOLD

A. I cannot try the patience of my public nor waste my own

time dealing with the problems of insensate animals. Already I have gone perhaps too far afield in the case of stuffed birds and cast-iron lawn dogs. Pretty soon I should be giving advice on wire-haired fox terrier weather-vanes.

Q. Mr. Jennings bought this beast when it was a pup in Montreal for a St. Bernard, but I don't think it is. It's grown enormously and is stubborn about letting you have anything, like the bath towel it has its paws on, and the hat, both of which belong to Mr. Jennings. He got it that bowling ball to play with but it doesn't seem to like it. Mr. Jennings is greatly attached to the creature.

MRS. FANNY EDWARDS JENNINGS

A. What you have is a bear. While it isn't my bear, I should recommend that you dispose of it. As these animals grow older they get more and more adamant about letting you have anything, until finally there might not be anything in the house you could call your own—except possibly the bowling ball. Zoos use bears. Mr. Jennings could visit it.

Q. Sometimes my dog does not seem to know me. I think he must be crazy. He will draw away, or show his fangs, when I approach him.

H. M. MORGAN, JR.

A. So would I, and I'm not crazy. If you creep up on your dog the way you indicate in the drawing, I can understand his view-

point. Put your shirt in and straighten up; you look as if you had never seen a dog before, and that is undoubtedly what bothers the animal. These maladjustments can often be worked out by the use of a little common sense.

Q. After a severe storm we found this old male raven in the study of my father, the Hon. George Morton Bodwell, for many years head of the Latin Department at Tufts, sitting on a bust of Livy which was a gift to him from the class of '92. All that the old bird will say is "Grawk." Can ravens be taught to talk or was Poe merely "romancing"?

Mrs. H. Bodwell Colwether

A. I am handicapped by an uncertainty as to who says "Grawk," the raven or your father. It just happens that "Arrk" is what ravens say. I have never known a raven that said anything but "Arrk."

Q. I have three Scotch terriers which take things out of closets and down from shelves, etc. My veterinarian advised me to gather together all the wreckage, set them down in the midst of it, and say "ba-ad Scotties!" This, however, merely seems to give them a kind of pleasure. If I spank one, the other two jump me—playfully, but they jump me.

Mrs. O. S. Proctor

A. To begin with, I question the advisability of having three Scotch terriers. They are bound to get you down. However, it seems to me that you are needlessly complicating your own problem. The Scotties probably think that you are trying to enter into the spirit of their play. Their inability to comprehend what you are trying to get at will in the end make them melancholy, and you and the dogs will begin to drift farther and farther apart. I'd deal with each terrier, and each object, separately, beginning with the telephone, the disconnection of which must inconvenience you sorely.

Q. My husband paid a hundred and seventy-five dollars for this moose to a man in Dorset, Ontario, who said he had trapped

it in the woods. Something is wrong with his antlers, for we have to keep twisting them back into place all the time. They're loose.

MRS. OLIPHANT BEATTY

A. You people are living in a fool's paradise. The animal is obviously a horse with a span of antlers strapped onto his head. If you really want a moose, dispose of the horse; if you want to keep the horse, take the antlers off. Their constant pressure on his ears isn't a good idea.

The Dog That Bit People

JAMES THURBER

Probably no one man should have as many dogs in his life as I have had, but there was more pleasure than distress in them for me except in the case of an Airedale named Muggs. He gave me more trouble than all the other fifty-four or five put together, although my moment of keenest embarrassment was the time a Scotch terrier named Jeannie, who had just had six puppies in the clothes closet of a fourth floor apartment in New York, had the unexpected seventh and last at the corner of Eleventh Street and Fifth Avenue during a walk she had insisted on taking. Then, too, there was the prize winning French poodle, a great big black poodle—none of your little, untroublesome white miniatures—who got sick riding in the rumble seat of a car with me on her way to the Greenwich Dog Show. She had a red rubber bib tucked around her throat and, since a rain storm came up when we were half way through the Bronx, I had to hold over her a small green umbrella, really more of a parasol. The rain beat down fearfully and suddenly the driver of the car drove into a big garage, filled with mechanics. It happened so quickly that I forgot to put the umbrella down and I will always remember, with sickening distress, the look of incredulity mixed with hatred that came over the face of the particular hardened garage man that came over to see what we wanted, when he took a look at me and the poodle. All garage men, and people of that intolerant stripe, hate poodles with their curious hair cut, especially the pom-poms that you got to leave on their hips if you expect the dogs to win a prize.

But the Airedale, as I have said, was the worst of all my dogs. He really wasn't my dog, as a matter of fact: I came home from a vacation one summer to find that my brother Roy had bought him while I was away. A big, burly, choleric dog, he always acted as if he thought I wasn't one of the family. There was a slight advantage in being one of the family, for he didn't bite the family as often as

276

he bit strangers. Still, in the years that we had him he bit everybody but mother, and he made a pass at her once but missed. That was during the month when we suddenly had mice, and Muggs refused to do anything about them. Nobody ever had mice exactly like the mice we had that month. They acted like pet mice, almost like mice somebody had trained. They were so friendly that one night when mother entertained at dinner the Friraliras, a club she and my father had belonged to for twenty years, she put down a lot of little dishes with food in them on the pantry floor so that the mice would be satisfied with that and wouldn't come into the dining room. Muggs stayed out in the pantry with the mice, lying on the floor, growling to himself—not at the mice, but about all the people in the next room that he would have liked to get at. Mother slipped out into the pantry once to see how everything was going. Everything was going fine. It made her so mad to see Muggs lying there, oblivious of the mice—they came running up to her—that she slapped him and he slashed at her, but didn't make it. He was sorry immediately, mother said. He was always sorry, she said, after he bit someone, but we could not understand how she figured this out. He didn't act sorry.

Mother used to send a box of candy every Christmas to the people the Airedale bit. The list finally contained forty or more names. Nobody could understand why we didn't get rid of the dog. I didn't understand it very well myself, but we didn't get rid of him. I think that one or two people tried to poison Muggs—he acted poisoned once in a while—and old Major Moberly fired at him once with his service revolver near the Seneca Hotel in East Broad Street —but Muggs lived to be almost eleven years old and even when he could hardly get around he bit a Congressman who had called to see my father on business. My mother had never liked the Congressman —she said the signs of his horoscope showed he couldn't be trusted (he was Saturn with the moon in Virgo)—but she sent him a box of candy that Christmas. He sent it right back, probably because he suspected it was trick candy. Mother persuaded herself it was all for the best that the dog had bitten him, even though father lost an important business association because of it. "I wouldn't be associated with such a man," mother said, "Muggs could read him like a book."

We used to take turns feeding Muggs to be on his good side, but that didn't always work. He was never in a very good humor, even after a meal. Nobody knew exactly what was the matter with him, but whatever it was it made him irascible, especially in the mornings. Roy never felt very well in the morning, either, especially before breakfast, and once when he came downstairs and found that Muggs had moodily chewed up the morning paper he hit him in the face with a grapefruit and then jumped up on the dining room table, scattering dishes and silverware and spilling the coffee. Muggs' first free leap carried him all the way across the table and into a brass fire screen in front of the gas grate but he was back on his feet in a moment and in the end he got Roy and gave him a pretty vicious

Nobody knew exactly what was the matter with him.

bite in the leg. Then he was all over it; he never bit anyone more than once at a time. Mother always mentioned that as an argument in his favor; she said he had a quick temper but that he didn't hold a grudge. She was forever defending him. I think she liked him because he wasn't well. "He's not strong," she would say, pityingly, but that was inaccurate; he may not have been well but he was terribly strong.

One time my mother went to the Chittenden Hotel to call on a woman mental healer who was lecturing in Columbus on the subject of "Harmonious Vibrations." She wanted to find out if it was possible to get harmonious vibrations into a dog. "He's a large tan-colored Airedale," mother explained. The woman said that she had never treated a dog but she advised my mother to hold the thought that he did not bite and would not bite. Mother was holding the thought the very next morning when Muggs got the iceman but she blamed that slip-up on the iceman. "If you didn't think he would bite you, he wouldn't," mother told him. He stomped out of the house in a terrible jangle of vibrations.

One morning when Muggs bit me slightly, more or less in passing, I reached down and grabbed his short stumpy tail and hoisted him into the air. It was a foolhardy thing to do and the last

Lots of people reported our dog to the police.

time I saw my mother, about six months ago, she said she didn't know what possessed me. I don't either, except that I was pretty mad. As long as I held the dog off the floor by his tail he couldn't get at me, but he twisted and jerked so, snarling all the time, that I realized I couldn't hold him that way very long. I carried him to the kitchen and flung him onto the floor and shut the door on him just as he crashed against it. But I forgot about the backstairs. Muggs went up the backstairs and down the frontstairs and had me cornered in the living room. I managed to get up onto the mantelpiece above the fireplace, but it gave way and came down with a tremendous crash throwing a large marble clock, several vases, and myself heavily to the floor. Muggs was so alarmed by the racket that when I picked myself up he had disappeared. We couldn't find him anywhere, although we whistled and shouted, until old Mrs. Detweiler called after dinner that night. Muggs had bitten her once, in the leg, and she came into the living room only after we assured her that Muggs had run away. She had just seated herself when, with a great growling and scratching of claws, Muggs emerged from under a davenport where he had been quietly hiding all the time, and bit her again. Mother examined the bite and put arnica on it and told Mrs. Detweiler that it was only a bruise. "He just bumped you," she said. But Mrs. Detweiler left the house in a nasty state of mind.

Lots of people reported our Airedale to the police but my father held a municipal office at the time and was on friendly terms with the police. Even so, the cops had been out a couple of times—once when Muggs bit Mrs. Rufus Sturtevant and again when he bit Lieutenant-Governor Malloy—but mother told them that it hadn't been Muggs' fault but the fault of the people who were bitten. "When he starts for them, they scream," she explained, "and that excites him." The cops suggested that it might be a good idea to tie the dog up, but mother said that it mortified him to be tied up and that he wouldn't eat when he was tied up.

Muggs at his meals was an unusual sight. Because of the fact that if you reached toward the floor he would bite you, we usually put his food plate on top of an old kitchen table with a bench alongside the table. Muggs would stand on the bench and eat. I remember that my mother's Uncle Horatio, who boasted that he was the third man up Missionary Ridge, was splutteringly indignant when he found out that we fed the dog on a table because we were afraid to put his plate on the floor. He said he wasn't afraid of any dog that ever lived and that he would put the dog's plate on the floor if we would give it to him. Roy said that if Uncle Horatio had fed Muggs on the ground just before the battle he would have been the first man up Missionary Ridge. Uncle Horatio was furious. "Bring him in! Bring him in now!" he shouted. "I'll feed the —— on the floor!" Roy was all for giving him a chance, but my father wouldn't hear of it. He said that Muggs had already been fed. "I'll feed him again!" bawled Uncle Horatio. We had quite a time quieting him.

In his last year Muggs used to spend practically all of his time outdoors. He didn't like to stay in the house for some reason or other—perhaps it held too many unpleasant memories for him. Any-

Muggs at his meals was an unusual sight.

way, it was hard to get him to come in and as a result the garbage man, the iceman, and the laundryman wouldn't come near the house. We had to haul the garbage down to the corner, take the laundry out and bring it back, and meet the iceman a block from home. After this had gone on for some time we hit on an ingenious arrangement for getting the dog in the house so that we could lock him up while the gas meter was read, and so on. Muggs was afraid of only one thing, an electrical storm. Thunder and lightning frightened him out of his senses (I think he thought a storm had broken the day the mantelpiece fell). He would rush into the house and hide under a bed or in a clothes closet. So we fixed up a thunder machine out of a long narrow piece of sheet iron with a wooden handle on one end. Mother would shake this vigorously when she wanted to get

Muggs into the house. It made an excellent imitation of thunder, but I suppose it was the most roundabout system for running a household that was ever devised. It took a lot out of mother.

A few months before Muggs died, he got to "seeing things." He would rise slowly from the floor, growling low, and stalk stiff-legged and menacing toward nothing at all. Sometimes the Thing would be just a little to the right or left of a visitor. Once a Fuller Brush sales-man got hysterics. Muggs came wandering into the room like Hamlet following his father's ghost. His eyes were fixed on a spot just to the left of the Fuller Brush man, who stood it until Muggs was about three slow, creeping paces from him. Then he shouted. Muggs wav-ered on past him into the hallway grumbling to himself but the Fuller man went on shouting. I think mother had to throw a pan of cold water on him before he stopped. That was the way she used to stop us boys when we got into fights.

Muggs died quite suddenly one night. Mother wanted to bury him in the family lot under a marble stone with some such inscrip-tion as "Flights of angels sing thee to thy rest" but we persuaded her it was against the law. In the end we just put up a smooth board above his grave along a lonely road. On the board I wrote with an indelible pencil "Cave Canem." Mother was quite pleased with the simple classic dignity of the old Latin epitaph.

The Horse That Played Third Base for Brooklyn

WILBUR SCHRAMM

The first day Jones played third base for Brooklyn was like the day Galileo turned his telescope on the planets or Columbus sailed back to Spain. First, people said it couldn't be true; then they said things will never be the same.

Timothy McGuire, of the Brooklyn *Eagle*, told me how he felt the first time he saw Jones. He said that if a bird had stepped out of a cuckoo clock that day and asked him what time it was, he wouldn't have been surprised enough to blink an Irish eye. And still he knew that the whole future of baseball hung that day by a cotton thread.

Don't ask the high commissioner of baseball about this. He has never yet admitted publicly that Jones ever played for Brooklyn. He has good reason not to. But ask an old-time sports writer. Ask Tim McGuire.

It happened so long ago it was even before Mr. Roosevelt became President. It was a lazy Georgia-spring afternoon, the first time McGuire and I saw Jones. There was a light-footed little breeze and just enough haze to keep the sun from burning. The air was full of fresh-cut grass and wistaria and fruit blossoms and the ping of baseballs on well-oiled mitts. Everyone in Georgia knows that the only sensible thing to do on an afternoon like that is sleep. If you can't do that, if you are a baseball writer down from New York to cover Brooklyn's spring-training camp, you can stretch out on the grass and raise yourself every hour or so on one elbow to steal a glance at fielding practice. That was what we were doing—meanwhile amusing ourselves half-heartedly with a game involving small cubes and numbers—when we first saw Jones.

The *Times* wasn't there. Even in those days they were keeping their sports staff at home to study for Information Please. But four of us were down from the New York papers—the *World*, the *Herald*, Tim, and I. I can even remember what we were talking about.

I was asking the *World*, "How do they look to you?"

"Pitchers and no punch," the *World* said. "No big bats. No great fielders. No Honus Wagner. No Hal Chase. No Ty Cobb."

"No Tinker to Evers to Chance," said the *Herald*. "Seven come to Susy," he added soothingly, blowing on his hands.

"What's your angle today?" the *World* asked Tim.

Tim doesn't remember exactly how he answered that. To the best of my knowledge, he merely said, "Ulk." It occurred to me that the Brooklyn *Eagle* was usually more eloquent than that, but the Southern weather must have slowed up my reaction.

The *World* said, "What?"

"There's a sorsh," Tim said in a weak, strangled sort of voice— "a horse . . . on third . . . base."

"Why don't they chase it off?" said the *Herald* impatiently. "Your dice."

"They don't . . . want to," Tim said in that funny voice.

I glanced up at Tim then. Now Tim, as you probably remember, was built from the same blueprints as a truck, with a magnificent red nose for a headlight. But when I looked at him, all the color was draining out of that nose slowly, from top to bottom, like turning off a gas mantle. I should estimate Tim was, at the moment, the whitest McGuire in four generations.

Then I looked over my shoulder to see where Tim was staring. He was the only one of us facing the ball diamond. I looked for some time. Then I tapped the *World* on the back.

"Pardon me," I asked politely, "do you notice anything unusual?"

"If you refer to my luck," said the *World*, "it's the same pitiful kind I've had since Christmas."

"Look at the infield," I suggested.

"Hey," said the *Herald*, "if you don't want the dice, give them to me."

"I know this can't be true," mused the *World*, "but I could swear I see a horse on third base."

The *Herald* climbed to his feet with some effort. He was built in the days when there was no shortage of materials.

"If the only way to get you guys to put your minds on this game is to chase that horse off the field," he said testily, "I'll do it myself."

He started toward the infield, rubbed his eyes and fainted dead away.

"I had the queerest dream," he said, when we revived him. "I dreamed there was a horse playing third base. My God!" he shouted, glancing toward the diamond. "I'm still asleep!"

That is, word for word, what happened the first day Jones played third base for Brooklyn. Ask McGuire.

When we felt able, we hunted up the Brooklyn manager, who was a chunky, red-haired individual with a whisper like a foghorn. A foghorn with a Brooklyn accent. His name was Pop O'Donnell.

"I see you've noticed," Pop boomed defensively.

"What do you mean," the *Herald* said severely, "by not notifying us you had a horse playing third base?"

"I didn't guess you'd believe it," Pop said.

Pop was still a little bewildered himself. He said the horse had wandered on the field that morning during practice. Someone tried to chase it off by hitting a baseball toward it. The horse calmly opened its mouth and caught the ball. Nothing could be neater.

While they were still marveling over that, the horse galloped thirty yards and took a ball almost out of the hands of an outfielder who was poised for the catch. They said Willie Keeler couldn't have done it better. So they spent an hour hitting fungo flies—or, as some wit called them, horse flies—to the horse. Short ones, long ones, high ones, grass cutters, line drives—it made no difference; the animal covered Dixie like the dew.

They tried the horse at second and short, but he was a little slow on the pivot when compared with men like Napoleon Lajoie. Then they tried him at third base, and knew that was the right, the inevitable place. He was a great wall of China. He was a flash of brown lightning. In fact, he covered half the shortstop's territory and two-thirds of left field, and even came behind the plate to help the catcher with foul tips. The catcher got pretty sore about it. He said that anybody who was going to steal his easy put-outs would have to wear an umpire's uniform like the other thieves.

"Can he hit?" asked the *World*.

"See for yourself," Pop O'Donnell invited.

The Superbas—they hadn't begun calling them the Dodgers yet—were just starting batting practice. Nap Rucker was tossing them in with that beautiful smooth motion of his, and the horse was at bat. He met the first ball on the nose and smashed it into left field.

He laid down a bunt that waddled like a turtle along the base line.
He sizzled a liner over second like a clothesline.

"What a story!" said the *World.*

"I wonder," said the *Herald*—"I wonder how good it is."

We stared at him.

"I wouldn't say it is quite as good as the sinking of the *Maine,*
if you mean that," said Tim.

"I wonder how many people are going to believe it," said the
Herald.

"I'll race you to the phone," Tim said.

Tim won. He admits he had a long start. Twenty minutes later
he came back, walking slowly.

"I wish to announce," he said, "that I have been insulted by my
editor and am no longer connected with the Brooklyn *Eagle.* If I
can prove that I am sober tomorrow, they may hire me back," he
added.

"You see what I mean," said the *Herald.*

We all filed telegraph stories about the horse. We swore that
every word was true. We said it was a turning point in baseball. Two
of us mentioned Columbus; and one, Galileo. In return, we got
advice.

THESE TROUBLED TIMES, NEWSPAPERS NO SPACE FOR FICTION,
EXPENSE ACCOUNT NO PROVISION DRUNKEN LEVITY, the *Herald's* wire
read. The *World* read, ACCURACY, ACCURACY, ACCURACY, followed by
three exclamation points, and signed "Joseph Pulitzer." CHARGING
YOUR TELEGRAM RE BROOKLYN HORSE TO YOUR SALARY, my wire said.
THAT'S A HORSE ON YOU!

Have you ever thought what you would do with a purple cow
if you had one? I know. You would paint it over. We had a horse
that could play third base, and all we could do was sit in the middle
of Georgia and cuss our editors. I blame the editors. It is their fault
that for the last thirty years you have had to go to smoking rooms or
Pullman cars to hear about Jones.

But I don't entirely blame them either. My first question would
have been: How on earth can a horse possibly bat and throw? That's
what the editors wondered. It's hard to explain. It's something you
have to see to believe—like dogfish and political conventions.

And I've got to admit that the next morning we sat around and
asked one another whether we really had seen a horse playing third
base. Pop O'Donnell confessed that when he woke up he said to
himself, *It must be shrimp that makes me dream about horses.* Then

all of us went down to the park, not really knowing whether we would see a horse there or not.

We asked Pop was he going to use the horse in games.

"I don't know," he thundered musingly. "I wonder. There are many angles. I don't know," he said, pulling at his chin.

That afternoon the Cubs, the world champs, came for an exhibition game. A chap from Pennsylvania—I forget his name—played third base for Brooklyn, and the horse grazed quietly beside the dugout. Going into the eighth, the Cubs were ahead, 2-0, and Three-Finger Brown was tying Brooklyn in knots. A curve would come over, then a fast one inside, and then the drop, and the Superbas would beat the air or hit puny little rollers to the infield which Tinker or Evers would grab up and toss like a beanbag to Frank Chance. It was sickening. But in the eighth, Maloney got on base on an error, and Jordan walked. Then Lumley went down swinging, and Lewis watched three perfect ones sail past him. The horse still was grazing over by the Brooklyn dugout.

"Put in the horse!" Frank Chance yelled. The Cubs laughed themselves sick.

Pop O'Donnell looked at Chance, and then at the horse, and back at Chance, as though he had made up his mind about something. "Go in there, son, and get a hit," he said. "Watch out for the curve." "Coive," Pop said.

The horse picked up a bat and cantered out to the plate.

"Pinch-hitting for Batch," announced the umpire dreamily, "this horse." A second later he shook himself violently. "What am I saying?" he shouted.

On the Cubs' bench, every jaw had dropped somewhere around the owner's waist. Chance jumped to his feet, his face muscles worked like a coffee grinder, but nothing came out. It was the only time in baseball history, so far as I can find out, that Frank Chance was ever without words.

When he finally pulled himself together he argued, with a good deal of punctuation, that there was no rule saying you could play a horse in the big leagues. Pop roared quietly that there was no rule saying you couldn't, either. They stood there nose to nose, Pop firing methodically like a cannon, and Chance crackling like a machine gun. Chance gave up too easily. He was probably a little stunned. He said that he was used to seeing queer things in Brooklyn, anyway. Pop O'Donnell just smiled grimly.

Well, that was Jones' first game for Brooklyn. It could have been a reel out of a movie. There was that great infield—Steinfeldt, Tinker, Evers, and Chance—so precise, so much a machine, that any ball hit on the ground was like an apple into a sorter. The infield was so famous that not many people remember Sheckard and Slagle and Schulte in the outfield, but the teams of that day knew them. Behind the plate was Johnny Kling, who could rifle a ball to second like an 88-mm. cannon. And on the mound stood Three-Finger Brown, whose drop faded away as though someone were pulling it back with a string.

Brown took a long time getting ready. His hand shook a little, and the first one he threw was ten feet over Kling's head into the grandstand. Maloney and Jordan advanced to second and third. Brown threw the next one in the dirt. Then he calmed down, grooved one, and whistled a curve in around the withers.

"The glue works for you, Dobbin!" yelled Chance, feeling more like himself. Pop O'Donnell was mopping his forehead.

The next pitch came in fast, over the outside corner. The horse was waiting. He leaned into it. The ball whined all the way to the fence. Ted Williams was the only player I ever sat hit one like it. When Slagle finally got to the ball, the two runners had scored and the horse was on third. Brown's next pitch got away from Kling a few yards, and the horse stole home in a cloud of dust, all four feet flying. He got up, dusted himself off, looked at Chance and gave a horselaugh.

If this sounds queer, remember that queerer things happen in Brooklyn every day.

"How do we write this one up?" asked the *Herald*. "We can't put just 'a horse' in the box score."

That was when the horse got his name. We named him Jones, after Jones, the caretaker who had left the gate open so he could wander onto the field. We wrote about "Horse" Jones.

Next day we all chuckled at a banner headline in one of the metropolitan papers. It read: JONES PUTS NEW KICK IN BROOKLYN.

Look in the old box scores. Jones got two hits off Rube Waddell, of Philadelphia, and three off Cy Young, of Boston. He pounded Eddie Plank and Iron Man McGinnity and Wild Bill Donovan. He robbed Honus Wagner of a hit that would have been a double against any other third baseman in the league. On the base paths he was a bullet.

Our papers began to wire us, WHERE DOES JONES COME FROM? SEND BACKGROUND, HUMAN INTEREST, INTERVIEW. That was a harder assignment than New York knew. We decided by a gentlemen's agreement that Jones must have come from Kentucky and got his first experience in a Blue Grass league. That sounded reasonable enough. We said he was long-faced, long-legged, dark, a vegetarian and a non-smoker. That was true. We said he was a horse for work, and ate like a horse. That was self-evident. Interviewing was a little harder.

Poor Pop O'Donnell for ten years had wanted a third baseman who could hit hard enough to dent a cream puff. Now that he had one he wasn't quite sure what to do with it. Purple-cow trouble. "Poiple," Pop would have said.

One of his first worries was paying for Jones. A strapping big farmer appeared at the clubhouse, saying he wanted either his horse or fifty thousand dollars.

Pop excused himself, checked the team's bank balance, then came back.

"What color is your horse?" he asked.

The farmer thought a minute. "Dapple gray," he said.

"Good afternoon, my man," Pop boomed unctuously, holding open the door. "That's a horse of another color." Jones was brown.

There were some audience incidents too. Jonathan Daniels, of Raleigh, North Carolina, told me that as a small boy that season he saw a whole row of elderly ladies bustle into their box seats, take one look toward third base, look questioningly at one another, twitter about the sun being hot, and walk out. Georgia police records show that at least five citizens, cold sober, came to the ball park and were afraid to drive their own cars home. The American medical journals of that year discovered a new psychoneurosis which they said was doubtless caused by a feeling of insecurity resulting from the replacement of the horse by the horseless carriage. It usually took the form of hallucination—the sensation of seeing a horse sitting on a baseball players' bench. Perhaps that was the reason a famous pitcher, who shall here go nameless, came to town with his team, took one incredulous look at Brooklyn fielding practice, and went to his manager, offering to pay a fine.

But the real trouble was over whether horses should be allowed to play baseball. After the first shock, teams were generally amused at the idea of playing against a horse. But after Jones had batted their star pitchers out of the box, they said the Humane Society ought to protect the poor Brooklyn horse.

The storm that brewed in the South that spring was like nothing

except the storm that gathered in 1860. Every hotel that housed baseball players housed a potential civil war. The better orators argued
that the right to play baseball should not be separated from the
right to vote or the responsibility of fighting for one's country. The
more practical ones said a few more horses like Jones and they
wouldn't have any jobs left. Still others said that this was probably
just another bureaucratic trick on the part of the Administration.

Even the Brooklyn players protested. A committee of them came
to see old Pop O'Donnell. They said wasn't baseball a game for
human beings? Pop said he had always had doubts as to whether
some major-league players were human or not. They said touché,
and this is all right so long as it is a one-horse business, so to speak.
But if it goes on, before long won't a man have to grow two more
legs and a tail before he can get in? They asked Pop how he would
like to manage the Brooklyn Percherons, instead of the Brooklyn
Superbas? They said, what would happen to baseball if it became a
game for animals—say, giraffes on one team, trained seals on a second and monkeys on a third? They pointed out that monkeys had
already got a foot in the door by being used to dodge baseballs in
carnivals. How would Pop like to manage a team of monkeys called
the Brooklyn Dodgers, they asked.

Pop said heaven help anyone who has to manage a team called
the Brooklyn Dodgers. Then he pointed out that Brooklyn hadn't
lost an exhibition game, and that the horse was leading the league
in batting with a solid .516. He asked whether they would rather
have a world series or a two-legged third baseman. They went away
muttering.

But his chief worry was Jones himself.

"That horse hasn't got his mind on the game," he told us one
night on the hotel veranda.

"Ah, Pop, it's just horseplay," said the *World*, winking.

"Nope, he hasn't got his heart in it," said Pop, his voice echoing
lightly off the distant mountains. "He comes just in time for practice
and runs the minute it's over. There's something on that horse's
mind."

We laughed, but had to admit that Jones was about the saddest
horse we had ever seen. His eyes were great brown pools of liquid
sorrow. His ears drooped. And still he hit well over .500 and covered
third base like a rug.

One day he missed the game entirely. It was the day the Giants
were in town, and fifteen thousand people were there to watch Jones

bat against the great Matty. Brooklyn lost the game, and Pop O'Donnell almost lost his hair at the hands of the disappointed crowd.

"Who would have thought," Pop mused, in the clubhouse after
the game, "that that (here some words are omitted) horse would
turn out to be a prima donna? It's all right for a major-league ball
player to act like a horse, but that horse is trying to act like a major-
league ball player."

It was almost by accident that Tim and I found out what was
really bothering Jones. We followed him one day when he left the
ball park. We followed him nearly two miles to a race track.

Jones stood beside the fence a long time, turning his head to
watch the Thoroughbreds gallop by on exercise runs and time trials.
Then a little stable boy opened the gate for him.

"Po' ol' hoss," the boy said. "Yo' wants a little runnin'?"

"Happens every day," a groom explained to us. "This horse
wanders up here from God knows where, and acts like he wants to
run, and some boy rides him awhile, bareback, pretending he's a
race horse."

Jones was like a different horse out there on the track; not
drooping any more—ears up, eyes bright, tail like a plume. It was
pitiful how much he wanted to look like a race horse.

"That horse," Tim asked the groom, "is he any good for racing?"

"Not here, anyway," the groom said. "Might win a county-fair
race or two."

He asked us whether we had any idea who owned the horse.

"Sir," said Tim, like Edwin M. Stanton, "that horse belongs to
the ages."

"Well, mister," said the groom, "the ages had better get some
different shoes on that horse. Why, you could hold a baseball in
those shoes he has there."

"It's very clear," I said as we walked back, "what we have here
is a badly frustrated horse."

"It's clear as beer," Tim said sadly.

That afternoon Jones hit a home run and absent-mindedly
trotted around the bases. As soon as the game was over, he disappeared in the direction of the race track. Tim looked at me and shook
his head. Pop O'Donnell held his chin in his hands.

"I'll be boiled in oil," he said. "Berled in erl," he said.

Nothing cheered up poor Pop until someone came in with a
story about the absentee owner of a big-league baseball club who
had inherited the club along with the family fortune. This individual

had just fired the manager of his baseball farm system, because the farms had not turned out horses like Jones. "What are farms for if they don't raise horses?" the absentee owner had asked indignantly.

Jones was becoming a national problem second only to the Panama Canal and considerably more important than whether Mr. Taft got to be President.

There were rumors that the Highlanders—people were just beginning to call them the Yankees—would withdraw and form a new league if Jones was allowed to play. It was reported that a team of kangaroos from Australia was on its way to play a series of exhibition games in America, and Pres. Ban Johnson, of the American League, was quoted as saying that he would never have kangaroos in the American League because they were too likely to jump their contracts. There was talk of a constitutional amendment concerning horses in baseball.

The thing that impressed me, down there in the South, was that all this was putting the cart before the horse, so to speak. Jones simply didn't want to play baseball. He wanted to be a race horse. I don't know why life is that way.

Jones made an unassisted triple play, and Ty Cobb accused Brooklyn of furnishing fire ladders to its infielders. He said that no third baseman could have caught the drive that started the play. At the end of the training season, Jones was batting .538, and fielding .997, had stolen twenty bases and hit seven home runs. He was the greatest third baseman in the history of baseball, and didn't want to be!

Joseph Pulitzer, William Randolph Hearst, Arthur Brisbane and the rest of the big shots got together and decided that if anyone didn't know by this time that Jones was a horse, the newspapers wouldn't tell him. He could find it out.

Folks seemed to find it out. People began gathering from all parts of the country to see Brooklyn open against the Giants—Matty against Jones. Even a tribe of Sioux Indians camped beside the Gowanus and had war dances on Flatbush Avenue, waiting for the park to open. And Pop O'Donnell kept his squad in the South as long as he could, laying plans to arrive in Brooklyn only on the morning of the opening game.

The wire said that night that 200,000 people had come to Brooklyn for the game, and 190,000 of them were in an ugly mood over the report that the league might not let Jones play. The Governor of New York sent two regiments of the national guard. The Giants were said to be caucusing to decide whether they would play against Jones.

By game time, people were packed for six blocks, fighting to get into the park. The Sioux sent a young buck after their tomahawks, just in case. Telephone poles a quarter of a mile from the field were selling for a hundred dollars. Every baseball writer in the country was in the Brooklyn press box; the other teams played before cub reporters and society editors. Just before game time I managed to push into Pop O'Donnell's little office with the presidents of the two major leagues, the Mayor of New York, a half dozen other reporters, and a delegation from the Giants.

"There's just one thing we want to know," the spokesman for the Giants was asking Pop. "Are you going to play Jones?"

"Gentlemen," said Pop in that soft-spoken, firm way of his that rattled the window blinds, "our duty is to give the public what it wants. And the public wants Jones."

Like an echo, a chant began to rise from the bleachers, "We want Jones!"

"There is one other little thing," said Pop. "Jones has disappeared."

There were about ten seconds of the awful silence that comes when your nerves are paralyzed, but your mind keeps on thrashing.

"He got out of his boxcar somewhere between Georgia and Brooklyn," Pop said. "We don't know where. We're looking."

A Western Union boy dashed in. "Hold on!" said Pop. "This may be news!"

He tore the envelope with a shaky hand. The message was from Norfolk, Virginia. HAVE FOUND ELEPHANT THAT CAN BALANCE MEDICINE BALL ON TRUNK, it read. WILL HE DO? If Pop had said what he said then into a telephone, it would have burned out all the insulators in New York.

Down at the field, the President of the United States himself was poised to throw out the first ball. "Is this Jones?" he asked. He was a little nearsighted.

"This is the Mayor of New York," Pop said patiently. "Jones is gone. Run away."

The President's biographers disagree as to whether he said at that moment, "Oh, well, who would stay in Brooklyn if he could run?" or "I sympathize with you for having to change horses in midstream."

That was the saddest game ever covered by the entire press corps of the nation. Brooklyn was all thumbs in the field, all windmills at bat. There was no Jones to whistle hits into the outfield and make sensational stops at third. By the sixth inning, when they had to call the game with the score 18-1, the field was ankle-deep in pop bottles and the Sioux were waving their tomahawks and singing the scalp song.

You know the rest of the story. Brooklyn didn't win a game until the third week of the season, and no team ever tried a horse again, except a few dark horses every season. Pittsburgh, I believe, tried trained seals in the outfield. They were deadly at catching the ball, but couldn't cover enough ground. San Francisco has an entire team of Seals, but I have never seen them play. Boston tried an octopus at second base, but had to give him up. What happened to two rookies who disappeared trying to steal second base against Boston that spring is another subject baseball doesn't talk about.

There has been considerable speculation as to what happened to Jones. Most of us believed the report that the Brooklyn players had unfastened the latch on the door of his boxcar, until Pop O'Donnell's Confidential Memoirs came out, admitting that he himself had taken the hinges off the door because he couldn't face the blame for making baseball a game for horses. But I have been a little confused since Tim McGuire came to me once and said he might as well confess. He couldn't stand to think of that horse standing wistfully beside the track, waiting for someone to let him pretend he was a race horse. That haunted Tim. When he went down to the boxcar he found the door unlatched and the hinges off, so he gave the door a little push outward. He judged it was the will of the majority.

And that is why baseball is played by men today instead of by horses. But don't think that the shadow of Jones doesn't still lie heavy on the game. Have you ever noticed how retiring and silent and hang-dog major-league ball players are, how they cringe before the umpire? They never know when another Jones may break away from a beer wagon or a circus or a plow, wander through an unlocked gate, and begin batting .538 to their .290. The worry is terrible. You can see it in the crowds too. That is why Brooklyn fans are so aloof and disinterested, why they never raise their voices above a whisper at Ebbets Field. They know perfectly well that this is only minor-league ball they are seeing, that horses could play it twice as well if they had a chance.

That is the secret we sports writers have kept all these years;

that is why we have never written about Jones. And the Brooklyn fans still try to keep it secret, but every once in a while the sorrow eats like lye into one of them until he can hold it back no longer, and then he sobs quietly and says, "Dem bums, if dey only had a little horse sense!"

How to Cure Bird-Watchers

John Fischer

One of our readers—a young woman living in Sacramento—has written to ask whether there is any known cure for bird-watching. Her father, she says, keeps gawking around the neighborhood with field glasses, often at unseemly hours. This causes embarrassment to her and her friends. Only last week a couple parked in a quiet lane was startled by the old gentleman at an unfortunate moment, and matters weren't helped much by his explanation that he was only looking for a spiny-toed nightingale.

The lady has come to the right place. This is a service magazine, in a soulful kind of way. We aim to help with the spiritual problems of our readers, just as *McCall's* takes care of the grosser human needs by printing all those articles about forty-three new ways to cook hamburger. Besides I have been plagued by birds for years, and while I can't say that I've learned to cope with them I at least know how to give them a good fight.

It is true that I have never suffered myself from bird-watching. Since childhood, when I was forced to take care of a herd of malevolent chickens, I have regarded all varieties of *Aves Neognathae* as smelly, noisy, feather-brained, hysterical little beasts, from which any sensitive man naturally averts his eyes. Nevertheless at a tender age I stumbled by accident on a sure-fire remedy for the affliction. The only difficulty is that the young woman will have to persuade her father to do his bird-watching, at least once, barefooted and along the banks of some southern stream. The Suwannee River would serve. Or Dead Man's Bayou.

My own discovery was made on Sweetwater Creek in northern Texas. I was after catfish, using a No. 6 hook baited with boiled potato. (This method is neither as sporting nor as efficient as dynamite, but my parents—who had never heard of Dr. Spock and permissive child-raising—discouraged me from playing with ex-

298

plosives.) So I was ambling along barefoot, brooding over parental tyranny and looking hard for one of those muddy backwaters where catfish hold their committee meetings.

All of a sudden my left foot came down on something unpleasant. I had never stepped on a water moccasin before, but somehow I knew right off what to do. The moccasin is a fat and sluggish snake, and before he knew what was squushing him I was ten feet in the air; and by the time he got his fangs cleared for action, I had hit the ground about five yards off in a high lope.

Ever since I have been a compulsive snake-watcher. Anyone, I believe, who has felt the coils of a water moccasin under his toes will thereafter keep his eyes firmly on the ground. Never again is he likely to be bothered with the sight of birds, aside from sandpipers and those little squinch owls that live in prairie-dog holes.

Even a reformed bird-watcher, however, is by no means out of the woods. With any decent animal—a grizzly, for instance—you can be reasonably sure that if you don't bother him, he won't bother you. But not birds; they seek out their victims with the vindictive persistence of the Kremlin's secret police. If you go to earth, so to speak, on the twenty-fourth floor of a Manhattan apartment, a posse of pigeons is sure to turn up at six the next morning to hoot and sneer at you from the window sill. Starlings will build a nest in the intake of your air conditioner. Or you will find, as one inoffensive New Yorker did recently, that something of the order *Columbiformes* has flown right inside and laid an egg on your bedspread.

Take the case of George and Helen Papashvily, sculptor and writer, who sought tranquillity in the upper fastnesses of Bucks County. They had hardly got the plumbing into their old stone farmhouse when they were beset by a retarded cardinal.

Like so many of his genus, he was belligerent as well as stupid. For weeks he carried on a running battle with his own reflection in the dining-room window—swooping into the pane like a *kamikaze* pilot, beating it with his wings, and pecking at it till his beak dripped blood. The round ended when he had knocked himself out or collapsed on the grass in exhaustion.

At this point the Papashvilys—who are kindly to the verge of simple-mindedness and constantly imposed upon by man and beast —would rise wearily from their dining-table and rescue the dope. After they had trickled brandy down his throat with an eye dropper,

plied him with smelling salts, and pressed cold towels to his forehead, he usually revived enough for another assault.

This might have kept up indefinitely, or anyhow until the
brandy ran out, if a she-cardinal hadn't come along one day and
diverted him to other interests. They are now, presumably, popu-
lating the thickets of northern Pennsylvania with generation after
generation of half-witted *Richmondena*.

Smart birds are even worse. Everything that wears feathers is
a criminal at heart—as Dr. A. C. Bent demonstrated in his classic
fourteen-volume *Life Histories of North American Birds*—but the
elite of this over-world obviously are the crows. They are as well
organized as the Mafia, and more cunning. Nobody has ever
rounded up a gang of crows in an Apalachin farmhouse.

The reason is that—unlike Barbara, Genovese & Co.—crows do
their conspiring in an open field, with guards posted to cover every
approach. These sentries apparently carry binoculars, and are
trained not only to spot a gun at five hundred yards but to tell
whether it is a rifle or shotgun; and they have learned the range of
each. Consequently, as every hunter knows, they are about the most
elusive game on this continent.

I once tried to beat their system by sneaking up on a crow con-
vention in a station wagon. They know that autos are harmless, and
ordinarily pay them no attention. So I pulled up, in an offhand way,
beside a pasture where maybe twenty-five of them were plotting their
next job.

Sure enough, after one contemptuous glance they went right on
with their scheming. I rolled down a window. Still no alarm. Then
I reached for the carbine I had hidden under a gunny sack, and
started to poke it—slowly and cautiously—over the sill. Not more
than an inch of the muzzle was sticking out when the nearest sentry
saw it, recognized instantly what it was, and blew the whistle. The
whole gang took off, jeering vulgarly, before I could get in a shot.

The only practical way to outwit a crow is with dynamite, the
sportsman's best friend on water or land. Here is a tested recipe,
bearing the Harper's Seal of Approval:

First you find a thicket of shinnery oaks where crows gather to
roost. These scrubby little trees grow in dense clumps all over the
Texas Panhandle; they make an ideal lair for crows, as they once did
for horse thieves and train robbers. As many as five thousand birds
may infest a single clump.

At daybreak they leave in small bands, scattering over miles of countryside on their criminal pursuits—stealing pheasant eggs, devastating grain fields, pecking the eyes out of newborn calves. As soon as you are sure they are all gone, you slip into the shinnery and start stringing up your dynamite. Half-sticks will do, tied to branches at about head height and spaced roughly five yards apart all through the thicket. Their detonators all have to be connected to a single wire, which runs to a hiding place a safe distance away—usually a neighboring patch of brush. There you wait, beside your storage battery and switch, until the enemy comes home at sundown.

This is the crucial moment. You have to lie well-ambushed and absolutely still; for if an advance patrol spots you, it will warn the whole flock—which at once will line out for another roost miles away. If you escape detection, however, you simply bide your time until the whole colony is assembled; then close the switch. The results are gratifying. A rain of black feathers, shinnery leaves, and crows' feet will cover the landscape for acres around.

In our struggle with the birds, the most dangerous chink in man's armor is sentimentality. They are alert for any sign of this weakness; and, as we have seen in The Papashvily Case, they know how to take instant advantage of it.

My aunt Annie was, I guess, the softest-hearted woman in Comanche County, Oklahoma. For many years she lived on a homestead there, keeping house for her widower father. One Christmas a neighbor gave her a jar of brandied cherries and—though Annie disapproved of liquor even in semi-solid form—the guests at dinner that night managed to put away the whole quart.

In her thrifty way, Annie saved the pits and fed them next morning to her flock of hens. This was meant in the kindliest spirit— Annie felt that even Plymouth Rocks deserved a Christmas treat— but it turned out to be a mistake. When Annie went out at noon to collect the eggs, she found every one of the chickens lying stone cold dead with its claws sticking up stiff in the air.

Crushed by grief as she was, she didn't mean to let those chickens go to waste. Annie couldn't bring herself to chop off their heads —that was man's work anyhow, and could wait till her father came in from plowing the northeast forty—but she could at least begin to get them ready for the cold-storage locker. With tears sliding down her nose, and muttering prayers against the evil of drink, she plucked them all—carefully saving the feathers for pillow-stuffing. Then she laid the corpses in a row along the shady side of the barn to await the axe.

Trouble was, they didn't stay dead. When her father brought in the team at supper time, he encountered a spectacle which, he said, beat anything he had seen since the night when a Kiowa war party scalped the whole village of Chillicothe. Twenty-three hens were staggering around the barnyard—over-hung, shivering, and naked as September Morn.

The sight so scandalized the mules—a high-strung pair at best— that it took him twenty minutes to get off the harness.

Annie worked all night, cutting up old burlap bags and sewing them into hen chemises, while her outraged flock huddled squawk- ing behind the stove. By morning they were the best-dressed chick- ens in Oklahoma; but they didn't seem to appreciate it. For the next six weeks, while they were growing a new crop of feathers, they wore their smocks with a look both sheepish and hang-dog—which, for chickens, is quite a trick. I am willing to grant (grudgingly) that they, anyhow, must have been birds worth watching.

Dogs

Ring Lardner

Every little wile you hear people talking about a man that they don't nobody seem to have much use for him on acct. of him not paying his debts or beating his wife or something and everybody takes a rap at him about this and that until finely one of the party speaks up and says they must be some good in him because he likes animals.

"A man can't be all bad when he is so kind to dogs." That is what they generally always say and that is the reason you see so many men stop on the st. when they see a dog and pet it because they figure that may be somebody will be looking at them do it, and the next time they are getting panned, why who ever seen it will speak up and say:

"He can't be all bad because he likes dogs."

Well friends when you come right down to cases they's about as much sence to this as a good many other delusions that we got here in this country, like for inst. the one about nobody wanting to win the first pot and the one about the whole lot of authors not being able to do their best work unless they are ½ pickled.

But if liking animals ain't a virtue in itself I don't see how it proves that a man has got any virtues, and personly if I had a daughter and she wanted to get marred and I asked her what kind of a bird the guy was and she said she don't know nothing about him except that one day she seen him kiss a leopard, why I would hold up my blessing till a few of the missing precincts was heard from.

But as long as our best people has got it in their skull that a friendly feeling toward dumb brutes takes the curse off of a bad egg, why I or nobody else is going to be a sucker enough to come out and admit that all the horses, rams and oxen in the world could drop dead tomorrow morning without us batting an eye.

Pretty near everybody wants to be well thought of and if liking dogs or sheep is a helping along these lines, why even if I don't like them, I wouldn't never loose a opportunity to be seen in their company and act as if I was having the time of my life.

But while I was raised in a kennel, you might say, and some of my most intimate childhood friends was of the canine gender, still in all I believe dogs is better in some climates than others, the same as oysters, and I don't think it should ought to be held against a man if he don't feel the same towards N.Y. dogs as he felt towards Michigan dogs, and I am free to confess that the 4 dogs who I have grew to know personly here on Long Island has failed to arouse tender yearnings anyways near similar to those inspired by the flea bearers of my youth.

And in case they should be any tendency on the part of my readers to denounce me for failing to respond whole heartily to the wiles of the Long Island breed let me present a brief sketch of some so as true lovers of the canine tribe can judge for themselfs if the fault is all mind.

No. 1

This was the dainty boy that belonged to Gene Buck and it was a bull dog no bigger than a 2 car garage and it wouldn't harm a hair of nobody's head only other animals and people. Children were as safe with this pet as walking in the Pittsburgh freight yards and he wouldn't think of no more wronging a cat than scratching himself.

In fairness to Mr. Buck I'll state that a pal of his give him the dog as a present without no comment. Well they wasn't no trouble till Gene had the dog pretty near ½ hr. when they let him out. He was gone 10 minutes during which Gene received a couple of phone calls announcing more in anger than in sorrow the sudden deaths of 2 adjacent cats of noble berth so when the dog come back Gene spanked him and give him a terrible scolding and after that he didn't kill no more cats except when he got outdoors.

But the next day De Wolf Hopper come over to call and brought his kid which the dog thought would look better with one leg and it took 5 people to get him not to operate, so after that Gene called up the supt. of a dogs reform school and the man said he would take him and cure him of the cat habit by tying one of his victims around his neck and leaving it there for a wk. but he didn't know how to cure the taste for young Hoppers unlest De Wolf could spare the kid the wk. after they was finished with the cat.

This proposition fell through but anyway Gene sent the dog to the reformatory and is still paying board for same.

No. 2

The people that lived 3 houses from the undersigned decided to move to England where it seems like you can't take dogs no more so they asked us did we want the dog as it was very nice around children and we took it and sure enough it was OK in regards to children but it shared this new owners feeling towards motorcycles and every time one went past the house the dog would run out and spill the contents, and on Sundays when the traffic was heavy they would sometimes be as many as 4 or 5 motorcycle jehus standing on their heads in the middle of the road.

One of them finely took offence and told on the dog and the justice of the peace called me up and said I would have to kill it within 24 hrs. and the only way I could think of to do same was drown it in the bath tub and if you done that, why the bath tub wouldn't be no good no more because it was a good sized dog and no matter how often you pulled the stopper it would still be there.

No. 3

The next-door neighbors has a pro-German police dog that win a blue ribbon once but now it acts as body guard for the lady of the house and one day we was over there and the host says to slap his Mrs. on the arm and see what happened so I slapped her on the arm and I can still show you what happened.

When you dance with mine hostess this sweet little pet dances right along with you and watches your step and if you tred on my ladys toe he fines you a mouth full and if you and her is partners in a bridge game he lays under the table and you either bid right and play right or you get nipped.

No. 4

This is our present incumbrance which we didn't ask for him and nobody give him to us but here he is and he has got the insomonia and he has picked a spot outside my window to enjoy it but not only that but he has learnt that if you jump at a screen often enough it will finely give way and the result is that they ain't a door or window on the first floor that you couldn't drive a rhinoceros through it and all the bugs that didn't already live in the house is moving in and bringing their family.

That is a true record of the dogs who I have met since taking up my abode in Nassau county so when people ask me do I like dogs I say I'm crazy about them and I think they are all right in their place but it ain't Long Island.

How Lillian Mosquito Projects Her Voice

ROBERT BENCHLEY

All the children came crowding around Mother Nature one cold, raw afternoon in summer, crying in unison:

"Oh, Mother Nature, you promised us that you would tell us how Lillian Mosquito projects her voice! You promised that you would tell us how Lillian Mosquito projects her voice!"

"So I did! So I did!" said Mother Nature, laying down an oak, the leaves of which she was tipping with scarlet for the fall trade. "And so I will! So I will!"

At which Waldo Lizard, Edna Elephant and Lawrence Walrus jumped with imitation joy, for they had hoped to have an afternoon off.

Mother Nature led them across the fields to the piazza of a clubhouse on which there was an exposed ankle belonging to one of the members. There, as she had expected, they found Lillian Mosquito having tea.

"Lillian," called Mother Nature, "come off a minute. I have some little friends here who would like to know how it is that you manage to hum in such a manner as to give the impression of being just outside the ear of a person in bed, when actually you are across the room."

"Will you kindly repeat the question?" said Lillian flying over to the railing.

"We want to know," said Mother Nature, "how it is that very often, when you have been fairly caught, it turns out that you have escaped without injury."

"I would prefer to answer the question as it was first put," said Lillian.

So Waldo Lizard, Edna Elephant and Lawrence Walrus, seeing that there was no way out, cried:

"Yes, yes, Lillian, do tell us."

"First of all, you must know," began Lillian Mosquito, "that my chief duty is to annoy. Whatever else I do, however many bites I total in the course of the evening, I do not consider that I have 'made good' unless I have caused a great deal of annoyance while doing it. A bite, quietly executed and not discovered by the victim until morning, does me no good. It is my duty, and my pleasure, to play with him before biting, as you have often heard a cat plays with a mouse, tormenting him with apprehension and making him struggle to defend himself. . . . If I am using too long words for you, please stop me."

"Stop!" cried Waldo Lizard, reaching for his hat, with the idea of possibly getting to the ball park by the fifth inning.

But he was prevented from leaving by kindly old Mother Nature, who stepped on him with her kindly old heel, and Lillian Mosquito continued:

"I must therefore, you see, be able to use my little voice with great skill. Of course, the first thing to do is to make my victim think that I am nearer to him than I really am. To do this, I sit quite still, let us say, on the footboard of the bed, and, beginning to hum in a very, very low tone of voice, increase the volume and raise the pitch gradually, thereby giving the effect of approaching the pillow.

"The man in bed thinks that he hears me coming toward his head, and I can often see him, waiting with clenched teeth until he thinks that I am near enough to swat. Sometimes I strike a quick little grace-note, as if I were right above him and about to make a landing. It is great fun at such times to see him suddenly strike himself over the ear (they always think that I am right at their ear), and then feel carefully between his fingertips to see if he has caught me. Then, too, there is always the pleasure of thinking that perhaps he has hurt himself quite badly by the blow. I have often known victims of mine to deafen themselves permanently by jarring their eardrums in their wild attempts to catch me."

"What fun! What fun!" cried Edna Elephant. "I must try it myself just as soon as ever I get home."

"It is often a good plan to make believe that you have been caught after one of the swats," continued Lillian Mosquito, "and to keep quiet for a while. It makes him cocky. He thinks that he has demonstrated the superiority of man over the rest of the animals.

Then he rolls over and starts to sleep. This is the time to begin work on him again. After he has slapped himself all over the face and head, and after he has put on the light and made a search of the room and then gone back to bed to think up some new words, that is the time when I usually bring the climax about.

"Gradually approaching him from the right, I hum loudly at his ear. Then, suddenly becoming quiet, I fly silently and quickly around to his neck. Just as he hits himself on the ear, I bite his neck and fly away. And, *voilà*, there you are!"

"How true that is!" said Mother Nature. "*Voilà*, there we are! . . . Come, children, let us go now, for we must be up bright and early to-morrow to learn how Lois Hen scratches up the beets and Swiss chard in the gentlemen's gardens."

Rufus

H. Allen Smith

Oct. 12—My most intimate friend died two days ago.

While the vet was putting him away, I went into the deep woods back of the house and wandered around for an hour, trying to fight off a sickish feeling and not succeeding at all. It was one of the worst hours I've ever had.

His name was Rufus and he had been my constant companion for all of the thirteen years of his life. He was a black cocker spaniel and during those years, from early morning to late at night, he was forever at my feet. As has been stated, my office is across a breezeway from the house and each morning, when I had finished breakfast, I'd address him as "Miss Blue"—recalling the secretary in the old Amos 'n' Andy radio show ("Miss Blue, buzz me!").

"All right, Miss Blue," I'd say, and head for the office, and he'd be right at my heels, ready for the day's work, ready to supervise everything I did. Sometimes there in the privacy of the office I'd talk to him. He was the first to hear the plots of two novels I wrote. He never said anything, one way or another, even after the books came out. I didn't expect him to. I didn't want him to. I wasn't looking for critical comment—I simply wanted to talk about those stories. He thought I was tetched. Whenever I talked to him at some length, he would twist his head to one side and keep it there, staring at me, telling me quite clearly that I was off my rocker. It never bothered me, because a lot of people look at me the same way.

On those occasions when I did leave the property for an hour or a day or a week, he would plant himself in the middle of the driveway and sit there staring patiently toward the road, until he heard my car horn beyond the curve. He could distinguish my horn from a hundred others and sometimes, on hearing it, he'd start racing around in a circle—he was that happy over my return.

Rufus had faults and failings that were almost human. He was, in fact, more of a "person" than many of my neighbors; he could be depended upon to react in certain definite ways to certain definite stimuli. He was a real oddball in many of his traits. For example, he was afraid of rabbits. Several times in his later years I saw him skulk in the presence of a rabbit. There was a reason for it. When he was younger he chased rabbits like any other dog. One day we were going down the hill to the mailbox when a cottontail took off across the field. Rufus gave it the old college try, running as hard as he could, and then something happened to his back legs. Both of them were somehow thrown out of joint and I had to carry him to the house and then to the vet. He couldn't walk for a couple of weeks and then the legs got better and pretty soon he was sound again. But he had learned something about rabbits, and he had no use for them after that. He had a feeling, I think, that a rabbit was possessed of a secret weapon—a sort of crippling ray. He had been a good fifty feet from that rabbit when the ray hit his back legs.

He was a real Milquetoast. He rarely left our property except for an occasional daring expedition up or down the road, traveling no more than a quarter of a mile and then he'd get frightened at the immensity of the world and come hurrying home. He could do a job of ferocious barking, usually at the wrong people; his most hysterical outbursts were always directed against the delivery truck which brought his meat. Because of his superficial ferocity everyone considered him to be a fine watchdog and said so. Yet he was the world's worst. He'd charge at any and all invaders, barking furiously, so long as I was on the scene to back him up. But we found out later that whenever we were away from the house he had a tendency to crawl off somewhere and hide. A friend arrived one day while we were in New York City, and she went searching for Rufus. Eventually she found him upstairs, under a bed, almost trembling with fright.

He used to go at the laundryman as if he meant to chew the guy to pieces; at the same time he would whine and tremble and cling to my side at a distant rumble of thunder. He didn't seem to know that more dogs have been knocked head over heels by laundrymen than by all the thunderclaps since time began.

My affection for Rufus was a little strange considering the fact that during the years in which I lived in New York City I was a dog-hater. It wasn't a mere distaste for dogs, but a wild and untrammeled bitterness, born of ten thousand meetings with them on the pavements and sidewalks of the city. In later years I realized that my animus wasn't actually directed against dogs, but rather against the people who owned them, and kept them in the prison of apartments, and put little raincoats and rubber booties on them when they walked them in the rain.

Then I moved to the country and almost immediately, by command of my children, I acquired Rufus. It came about through my reading of a classified ad in the local paper, an ad that was somewhat confusing in its terminology. After studying it for quite a while I concluded that a man named Paul Ganz was giving away cocker spaniels. He lived over in Yorktown, on Baptist Church Road, and when I telephoned him and asked him if it was true, he said it certainly was not true. What the ad meant was that he had some girl dogs that he wanted to stash around at different homes, and they wouldn't really belong to the people who kept them, and occasionally Mr. Ganz would come around with boy dogs, and then something would happen that I never did quite understand, and that's all there was to it, except that there was some mention of puppies. This didn't sound good to me—I said I just wanted to buy a dog, not operate a house of ill fame. So Mr. Ganz drove over one evening, walked into the living room, reached into his coat pocket and pulled out a little black ball and set it on the floor and it promptly peed on the carpet.

A few days later Mr. Ganz sent me a certificate of pedigree—a thing I didn't even have for myself. I didn't like the looks of that pedigree. The dogs involved in the production of Rufus all seemed to be close relatives—first cousins and uncles and aunts and brothers and sisters—and the more I studied the thing the more I thought that I might have an idiot dog on my hands. Rufus was a My Own Brucie cocker. Of his eight great-grandparents, two were My Own Brucie— the same fellow both times—and one was My Own Miss Brucie, and one was Blackstone Brucie (a dog lawyer?) and one was My Own Old Lace, and one was My Own Clear Doubt. Kinfolks. Close-knit. Clannish. Carrying on under the same roof. Then one of the grandfathers named Pooh-Bah of Angelfear romanced My Own Clear Doubt and to this union was born Rustum of Angelfear and Rustum of Angelfear fell in love with Rebel Beauty of Angelfear (could they have been brother and sister?) and they begat Rufus and Rufus peed on the carpet. His real name was Black Rebel of Mount Kisco but I don't think he ever knew it. He was named Rufus after my friend Rufus Blair of Hollywood. Rufus Blair's daughter, Sandra, when she was about twelve, developed a deep resentment over my having named a dog for her father. She got back at me. One day she came home with an ancient tomcat, and announced to the family that its name was H. Alley Cat.

Any dog that has My Own Brucie for a great-grandfather, twice over, has something to be genuinely proud about, but I'm sure Rufus never gave the matter any thought. He was as common as dirt. He didn't act superior, was opposed to bathing, and ate sticks. It took a long time to get him housebroken. Bluebloods are harder to train in that respect than ordinary dogs; whether this also applies to people is a thing I wouldn't know. After we did get him housebroken it turned out that he was broken to only one house. Whenever he got into a house other than his own, the first thing he looked for was the piano. He seemed to have some prejudice against pianos, or perhaps against music generally. If he couldn't find a piano, he'd use people. One evening when he was still a puppy we had company in, and among the guests was a lady of considerable dignity and poise. She was standing by the fireplace with a cocktail in her hand, gassing about Henry James, when her left foot began to feel warm-ish. She took a sip of her drink and then glanced down at her foot and Rufus was there, just finishing up a great job of work. He had filled her shoe, but there was a saving circumstance. She had on open-toed slippers, and it all ran down and out through the vent in the front. This is the only time I ever saw an application of the practical value of open-toed shoes.

(I wrote a few things about Rufus once in a book, including the incident of the open-toed shoe. Maureen McKernan told me later that there was an 80-year-old priest down-country who, about once every two or three months, would call his assistant and say, "Get the book and read me the part about Rufus and the shoe again." He expressed the wish to meet Rufus before he died, but unhappily I didn't know about it so it never came to pass.)

I must mention that at the same time we got Rufus we acquired two cats and he grew up with them and for a long time I'm sure he believed himself to be a cat. He acquired certain cat habits, the most noteworthy of which was the expert use of his paws. He boxed and slapped with his paws, the way a cat does, and showed a certain dexterity in handling objects with his paws. And he did more licking of his pelt, cat fashion, than any other dog of my acquaintance.

He knew no tricks. He jumped through no hoops. We never tried to get him to heel by saying "heel" to him. That would only have bewildered him because we used the word in another connection at our house. He had an extensive vocabulary, insofar as understanding words was concerned, and we sometimes had to spell out things that we didn't want him to hear. Like most dogs he was daffy about riding in automobiles, and knew the word "car" and when he heard it, he'd get so excited he'd almost swoon. Consequently it was necessary for us sometimes to refer to the c-a-r in his presence. It will not be generally believed, but I take oath that eventually he learned to understand the word when it was spelled out.

I did things for him that I shouldn't have done. I often fed him things that were forbidden. I blush to confess that on several occasions I sprinkled Accent on his horse-meat to make it taste better. My attitude toward him was much the same as that of an old man I knew when I was a boy—Old Man Carter. He lived alone with a venerable hound named Jeff and the two of them were inseparable. On Saturday nights Old Man Carter would get loaded on home brew and then he'd take to grieving over the plight of his dog in *merely being a dog*. He'd get to weeping, beerily, and talking to Jeff, and he'd wail, "You're nothin' but a dog—jist a dog—you won't never be nothin' else but a dog—I'd do somethin' about it if I could, but I cain't—Oh God I woosht I could do somethin' about it!"

As I have mentioned, I regarded myself as a dog-hater before Rufus came into my life. And then one evening I realized to the full just how drastically I had changed. We were playing cards in the living room and Rufus was lying at my feet. At the conclusion of the game I stood up and lifted the chair away from the table. It came down on Rufus's paw and being a heavy chair, hurt him. He let out a yell, jumped about three feet across the carpet, and then began crying, looking at me as if I were the most unprincipled villain on earth.

I confess that I went a little out of my head, and got panicky. I was *so* distraught, *so* upset about it, *so* sorry. I hadn't done it on purpose. And the feeling that took possession of me was a desperate desire to let him know, somehow, that it was an accident, that I loved him, that I would never be capable of hurting him deliberately. I just *had* to get it across to him . . .

So I whipped the chair.

Another dog? Certainly not. What would I want with a dog? Rufus was not a dog. He was Rufus.

Horse in the Apartment

FRANCES EISENBERG

Ever since Miss Piper was a little girl she had loved animals and had cherished them to the best of her ability. People looking at her might have thought with dismay of the kind of a little girl she must have been, and to tell the truth, Miss Piper at thirty-eight was rather peculiar looking, with her long nose which grew red in winter, and her longish hair which continually dangled in a loose knob at the back of her head; and her clothes, which looked as if they were about to blow off, a petticoat tagging untidily below her skirt, and a little hat set askew over one eye. But in spite of all this, Miss Piper *had* been a little girl once, and a very affectionate little thing, though homely; always dragging in wet dogs and weak-eyed kittens that anyone else would have shuddered to have touched. At one time she had had a rooster for a pet named Goliath, and she had pulled him around in a red cart; she had had numerous rabbits for whom she spent hours on her knees grubbing up clover. She had even had, at intervals, jelly glasses full of tadpoles scooped out of the creek, which she fed lovingly with bugs and crumbs. And I suppose you will agree that a child who could love a tadpole is truly catholic in her taste in animal friends.

As Miss Piper slowly grew up and passed through high school and a girls' college and finally became a cataloguer in the city library, she had changed in many ways. She had grown even homelier and more lanky, and more careless about her clothes until people on the street looked at her in amusement or pity. But her passion for animals stayed the same, only becoming stronger, if anything, with the years. It had been a long time since she had had an animal of her own because now that her family was dead (except a brother who lived in Oklahoma), she had lived in furnished rooms and her various landladies had always discouraged pets. Sometimes Miss Piper, prowling around the windows of pet shops during her lunch hour, would think

315

wistfully, "Maybe if I got a Pekingese or something small she wouldn't mind." But her common sense told her that there was no one to take care of the dog while she was at work, and with a pang she would remember what had happened to her goldfish.

She had got some once, thinking that a landlady couldn't object to anything as quiet and unassuming as fish, but on the contrary, although she didn't actually ask Miss Piper to get rid of them, the current landlady had made several disparaging remarks about them, saying that the splashing of the fish kept the other roomers awake at night. And one day when Miss Piper came home the fish bowl was empty, and the landlady told her with a false sympathetic smile that it had got turned over that morning when she was cleaning up the room. That was Miss Piper's last attempt to get something of her own that she could love, and she had to admit that the goldfish hadn't been very satisfactory. They had apparently never learned to recognize her and had returned all of her affectionate words with looks of indifference.

Miss Piper, denied a specific animal of her own, loved animals in general. She carried with her a little oilcloth bag, and into it she put the bread from all her meals to feed any birds that she met. Naturally she herself was a vegetarian, but she bought bones at a nearby butcher's shop and these she proffered to stray dogs. In her bag she also carried several small cans of sardines, the kind you open with a key. Whenever she saw a forlorn and bony cat she put down her things then and there, and unwound a can of fish and fed it to the incredulous creature.

I should like to be able to say that Miss Piper was beloved by all her furred and feathered friends, and that everywhere she went she was followed by a grateful flock of them, but the truth is that they ate her food and received her caresses with an automatic wag of the tail or a loud insincere purring, then went off to further fields and alleys and forgot all about her.

The pigeons always came in droves, but she never knew if they were the same ones; although she thought she recognized some of them each time, still she could never be sure.

It was one afternoon late in February when Miss Piper's assistant, Miss Snodgrass, who was helping her catalogue some new books, suddenly asked her if she would be interested in subletting a furnished apartment for three months. "It belongs to my sister and brother-in-law," Miss Snodgrass explained. "And Bill, that's her husband, got a three months' leave of absence, and they want to go to Florida if they can find somebody to live in their apartment. The rent would pay their train fare, you see."

Miss Piper's first impulse was to say no because she didn't like change, and she had only lived in her present room since her summer vacation. Besides, it frightened her to think of having a whole apartment of her own. And yet she did like to be obliging, and she was fond of Miss Snodgrass, who was a nice quiet girl. Miss Piper thought she would like to do Miss Snodgrass' sister a favor. She asked what the rent would be, and finding it very low she hesitated, but finally said yes, she wouldn't mind having the apartment while they were gone.

When Miss Piper saw the happy look on Miss Snodgrass' face she felt a glow of satisfaction for having promised to take the apartment.

"Oh, Miss Piper, you sweet thing!" Miss Snodgrass cried in her girlish way. "I must go call my sister this minute and tell her the good news."

Miss Piper looked intently through her glasses at the card she was filing, trying to hide the flush of pleasure that mounted to her face. It wasn't often that anybody spoke to her so affectionately. She felt happy, though confused, and it was not until after she had got home that night and had broken the news to the landlady, who took it with ill-concealed displeasure, that Miss Piper suddenly thought of a glorious advantage of living in an apartment.

She was taking off her things, getting ready for bed—"I can have a dog!" She was so surprised at the thought that she stood still in her black cotton petticoat, with the drawstring at the top, not noticing how cold the room was. "Or two dogs!" It seemed too wonderful to be true, that she could actually have an animal of her own.

She slid her nightgown over her head and climbed between the cold sheets thinking happily about the dogs she would get. If it was a very large apartment she thought she might get two of those sheepy-looking ones with long hair that she had seen once in a dog show. They had such affectionate expressions. Short-haired dogs like greyhounds and different kinds of terriers were more likely to be supercilious . . . she thought the untidy, good-humored ones would be more congenial.

The next Sunday Miss Piper went to see the apartment. To her relief it was in a rather shabby neighborhood, although the building

itself was quite nice. She had been a little nervous thinking about
the doorman because all her life she had lived very simply, and had
scarcely even been inside an apartment house before. But after all
there was no doorman nor even an elevator man. You could either
walk up or take yourself up in a little elevator which rose when the
door was closed and stopped obediently at the right floor when you
pushed a thing showing where you wanted to get off.

The Wilkersons—Miss Snodgrass' sister and her husband—were
very nice and grateful to Miss Piper. They told her not to hesitate to
use everything she needed, even the kitchen utensils and the bathroom towels.

They thought Miss Piper was nice too, but a little eccentric because of her looks and because when she dropped her bag a large
bone fell out. However, they had been warned by Miss Snodgrass
that Miss Piper was rather peculiar so they did not act surprised and
Mr. Wilkerson picked the bone up and handed it to her with a little
bow. Miss Piper took it without embarrassment, and right in the
middle of what Mrs. Wilkerson was telling her about the bathroom
taps, she suddenly asked, "Do you object to dogs?" When the Wilkersons said no, Miss Piper said, "All right then," and handed them
the three months rent all in one dollar bills. "Good-bye," she said,
and went out leaving the Wilkersons slightly surprised.

Miss Piper got downstairs on the elevator all right and it made
her feel exhilarated. She would have liked to have gone up again
and have done it over, but she felt that would not be dignified for
a person with an apartment of her own.

She walked down the street, musing on her new status, until
the sight of the circling pigeons reminded her that she had not
scattered crumbs for them. Presently the icy wind which blew her
coat behind her like a banner, made her eyes sting, and blew the
birds' feathers backwards, made her realize how cold it was. She
bought a package of hot roasted peanuts from a vendor on the corner and flung them to the birds, who ate them greedily, but without
any outward expression of gratitude at Miss Piper's thoughtfulness.
But Miss Piper, who could see below the surface, did not judge their
inner feelings by their outward demeanor. She was thinking, as she
scattered the hot nuts, that she might be able to have a pigeon cote
on the roof of her new apartment house where homeless pigeons
might have a warm place to spend rainy nights.

On Tuesday the Wilkersons left for Florida, and when she left

the library at six p.m. Miss Piper carried two bulging suitcases over
to Terry Street. She went up alone in the elevator with much satisfaction, and let herself in with the key given her that morning by
Miss Snodgrass.

That night for the first time in years Miss Piper had soup for
supper that was really hot. Afterward she hung up her clothes in
the Wilkersons' empty bedroom closet. When she saw how few
dresses she had she thought she must get a new one sometime, but
that there was no hurry. First she would find herself some dogs so
that she could be enjoying them. Clothes you could get anytime.

Miss Piper went to bed at about eight because she meant to get
up early in the morning and look for a good place nearby where she
could buy her bones. She lay cosily in the dark in the Wilkersons'
bed listening to the wind shrieking around the corner of the building, and letting drowsy thoughts flow through her mind. In her old
room on a night like this, she would have lain cold and miserable
thinking of all the homeless dogs shivering in alleys, and the lean
cats with caved-in sides rooting desperately in garbage cans, and
birds huddled on quaking limbs; but now that she was going to have
some animals of her own, she did not worry much about the others.
Instead, she thought of herself leading her dogs through the park
on Sunday afternoons. How nice it would be to be able to stop and
compare them with other people's instead of having to look at and
admire dogs she didn't own. She tried to think up some good names,
but before she got very far she was asleep.

The next morning Miss Piper cooked herself a large dish of
oatmeal without any lumps, and then she put on her hat and coat
and wound the scarf around her neck and went out to explore the
neighborhood a little before time to go to work. It was very early,
and so foggy that it looked even earlier than it was. The street lights
were still burning. Miss Piper seemed to be the only person about.
She pulled her collar up around her ears to keep the cold from
settling in them.

Just around the corner from her apartment she was glad to see
that there was a butcher's shop, and a few doors down a grocery
store, in which she was also interested, since she was going to do her
own cooking. In front of the grocery store was a milk wagon, and
Miss Piper was thinking how few milk wagons you see nowadays
when everything is delivered in trucks. She glanced with instinctive
sympathy at the horse which was hitched to the wagon. What a hard
life he must lead, she thought, pulling a milk wagon through all sorts

of weather. The horse seemed rather ill at ease, and when he felt
Miss Piper's eyes on him he looked nervously away, and chewed on
his bit.

"Poor thing," Miss Piper thought compassionately. She reached
over to stroke his neck, but at that the horse jerked his head back
and shuffled his feet in acute embarrassment.

"Good horsie, nice horsie," said Miss Piper in the high soothing
voice that she always used on animals. She wished she had something to feed him, but it had never occurred to her that she might
meet a hungry horse, and she hadn't prepared for the possibility.

Then through the window of the store she could see the milkman coming toward the door with his basket of empty bottles, so she
gave the horse a last pat, and quickly walked away. When she had
gone a few feet she looked back and saw that the horse was watching her furtively, but when he saw her looking he turned his head
and stood staring at the ground, the very picture of dejection.

All day long as she worked on cards and filed them in the
drawers, the horse haunted Miss Piper. She thought of him pulling
the heavy wagon through rain and sleet. Undoubtedly he had been
mistreated, too. His master must be a brute, or the animal would not
act so subdued. By night Miss Piper had become convinced that she
must do something about the horse. She felt that the poor creature
deserved to spend his last days in comfort and serenity, and the more
she thought of it the more the idea possessed her. What was the use
of the horse ever having lived at all if all he was ever to know was
drudgery?

"At least I can give him a few pleasant memories," she thought.
On her way home that night she bought a large red apple, and put
it in the basket with the bones. She was thinking so hard about the
horse that she completely forgot her usual habit of going through the
park to scatter crumbs to the birds. She even forgot to look out for
a suitable dog for herself. In fact, dogs and birds and cats seemed
rather dull and unimportant beside the horse.

She set her alarm for five-thirty and she could hardly wait to get
her clothes on and eat her breakfast the next morning, for anticipat-
ing the pleasure she was going to bring to the poor friendless animal.
All the other occupants of the apartment house seemed to be still
asleep, and outside it was almost dark; the streets were empty. When
she got to the grocery store the milk wagon was not there, but when
she had walked a block then circled back around, shivering a little

in the biting air, she could see the horse standing in the same place, his head lowered mournfully and misery in every line of his drooping body.

A throb of pity smote Miss Piper and hastily she took out the apple. Walking slowly and quietly toward the horse so she would not startle him, and at the same time looking as kind and harmless as possible, she gently thrust out the apple to him. She murmured soothing sounds also, but the horse jerked his head up and rolled his eyes in fright. His front knees knocked together and he looked both to the right and to the left, trying to avoid seeing Miss Piper. But she kept holding the apple under his nose until she saw that the poor thing was in an agony of embarrassment, then she laid it on the curb and retreated a few steps. The horse gave Miss Piper several terrified looks, then after a moment he touched the apple with his nose, looked anxiously around, then with a sudden bite he snatched up the apple and demolished it with a few crunches. Then he stood as humbly as before, with lowered head, staring at where the apple had been.

Miss Piper felt a sudden glow of happiness that warmed her all over. The horse had eaten her apple, and now no matter what happened to him, he would always have it to remember. She went down the street swinging her bag a little and smiling triumphantly, with her hat sliding over one eye. Her success with the apple made her eager to do something more for the horse; she was turning all kinds of schemes over in her mind.

By noon she had entirely abandoned her former plan of adopting some dogs and her vaguer one of providing a quiet haven for pigeons. She could think of nothing but the horse. Over and over she saw how he had snatched the apple, and she thought of him plodding along on his rounds with the day not quite so dark because of it.

All day long at her desk Miss Piper rehearsed the morning's adventure, and that afternoon, in the middle of a list of books that she was typing, she suddenly knew what she was going to do. She knew it in a calm, cold-blooded way; it was inevitable.

It was daring, too, but Miss Piper felt a mounting confidence in herself, and she knew she could carry her plan through. First she must think out every move, and not make even one small slip; then she must do each thing as she had planned it, and she couldn't fail.

She thought back to the morning. Had she met anyone on her way out of the apartment? Had there been a janitor or a maid anywhere around? Had anyone passed her in the street? No, there had been no one. The milkman had been talking to the sleepy-looking grocer in the back of the store. Their backs had been turned toward the window.

It was too much to expect that it would all be repeated like that again, but with luck it might. And if something happened, then she would simply have to keep trying until the opportunity came again.

"I got a card from my sister today," Miss Snodgrass told Miss Piper when they were down in the locker room getting ready to go home. "She wrote it from Atlanta, and she wanted me to ask you if you were comfortable, and if everything was all right in the apartment."

"Oh yes," Miss Piper said, bending down to put on her rubbers. "Oh yes, yes indeed." She was thinking so hard that she went on murmuring, "Yes, yes, yes indeed," until it sounded like a song. Miss Snodgrass looked rather alarmed. But Miss Piper, coming to suddenly, gave her a reassuring smile and added, "And the elevator too, the elevator," which didn't seem to make Miss Snodgrass feel any better. She stood a moment, staring at Miss Piper with her mouth open, then said "Goodnight" in a frightened voice and hurried up the stairs.

Miss Piper hardly noticed that she was gone. With her overshoes on the wrong feet and her hat perched on top of her head and the scarf wound three times around her neck, she went leisurely out into the windy twilight and along the street under the leafless trees. The sky between the buildings was pink and gold and Miss Piper felt very much alive and happy.

She went through the park because the dusk was beautiful and she was excited and wanted to walk. Seeing the pigeons fluttering down she remembered them, and stopped and tossed out to them all the crumbs left in her bag. She did this without love, and she scarcely looked at the birds as they snatched greedily at the bread. She emptied the last of the crumbs on their backs, then she hurried away without watching them eat. "Pigeons, what are pigeons?" she thought scornfully.

It was hard for Miss Piper to sleep that night, knowing what she meant to do the next day. She kept going over and over every detail of her plan in her mind, reminding herself again that one slip would be fatal. And she remembered what she had read so many times that there is no such thing as a perfect crime, and that worried

Miss Piper somewhat. But she resolutely drank a glass of warm milk and went to bed, and managed to float off into some highly colored dreams, until she awoke with a jerk while it was still dark. She saw that the shining hands of the alarm clock pointed to five.

Through the window Miss Piper could see that it was raining outside; the pavement under the street lamp gleamed wetly.

Trembling a little with excitement, she put on her clothes and drank two cups of coffee while standing up. Exactly at five-thirty she switched off her light, opened the door of her apartment stealthily, and peered up and down the hall. When she saw that it was quite empty and that by the dim light the doors had a withdrawn look as if everyone behind them was asleep, she closed her own door quietly, pushed the elevator button, slid noiselessly downward, and in a moment she was in the silent empty street.

She walked as slowly as possible. Now her excitement was gone and she felt quite calm and cool.

When she had rounded the corner and had gone halfway down the next block she could see the dim shape of the milk wagon in front of the grocery store, and the white form of the horse. It was still so dark that she could only imagine the look of mingled fright and misery that he wore.

Glancing behind her she saw that no one was in sight. When she got even with the grocery store she could see the milkman inside, bundled up in a black raincoat, with his back to the window. The grocer, who still wore his hat and coat, was handing the milkman a flat bottle, and Miss Piper, peering from the sheltering gloom saw the milkman tilt it to his lips while the grocer watched him. Miss Piper knew that the bottle did not contain milk, and she deduced immediately why it took the milkman so long to deliver milk in that store every morning.

Hurriedly, and yet calmly too, she unhitched the horse from the wagon. In the dim light from the window she could see his frightened eyes glaring wildly at her, and she could tell that he was shaking like a leaf, but she murmured a few reassuring words and when she tugged at the leather thing on his face, he followed her obediently. For all his timidity, he seemed to be an intelligent animal; he stayed in the shadow, and his feet made scarcely a sound on the pavement.

Miss Piper held her umbrella over the horse's head to protect him from the cold drizzle, but that seemed to make him more uneasy than comfortable. He twisted his neck from side to side and made nervous coughing sounds, but Miss Piper continued to hold the umbrella firmly in place.

Their luck was almost unbelievable. No one passed them during the whole two blocks.

Miss Piper stopped before the door of her apartment house, slid her key noiselessly into the lock, then with the horse following, his shoes clicking a little on the stone floor, she hurried across to the elevator and inside it. The horse cowered in a corner, his breath coming in terrified gasps, but he made no noise of any kind except a few muffled snorts as the elevator rose slowly upward.

Now that the most dangerous part was over, Miss Piper felt a relief that was almost like intoxication. Only that little stretch of hall. She tiptoed warily down it, but the carpet deadened the sound of their footsteps, and the doors were as remote and the lights as dim as when she had left, nearly twenty minutes before. A door might open, and she might be seen bringing in a stolen horse, but it wasn't likely, and Miss Piper was positive that now she was safe. And sure enough, in a moment they were on the other side of her apartment door, in her own living room.

She took off her wet raincoat and put the umbrella in the bathtub to drip, then she hastened to rub down the horse with a large bath towel. The poor creature's teeth were chattering violently, either from cold or excitement, and he cowered timidly in the warmth, at the same time looking curiously and fearfully around the room.

Miss Piper cooked a double boiler full of nourishing cornmeal mush, at the same time making a mental note that she must remember to get some hay, and hastily pouring it in a bright new dishpan she took it in to the horse and set it before him. She had expected to see him devour the wholesome mixture with an expression of gratitude, but instead he sniffed cautiously at it, then turned his head meekly and gazed out of the window.

Miss Piper was alarmed. It would be ironical indeed if, having abducted the horse to give him a taste of happiness, he should get ill and die of pneumonia. She took off the woolen blanket that was folded across the foot of her bed, and wrapped it around the horse and pinned it in front with a safety pin. Then she tempted his appetite with everything she could find, even a bit of fruit cake left over from a Christmas box sent her by her brother. But the horse, after smelling of each thing, turned his long sad countenance briefly toward Miss Piper, then looked away, more in sorrow than in anger.

Miss Piper began to feel very guilty. "There's something he wants," she thought anxiously. "Now what can it be, I wonder?"

Then she happened to think that maybe it was an apple, and although it was growing late and almost time for her to start to the library, she put on her coat and went out with the umbrella down to the corner fruit market, and got a beautiful red apple as large as a grapefruit.

When she offered it, breathlessly, to the horse, she was delighted to see that after a cautious sniff or two he began to nibble at the fruit, casting at the same time a look of almost painful gratitude at Miss Piper.

Now it was quite light outside, so with many a soothing word to the horse, Miss Piper wound her scarf around her neck and put on her rubbers and hurried, for the third time that morning, out into the cold rain. All the way in on the bus she ignored the smell of wet wool and the shoves of the other passengers. Someone behind her kept jabbing her with an elbow, and people pushing past to get off stepped on her feet, but Miss Piper braced herself firmly and concentrated on the horse. She felt quite strong and extroverted when she thought that she alone was responsible for the happiness of the poor frightened animal, and she began to think of ways that she could reassure it and adjust it and make it realize that men were its friends. She thought that she would begin very gently with kind words and little gifts, and gradually win it back to its lost faith in people. When the first warm days of spring came, it might be possible to get the horse out of doors sometimes on Sundays for walks, or out in the country even. That would give it a more healthful view of life.

All day long Miss Piper thought along this line, and looked forward to going back to the apartment so she could take up her missionary work at the point where she had had to leave it that morning.

She hoped that a long quiet day of solitude had done the horse good, and indeed, when she went in that night he did seem to be much calmer. He was still by the window, looking down into the street, and when he heard the door latch click he jumped only slightly. When he saw who it was, it seemed to Miss Piper that his eyes lit up and a brighter expression came on his face.

Miss Piper talked kindly to him as she prepared her supper, and as he did not seem to want to leave the living room she brought her supper in there. She had got a whole bushel of apples, (although they were rather expensive) and they ate their suppers together in companionable silence, broken only by the sounds of crunching.

"Now, isn't this cosy?" Miss Piper thought when she had settled down after supper with a magazine. Outside she could hear the dripping of the rain, but inside it was warm and bright. When she ran across an interesting bit she read it aloud, knowing of course that the horse could not understand the words, but that he could tell by the inflection of her voice that she was being friendly.

The only response that the horse made was a loud asthmatic breathing, but looking up occasionally Miss Piper caught a grateful expression in his eyes that more than paid her for her trouble.

At nine o'clock she fixed a bed of blankets in the bathroom, and although the horse lay down meekly, something seemed to be wrong; he kept rolling his eyes and shifting his feet around.

After Miss Piper had gone to bed she could hear his hoofs bumping on the floor and presently she was aware of low groans which increased in volume until it sounded as if the horse was in an agony of pain.

She leapt out of bed and hurriedly clicked on the bathroom light, and the horse gazed humbly up at her and continued to groan most heartrendingly.

"Could it be the apples?" thought Miss Piper anxiously. He had only eaten three and they had seemed very ripe. She covered him up with an extra blanket, but his moanings did not subside. He began to bite feebly at the blanket under him, and finally it occurred to Miss Piper that perhaps the floor was cold through such a thin covering. So she pulled the mattress off her bed and dragged it with much difficulty into the bath room and settled the poor creature on it.

The look in the animal's eyes was enough to touch the hardest heart. Miss Piper felt well repaid for her sacrifice as she settled herself on the studio couch, which was lumpy and full of drafts.

She spent a wakeful night, but the thought of the horse sleeping so soundly and comfortably without having to think of getting out in the cold in the middle of the night made her feel very philanthropic. Toward morning she fell asleep, and was wandering in a confused dream in which the Wilkersons had suddenly come back to their apartment and ordered her and the horse out into the rain.

When she awoke she found to her dismay that it was almost seven. She got up hastily, aching in every limb. She made herself a cup of coffee, and then she looked in to see how the horse was doing. He seemed to be sleeping very soundly, so she tiptoed in and laid three apples under his nose where he would be sure to see them when he awoke. She closed the apartment door as softly as she could on her way out so he shouldn't be disturbed. That night Miss Piper stopped by a feed store to see about some hay. She found that although it wasn't very expensive, a bale made quite a large bundle, and at the moment she couldn't think of any pretext to use to have it sent to the apartment. If the neighbors saw a bale of hay being carried in they might suspect something. So she asked if she might have a small sample, and the clerk, looking as if he thought it was highly irregular, pulled out a handful of sprigs; enough to make the horse a good meal.

However, when Miss Piper got home, she was alarmed to find the three apples lying where she had left them that morning, and the horse sitting in his favorite place, weakly gazing out of the window. He seemed very feeble, and when she came in he gave a loud melancholy cough and scarcely lifted his eyes.

Miss Piper put her things down and offered him the bunch of hay that she had brought, but he made no move to eat or even to sniff at it. When he saw what it was he turned away and kept staring out at the sunset, looking gaunt and patient.

The sight of him struck Miss Piper to the heart. She offered him the apples one by one, but he glanced once at them without interest, gave a gentle apologetic cough, and paid no more attention to Miss Piper.

Now Miss Piper began to be really frightened. Still wearing her coat and rubbers she went into the kitchen and heated some milk, but in vain. The horse was meek but indifferent. While she was racking her brain wondering what to do next, she saw him give a sidelong glance toward the apples, and eagerly she proffered them for the second time, but the horse refused them again with a mute twist of his head.

Then Miss Piper had an inspiration. She peeled the apples and cut them up in quarters, and to her joy the horse ate them readily when she fed them to him one by one. She was greatly relieved, although in the back of her mind was the thought that a diet of sliced apples might prove expensive as well as troublesome. Yet surely that was a very minor matter if it would make the horse happy. And she thought that it was an encouraging sign for the animal to show such definite likes and dislikes. It showed that he was putting a new evaluation upon himself.

However, she was rather annoyed that night when she was

awakened by the horse's groans and found, by the process of elimination, that he wanted the pink woolen comforter that she had instead of the brown army blanket that she had spread over him. And the next morning she was five minutes late (for the first time in her life) because of the extra time it took to prepare the horse's breakfast. There were other unpleasant difficulties too, and although Miss Piper kept telling herself that it was a rare privilege to be able to restore a dumb creature's faith in mankind, she did wish that the apartment was not quite so small, and that she had a barn to keep the animal in. As time went on the horse developed other idiosyncrasies. He was allergic to a certain dress that Miss Piper had hitherto worn a great deal and was very fond of—a brown wool dress with green glass buttons down the front. But now when she put it on the horse would turn his head and refuse to look at her, giving low groans at intervals. So with a sigh of regret Miss Piper had to put the dress away, and although she was rewarded by a look of almost passionate gratitude from the horse, she thought of it lying there unused, and it seemed a pity.

Another thing, Miss Piper found that in order to make the horse happy the temperature of the room had to be kept at about eighty-five degrees, and since she was subject to occasional hot flashes, she was very uncomfortable. But when she turned off the heat the horse hovered over the cold radiators with such a look of dumb misery that Miss Piper couldn't bear it, and she would turn them back on and stand it as best she could.

The horse did not like a draft so the windows had to be kept down all night because he could feel the air even through the closed bathroom door. Miss Piper would awake every morning feeling stuffy and aching in every limb from the hard couch, but she kept assuring herself that it was for a good cause, and the horse was certainly gaining in self-respect every day.

It was lucky that Miss Piper did her own cleaning because if she had a maid, like most of the other people in the house, it would have been no time until everyone would have known about the horse. As it was, rumors began to spread around that Miss Piper's apartment was haunted. People reported seeing a mysterious white figure in the window, and those passing the door sometimes heard strange groans and thumpings. But luckily for Miss Piper, the people in that apartment house believed in tending to their own business, and letting their neighbors alone, so no one investigated. They merely talked about it in lowered voices, shivered pleasantly, and let it go.

At the library Miss Snodgrass gave Miss Piper daily reports of her sister and brother-in-law, and asked politely if Miss Piper was enjoying the apartment. Miss Piper always said, "Oh yes indeed," but the truth was that she was getting haggard and thin never knowing what whim the horse was going to take next, and wondering what she was going to do with him when the Wilkersons came back and claimed their apartment. The weeks were going by very fast, and she had to begin thinking of the future.

As Miss Piper grew thinner and more harassed, the horse grew sleeker in spite of his diet of apples; but he stayed as sensitive as ever. Sometimes Miss Piper would feel a little resentful when she thought of all the things she had given up for the horse. There were certain foods that he couldn't bear the smell of, such as fried onions or cauliflower, and when Miss Piper had them for her dinner he had groaned and worn such an agonized expression that she had to stop cooking them.

Again, the horse could enjoy only the most classical music on the radio, and when Miss Piper tuned in on the kind of programs she liked, such as Major Bowes and good organ music on Sundays, and such songs as "Let Me Sit in a House by the Side of the Road," or poetry read to music, the horse sat by the window staring mournfully out, and he would not look at Miss Piper nor eat his apples for several hours afterward. So out of respect to his taste and for her own peace of mind, she had to listen to symphony orchestras, if anything, and they made her head ache, although the horse would stare dreamily into space with his eyes half-closed, the very picture of ecstasy.

Sometimes late at night Miss Piper, unable to sleep because of the bumps and hollows in the studio couch, would think about the milkman and wonder how he was getting along without his horse. Gradually the thought began to creep into her mind that she had done very wrong to take away the means, or part of the means, of his livelihood. Perhaps he had a lot of little children to feed and clothe and educate, and perhaps the disappearance of the horse was an irreparable loss to him. She was always intending to get up early some morning and walk by the grocery store to see if he had got another one, but after she had tossed and tumbled the first part of the night, she usually fell asleep about dawn, and woke just in time to get to the library by eight, and of course the milkman by then had gone hours ago.

But she began to feel more and more sorry for him and his family, and very guilty for being responsible for their probable difficulties. Her imagination showed her pictures of his children unable to go to school because their shoes were worn out, and she could see the milkman, with his head in his hands, overcome by despair, with perhaps a mortgage on his farm that he was unable to pay because his horse was gone and he couldn't deliver the milk.

The idea began to prick at her mind that the only way she could make amends was to take the horse back where she had got it; otherwise her conscience would never give her any peace. The grocer would see that the milkman got the horse, she thought. It might be hard on the horse, but after all he had had a nice long rest and the best of care, and a little hard work might be a good thing; he needed to get his mind off of himself.

One morning Miss Snodgrass, with a beaming face, said to Miss Piper, "Sister will be home next week, and she sends you her regards, and I don't need to tell you how much we appreciate your taking such good care of the apartment. Sister says she's had a grand time, and never a minute's worry because she knew her things were in such good hands."

Miss Piper blushed modestly and made some suitable reply, but at the same time she thought with some trepidation that Miss Snodgrass' sister might not have liked it much if she had known that Miss Piper had kept a horse in her apartment the whole time they were gone. And after all, the Wilkersons had trusted her with all their furniture, and even their cooking utensils, and she had taken the liberty of bringing in a horse with never a thought of whether or not they would like it. This thought fused with what she had already been thinking about the milkman, and from the two came the conviction that the only honorable thing would be to return the horse. "Much as I would like to keep him," she assured herself.

On the horse's last night she tried to make it as pleasant as possible so as to leave a happy memory. She kept the heat up to ninety-two degrees, he had his favorite kind of apples—Winesaps—served on a lovely pink china plate, and she turned the radio on to a symphony orchestra, which as providence would have it, played Beethoven's sixth symphony, which the horse liked best of all. Miss Piper set her alarm and went to bed early after fixing the horse's bed for the last time. She was ashamed of herself because instead of feeling sad at the thought of losing him she felt quite cheerful. "It's only because such a weight will be off my conscience," she kept excusing herself. "And for the sake of the milkman, and because I think it's really best for the horse . . . ." But she could not deny that it would be nice to be able to open the window at night, and to sleep in a bed on a real mattress, and not to have to slice up another apple. Never to have to look at an apple again!

The next morning she got up at four because it was light earlier now, being the middle of April, and she had to get the horse out under the cover of darkness. She waited until the last minute to arouse him, out of respect for his feelings, and then she awoke him as gently as possible.

At first he seemed unable to believe that she meant for him to get up at this hour, and he began to give long agonized moans, but Miss Piper was adamant. Gently but firmly she prodded him with her foot until he struggled up and stood swaying as if he were about to fall; but even that did not cause Miss Piper's resolution to falter. The horse seemed to realize at last that nothing he could do would stop Miss Piper, so after a moment he was silent, merely staring at her with reproachful eyes, and moving his lips a little as if in prayer.

But that did no good either. Miss Piper opened the door, looked up and down the hall, then seeing nobody, she pushed the horse out and along the hall toward the elevator. She pressed the button almost gaily, and the horse cowered in a corner, giving long-drawn sighs, and rolling his eyes in an agony of self-pity as the elevator sank slowly downward. Miss Piper hummed a little tune under her breath, and pretended not to notice.

"He'll be all right," she assured herself. "What he needs is some good hard work out in the open air."

Again they were lucky and met no one on their way out of the apartment house. The horse kept holding back, and even when Miss Piper gave him a poke in the ribs he would move only slightly faster, moaning quaveringly under his breath as he crept along. Miss Piper did not try to hurry him much, because they had plenty of time. The only danger was that they might be seen, and even for that she didn't care much, because she had nothing to lose now that she was doing her duty and taking back the horse.

When she rounded the corner she could see the milk wagon just pulling up into the dim patch of light cast through the grocery store window. The sight disappointed her in some strange way. After all her worrying it was somewhat of a let-down to see that the milkman had got himself another horse and was going ahead as if nothing had happened. She halted in the shadows and watched the man get out, rather slowly and heavily, she thought, with his bottles, and go into the store.

Poor man, she thought, with a sharp stab of guilt. She gave the horse a last prod, and he, realizing that there was nothing else to do now, crept hopelessly forward with downhanging head toward the milk wagon. In every line of his body was reproach for Miss Piper. But her heart felt cheerfully hard. She watched from the shadows for a moment, and when she was sure that he was going to stay there in front of the door, where the milkman could see him first thing when he came out, she turned and started back toward the apartment.

The Story of the Young
Man and the Mouse

William Saroyan

A week of drinking turned the young man's fancy to mice, *the* mouse, the one and only, the mouse of all mice, the city mouse, the brilliant mouse, the genius of mice, the Great Northern Hotel mouse.

He, or it, arrived one night prancing in the manner of an over-joyed retriever. The mouse came fearlessly to the young man and dropped the money at his feet. The money was four ten-dollar bills which the mouse carried in its mouth. The mouse carried the money so dexterously, or rather so magnificently, so thoughtfully, so deli-cately that not even slight teeth marks impaired the beauty of the money. The young man picked up the money casually, examined it, and studied the mouse, which stood by in perfect harmony with everything.

The young man moved two paces and also stood by in perfect harmony with everything.

"Well," he said. "This *is* delightful."

He looked at the mouse thoughtfully.

"Stealing, hey?" he said.

The mouse nodded the way a clown nods when he acknowledges the commission of some petty but delightful crime.

"All right," the young man said. "I believe in live and let live. You bring me money this way so I can live and I'll try not to improve your morals. If you want to steal, that's all right with me."

This arrangement appeared to be all right with the mouse, which continued exploring the rooms of the hotel, going to those places where traveling people or retired army officers or people tak-ing a shower like to leave their folding money. Almost every day the mouse returned to the room of the young man to deposit various foldings of American currency: sometimes tens, sometimes fives,

333

sometimes a five and a couple of ones, and one day four ones, which was a crisis and a bitter disappointment to the young man, who was drinking a great deal.

"Live and let live of course," he said to the mouse, "but you can do better than that. Now, let me explain. This number. That's ten. That's good. Get that kind when you can. This is five. Half as good. If you can't get tens, get fives. This is a two. Bad luck. Don't leave them, but they aren't so good. This is one. Awful. Try for tens."

The mouse accepted this simple instruction and was lucky enough to enter rooms where guests who were having showers had left big folding money lying around here and there, so that for many days the young man lived pretty much like a king. He bought clothes. Odds and ends. Ate well. And drank exceptionally well.

The mouse, however, lived on very feeble fare. Old stockings.

"Now," the young man said one day to the mouse, "this may get around. Folks may begin to get suspicious. There is no law against a mouse stealing money, and you'll always be innocent according to the statutes. There isn't a jury in the country that would convict you. But some busybody somewhere may take a long-shot chance and set a trap. They're horrible things, but very attractive outwardly. Cheese is involved. With only one of these pieces of paper which you have just fetched I could buy, I believe, close to twenty pounds of the finest cheese imaginable—which, I daresay, you wouldn't like. They'll try to attract you with cheap cheese. Ten cents a pound. Something like that. Something I haven't eaten in months. Don't be a fool. Don't get taken in. Don't swoon and move into the trap because the smell of the cheese is so wonderful. I'm counting on you to stay in good health."

The mouse had never heard.

Cheese?

Traps?

He didn't know. It was all very exciting.

Money, for some reason, he *did* know. It didn't smell good. It was tasteless and official, but even so.

The young man might have furnished the mouse a little cheese, but he was afraid that if he did the mouse would cease to appreciate anything but food. That, he didn't want. It would be better for the mouse to fend for itself.

"But," he said clearly, "stay away from little pieces of cheese artfully attached to gadgets which appear to be perfectly static and harmless. Once you swoon, you're a goner. It may mean death."

Death?

The mouse hadn't heard.

The drinking continued. Many times the mouse went away and returned with money, but one day the mouse didn't return. Soon the young man began to be poor again. He began to be a little worried, too. First he worried about how he was ever going to be able to keep up appearances without money, but little by little he began to worry about the mouse. In a psychic or alcoholic way, he was able to trace the mouse's course from his room two days ago to where it had fallen into a trap.

This was room 517, one floor down, two doors to the left. The room was inhabited by an old woman whose children sometimes took her to Larchmont for week-ends.

It was a little difficult getting in through the window, but he made it, and sure enough in the corner of the room was the mouse. The old woman was in Larchmont.

The young man burst into tears.

"I told you," he wept. "You see what happens? Now look at you. Here. Let me get you out of this God-damned gadget."

He got the mouse out of the trap and carried it carefully in the palm of his left hand to his room, taking the elevator and weeping.

The elevator boy burst into tears with the young man, but suggested heat and quiet.

Heat and quiet were provided the mouse, and five cents' worth of cheese, which the mouse did not wish to eat.

This frightened the young man.

"Those ungodly people," he said again and again.

The mouse watched the young man quietly for five days and five nights, and then it died.

The young man wrapped it carefully in hotel stationery, appropriately white, and carried it to Central Park where he dug a small grave with the toe of his right shoe, and buried it.

He returned to the hotel and checked out, complaining bitterly about the type of people inhabiting the world.

Pigs Is Pigs

Ellis Parker Butler

Mike Flannery, the Westcote agent of the Interurban Express Company, leaned over the counter of the express office and shook his fist. Mr. Morehouse, angry and red, stood on the other side of the counter, trembling with rage. The argument had been long and heated, and at last Mr. Morehouse had talked himself speechless. The cause of the trouble stood on the counter between the two men. It was a soap box across the top of which were nailed a number of strips, forming a rough but serviceable cage. In it two spotted guinea-pigs were greedily eating lettuce leaves.

"Do as you loike, then!" shouted Flannery, "pay for thim an' take thim, or don't pay for thim and leave thim be. Rules is rules, Misther Morehouse, an' Mike Flannery's not goin' to be called down fer breakin' of thim."

"But, you everlastingly stupid idiot!" shouted Mr. Morehouse, madly shaking a flimsy printed book beneath the agent's nose, "can't you read it here—in your own plain printed rates? 'Pets, domestic, Franklin to Westcote, if properly boxed, twenty-five cents each.'" He threw the book on the counter in disgust. "What more do you want? Aren't they pets? Aren't they domestic? Aren't they properly boxed? What?"

He turned and walked back and forth rapidly, frowning ferociously.

Suddenly he turned to Flannery, and forcing his voice to an artificial calmness spoke slowly but with intense sarcasm.

"Pets," he said. "P-e-t-s! Twenty-five cents each. There are two of them. One! Two! Two times twenty-five are fifty! Can you understand that? I offer you fifty cents."

Flannery reached for the book. He ran his hand through the pages and stopped at page sixty-four.

"An' I don't take fifty cints," he whispered in mockery. "Here's the rule for ut. 'Whin the agint be in anny doubt regardin' which of two rates applies to a shipment, he shall charge the larger. The con-sign-ey may file a claim for the overcharge.' In this case, Misther Morehouse, I be in doubt. Pets thim animals may be, an' domestic they be, but pigs I'm blame sure they do be, an' me rules says plain as the nose on yer face, 'Pigs Franklin to Westcote, thirty cints each.' An', Misther Morehouse, by me arithetical knowledge two times thirty comes to sixty cints."

Mr. Morehouse shook his head savagely. "Nonsense!" he shouted, "confounded nonsense, I tell you! Why, you poor ignorant foreigner, that rule means common pigs, domestic pigs, not guinea-pigs!"

Flannery was stubborn.

"Pigs is pigs," he declared firmly. "Guinea-pigs or dago pigs or Irish pigs is all the same to the Interurban Express Company an' to Mike Flannery. The' nationality of the pig creates no differentiality in the rate, Misther Morehouse! 'Twould be the same was they Dutch pigs or Rooshun pigs. Mike Flannery," he added, "is here to tind to the expriss business and not to hould conversation wid dago pigs in sivinteen languages fer to discover be they Chinese or Tipperary by birth an' nativity."

Mr. Morehouse hesitated. He bit his lip and then flung out his arms wildly.

"Very well!" he shouted. "You shall hear of this! Your presi-dent shall hear of this! It is an outrage! I have offered you fifty cents. You refuse it! Keep the pigs until you are ready to take the fifty cents, but, by George, sir, if one hair of those pigs' heads is harmed I will have the law on you!"

He turned and stalked out, slamming the door. Flannery care-fully lifted the soap box from the counter and placed it in a corner. He was not worried. He felt the peace that comes to a faithful servant who has done his duty and done it well.

Mr. Morehouse went home raging. His boy, who had been awaiting the guinea-pigs, knew better than to ask him for them. He was a normal boy and therefore always had a guilty conscience when his father was angry. So the boy slipped quietly around the house. There is nothing so soothing to a guilty conscience as to be out of the path of the avenger.

Mr. Morehouse stormed into the house. "Where's the ink?" he shouted at his wife as soon as his foot was across the doorsill.

Mrs. Morehouse jumped guiltily. She never used ink. She had not seen the ink, nor moved the ink, nor thought of the ink, but her husband's tone convicted her of the guilt of having borne and reared a boy, and she knew that whenever her husband wanted anything in a loud voice the boy had been at it.

"I'll find Sammy," she said meekly.

When the ink was found Mr. Morehouse wrote rapidly, and he read the completed letter and smiled a triumphant smile.

"That will settle that crazy Irishman!" he exclaimed. "When they get that letter he will hunt another job, all right!"

A week later Mr. Morehouse received a long official envelope with the card of the Interurban Express Company in the upper left corner. He tore it open eagerly and drew out a sheet of paper. At the top it bore the number A6754. The letter was short. "Subject— Rate on guinea-pigs," it said. "Dr. Sir—We are in receipt of your letter regarding rate on guinea-pigs between Franklin and Westcote, addressed to the president of this company. All claims for over-charge should be addressed to the Claims Department."

Mr. Morehouse wrote to the Claims Department. He wrote six pages of choice sarcasm, vituperation and argument, and sent them to the Claims Department.

A few weeks later he received a reply from the Claims Depart-ment. Attached to it was his last letter.

"Dr. Sir," said the reply. "Your letter of the 16th inst., addressed to this Department, subject rate on guinea-pigs from Franklin to Westcote, rec'd. We have taken up the matter with our agent at Westcote, and his reply is attached herewith. He informs us that you refused to receive the consignment or to pay the charges. You have therefore no claim against this company, and your letter regard-ing the proper rate on the consignment should be addressed to our Tariff Department."

Mr. Morehouse wrote to the Tariff Department. He stated his case clearly, and gave his arguments in full, quoting a page or two from the encyclopedia to prove that guinea-pigs were not common pigs.

With the care that characterizes corporations when they are systematically conducted, Mr. Morehouse's letter was numbered, O.K'd, and started through the regular channels. Duplicate copies of the bill of lading, manifest, Flannery's receipt for the package and several other pertinent papers were pinned to the letter, and they were passed to the head of the Tariff Department.

The head of the Tariff Department put his feet on his desk and yawned. He looked through the papers carelessly.

"Miss Kane," he said to his stenographer, "take this letter. 'Agent, Westcote, N. J. Please advise why consignment referred to in attached papers was refused domestic pet rates.'"

Miss Kane made a series of curves and angles on her note book and waited with pencil poised. The head of the department looked at the papers again.

"Huh! guinea-pigs!" he said. "Probably starved to death by this time! Add this to that letter: 'Give condition of consignment at present.'"

He tossed the papers on to the stenographer's desk, took his feet from his own desk and went out to lunch.

When Mike Flannery received the letter he scratched his head.

"'Give prisint condition'," he repeated thoughtfully. "Now what do thim clerks be wantin' to know, I wonder! 'Prisint condition,' is ut? Thim pigs, praise St. Patrick, do be in good health, so far as I know, but I niver was no veternairy surgeon to dago pigs. Mebby thim clerks wants me to call in the pig docther an' have their pulses took. Wan thing I do know, howiver, which is, they've glorious appytites for pigs of their soize. Ate? They'd ate the brass padlocks off of a barn door! If the paddy pig, by the same token, ate as hearty as these dago pigs do, there'd be a famine in Ireland."

To assure himself that his report would be up to date, Flannery went to the rear of the office and looked into the cage. The pigs had been transferred to a larger box—a dry goods box.

"Wan,—two,—t'ree,—four,—foive,—six,—sivin,—eight!" he counted. "Sivin spotted an' wan all black. All well an' hearty an' all eatin' loike ragin' hippypottymusses." He went back to his desk and wrote.

"Mr. Morgan, Head of Tariff Department," he wrote, "why do I say dago pigs is pigs because they is pigs and will be til you say they ain't which is what the rule book says stop your jollying me you know it as well as I do. As to health they are all well and hoping you are the same. P.S. There are eight now the family increased all good eaters. P.S. I paid out so far two dollars for cabbage which they like shall I put in bill for same what?"

Morgan, head of the Tariff Department, when he received this letter, laughed. He read it again and became serious.

"By George!" he said, "Flannery is right, 'pigs is pigs.' I'll have to get authority on this thing. Meanwhile, Miss Kane, take this letter: Agent, 'Westcote, N.J. Regarding shipment guinea-pigs, File No. A6754. Rule 83, General Instructions to Agents, clearly states that agents shall collect from consignee all costs of provender, etc., etc., required for live stock while in transit or storage. You will proceed to collect same from consignee.' "

Flannery received this letter next morning, and when he read it he grinned.

" 'Proceed to collect',," he said softly. "How thim clerks do loike to be talkin'! *Me* proceed to collect two dollars and twinty-foive cints off Misther Morehouse! I wonder do thim clerks *know* Misther Morehouse? I'll git it! Oh, yes! 'Misther Morehouse, two an' a quarter, plaze.' 'Cert'nly, me dear frind Flannery. Delighted!' *Not!*"

Flannery drove the express wagon to Mr. Morehouse's door. Mr. Morehouse answered the bell.

"Ah, ha!" he cried as soon as he saw it was Flannery. "So you've come to your senses at last, have you? I thought you would! Bring the box in."

"I hev no box," said Flannery coldly. "I hev a bill again Misther John C. Morehouse for two dollars and twinty-foive cints for kebbages aten by his dago pigs. Wud you wish to pay it?"

"Pay—Cabbages—!" gasped Mr. Morehouse. "Do you mean to say that two little guinea-pigs——"

"Eight!" said Flannery. "Papa an' mamma an' the six childer. Eight!"

For answer Mr. Morehouse slammed the door in Flannery's face. Flannery looked at the door reproachfully.

"I take ut the con-*sign*-y don't want to pay for thim kebbages," he said. "If I know signs of refusal, the con-*sign*-y refuses to pay for wan dang kebbage leaf an' be hanged to me!"

Mr. Morgan, the head of the Tariff Department, consulted the president of the Interurban Express Company regarding guinea-pigs, as to whether they were pigs or not pigs. The president was inclined to treat the matter lightly.

"What is the rate on pigs and on pets?" he asked.

"Pigs thirty cents, pets twenty-five," said Morgan.

"Then of course guinea-pigs are pigs," said the president.

"Yes," agreed Morgan, "I look at it that way, too. A thing that can come under two rates is naturally due to be classed as the higher. But are guinea-pigs, pigs? Aren't they rabbits?"

"Come to think of it," said the president, "I believe they are more like rabbits. Sort of half-way station between pig and rabbit. I think the question is this—are guinea-pigs of the domestic pig family? I'll ask Professor Gordon. He is authority on such things. Leave the papers with me."

The president put the papers on his desk and wrote a letter to Professor Gordon. Unfortunately the Professor was in South America collecting zoological specimens, and the letter was forwarded to him by his wife. As the Professor was in the highest Andes, where no white man had ever penetrated, the letter was many months in reaching him. The president forgot the guinea pigs, Morgan forgot them, Mr. Morehouse forgot them, but Flannery did not. One half of his time he gave to the duties of his agency; the other half was devoted to the guinea-pigs. Long before Professor Gordon received the president's letter Morgan received one from Flannery.

"About them dago pigs," it said, "what shall I do they are great in family life, no race suicide for them, there are thirty-two now shall I sell them do you take this express office for a menagerie, answer quick."

Morgan reached for a telegraph blank and wrote:

"Agent, Westcote. Don't sell pigs."

He then wrote Flannery a letter calling his attention to the fact that the pigs were not the property of the company but were merely being held during a settlement of a dispute regarding rates. He advised Flannery to take the best possible care of them.

Flannery, letter in hand, looked at the pigs and sighed. The dry goods box cage had become too small. He boarded up twenty feet of the rear of the express office to make a large and airy home for them, and went about his business. He worked with feverish intensity when out on his rounds, for the pigs required attention and took most of his time. Some months later, in desperation, he seized a sheet of paper and wrote "160" across it and mailed it to Morgan. Morgan returned it asking for explanation. Flannery replied:

"There be now one hundred sixty of them dago pigs, for heaven's sake let me sell off some, do you want me to go crazy, what?"

"Sell no pigs," Morgan wired.

Not long after this the president of the express company received a letter from Professor Gordon. It was a long and scholarly letter, but the point was that the guinea-pig was the *Cavia aparoea*, while the common pig was the genus *Sus* of the family *Suidae*. He remarked that they were prolific and multiplied rapidly.

"They are not pigs," said the president, decidedly, to Morgan. "The twenty-five cent rate applies."

Morgan made the proper notation on the papers that had accumulated in File A6754, and turned them over to the Audit Department. The Audit Department took some time to look the matter up, and after the usual delay wrote Flannery that as he had on hand one hundred and sixty guinea-pigs, the property of consignee, he should deliver them and collect charges at the rate of twenty-five cents each.

Flannery spent a day herding his charges through a narrow opening in their cage so that he might count them.

"Audit Dept.," he wrote, when he had finished the count, "you are way off there may be was one hundred and sixty dago pigs once, but wake up don't be a back number. I've got even eight hundred, now shall I collect for eight hundred or what, how about sixty-four dollars I paid out for cabbages."

It required a great many letters back and forth before the Audit Department was able to understand why the error had been made of billing one hundred and sixty instead of eight hundred, and still more time for it to get the meaning of the "cabbages."

Flannery was crowded into a few feet at the extreme front of the office. The pigs had all the rest of the room and two boys were employed constantly attending to them. The day after Flannery had counted the guinea-pigs there were eight more added to his drove, and by the time the Audit Department gave him authority to collect for eight hundred Flannery had given up all attempts to attend to the receipt or the delivery of goods. He was hastily building galleries around the express office, tier above tier. He had four thousand and sixty-four guinea-pigs to care for. More were arriving daily.

Immediately following its authorization the Audit Department sent another letter, but Flannery was too busy to open it. They wrote another and then they telegraphed:

"Error in guinea-pig bill. Collect for two guinea-pigs, fifty cents. Deliver all to consignee."

Flannery read the telegram and cheered up. He wrote out a bill as rapidly as his pencil could travel over paper and ran all the way to the Morehouse home. At the gate he stopped suddenly. The house stared at him with vacant eyes. The windows were bare of curtains and he could see into the empty rooms. A sign on the porch said, "To Let." Mr. Morehouse had moved! Flannery ran all the way back to the express office. Sixty-nine guinea-pigs had been born during his absence. He ran out again and made feverish inquiries in the village. Mr. Morehouse had not only moved, but he had left Westcote. Flannery returned to the express office and found that two hundred and six guinea-pigs had entered the world since he left it. He wrote a telegram to the Audit Department.

"Can't collect fifty cents for two dago pigs consignee has left town address unknown what shall I do? Flannery."

The telegram was handed to one of the clerks in the Audit Department, and as he read it he laughed.

"Flannery must be crazy. He ought to know that the thing to do is to return the consignment here," said the clerk. He telegraphed Flannery to send the pigs to the main office of the company at Franklin.

When Flannery received the telegram he set to work. The six boys he had engaged to help him also set to work. They worked with the haste of desperate men, making cages out of soap boxes, cracker boxes, and all kinds of boxes, and as fast as the cages were completed they filled them with guinea-pigs and expressed them to Franklin. Day after day the cages of guinea-pigs flowed in a steady stream from Westcote to Franklin, and still Flannery and his six helpers ripped and nailed and packed—relentlessly and feverishly. At the end of the week they had shipped two hundred and eighty cases of guinea-pigs, and there were in the express office seven hundred and four more pigs than when they began packing them.

"Stop sending pigs. Warehouse full," came a telegram to Flannery. He stopped packing only long enough to wire back, "Can't stop," and kept on sending them. On the next train up from Franklin came one of the company's inspectors. He had instructions to stop the stream of guinea-pigs at all hazards. As his train drew up at Westcote station he saw a cattle-car standing on the express company's siding. When he reached the express office he saw the express wagon backed up to the door. Six boys were carrying bushel baskets full of guinea-pigs from the office and dumping them into the wagon. Inside the room Flannery, with his coat and vest off, was shoveling guinea-pigs into bushel baskets with a coal scoop. He was winding up the guinea-pig episode.

He looked up at the inspector with a snort of anger.

"Wan wagonload more an' I'll be quit of thim, an' niver will ye catch Flannery wid no more foreign pigs on his hands. No, sur! They near was the death o' me. Nixt toime I'll know that pigs of whativer nationality is domestic pets—an' go at the lowest rate."

He began shoveling again rapidly, speaking quickly between breaths.

"Rules may be rules, but you can't fool Mike Flannery twice wid the same thrick—whin ut comes to live stock, dang the rules. So long as Flannery runs this expriss office—pigs is pets—an' cows is pets—an' horses is pets—an' lions an' tigers an' Rocky Mountain goats is pets—an' the rate on thim is twinty-foive cints."

He paused long enough to let one of the boys put an empty basket in the place of the one he had just filled. There were only a few guinea-pigs left. As he noted their limited number his natural habit of looking on the bright side returned.

"Well, annyhow," he said cheerfully, " 'tis not so bad as ut might be. What if thim dago pigs had been elephants!"

The Duck That Flew Backwards

DON TRACY

Millard was born in a Canadian marsh. That wasn't his real name, of course; his real name started with a high-pitched quack that sank, quavered and went up at the end. Absolutely unspellable. For purposes of convenience, call him Millard; Millard the Mallard.

He was one of a clutch of four ducklings, and the only drake in the lot. His three sisters, also renamed for convenience, were Millie, Maggie and Melissa, all nice girls. Millard's pop—name him Mike—had wanted four boys and he didn't bother to hide his disappointment very much at getting only one. Minnie, the mother, knew that having three girls and only one boy was a severe pain in the crop to her husband, but what was a poor hen to do? She just laid the eggs, she didn't call the shots; and let Mike glower at her after looking over the brood and finding only one drake, if he found any satisfaction in it.

Mike looked over the ducklings quite often, unsmilingly, the first few days after the little ones were out of the eggs, and once he said "Nuts!" loudly. Minnie ruffled her feathers. After all, she had been born a Saskatchewan mallard and no mere York Stater whom she'd met on a blind date in Louisiana and hadn't had the sense to give the brush-off at the start was going to say "Nuts!" to her efforts, and get away with it.

"You ought to be proud," she told Mike, her voice edgy, "to have three beautiful daughters. Most fathers would be sticking out their chests at the idea of having all the eggs hatch, instead of going around muttering like a heron that's stepped on a hard crab."

"Most wives," Mike retorted, "would have arranged at least a fifty-fifty split. I had two brothers in my hatching and God knows how many half-brothers, later. My family runs to drakes. It must be your folks that turn out the hens."

"That's right," Minnie snapped. "Blame it on my people! I only

345

hope to heaven the boy doesn't turn out like his father, Gawd forbid. Coseying up to that—"

"All right, all right!" Mike cried. "Nothing came of it, I tell you!"

"I know it didn't," Minnie admitted, "because—ha ha *ha-a-a*— her drake chased you halfway to Nichikum Lake before you stopped yelling uncle. Good old Mike, the fine-feathered Lothario."

"Women!" Mike snorted. He waddled down to the water and paddled away, gabbling bitterly to himself.

Millard looked like any other mallard duckling and acted like one until it came time for his first swimming lesson. Minnie and Mike took the girls first, because with ducks, as with humans, it pays to start the girls off early in learning how to be fleet of foot. Millie, Maggie, and Melissa took to swimming like a duck takes to—er— they all picked up swimming very rapidly indeed.

Then came Millard's turn. He got down to the water's edge all right and he plunged in fearlessly, but there all resemblance to his sisters stopped. Mike, who was supervising from the bank, stared and swallowed.

"What the hell?" he asked.

For Millard was swimming all right, but backwards. His little stern was pushing through the water at a fine clip. If he had been a boat and if his position had been reversed, he might have been described as having "a bone in his teeth." As it was, the quaint old phrase didn't fit at all.

"Turn around!" Mike yelled from the bank. "You're in reverse, you dope!"

Millard tried valiantly to turn around. He managed to get his green head pointed in the direction he wanted to go, but when he paddled his feet he started moving backwards again. He wound up with a jarring bump against a tree stump near the shore.

"Now listen!" Mike roared, clambering down the bank and splashing into the water. "If you think this is funny, you can—"

"Easy, Mike," Minnie cautioned. "The poor boy is just confused. Come on, Millard, and watch mommie."

She paddled back and forth in front of the duckling, using slow, elaborately distinct strokes of her webbed feet to show the youngster how it should be done. Millie, Maggie and Melissa, on the shore, looked smug. Mike scowled thunderously.

"Now try it, dearie," Minnie urged. "Slow and easy does it."

Millard tried it slow and easy, then fast and furiously. Because his rear was still firmly lodged against the stump, he didn't move. He churned the water with his little paddles but he succeeded only in covering the surface of the pool with foam.

"Forward, you fool!" Mike yelled.

"I can't," Millard squeaked. "I'm trying to go forward, but all I can do is go backwards."

"I have one son and he turns out to be a filliloo bird!" Mike said, rolling his eyes upward.

"What's a filliloo bird, papa?" chorused Millie, Maggie and Melissa.

"A bird that flies backwards because he doesn't care where he's going but wants to see where he's been and—Shaddap! Get back in the nest where you belong!"

You see, Mike could not bear to have these hens, daughters of his though they might be, witness the shame of his only son, Millard. In Mike's book, no hen should ever be given the chance of laughing at a drake, even if said drake was a schmoe who swam backwards.

With the three little hens gone from the scene, Mike took a hand in trying to unmesh Millard's reverse gear. He and Minnie worked hard that day, and the next, and the next, before Mike finally called it quits. By that time, Millard had learned to roll his eyes back far enough to see where he was heading—or tailing, maybe—and dodge the larger obstructions. Still, despite Mike's imprecations, which would have fitted solidly on a Walt Disney sound track, Millard had yet to move a single foot in the normal forward direction.

"This should happen to me," Mike groaned. "Wait till the boys get hold of this! It'll be the talk of the flyways."

"I," said Minnie, stanchly, "think it's kind of cute."

"Cute!" Mike grated. "What's cute about it? What do you suppose the good Lord put that beautiful green head on that schnook for—to watch his own wake when he's swimming? Get a load of him sailing up to join a rick of strangers. I can hear them now: 'Don't look, guys, but it's either a decoy that's broken loose or one of them dipper-ducks playing wise again. Either way, let's give it the works.' That's what they'll say and——"

A horrible thought struck him and his eyes glazed. "Suppose," he said. "Suppose—when he flies—good Lord, what if he flies like he swims?"

"Don't be silly, Michael," Minnie said, in a wifely manner. "Who ever heard of a duck flying backwards?"

"Who ever heard of a duck swimming backwards?" Mike countered. "C'mon, let's teach him to fly—quick!"

Minnie demurred. "He's not old enough to learn to fly," she said. "It's liable to make him bow-winged."

"Bow-wings be hanged!" Mike said. "Let's learn the worst as soon as possible. Hey, Millard! Turn your little back bumper this way and come on over. Mummie and daddy want to show you something."

Getting Millard into the air required more time than it had taken to get the little drake into the water, but Millard finally did manage to take off, solo. It was, all in all, a creditable flight for a fledgling. Millard left the pool beside which he had been born, circled around the tall pine to the north, came back over the inlet, swooped low and zoomed again, rounded the point by the beaver dam and returned to the starting place. Yes, it was an admirable flight for one so young—excellent take-off, fine turns, superior control of speed and a neat landing.

There was only one trouble with Millard's first solo. He flew backwards, all the way.

"I've lived right," Mike said, staggering away, "and tried to serve my king and country—and I get this!"

"Where are you going?" Minnie called.

"If I was human, and if I had one of those bottles I've seen in duck blinds, flying over," Mike replied, "I'd go out and get drunk. As it is, I think I'll hunt up a nice hungry weasel."

He didn't, though, because he was back in the nest just before dark, growling to himself. In the weeks that followed, he gave himself over more and more to dark spells of brooding and he even lost a little of that jaunty brashness that had marked him up till the time of Millard's first swimming and flying lessons. At intervals, he would rouse himself from his black mood and try again.

"C'mon, Hindsight," he would call to his son. "Let's have another fling at trying to get it through your skull that you're supposed to be going somewhere, not coming from someplace. Here, watch me."

Millard would watch obediently while Mike went through some beautiful wing work. Then, clenching his bill with determination, the little drake would try to do exactly as pop had done. Once, he actually managed to propel himself forward over the water for a space of four feet before he jibbed, went under and headed for the bottom. Mike had to dive for him that time and if it was noised about that he had waited quite a while before going to the rescue, that probably was just some merganser gossip.

These practice sessions always wound up with Mike hoarse and livid with rage and little Millard as close to tears as a duck ever could get. In the end, Minnie put a stop to Mike's lessons.

"For heaven's sake," she clacked, "leave the boy be. After all, flying backwards is—distinctive. Not every family can boast a drake that can fly backwards faster than most ducks can fly frontwards."

"A monstrosity," Mike moaned. "I'll be the laughing stock of Currituck Sound. Even the cormorants will snicker. I'll——"

"It's always you, you, you!" Minnie said, sharply. If she had been human, she would have had her arms akimbo by this time. "Now you listen to me, Mike Mallard! Instead of feeling sorry for yourself, the way you've been doing, it might be a good idea to start thinking of training Millard so he can take care of himself, lead a useful life. It's our duty to see to it that he gets schooled to meet some of the facts of life he'll meet up with, backward or forward."

So Millard went out that day with Millie, Maggie and Melissa when Mike and Minnie took their brood on their first group-training flight. Millard, by common consent, flew in the center of the formation so that Mike, leading the flight, could steer him away from high trees, mountain ranges and other obstacles he might encounter, looming up in front of his stern.

As a matter of fact, Millard did not need this guidance. As he had grown, he had developed the knack of walling his eyes so that he could see in front of him—that is, in the direction he was going —almost as well as he could see back of him—or where he had been. He had kept this accomplishment to himself; Mike's ever-present scorn had made the kid timid about ever opening his bill.

He tooled along with Mike in front of him, Minnie behind him and his sisters on either side of him, changing position every so often as Mike snapped back orders, while pop kept up a running fire of comment, mostly sarcastic.

"Look out for this fir tree, Useless," Mike would call back. "Ram into that thing and all they'd have to do is revolve the tree to make you look like something in a rotisserie window."

Or: "Try bumping this hill, Little Chief Looking-Backwards, and you'll have some black-and-blue decorations to go at the opposite end of your little green knot-head."

"Stop it, Mike!" Minnie would call crossly. "Pay attention to your flying, for pity's sake!"

"Back-seat flying," Mike would grumble. "Always the yaddega-yaddega from the back seat."

The flight had been in the air a little over an hour when Millard broke radio silence. "Falcon!" he cried, in his high-pitched voice. "About seven o'clock high!"

Minnie and Mike cast startled glances over their shoulders. Yep, there was the falcon, starting his power dive and already debating whether he'd take his mallard back to his nest to share with the old lady or hold out on his wife and dine alone. If it had not been that Millard was keeping watch over the rear of the flight, that falcon would have been a cinch to put at least one member of the family out of immediate circulation. As it was, Millard's screeched warning came in time for Mike, a fair hand at elusive action, to lead his flight into a series of dizzy swerves that sent the falcon catapulting past them, far wide of his target, and cursing. By the time the feathered dive-bomber had recovered himself, Mike, Minnie and the family were safe.

"Now," said Minnie, in a heavy voice, "perhaps you'll stop this inhuman heckling of your son. If it hadn't been for Millard——" She left the sentence hanging and gave a delicate shudder.

"He did all right," Mike said grudgingly. "Of course, I could've gotten us out of that jam without him, but——"

"Of course!" Minnie said witheringly. "In a widgeon's eye, you could have! You were so busy playing Donald up front you wouldn't have seen a condor till he had all of us."

The falcon episode might have softened Mike's attitude toward Millard, but not too much. He still was given to spells of bleak pondering. He would watch his son swimming or flying backwards and, after shaking his head, he would get up with a grunt and stamp off into the deep marsh grass.

"Y'know," he told Minnie one day. "I've been doing some think-ing. The only thing I can bring to mind that travels backwards most of the time is a crab. Now, how in the hell could a crab——"

"Mich-ael Mal-lard!"

He recognized the tone. He shut up.

Came autumn and, after the Indian summer, the nipping winds that told Mike it was time to head south for Louisiana. He hated the prospect, even though the annual flight, till now, always had been something to look forward to. There were old friends to be met on the yearly pilgrimage, acquaintances to be renewed, new people to meet; there was always a dizzy redhead who could be convinced that it wasn't necessarily true that a duck had to keep to her kind in making back-bayou dates.

This year, though, there was Millard. In the Canada establishment, Mike could keep Millard more or less under cover. The nearest neighbors in the marsh were a rick of black ducks who kept to themselves pretty much and, as everybody knew, blacks were too dumb to think anything about a duck flying backwards even if they might have happened to glimpse Millard skittering overhead. Once the trek south began, however, Millard perforce would have to be seen by a good many ducks. There were only two flyways out of Eastern Canada: the East Coast and the Mississippi Valley routes, and both would be crowded, as usual. A hundred thousand ducks, not counting coots, would see and laugh at Millard—and Millard's father—before the little family hit their winter home in Louisiana.

The more Mike thought about this, the less he liked it. One day, therefore, he got Millard aside and laid a wing on the boy's back.

"Millard, m'boy," he said, "I've been thinking. You've grown up to be quite a drake—strong, big-winged—smart."

"Thanks, pop," said Millard warily.

"Um-m, yeah. Well, I was thinking that perhaps you were the duck to do what I wanted to do, but couldn't; what every ablebodied duck I've ever known has wanted to do but couldn't."

"What's that?"

Mike's voice went into a deep tremolo. "Why, make your first southern flight alone," he said.

He stepped back to watch his son's face break into an expression of ecstatic excitement. Millard stared back at him, dead-pan.

Mike took a deep breath. "Just think of it!" he said, waving his wings. "There you are, a youngster just out of your shell, winging your way southward, southward, covering mile after mile on tireless wings—and on your own! Do you need an old drake like me to show you the way, slow you up? No! Do you need a fussy hen quacking at you if you so much as swing off a mile or so to see the country? No! No, there you'll go, as free as the air you travel, without a care in the world. Down over Massachusetts Bay, Sandy Hook, the Jersey marshes, the Susquehanna Flats! On you'll go, over Currituck and Pamlico Sound, Ocracoke Inlet and—"

"Uh-uh," Millard said flatly.

ABOUT THE AUTHORS

ANONYMOUS. "The Dog That Was Pensioned by the Legislature" is from an *omnium-gatherum* entitled *Funniest Books of All; Sketches of the Popular Humorists of the Day* (Chicago: Rhodes and McClure, 1882)

ANDERSON, DILLON. Both "A Buffalo Named Woodrow" and "Billingsley's Bird Dog" appeared in the *Atlantic Monthly* (March 1954 and December 1955). The author, a native Texan, is reputed to be one of the ablest lawyers in Houston. During World War II he served in the Middle East and on the War Department General Staff. He confesses to having a special fondness for poker and bird dogs. His other writings include two books: *I and Claudie* and *Claudie's Kinfolks.*

ARROWOOD, CHARLES F. (1887-1951), a native North Carolinian and late Professor of the History and Philosophy of Education, University of Texas. "The Blue Quail Dog" is reprinted from *Backwoods to Border*, and "The Indestructible Razorback" from *In the Shadow of History*, publications of the Texas Folklore Society.

ASWELL, JAMES R. "Young Melvin" is from *God Bless the Devil!* (Chapel Hill: University of North Carolina Press, 1940), a collection of Tennessee Federal Writers' Project stories edited by Aswell. The author is a native of Tennessee. He also edited *Native American Humor* and the *Tennessee Guide* in the American Guide Series, and has had short stories published in a number of national magazines.

BAILEY, JAMES M. (1841-1894). "A Very Friendly Horse" is from the author's *Life in Danbury* (Boston: Shepard and Gill, 1873). Bailey was a native of New York, but after the Civil War settled in Danbury, Connecticut, where he edited the *News* and wrote several highly popular volumes of Danbury sketches and recollections of his youth. James Aswell describes his writings as "belonging to the late nineteenth century, or house-broken, stage of American humor."

BARRERA, GENOVEVA. "How the Burro Tricked the Buzzard" is from *Texian Stomping Grounds*, a Texas Folklore Society publication. At the time of writing, Miss Barrera was a student at Texas College of Arts and Industries, Kingsville. The story, she reports, was heard from one of her kinsmen.

BENCHLEY, ROBERT (1889-1945). "How Lillian Mosquito Projects Her Voice" is from the author's *Love Conquers All* (New York: Holt, 1922). Benchley was born in Worcester, Massachusetts, and educated at Harvard. He served as drama critic of the old *Life* and later of the *New Yorker*. His humorous sketches, collected in numerous volumes, belong to the *non-sequitur* or nonsense school.

BILLINGS, JOSH (Henry Wheeler Shaw, 1818-1885). "The Mule" first appeared in *Josh Billings, His Sayings* (New York: Carleton, 1865), and "The Poodle" is in *Josh Billings, His Works Complete* (1880). Shaw, a native of Massachusetts, was for some years a farmer and auctioneer in the West, then returned east to become an auctioneer and land agent at Poughkeepsie, New York. In 1860, he began publishing his humorous sketches written in farmer's dialect, in an era when misspelling was considered excruciatingly funny. His crackerbox philosophy, in a similar vein, delivered from the lecture platform was equally popular.

BOATRIGHT, MODY C. "Pecos Bill and the Mountain Lion" is from the author's *Tall Tales from Texas* (Dallas: Southwest Press, 1934). Boatright, a native of Texas, has been on the English faculty of the University of Texas since 1926, and has long been a leader in the Texas Folklore Society's collecting activities. He is author or editor of *Gib Morgan, Minstrel of the Oil Fields, Folk Laughter on the American Frontier, Folk Travelers, The Golden Log*, etc.

BUTLER, ELLIS PARKER (1869-1937), was born in Muscatine, Iowa. His *Pigs Is Pigs* (New York: Doubleday, 1906) has become a classic of American humor; though he subsequently wrote a number of other humorous works, none rivaled the first in popularity.

BYRAM, GEORGE. "The Wonder Horse" is from the *Atlantic Monthly* (August 1957). Byram, who operates a small ranch in Colorado, says that the idea for the story "came about quickly one evening when I was studying genetics in regard to my own horse-breeding program (crossing Arabians on Quarter Horses). Like any horse-breeder, I began dreaming what kind of mutation I would like to have happen." The tale is so realistic that the first editor to whom it was submitted took it literally and rejected it as impossible, failing to recognize the marvelous fantasy and humor.

CORBETT, SCOTT. "The Perfect Bait" originally appeared in the *Atlantic Monthly* (August 1955). The author, born in Missouri, formerly made his home among the bass fishermen of Cape Cod. He is now a resident of Provincetown, Massachusetts. His books include *We Chose Cape Cod, Cape Cod's Way, The Reluctant Landlord, Sauce for the Gander*, and *The Sea Fox*.

CROCKETT, DAVY (1786-1836). "Grinning the Bark Off a Tree" is from *Sketches and Eccentricities of Col. David Crockett of West Tennessee*

(New York: Harper, 1833). A famous backwoodsman, Crockett served under Andrew Jackson against the Creek Indians, was elected to Congress for three terms, starting in 1826, and was among the American heroes who died at the Alamo, in the Texas war for independence. The tall tales that clustered around his name have transformed Davy into a comic demigod.

CRONYN, GEORGE. "Harold Peavey's Fast Cow" is from *Story* (July 1935). Cronyn, formerly business manager of *Story* magazine, is author of *The Fool of Venus, The Path on the Rainbow* (an anthology of songs and chants from the North American Indians), *The Sandbar Queen,* etc.

DORSON, RICHARD M. "Major Brown's Coon Story" is from Dorson's *Jonathan Draws the Long Bow* (Cambridge: Harvard University Press, 1946), printed from a mid-nineteenth century manuscript found in the archives of the Vermont Historical Society. Dorson is one of the most indefatigable collectors and critical writers on American folklore, as his numerous books and articles on the subject attest. He is at present professor of history and folklore at Indiana University and editor for the American Folklore Society.

EISENBERG, FRANCES. "Horse in the Apartment" originally appeared in *Story* magazine (July-August 1940). Miss Eisenberg, a native of Knoxville, Tennessee, was a member of Whit Burnett's short-story seminar at Columbia University, and at the time of writing the story was a school teacher.

FISCHER, JOHN. "How to Cure Bird-Watchers" is from *Harper's Magazine* (August 1959). A native of Oklahoma, the author filled a variety of positions as newspaper reporter in the United States and Europe, 1928-37, and important posts in the Federal Government, 1937-44, before joining *Harper's* in 1944 as associate editor, and more recently as editor-in-chief.

FISHER, VARDIS. "A Family Pet" is from *Idaho Lore* (Caldwell, Idaho: Caxton Printers, 1939), a collection of folktales assembled by the Federal Writers' Project under Fisher's direction. Vardis Fisher is a native of Idaho and a prolific novelist, chiefly on Western themes.

FORD, JESSE HILL. "The Surest Thing in Show Business" is from the *Atlantic Monthly* (April 1959). Ford, a thirty-four-year-old Tennessean, graduate of Vanderbilt and the University of Florida, is a free-lance writer and has engaged in public relations work.

HARRIS, JOEL CHANDLER (1848-1908). "The Doodang" is from *Uncle Remus and the Little Boy* (New York: Dodd, Mead, 1910). Harris's famous Uncle Remus stories, starting the vogue for Negro folk literature in the United States, began publication in the *Atlanta Constitution,* with which he became associated in 1876. The first collection in book form appeared in 1880.

HELFER, HAROLD. "The Sea Serpent of Spoonville Beach" is from

Story; the Magazine of the Short Story in Book Form (New York: McKay, 1953). Helfer, a free-lance fiction writer, newspaper reporter, and columnist, resided in Washington, D.C., at the time the story was written. He was a war correspondent with the United States Marine Corps during World War II. No locale for the yarn is given, but it seems naturally to belong to the New England coast.

HENDRICKS, WILLIAM C. Hendricks was State Supervisor of the Federal Writers' Project for North Carolina, and edited *Bundle of Troubles and Other Tarheel Tales* (Durham, N.C.: Duke University Press, 1943), in which "Uncle Heber's Flytrap" and "Bear Hunt in Reverse" appear. The story of the laziest man in North Carolina was told by William Wilson, drawbridge tender in the Brice's Creek section of Craven County, eastern Carolina, and the bear story by a Negro huckster of Durham.

HOIG, STAN. "Cow Country Critters" is a chapter from *The Humor of the American Cowboy* (Caldwell, Idaho: Caxton Printers, 1958). Hoig is a native Sooner, born at Gage, western Oklahoma, near the Texas border, an area rich in lore of the American Indian wars and of the early cattle trails. The author has published short stories in various western and other magazines. He is now an industrial editor, living in Houston, Texas.

LARDNER, RING (1885-1933). "Dogs" is a sketch from *First and Last* (New York: Scribner, 1938). Lardner was a sports reporter for newspapers in Chicago, St. Louis, and Boston from 1907 to 1919. His sardonic humor, with its highly characteristic sports idiom, first appeared in collected book form in *You Know Me, Al*, 1916, followed by a series of similar devastating satires on American social foibles.

LEWIS, LLOYD (1891-1949). "Old Mitts" is from Lewis's *It Takes All Kinds* (New York: Harcourt, 1947). The author was born in Indiana, and in the course of his varied career was a newspaper reporter, critic, sports editor, columnist, and lecturer and author of a number of books on American history, chiefly relating to the Civil War and after.

MENCKEN, H. L. (1880-1956). "Memoirs of the Stable" is an excerpt from Mencken's boyhood recollections (around 1891) contained in his *Heathen Days, 1890-1936* (New York: Knopf, 1947). Mencken was a native and devoted son of Baltimore, Maryland. His long career as newspaper reporter and editor began there in 1899. He is most widely known, of course, for his iconoclastic attacks on American beliefs and institutions.

MOTT, EDWARD HAROLD (1845-1920). "The Intelligent Steer" is from *Pike County Folks* (New York: John W. Lovell Co., 1883), a series of sketches of Pike County, Pennsylvania, where Mott was born. The author filled newspaper editorial positions in Pennsylvania, New York, and Texas, and wrote several other books: *The Black Homer of Jimtown, The Erie Route, The Old Settler,* etc.

PENN, A. W. "Tall Tales for the Tenderfeet" is from *Follow de Drinkin' Gou'd,* a Texas Folklore Society publication. At the time the stories were written, 1928, the author was a young business man of Austin, Texas.

RANDOLPH, VANCE. The best-known collector of authentic Ozark folklore, folktales, and anecdotes—a task to which he has devoted himself since 1920. The "Randolph Carnival" is drawn from the following sources, all issued by the Columbia University Press: "The Toadfrog," from *The Devil's Pretty Daughter* (1955); "What Cows Do on Christmas" and "Grandpap Hunted Birds," from *Sticks in the Knapsack* (1958); "The Talking Turtle," "Tobey the Kingsnake," "The Big Rabbits," and "Wolves Are My Brothers," from *The Talking Turtle* (1957); "Fabulous Monsters," from *We Always Lie to Strangers* (1951); and "The Mare with the False Tail," from *Who Blowed Up the Church House?* (1952).

SALE, JOHN B. "Why Brer Rabbit Doesn't Have to Work Any More" is from *The Tree Named John* (Chapel Hill: University of North Carolina Press, 1929). This Negro folktale is recollected from the author's boyhood in Columbus, Mississippi, during the eighteen nineties.

SAROYAN, WILLIAM. "The Story of the Young Man and the Mouse" is from the author's *Dear Baby* (New York: Harcourt, Brace, 1944). Saroyan is a Californian of Armenian descent. The instant success of his first book *The Daring Young Man on the Flying Trapeze* (1934) has been followed by a steady stream of novels, short stories, plays, and essays. Edmund Wilson characterized Saroyan as "an agreeable mixture of San Francisco bonhommie and Armenian Christianity."

SCHRAMM, WILBUR. "The Horse that Played Third Base for Brooklyn" appeared in the author's *Windwagon Smith and Other Yarns* (New York: Harcourt, Brace, 1941). Schramm's versatile career began as a newspaper reporter, and continued as editor, university professor, holder of important assignments in the Federal Government, communications expert, and prolific author. He is now Professor of Communications and Journalism and a member of the Institute of Communications Research, Stanford University.

SCUDDAY, ROY. "The Musical Snake" appears in *From Hell to Breakfast,* a Texas Folklore Society publication. The author is a native of Sweetwater, Texas, and an alumnus of the University of Texas.

SMITH, H. ALLEN. "Rufus" is a nostalgic sketch from *Let the Crabgrass Grow* (New York: Random House, 1960). The author, a native of Illinois, started working on newspapers at the age of fifteen. Since the late nineteen thirties, he has been delighting his multitude of faithful fans with such books as *Low Man on a Totem Pole, Life in a Putty Knife Factory,* and *Lost in the Horse Latitudes.*

STORM, DAN. "Señor Coyote and Señor Fox" is from *Coyote Wisdom,* a Texas Folklore Society publication. Storm has lived in Mexico, spent much time with Indians in New Mexico, and maintains a home in Austin, Texas. He is a journalist by profession.

STUART, JESSE. "Red Rats of Plum Creek" was published in *Story; the Magazine of the Short Story in Book Form* (New York: McKay, 1953). The author is a native of Kentucky and prolific writer of novels, short stories, and poems. His favorite locale is the Kentucky mountains, his home base.

THURBER, JAMES (1894-1961). "Prehistoric Animals of the Middle West" is from *The Beast in Me and Other Animals* (New York: Harcourt, Brace, 1948); "The Pet Department" from *The Owl in the Attic* (New York: Harper, 1931); and "The Dog That Bit People" from *My Life and Hard Times* (New York: Harper, 1933). Thurber was born and grew up in Columbus, Ohio, a town that he made famous in his *My Life and Hard Times* and other writings. His early career was spent as a newspaperman in Columbus and Paris. From 1926 until his death, he was associated with the *New Yorker* in various capacities—as managing editor, conductor of the "Talk of the Town" department, and in later years as a regular contributor.

TRACY, DON. "The Duck That Flew Backwards" first appeared in the *Saturday Evening Post* (May 1, 1937). The author was born in Connecticut and now lives in Florida. He has been a frequent contributor of short stories to magazines of national circulation: *Saturday Evening Post, Good Housekeeping, Collier's, American Magazine,* etc.

TWAIN, MARK (Samuel L. Clemens, 1835-1910). "Jim Baker's Bluejay Yarn" and "Ants" are from *A Tramp Abroad* (Hartford, Conn.: American Publishing Co., 1880). The career of Mark Twain, greatest American humorist, is too well known to require review here. It should be noted, however, that the first step in his climb to fame was a tall tale in the animal category—"The Jumping Frog of Calaveras County." The extravagant bluejay concoction was told to Twain by Jim Gillis, a California miner with whom he camped for several months.

VANN, WILLIAM H. "The Animals' Spring" and "How Mr. Rabbit Fooled Mr. Possum" are from *Backwoods to Border,* a Texas Folklore Society publication. The author has been prominent in Texas literary circles and taught English in a number of Southern colleges. The two stories came to him through his father, who in turn had heard them from Negroes on his plantation in eastern North Carolina, in the decade before the Civil War.

WHITE, E. B. "A Boston Terrier" is from *One Man's Meat* (New York: Harper, 1942), and "The Hour of Letdown" from the *New Yorker* (December 22, 1951). Though born in Mt. Vernon, a suburb of New York City, White has become a confirmed Down Easterner, a resident of Brooklin, Maine. Almost from the beginning of that magazine, he has been a contributing editor of the *New Yorker*, and for eleven years wrote most of its "Talk of the Town." James Thurber observed of him, "He understands begonias and children, canaries and goldfish, dachshunds and Scottish terriers, men and motives." White is one of the great stylists of American literature.

WILLIS, PRISCILLA. *Harper's Magazine* originally published both "A Little Wine of the Country" (December 1955) and "Just a Simple Country Boy" (September 1958). Mrs. Willis spends much of her time on a farm where her husband, a Chicagoan, breeds and raises cattle. She has served as a reporter on a weekly sporting paper devoted to country living, and has written other short stories and juvenile books. Her agricultural training was received at a midwestern university, where her husband sent her to study animal husbandry.

YATES, NORRIS. "The Angry Sailor" is from the *Journal of American Folklore* (April–June 1949). The tale was told to Yates, a member of the English and Speech faculty of Iowa State University (Ames), by Marine Corporal Richard T. Davis, then at Camp Lejeune, North Carolina.